THE KING'S SUCCESSOR

The Divalian Chronicles

Book 4

S. T. Hobbs

Book and Cover design by germancreative
ISBN: 979-8-9857217-5-1
First Edition: December 2022
10 9 8 7 6 5 4 3 2 1

Table of Contents

Chapter 1

A S MUCH AS HE KNEW THIS DAY would eventually come, it still felt as if the ground beneath his feet had just been swept away by Captain Lupin's words. Aki's eyes fixed on a knot in the smooth wooden surface of the captain's desk, taking in the dark swirl that marred the otherwise even grain of the wood.

Captain Lupin was waiting for him to speak, waiting for some acknowledgement of the news he'd just delivered but Aki's mind had momentarily emptied itself of any coherent thought.

When it became clear that he wasn't going to say anything, that he couldn't say anything, Captain Lupin said, "You'll want to leave for home right away, I assume. I'll take care of letting Atticus and Colin know so you don't have to worry about that. You may leave as soon as you're ready."

Nodding his understanding and thanks, still incapable of speech, Aki slid his chair away from the desk, the scraping of its legs against the floor loud and harsh in the silence. Crumpled in his hand was the letter that Captain Lupin had given him to accompany his words. A letter from Alina. The words had blurred before his eyes when he'd tried to read it and he didn't have the heart to try again.

Outside, the late summer sun was casting shadows as clouds danced intermittently across the sky in front of it. The hard packed dirt of the arena was dry, and a little puff of dust followed each footfall as he crossed it towards his room.

The dormitory was a mirror to the emptiness inside him. None of the others were there and Aki was glad of it. He went through the motions of packing like a puppet on a string, watching his hands move with complete detachment.

Once on the road outside Bren, Aki spurred Sky into a canter. Even though he knew he couldn't keep her at that speed for the entire trip, he couldn't endure the thought of plodding along just now. With the wind in his ears, there wasn't as much pressure to think. Even so, the cadence of her hoofbeats matched the words that repeated themselves endlessly in his mind, the words Captain Lupin had spoken - *Stephan is dead.*

Chapter 2

AKI STOOD NEXT TO SASHA, his mind wandering as Stephan's grave was filled in. He ought to have been by Alina, but her own children were there, and he didn't feel he had the right to intrude on their familial privacy. He drew in a ragged breath as the weight of Sasha's hand fell on his shoulder.

"Are you alright?" Sasha's voice was a whisper and did not disturb the quiet grieving of those around them.

Aki bit down on his lip as he nodded. He glanced over at Alina again. Hamo and Aldrid were with her, as well as the daughter he'd only met once, Sabina. Seeing them together was almost worse than the grave in front of him.

"I would have sent for you sooner if I'd known," Sasha continued, and Aki nodded wordlessly once more. It happened suddenly. That's what everyone said. Stephan had been in good health, although his age had begun to show in his movements. And then, one morning, he was gone. Aki wasn't sure if knowing ahead of time would have made anything better or easier. "Did you two ever...?"

Sasha didn't need to finish his question for Aki to give an emphatic shake of his head. No, they never had. Even a whole year later, there had been things amiss between him and Stephan, things he hadn't been able to put to right. Dagmar's death, his own cowardice had hung like a curtain between them, dividing them, holding them apart. Now, the chance to tear down that curtain was gone forever.

"I'm sorry."

This time, Aki didn't even bother to nod. He just walked away.

The woods surrounding most of Stephan's farm had always been a haven for him and he found himself drawn deep within them now. Putting one foot in front of the other with no other goal in mind except to lose himself for a few hours, Aki crossed the spring that was now mostly dried up with summer's heat. He rarely ventured this far into the forest and paused before deciding he could stand just a little bit more distance between himself and everyone else.

He should have come home before, Aki thought as he tore off a leaf that brushed against his hand and began picking it into pieces that scattered onto the ground behind him. Captain Lupin and Master Wehr had both offered on many occasions to give him time at home during this past year. Every time, he'd turned them down without a second thought.

He thought they had only offered out of sympathy for the difficulties he had faced coming back to the academy. Now he wondered if perhaps they had known what was coming somehow and wanted to give him one more chance to make his peace. Looking back, he should have taken it. Perhaps then the guilt that lodged itself like a stone in his heart would be gone, leaving room for sorrow.

With the thick canopy of leaves over his head it was hard to keep track of the time. The sun was hidden from view and the shadows were always long beneath the leaves of the trees.

As he picked his way home, it became obvious that he would not reach it until after dark. As the sun set somewhere beyond the trees, the noise of the forest changed. Golden orbs blinking in the shadows revealed the presence of the nocturnal animals that inhabited the trees. They were more disturbed by Aki's presence than he was by theirs.

It was harder finding his way back in the dark, but Aki's sense of direction had only improved since he began training as a courier and nearly an hour after the sun had disappeared completely, he approached Stephan and Alina's house.

The front door was open, soft yellow light spilling out onto the covered porch. Aki saw Alina sitting on her favorite chair there before she saw him. He climbed the first two steps and sat down on the uppermost one, leaning his head against the rail at his side, his back to Alina.

"I was beginning to wonder whether you were going to come back at all," Alina said softly.

He turned his head to look at her. And promptly regretted it. Her eyes were heavy with pain as she met his. He tried to think of something to say that would ease her sorrow, but words were useless against that sort of pain. He knew that all too well.

"I'm sorry. I shouldn't have left this afternoon."

For a while they sat, listening to the chirping of a million crickets. Aki wanted to add to his apology, wanted to explain that he thought she would prefer to be with her real children, that he didn't think she would notice his absence, that he hadn't meant to make her feel any worse. But his tongue was tied up in knots and no matter how many times he rehearsed the words over in his head, when he opened his mouth to speak them, he failed.

As if reading his mind, Alina leaned forward and said, "You're as much a part of this family as any of the others. Don't ever think otherwise."

That was enough. Aki could speak now that she had spoken. "Did he still think so badly of me in the end?"

Alina gave him a small, sad smile and shook her head. "Stephan never thought as badly of you as he let on. Unfortunately, he never took the chance to tell you that. More than anything, he thought he'd failed you."

"How could he possibly have thought that? You both gave me everything. I was the one who messed up."

"You were afraid of us, Aki. He hated that. He hated that you were afraid of what we might think if you told us the truth. He blamed himself for that."

Aki bent down and plucked up a pebble from the ground. He rolled it around between his fingers and stared into the darkness that shielded the barn from sight. Alina's words weren't what he expected. He couldn't decide if they were better or worse yet.

"Why didn't you come home at all this last year?"

Aki winced. That was the last question he wanted to answer. Turning to lean his back against the rail and drawing his feet up onto the step with the rest of him, he shut his eyes and answered, "I wanted to prove that I wasn't the same anymore, that I could do better. And I wanted to do that before I saw you both again. Before I had to face him again."

The soft rustle of fabric shifting alerted him to Alina's movements and Aki opened his eyes. She nudged his legs off the step and sat down next to him.

"We missed you," she said, her hand on his face. Aki flinched. He didn't mean to. The gesture reminded him too much of Mara. He felt awful the next instant, but it was too late. Alina withdrew her hand. "I missed you. Has it been so hard going back?"

Aki shrugged. "I guess it's no worse than I imagined it would be."

Her lips pressed into a thin line as she considered his answer. There was a lot he wouldn't say, and she must have sensed that because she didn't press him for any details. She didn't need to know that the only person at the academy who would have anything to do with him was Oscar. She didn't need to know that he spent almost all of his free time alone in his room, avoiding the presence of anyone else. She didn't know the hours and hours he spent studying or practicing because otherwise the loneliness and the guilt were more than he could bear.

The letters he'd written home had brushed over those parts, ignoring the friends he didn't make, ignoring the people who still looked at him with distrust and betrayal, ignoring the sleepless nights.

"Come, you look tired."

He couldn't argue with that. Getting to his feet, he held out a hand to help her.

Tired as he was, it took a long time for Aki to fall asleep. Without Stephan's presence, the house seemed empty, and Aki considered for the first time what Stephan's death might mean for Alina. Hamo and Aldrid were near enough to take care of her, but it wasn't likely that they would maintain the farm.

He could stay.

The thought crossed his mind and arrested all other thoughts. He could give up the academy where he was mostly unwanted anyway and stay here. He certainly knew how to care for the horses. It would be so easy. And Alina wouldn't argue with him. She would most likely be relieved by such a choice.

He was still tossing the idea around when hoofbeats came up the drive. Whoever it was, they were in a hurry. Aki tossed his blankets off. By the time he'd made it to the front door, the rider was already knocking. Aki lifted the latch as Alina came out of her room.

"Who is it, Aki?"

Instead of answering, he opened the door. "Colin?"

Colin wasted no time on a greeting. "I know you planned on staying a few days at least, but something's come up. You're going to have to come back with me."

"What's going on, Aki?" Alina asked again.

"I'll be out in a minute," Aki said to Colin. Then he shut the door and turned to face Alina. "They need me back."

"Already? You've only been here a day."

"Colin said something came up."

Alina didn't bother to hide her disappointment and Aki wanted nothing more than to tell Colin he wasn't coming back for any reason. Sensing his hesitation, she waved the idea away. "Of course. I shouldn't be so selfish to think that I could keep you here."

Aki dressed for the long ride ahead of him and pulled his courier's jacket over his shirt. He had only recently earned the scarlet band on the cuffs that marked the completion of his first year. He was the only one to earn it so late. The rest of his group had theirs given to them almost four months ago. Throwing the few things he'd brought back with him into his saddlebags, he hurried out of his room.

"For the road," Alina said, pressing a small bundle into his hands before embracing him. "Don't stay away for so long, Aki. I couldn't bear it."

"I'll be back before you know it. I promise."

Chapter 3

DESMOND TWISTED THE RING on his finger. Round and round it went as the voices around him droned on. It had been hours since the arrival of the dust-covered courier and the small gathering of resident council members had yet to disband.

He shifted ever so slightly in his chair, earning a reprimanding glance from his father. Desmond straightened and tried to pay attention to the red-haired man who was currently standing and speaking.

"It's an act of war, Your Majesty. It should be met with force, not negotiation," Baron Orlander finished saying and sat down, the chair groaning as he settled his weight into it.

Desmond looked toward his father, hoping for some sign that the meeting was nearing its end. It was only on his father's insistence that he'd even begun attending these. King Darien met his eyes and gave him a slight nod. Resting his hands flat on the table before him, the king stood.

"Gentlemen, regardless of whether this was an act of war or merely the act of a few rogue individuals, I must remind you that we cannot respond in force without the vote of the fully assembled council. What we can do is retire for the night and in the morning, we can revisit the subject of sending a party out to initiate negotiations. It is imperative that every effort is made to recover those lost. That is our first priority."

There was a scraping of chairs and shuffling of feet mingled with a few grumblings from one or two of the council members. Only Desmond remained in his seat at a sign from his father. As the half dozen council members exited the room, King Darien sat once again.

"He's right, you know."

"Baron Orlander?"

Desmond nodded. "The best way to deal with a threat like this is to react swiftly."

King Darien smiled in bemusement. "And you know that because you've done it so many times, is that it, Des?"

"It's Desmond, please. You know I hate being called that. It makes it sound like I'm a child. And I don't have to have done it so many times to know that Orlander is right. If we march straight up there and show them we aren't easily bullied, they'll think twice before attempting such a thing again. If it were up to me, I'd..."

"But it's not. Not yet at least." Darien sighed and drummed his fingers on the table as he studied his son. The youngest of his four children and his only son, Desmond was the undisputed heir to his throne. Desmond bit his tongue at the rebuke but didn't otherwise bother to hide his annoyance. "When you inherit this throne, I hope it will be with the realization that you are responsible for the lives of everyone you rule. Including the innocent people who might be lost if we react violently. We have made our peace with Aruuk, and we cannot allow one act to destroy that."

"But if we do nothing..."

"We're not doing nothing. Like I said, we'll organize a party in the morning. We will bargain for our people to be returned and find out who is behind this. If it is a true threat to our kingdom, we will act on that knowledge. If it is not, we will have spared the lives of many soldiers and the sorrow of many families. That is worth waiting for, I think."

King Darien stood up and started for the door. Desmond cleared his throat and his father turned back to him.

"Who are you sending?"

The first real expression of frustration that he'd shown all night flashed across King Darien's face at the question.

"I don't know, yet. It would normally be one of the council members. Baron Orlander is the senior most member here, but he's not exactly good at the whole negotiating process."

"Send me."

"What?"

"I said, send me."

"Oh, I heard what you said just fine. And absolutely not. You're not ready for something like that. Diplomacy is a delicate and tedious matter, not one I'm sure you're prepared for."

"Father, you always say that. I've trained my entire life for these sorts of things. You don't have to send me alone, but you can't just keep me locked away in the castle."

After a pause, King Darien nodded. "I'm not agreeing to it, but I will consider it."

Desmond stayed alone in the meeting room for some time after his father left. Now that he'd mentioned the idea, he was set on it. Father couldn't deny him a chance to prove himself. Almost his entire life had taken place within the walls of the castle or within the confines of Bren. A chance to travel all the way to the northernmost end of the kingdom was an opportunity he couldn't bear to pass up.

When they gathered again in the morning, Desmond hazarded a searching glance at his father's face. He recognized immediately the dark shadows beneath his father's eyes. He'd barely slept himself the night before. Looking around the room, he knew no one there had. Aside from the half dozen council members who resided in or near enough the castle to be present, there were two or three others now in the room that he did not recognize immediately. His attention was drawn back to his father as King Darien cleared his throat. The murmur of conversation died away at once.

"For those who were not present last night, I will briefly explain our situation. Last night we received word that there was an attack on one of the mountain settlements by a group that we can only assume came from Aruuk." King Darien paused to let the news sink into those who had not heard it before. "As you all know, we have a treaty with them, one that I don't believe they would be in a hurry to break. It is quite likely that the group responsible for this acted on their own, without the support of their governing body. In the attack, there were at least twenty of our citizens that were taken captive. Getting them back is our first priority. Discovering who is behind the attack is second. To address both those needs, I have decided to send a delegation to Aruuk."

A few heads nodded, but most in the room took the news without reacting. Desmond kept his eyes fixed on his father. The next stage of this meeting would be to discuss who would be sent. It was for that part that Desmond held his breath. As if sensing his anxiety and impatience, King Darien allowed his gaze to flicker briefly in his direction.

"Who do you intend to send, Your Majesty?" Baron Orlander said from across the room. Having argued for more forceful action before, Desmond would have expected at least a little disappointment from him, but the baron appeared completely resigned to the king's decision.

"Gregory Carrellis," King Darien nodded in the direction of his choice, "will accompany my son, Desmond. Together, they will be responsible for the negotiations."

"Your Majesty, if I may," Gregory spoke up, a slightly pained expression on his narrow face, "we have not sent a delegation to Aruuk in, well, in more than forty years. Neither your son nor I speak their language or have any familiarity with their customs. They are not a country we have had the opportunity of getting to know. That will make negotiations most difficult."

"Well, then it's a good thing I'm not sending you two alone, isn't it?"

"Your Majesty?"

"You will take a contingent of soldiers as well as an interpreter and guide. Aki Turston will be joining you."

There was a hush in the room followed immediately by a small, "Me?"

Desmond looked toward the source of the voice. He was one of the three in attendance who wasn't a part of the council. Desmond hadn't paid them much notice before but now he noticed that all three wore the coats that marked them as couriers. One was the man responsible for bringing the news. The one who'd spoken out was two or three years younger than himself and Desmond had only seen him one other time before today – at a trial where the courier was accused of being an accomplice to treason. Desmond frowned. Not exactly who he would have picked to accompany them.

"Yes, you," King Darien answered, turning to face Aki. "You understand their customs. You know the mountains. And most importantly, you speak their language."

"Like a native," Baron Orlander muttered just loud enough for everyone to hear, "because he is one."

"Which is, in fact, what we need." King Darien stood, ending any hopes of arguing. "Gregory and Desmond, make whatever preparations you need to. I will speak with both of you before you leave. The soldiers accompanying you will be ready by this afternoon. I expect you to be as well."

Chapter 4

DOES IT MATTER IF I DON'T want to go?"

"No. Not at all. Imagine if the king had to take into account what everyone wants or doesn't want. It would be catastrophic, and nothing would ever get done. Is there any particular reason why you don't want to go?"

Aki sat on his high stool in the front room of Master Wehr's, his feet hooked onto the rungs, his face cupped in his hands. His own preparations took very little time and rather than sit in his room with nothing but his thoughts to keep him company, he'd wandered to Master Wehr's. If it was sympathy he was seeking, Master Wehr appeared to have a very short supply that day.

When he didn't answer right away, Master Wehr glanced over the top of the paper he was reading. His eyesight was failing after all these years, but it didn't take sharp eyes to read the glum expression carved onto Aki's face. He opened his mouth, then closed it with a shake of his head.

"There's something you're not telling me," Aki finally said. He lifted his head and met Master Wehr's eyes.

"What makes you say that, Aki?"

"I'm not being trained the same as the rest of them. And this whole thing with being an interpreter. That's not what couriers do. We take messages, relay orders. Not go on diplomatic missions as interpreters."

"Are you going to say that to the king?"

"No, absolutely not."

"Hmmm...well, then I guess you'd better accept the fact that you're going and make the best of it."

Master Wehr went back to his reading, but Aki continued to watch him with interest. His eyes narrowed as he studied his teacher. It wasn't like Master Wehr to deliberately ignore something he'd said. Aki considered the possibility of Master Wehr having a rare moment of absentmindedness. He threw the thought out almost immediately. Despite his attempt to look disinterested and relaxed, Aki could see the tension his words had caused in Master Wehr's rigid posture and the way he forced his eyes to stay on the paper before him.

"I guess I should head up to the castle. They'll be getting ready to leave soon," Aki said, sliding off his stool, his eyes still fixed on his teacher.

Master Wehr glanced up and gave him a rather distracted and fleeting smile. "I expect you'll be gone for some time. Use the time well, Aki."

Aki mulled the words over in his mind as he led his mounts toward the castle. It wasn't so much what Master Wehr said as the way he said it. There was weight in the words, a reminder that Aki didn't understand.

The courtyard was crowded with men and horses. Aki guided Sky and his replacement mount to an empty corner to wait. In the center of the courtyard, a cart stood harnessed to a team of horses and was being loaded down with provisions. Aki grimaced when he saw it. They would not reach the mountains until the heavy autumn rains. A cart would be nothing but a dead weight in the narrow mountain passes and would likely have to be abandoned.

Aki turned his attention to Sky, lifting each leg and inspecting each hoof to ensure no stones had lodged themselves inside. Bending over, he felt an intense gaze boring into him from behind. Setting Sky's leg down, he turned to find Halle watching him. Even at a distance, Aki could see how thin Halle was, how bruised and gaunt his face was. Halle clearly wasn't faring well on his own with his fellow indentures. Aki turned away again. There was nothing he could do about it now and Halle's year was almost up.

"There you are. I've been looking all over for you," Colin said as he crossed the courtyard toward him. "You've brought your weapons, haven't you?"

Aki gestured to the sword at his side and the bow and quiver of arrows secured to his pack horse. He didn't even bother to reveal the knives he carried, that Colin and Master Wehr insisted he carry. He was the most heavily armed courier he'd ever met - part of the difference that Master Wehr elected to ignore that morning.

"Good." Colin nodded. "There's no telling what you're walking into. Strictly speaking, you're only along as an interpreter and guide." He lowered his voice and continued, "No matter what you heard King Darien say, your first priority - everyone's first priority - is to make sure Prince Desmond returns alive. Understand?"

"Isn't that what the soldiers are for?"

"Naturally. But you know how to fight, Aki, and you'll be at the prince's side more than the soldiers will be. Protect the prince."

Colin started to walk away but Aki called after him. "Aren't you coming too?"

"No. I'm a courier. They don't need me for this."

His words hit Aki like a punch, robbing him of breath for a moment. By the time he'd recovered himself enough to speak, Colin was gone, and the captain was shouting out the order to mount up.

Aki shut his eyes and took a deep, steadying breath. Now wasn't the time, he told himself. It wasn't the time to worry about what Colin meant, about what Master Wehr's strange behavior meant. When he returned, though, he would pester them until they explained.

It wasn't until they were outside of Bren that they could break out of the single file that the narrow streets in town confined them to. Aki held Sky back, keeping her towards the rear of the group. Keeping his head down made it easy for him to be ignored by all the others, which was exactly the way he preferred it.

Their pace was plodding, set by the horses harnessed to the heavily loaded cart. Having slept little in the past two days, Aki found himself nodding off in his saddle. He'd learned long before that it was possible to doze sitting up and Sky was a competent enough mount that she didn't wander off. It was the snorting of another horse beside him that roused Aki. He straightened up, blinking and found that he was no longer by himself at the back. Prince Desmond rode on one side of him and Gregory on the other.

Aki looked between them, a question in his eyes.

"You are from Aruuk?" Gregory broke the silence first.

Aki sighed and tried not to roll his eyes at the unnecessary question. "Yes, I am. But I haven't been there in almost five years."

"People don't change that much in five years. What can we expect when we get there?"

"That depends on how you plan to approach them."

"What do you mean?" Prince Desmond asked.

"Well, Your Highness, are you going straight to Illsen to speak to the leaders or are you going to try to find the band responsible and free their captives on your own?"

Neither Gregory nor Prince Desmond answered right away, and Aki guessed that they hadn't given it much thought yet. He started to add what he knew but decided to wait instead. He wasn't about to give them unasked for opinions. It was obvious they resented his presence already. He was a necessary evil to be endured for the sake of their mission, nothing else.

"And what would you suggest we do?" Prince Desmond asked after exchanging a look with Gregory.

Aki ran his fingers through Sky's mane as he considered the options. "If you go after the group that attacked in hopes of getting your people back, you'll never find them. Unless, of course, they want to be found."

"So, you would go straight to Illsen if it were up to you?"

Going to Illsen was the last thing Aki ever wanted to do. His hand tightened its grip on the reins causing Sky to toss her head in frustration. He felt the eyes of the other two on him. Quietly, he said, "Illsen is your best chance."

"And can you get us to Illsen?" Gregory queried.

"If that's where you decide to go."

"We haven't decided anything yet," Desmond said, giving Gregory a pointed look that Aki couldn't miss. "We have time to discuss it still before we even set foot in the mountains."

Aki raised an eyebrow as he watched them ride back up to the front. Desmond's meaning was clear. Whatever decision they made would be without him present. What didn't need to be put into words was that neither Gregory nor Desmond trusted him.

Chapter 5

T HE VOID HAD CEASED TO FIT ITS name for several years. At a glance it was mile upon mile of endless flat land. Hidden by the tall grass that grew thick and unhindered were the dips and rises that were all that remained of the great war. In the spring and early summer, the land resembled a covering of rich green velvet. After weeks of unrelenting sun and heat, the grass was dried, the dirt parched and cracking and a dull, pale brown was the prominent color. In a short time, heavy rains would turn into a mire almost impossible to cross.

Desmond thought he'd never seen a more depressing place. A ceaseless, whining wind cut across the open ground. It wasn't cold. Not yet. He couldn't imagine what it must be like to be stuck out here in the winter, though, when the wind turned bitter and drove the snow from the mountains down in a blinding swirl of white. The thought sent a chill down his spine, and he turned to Gregory.

"How many weeks before we can expect the weather to turn?"

"With luck, we'll be home before the snow flies, Your Highness. Our biggest worry will be the rain."

Not reassuring news, Desmond thought. Rain driven by this relentless wind would be just as miserable as snow.

"Can we not move faster? This is an easy road. There's no reason we can't push the horses and men a little more."

It was Captain Tyrrel who spoke up this time. "We move no faster than this. There are many days of riding ahead of us yet, and we can't tire the horses out before reaching the mountains."

Desmond gave a casual glance around, ensuring that no one else was within hearing before speaking again. "And where are we headed once we reach the mountains?"

"Illsen. We make for Illsen," Gregory said without hesitation.

Desmond's mouth tightened into an impatient frown of displeasure. "This was meant to be a discussion, Gregory. And don't forget, that the decision is mine to make, not yours."

"Of course, Your Highness." Gregory lowered his head but not quick enough to hide his irritation. "And where is it that you think we should go?"

"Didn't my father say that recovering the captives was our priority? I say we hunt them down."

"The courier said we'd never find them."

"He doesn't know that. And who's to say we should trust him? These are his people we're going to."

Once again it was the captain who responded. "Your Highness, whether you trust him or not, he's right. If the raiding party has disappeared into the mountains, we will not find them on our own. Ignoring that warning would be a mistake."

Desmond clenched his teeth together and stared straight ahead as he attempted to rein in his temper. It was always getting him in trouble. He wasn't going to let it this time, not with so much at stake. Father was counting on him, trusting him. Both Captain Tyrrel and Gregory were watching him, waiting for his answer. He rubbed a hand across his jaw, forcing it to relax.

"We'll search for them first. It may be that they are near the border still." He heard both men sigh, and his back went rigid with the anger he was barely keeping to himself. "If we see no sign of them, we move on to Illsen, but I don't want to pass up a chance to recover the captives if they are near at hand."

"Very well, Your Highness. It will be as you say," Gregory responded for them both.

Desmond didn't think he'd ever heard sweeter words. They were enough to melt away his anger and he smiled to himself.   Father would have been pleased at his decisiveness.

They stopped, as they had every night, around an hour before sundown. A week into their journey, everyone knew what part they had to play in order to make camp for the night.

Desmond sat back and watched as the camp took shape. A fire was started, and the smell of food soon filled the air. The horses were unsaddled and staked out together in the long grass. They had stopped near a creek tonight and most of the men were taking advantage of it to wash. Desmond was tempted to join them. The heat of the day lingered still, and the cool water looked refreshing. In the end, he decided it was beneath him.

He wasn't the only one to come to that decision, either, he realized. Aki sat alone on top of a rise in the ground, watching the others. Aside from their brief conversation on the first day, Desmond had seen little of him. Now, bored with the tedium of travel, he made his way over and lowered himself onto the ground next to Aki.

Aki glanced over at him but couldn't be bothered to rise. "Your Highness?"

"How long will it take us to reach Illsen once we've entered the mountains?"

"Seven, maybe eight, days. Unless the autumn rains come and then it will take a bit longer. We'll have to leave the cart behind then, as well."

Desmond let out a huff of air. "We're not leaving anything behind. Your people manage to move entire armies around in the mountains. You can't tell me they don't use any wheeled vehicles to do that."

"My people," Aki bit the words off with obvious irritation, "don't move armies during the spring or autumn rains. They either do it in the winter and use sleighs or in the summer when the ground is solid."

"I see. Does it bother you to remember that you belong to them? I'm surprised Father trusted you enough to send you with us." Desmond watched Aki out of the corner of his eye. He heard his sharp intake and saw him shift slightly. "What can we expect when we reach Illsen?"

"A town. With people in it," Aki responded dryly.

"Besides that?"

"I have no idea. I haven't been there in five years. I've been told it's changed greatly since I was there."

Desmond sighed. His own initial excitement at being chosen by Father was wearing thin after just a few days. It was quickly turning into impatience.

"I wish we would move faster," he muttered.

"The horses will need their strength when we reach the mountains," Aki reasoned, although Desmond hadn't really meant for him to hear.

"Yes, yes, I know. The captain has already explained all that to me. But we're barely crawling across these plains, and I, for one, am sick and tired of listening to nothing but wind howling all day. I say we could push them just a little harder and they'd be fine." Desmond paused and frowned. Father would have been annoyed by such an outburst. He would have said Desmond lacked the ability to control himself and that was the one thing that Desmond needed to prove on this trip. Worse still was that the reaction he'd been hoping to elicit from Aki wasn't forthcoming. Aki simply shrugged his words off, not rising to the bait of an argument.

Aki's only response was, "Whatever you decide, Your Highness."

Whatever he decided. Desmond appreciated the sound of those words as he contemplated them. He only had to say the word and they would set a faster pace. The captain would grumble, and Gregory would advise against it, but in the end, he was the prince and his word was law for this expedition. Still, he was upset at Aki's lack of reaction. He turned to study the courier and noticed the sword he wore at his side.

"You know how to use that?"

Aki followed his eyes to the sword and nodded.

"He knows how to use it well." Captain Tyrrel's voice came from just behind them and Desmond jumped in surprise. "At least, he holds his own every time I've seen him. You missed your calling, courier. You would have been a great soldier."

"Except for one small matter," Aki responded in a tone that made Desmond think they'd repeated this exact conversation many times before.

"And what small matter would that be?" Desmond said with a laugh. "A bit reluctant to put your life at risk for this kingdom? I'm surprised you're even allowed to carry a weapon."

"I hate fighting."

"Ah, well that might be a problem," Captain Tyrrel said.

Aki twisted around to study the captain, bothered by the tone in which he said the words. The captain said nothing more to clarify and Aki turned back to face the creek again.

Desmond hated the silence. He hated Aki's sullenness. He hated the boredom that gnawed into him, eating away reasonable thought. He was restless and aching to do something other than sit here and try to goad a reaction out of his interpreter. Pushing to his feet, he said, "I think I'd like to see how well you know how to fight. After all, with your history, you're as likely to use that on me as on our enemies and I'd like to know what I'm up against. Come on, let's go a round. I could use some practice myself."

Aki stared up at him in horror and shook his head. "That is absolutely the worst idea, Your Highness."

"He's right, Your Highness," Captain Tyrrel said. "If you want to see him fight, he can spar with one of my men like he's done before. If you want the practice, you can practice with me. I've seen both of you fight and he will destroy you."

Desmond looked between the two of them, a bit unsettled by the vehemence of their reaction and considering overriding both their words. He could. He was the one in charge. But something in both their faces stopped him. It wasn't fear. He pounded that into his head. He wasn't afraid of losing, especially not to an apprentice courier who didn't look remotely impressive. But he was curious. Very curious. He smiled tightly at the captain and said, "I'll settle for just watching him then."

"Very well, Your Highness. Courier?"

"Must I?"

"You wouldn't want to disappoint our prince," the captain said, his voice dripping with condescension. "Or rob him of his entertainment."

Aki grimaced at the words and shot an annoyed look in Desmond's direction as he got to his feet. Desmond got the uncomfortable feeling that the captain's words were a stab at him and not Aki. He watched as Aki withdrew his sword with a heavy sigh. He held it lightly, easily, but with its tip lowered to the ground. Every inch of him screamed reluctance as he waited for the captain.

"I thought you said I would face one of your soldiers, not you," Aki said when Captain Tyrrel drew his own weapon.

"Apparently, the prince doesn't need me to practice with. And it's not like you can't hold your own against me."

Desmond frowned. The captain was definitely irritated with him. He wondered if the man had been standing behind him while Desmond complained to Aki about their pace. Or maybe it was just the fact that he thought Desmond was making a spectacle of them for his own entertainment. He wasn't, of course. He would prove it too. He'd call off the whole thing and tell them he wasn't that interested.

He opened his mouth to do it, but the captain was already attacking, his sword cutting through the air towards Aki's still lowered one. A brief nightmare flashed before Desmond's eyes as he considered the possibility of having to go home to his father and tell him his interpreter was dead, killed by his own captain.

The sharp clang of metal on metal cleared the vision and Desmond stared in stunned disbelief at the speed with which Aki blocked.

Chapter 6

THERE WERE FEW THINGS AKI hated worse than being made a spectacle of. He didn't have any time to dwell on his anger, though. Captain Tyrrel was too quick, the ground too uneven for him to indulge in any thought except for the silver blade dancing before his eyes and how to stop it.

It wasn't the first time he'd faced the captain. Colin had hauled him out to the barracks one day and told him that from now on he was to practice with the soldiers there.

That had been after Colin discovered that Aki spent every spare moment in the weapons room. He hadn't asked Aki why, and Aki hadn't volunteered a reason. He didn't think Colin would understand his need for the distraction, the exhaustion. It was the only way to sleep at night and to keep his thoughts where they belonged during his waking hours. When he controlled a weapon, he controlled himself. And he needed that control more than anything.

He held Captain Tyrrel's eyes, reading the anger in them and realizing that it actually wasn't directed at him. He retreated, parrying every swipe of the captain's sword but putting little effort into taking the offensive. He was lighter, smaller, quicker on his feet than the captain and he used that to his advantage on the uneven ground.

"You're holding back," Captain Tyrrel said softly.

Aki leaped lightly out of his reach and shrugged. "I said I didn't want to do this."

"Do it anyway."

One look at the captain and Aki knew the match wouldn't end until Aki ended it. When Captain Tyrrel's sword connected with his again, he didn't back away. Inch by inch, he drove the captain back across the same ground they'd just covered. A small smile of satisfaction tugged at the captain's mouth and Aki found himself mirroring it.

There was a savage pleasure to be had in a fight, and for once he gave into it and began to enjoy himself. He let himself fall into the rhythm of it completely. He sped up. Each stroke, each thrust, each parry came faster than the one before it. The sword became an extension of him, every flick and twist of his wrist carried through the blade as it sang through the air. He had control over this. It was orderly, neat, precise. Unlike anything else in his life.

"Enough." Captain Tyrrel stepped out of his reach and lowered his sword.

Aki backed up a pace, breathing hard. He brought his arm up and rubbed his sleeve over his forehead. His sword slid back into its scabbard with a soft clank, and he noticed for the first time that Desmond was no longer their only observer. The others had formed a loose ring around them. The soldiers he was already used to practicing with and around and their presence did not bother him nearly as much as Gregory's, who was watching him with a troubled frown on his face.

"Like I said, courier, you missed your calling," Captain Tyrrel said, gesturing to Aki with his sword before putting it away. Then his face returned to stone as he turned toward the prince. "Was that entertainment enough for you, Your Highness? Or is there something else you'd still like to prove?"

"I wasn't... I was just bored. It was nothing."

"This trip isn't for your amusement. The men around you aren't here for your amusement. So, unless it serves some purpose greater than your personal diversion, I'd suggest you quit trying to goad anyone else into doing what you want."

Aki watched as the captain's words registered. Prince Desmond's face underwent a series of changes and grew redder by the minute. He leaped to his feet; his hands clenched tightly at his sides. Everyone, including Aki, pretended to look at anything but him and the captain. Only the captain maintained his intense gaze, daring the prince to answer him.

"Are you forgetting who I am, Captain?"

"Not in the least, Your Highness. It's hard to forget when you behave as if everything is about you."

Aki wanted to crawl into a hole in the ground for the prince. Casting a surreptitious glance at the others, he knew the sentiment was shared. He wondered how Captain Tyrrel had the nerve to speak like that to a member of the royal family. Prince Desmond was probably wondering the same thing.

"You have no right to speak to me like this. You answer to me, not the other way around."

"I answer to the king. And you are not that yet, thank goodness. Right now, you are nothing but an arrogant boy who can't bother to listen to the sound advice given to him by those who know better."

Prince Desmond met Aki's eyes and Aki knew what he was going to say before he even opened his mouth. A hole in the ground was becoming an ever more appealing idea. "At least I'm not a traitor. Tell me, Captain Tyrrel, what is your advice regarding him?" Prince Desmond waved a hand in Aki's direction, successfully shifting the attention of the group from himself to Aki. "Should we listen to him when he was one of the ones who plotted against my sister? Perhaps he is leading us into a trap."

Captain Tyrrel lowered his voice so that only those nearest heard his response. "He is bound in service to the king for the rest of his life for that crime and if your father trusts him with this task, I would suggest you figure out how to do the same. We'll get nowhere without that."

It was all Aki could do to keep from speaking out. He'd stopped listening after the captain's first words. They pounded through him like a second pulse, breathing life into every question, every doubt that had been planted in him over the last few months. Every time his training had deviated from the other apprenticed couriers. Every time Colin had dragged him through the darkened streets of town with no obvious purpose other than to stay out of sight. Every lesson Master Wehr taught that had no obvious bearing on his service as a courier. Every time he trained with the captain and his men until there wasn't a weapon he touched that he didn't know how to use expertly.

He stared at the dried grass beneath his feet as Captain Tyrrel waved the others off. He waited until everyone else had drifted away and only the captain stood still in front of him. Then he lifted his eyes, a question on his lips. But the captain held up a hand and forestalled him. "Don't ever ask me about what I just said. It's not for me to tell you."

And then the captain was walking away, leaving him to his thoughts. Aki's hand slid down to the hilt of his sword. Now was the sort of time when he liked to use it. There was nothing better for reining in his out-of-control thoughts than cutting and swinging and hacking until his arms shook and his lungs screamed for breath. If there had been a tree nearby, he would have unleashed himself on it. Instead, he was forced to retire with the rest of the men.

The wind had died down, settling into a gentle breeze, barely strong enough to rustle the dry grass. Aki lay still on his blanket staring up at the sky full of stars.

A murmur of voices carried through the darkness and Aki turned his head enough to see Gregory and the prince huddled near the last of the fire. They were too far away for him to hear the topic of their conversation, but he had a good guess. His name was probably being thrown around and quite possibly that of the captain.

Aki would have been bothered the night before. Tonight, though, he was beginning to feel as if getting to Aruuk and back in one piece and retrieving the captives were the least of his problems. He fell asleep still pondering the captain's words.

Chapter 7

RUMORS.

That's all she'd been able to find in this wretched town. No one knew anything for certain. Yes, there'd been a plot against the king's daughter. Yes, men from Aruuk and Karu had been a part of it. But the one name she was seeking was never mentioned. In fact, no names were. It was as if the people in this town were too far removed from the events happening in their own kingdom. Someone was hanged. Others were killed in the brief fight that ensued. A few were locked away. Most had made their way back to her mistress.

Karina tossed the core of the apple she'd been eating over her shoulder and stalked down the narrow street. She was running out of time. She was running out of money. But most importantly, she was running out of options.

Every day, she toyed with the idea that she would need to cross the great plains that divided the province of Dorsten from the rest of the kingdom. The plan was fraught with problems, and she didn't have the patience to work out solutions.

If there was one thing the people of this town agreed on, it was that the great plains couldn't be crossed alone and on foot. Although the smell of death had faded beyond a human's ability to sense, it still lingered enough to keep the land barren of animals. Any food that was needed on the journey across had to be carried. And one person, on foot, couldn't carry enough food to last them.

But Karina hated horses. And she didn't trust anyone. Those two facts were a stone wall that she battered her mind against every day.

The street ended in a much wider one. Karina stood in the mouth of it, watching the large party of horsemen as they rode past. Not one of them glanced in her direction and Karina let out a sigh of relief. It didn't matter how many times she told herself that there was nothing suspicious about her presence in Dorsten, that she looked just like any number of other innocent people out on the streets during the day. She still couldn't shake the habit of watching over her shoulder, of searching each face for signs of suspicion.

Confident that none of the party noticed her in particular, she took her time studying them as they rode past. There were more than twenty, but she didn't bother to get a more accurate count. They moved through the street quickly, carrying with them a strong sense of purpose and authority.

Whispers flew around Karina, and she soaked them up, filtering through them to learn what she could of the group. It was the prince, one person said. Another commented on the recent raid that had left the townspeople shaken.

Karina had already heard all about the raid. It had happened the same day she arrived. A group of men had swept down from the north on a small mountain hamlet, killing or carrying away captive the entire population. It was the work of Aruuk, most said. A break in the treaty that the king had signed with them. Karina wasn't sure what to believe and had reached the decision that it didn't matter to her. Her task remained unchanged by the events.

When it became obvious that the party was not stopping in town but heading for the unoccupied castle above it, she decided the rumor about the prince traveling with them was true. Only a prince would choose the dark and unwelcoming castle as a place to rest.

Using the distraction, Karina snatched a loaf of bread off the baker's wagon and disappeared once more into the alleys. No one followed her.

Time. She needed more time. Her mistress would run out of patience soon and Karina knew nothing in the world would save her if that happened. The woman's parting words rung in her ears.

"Return with my son, or not at all, Karina," her mistress had said.

To most people, the threat would have meant nothing. But to Karina...

Karina couldn't fathom a life without her mistress's protection. It was the only thing that had kept her alive so far. She had no skills, no knowledge to make it on her own. The last two weeks had proved that beyond a doubt. Karina had to make it back to her, but more importantly, Karina had to find the lost son first. The son was her way home.

Chapter 8

NOTHING HAD PREPARED DESMOND for the size of the mountains. A little thrill ran through him as they approached. They were so different from anything around Bren.

As the towering peaks closed in around them, Desmond thought of Aki's words when they first spoke.

For the first time, Desmond was forced to acknowledge the truth in them. There was no way they could scour all the hidden places of the mountains. He looked out of the corner of his eye to where Gregory rode beside him.

"So, are we still going to search for them first, Your Highness?" Gregory asked, an annoying smirk on his face as if he'd been able to read Desmond's mind.

Desmond bristled and changed his mind. Captain Tyrrel's lecture had eroded what little respect the men had for him. He'd sensed the change in them from that day onward. They stayed out of his way, but he caught their looks, their amused smiles, their whispers when they thought he wasn't watching. They treated the courier with more deference than they did him, he thought. A traitor held in higher regard than their prince.

"Aki!" he twisted around in his saddle and called.

A moment later he heard the courier's horse coming up beside him.

"Your Highness?" Aki didn't even look at him when he spoke. He seemed intent on the landscape.

"My father sent you along as both interpreter and guide. You can't very well guide us from the back, can you?"

"I suppose not, Your Highness," Aki answered evenly.

Desmond gritted his teeth. He could see that the way he addressed the courier bothered him, but he wouldn't react. Desmond envied him that level of control. Father was forever complaining about how easily Desmond let his temper fly. His mother was always chiding him for his lack of temperance. Perhaps that's why Father had taken such an interest in the young courier. Perhaps he was what Father wanted in a son. The thought made him hot all over.

"Is there a problem, Your Highness?" Gregory asked from his other side.

"No, no problem. I'm just reminding our courier that we're relying on him to get us to our destination."

"And what is our destination, Your Highness?" Gregory pressed.

He couldn't admit defeat. Not after all the respect he'd already lost. He needed to make his own decision, not the one everyone expected of him. "We search, just like I said we would. And if we find no sign of them, we ride for Illsen."

"As you wish, Your Highness."

Desmond wanted to yell at Gregory, at everyone. They stuck his title onto every sentence addressed to him, throwing it back in his face after the captain had humiliated him. It had ceased to mean anything but a mockery.

The jingle of a horse's bridle as it came up behind them alerted Desmond to Captain Tyrrel's approach. The captain's face didn't reveal if he'd heard any part of their conversation. His eyes, like Aki's, were drawn instead to the landscape around them. Desmond wasn't sure what it was they were looking for. So far, he hadn't seen a soul outside of their group.

"You should ride in the middle, Your Highness."

"Is there any danger, Captain?"

"There's always danger," the captain said cryptically, then added, "these mountains hold a lot of good hiding places for an ambush. If you're in the middle, there's a smaller chance of you being hit if we're attacked. Gregory, the same goes for you."

"What about him?" Desmond pointed to Aki who was still looking at everything except the people around him. It was starting to make Desmond nervous, as if he could see something that the others couldn't.

"He's the guide. We follow him."

Two days brought them to the border. Although the border was guarded on their side, they ran into no one from Aruuk. Desmond almost laughed. All his life he'd heard about how fearsome their enemies to the north were, but not a single guard was there to prevent them from entering. They could have marched an entire army through and no one in Aruuk would have been any the wiser.

Desmond was pleased to still have the cart rattling along behind them. The mountain road they were following was narrow and deeply rutted, but it was dry and firm.

Until the third day.

They woke to the pattering of rain on their tents. Desmond groaned as he pulled the flap open and saw outside. Dense, dark clouds shielded the tall peaks from view and there was no end of them in sight. Worse still, the rain leached the warmth right out of the air and a damp chill settled over him even inside his tent.

Pulling the courier aside as they prepared to mount up for the day, he asked, "How long will it keep up like this?"

Aki shrugged and gave him an odd look. "It's the weather. It does what it wants. We'll have to leave the cart behind, though. It will get bogged down in the mud."

"I already told you; we're not leaving anything behind."

It was a miserable day. Desmond had put on his heavier clothes, and they were still soaked through within an hour. His saddle squeaked loudly with every step, the wet leather chafing against him. Steam rose off his horse's drenched neck. Water ran down the steep slopes surrounding them, pooling in the deep cart tracks, and turning them into thick sludge.

Late in the afternoon, the rain came down harder. Desmond had pulled his hood up over his head and could see nothing but what was directly in front of him and even that was blurred by the steady streams of rain falling from the sky. A shout came from behind him. Twisting around in his saddle, and grimacing as a cold rivulet of rainwater trickled down a gap in his clothes, Desmond looked for the source of the sound. The grimace turned into a scowl as he realized the meaning of the shout. Behind two straining horses, the cart sank into the mire.

"Get down and push it out. We're not leaving it behind."

It took almost an hour to free it and by then, there wasn't enough daylight left to keep going. Desmond didn't dare look in Aki's direction.

Sleep was difficult to come by that night. Everything was wet. The ground, the tent, the blankets. As he huddled beneath his blankets, a deep appreciation for his title and position settled over him. All the other men took their turns on watch at night, except for him and Gregory. A small corner of his mind whispered that the others resented him for his privilege, and on a less miserable night he would have agreed. Tonight, though, he was just thankful to be spared the discomfort.

For two more days they struggled on, stopping often to free the cart from the mud. Desmond, even with his inexperience, could see the effects on the men and horses. Their progress, never fast to begin with, was almost nothing.

When the cart stuck fast once more and half the men were working to push it out, Desmond rode ahead to where both Captain Tyrrel and Aki were sitting still on their horses. Neither looked at him at his approach. He realized that they were both staring through the rain at the same thing - although, what that thing was, he couldn't imagine.

"How much farther is it, courier?"

Aki whipped his head around at the sound of his voice. His eyes took in the cart behind them, and he sighed audibly. "At this rate, more than a week, Your Highness."

"That's too long."

"Then leave the cart, Your Highness," Captain Tyrrel interrupted. "We can divide the load between the horses. We'll move a lot faster and at this point, that is imperative."

"Why?"

"Because when this rain finally does let up it will only be because snow has set in and I, for one, do not wish to be trapped in these mountains for an entire winter."

"We're being watched," Aki said quietly before Desmond had a chance to answer the captain.

"By whom? How long have they been there?" Desmond followed Aki's eyes, but the rain blurred and distorted everything. He thought he saw a hazy shape moving against the dark mountainside, half hidden by the evergreens that grew along the lower slopes, but he could just as easily have been mistaken.

"I would imagine they are Aruuken soldiers, and they've been there since we crossed the border."

"Nonsense. There was no one when we crossed." Neither Aki nor the captain said anything, and Desmond went on. "And if they have been there that long, why am I just now hearing about it?"

"I did tell you to ride in the middle of the group for your own protection, Your Highness."

"That's not the same as telling me we're being followed." Desmond raised his voice, and turned to Aki, "And you never said a word about anything at all."

Aki shrugged. "Your father sent me along as a guide and interpreter. Not a guard."

Desmond's face went red, and he looked down. There was no mistaking the tone in Aki's voice as he threw Desmond's own words back at him.

"Besides," Aki continued, "they aren't a threat. If they were, we wouldn't have made it past the first night. They're just keeping an eye on us to see what we'll do."

Admitting defeat was hard, but Desmond saw the relief on the men's faces when he announced that they would leave the cart and carry the rest of the supplies with them on the horses.

His own sense of relief came when, almost a week later, Aki, once more out front, stopped abruptly at the top of a rise. Desmond broke out of the center of the group where he'd been content to ride since he'd learned of their followers. He brought his horse to a stop next to the courier's. Through the mist of rain, he could make out the dark shapes of buildings clustered together in a small valley.

"Illsen?"

"Illsen."

There was something in the way Aki said the word that caused Desmond to search his face. It was hard to accomplish since both of them had their hoods up, but he didn't need much of a look to see the paleness in Aki's face, the tremor in his hands as he gripped his reins.

"You really don't want to be here, do you?" The thought had never occurred to Desmond. These were Aki's people. If anything, Desmond had been half-expecting him to spring some trap on the group.

"If you trust nothing else I say, Your Highness, trust this - that there is absolutely nothing I want about this place," Aki said softly, his voice almost carried away in the rain. "I would rather be anywhere but here."

"Will they know you here?"

Aki was quiet for a long time. "I hope not, Your Highness."

Chapter 9

WELCOME HOME, AKI GUNDARSON," the older man who met them inside the Chief's house said, inclining his head as he spoke. "It is a great honor to receive the representatives of Dival. But may I ask the reason?"

Aki's heart dropped when he heard his name. It had been too much to hope for that no one would recognize him. At least it was just Faramund. Of all the people Aki knew in Illsen, he was one of the few Aki didn't attach to any horrible memories. The older clansman from Jarle had never been anything but civil to Aki once he'd been acknowledged as a son of Chief Gundar and he'd had absolutely nothing to do with Aki before that. Aki explained in a few words their purpose for coming and Faramund nodded solemnly along.

"We've heard of no such raids, and we certainly have not condoned such raids. It was part of the agreement we reached with your brother, Sasha, and the king of Dival." Faramund motioned for him to follow him through the entry hall and into a large room. Aki recognized the room. It was where Gundar met with his clansmen to plan their yearly raids. The irony of using it now to settle a misunderstanding was not lost on him. "Please, sit. Tell us what you know of the attack and perhaps that will shed some light on the culprits."

For the next hour, Aki translated Prince Desmond, Gregory, and Captain Tyrrel's words to Faramund and two other clansmen who had joined them. Aki only recognized one of them. He spent the entire hour with his head down, hoping the man didn't recognize him. Cadoc's was a face he would never forget for it haunted his darkest memories, the ones he'd buried so far down that he could imagine they never happened. Until, that is, he was sitting in the presence of the man responsible.

Faramund's face had grown very grave as Aki related the words of the other men and Aki knew him well enough to know it was no act on his part. Faramund truly had no idea.

"That is troubling news indeed. You were wise to come here first, though. To assume we were responsible would have been a grave mistake when the peace between our two countries is already so fragile. We have no desire for war with Dival."

Aki repeated the words for the other three.

"Do you think he's telling the truth?" Gregory asked.

"He is."

"Then we've wasted our time coming here," Prince Desmond said, throwing his hands up in frustration. "We could have been out there looking for the captives already."

"We're not wasting our time if they're willing to help us," Captain Tyrrel said. "Courier, ask him if, as proof of their innocence, they will join us in searching for the rogues responsible for this. Their people will know these mountains. They'll know where hidden things can be found."

Aki tried to keep his irritation hidden. Despite all the times he had been at the barracks, training with the captain and his men, the man still refused to call him by his name.

When he asked Faramund, the man was quick to agree.

"I will send out men right away."

"We'll go with them," Aki said.

"No, your men and horses need rest."

Aki couldn't very well argue with that. Just sitting in a warm, dry room for the last hour was enough to make him want to fall into a bed. He wasn't sure how to convey the suggestion to Prince Desmond, however. The prince seemed determined to do everything Aki advised against and even the captain couldn't overrule.

Faramund stood up before he had the chance and said, "Tell them they are welcome to stay the night. I have had rooms prepared for your entire party. They may decide in the morning whether or not to join our men in the search, although I advise very strongly against it."

Aki stood in front of the door to his old room, hands clenched tightly at his sides. Whose idea was it to put him here? If it was Faramund's, it was easily forgiven, but Aki had briefly met Cadoc's eyes as they were leaving and the darkness he'd read in them made him worry the man had recognized him as well.

Brushing past the man who'd escorted him, he stepped inside the old, familiar space. The prince, he knew, occupied the room to his right and Gregory's was just beyond the prince's. Captain Tyrrel and his men were sharing the rooms to his left. Although the Chief's family no longer occupied this house, it was still the center of the Aruuken government and was well-designed for its purpose.

Not much had been altered since he'd left with Gundar almost five years before. The bed, the set of drawers, everything was exactly where he'd left it. As he pushed the door shut behind him, Aki tried to stave off the wave of homesickness that threatened to undo him. He had never known such an intense desire to return to anywhere. But now, all he could think about was his small, but very comfortable room at Stephan and Alina's. Just Alina's now, he remembered, and the loneliness overran his efforts to control it.

Stephan was gone forever.

And so much had been left unsaid between them. He'd been able to push all thoughts of his loss away since Colin had shown up on his doorstep that night, but here, alone in a room that held nothing but the worst memories of his life and surrounded by people who either disliked or distrusted him, his resolve was too weak.

For a long time, he just sat on the floor in front of his door. He was still in his wet clothes, chilled through and through by the rain, but more than an hour went by before he could find the strength of will to push himself off the floor to change into something dry and warm. Tossing his wet clothes into a heap in the corner to be dealt with later, he sank onto the bed.

In the hour he'd spent sitting doing nothing but trying to rein his thoughts and emotions back in, the last of the daylight had fled. Aki didn't bother to grope around in the gloom, searching for the lamp and matches he knew were in the room. He welcomed the darkness. He liked the way it closed in around him, shutting out the rest of the world. Within the darkness, he could imagine himself anywhere but here.

Laying back on the pillow, Aki was sure he'd never be able to fall asleep in this room. It was surprising to him, then, when a shift in the room made him stir and he realized he was just waking up.

And he wasn't alone.

Breathing, measured and quiet in the stillness, reached his ears. The floor right next to his bed creaked.

Aki tried to roll over, tried to sit up. A hand clamped over his face. It shoved him back onto his pillow. The bed beneath him shifted with the weight of a man climbing on, pressing Aki's body against the mattress, and pinning him in place. The hand covering his mouth and nose pressed down, smothering him, and preventing him from making any sound. Aki felt the hot breath of the man against his ear as he leaned down and whispered, "You didn't think I could forget you, did you? I never forget my favorites."

Cadoc.

Aki's blood ran cold.

His voice was exactly as Aki remembered it, the same slur in his whispered words, the same lust. He struggled beneath the much heavier man. Cadoc's free hand slipped between them, fumbling with Aki's trousers, his fingers working their way inside. Aki's lungs threatened to explode. Blood pounded in his ears as he tried to twist away, tried to slide a hand beneath his pillow.

"You didn't use to fight, Aki," Cadoc hissed in his ear as Aki writhed beneath him.

Aki's fingers brushed against something hard under his pillow and he wrapped them tightly around it. He pulled it free.

In a single, desperate motion, he brought the knife down and jabbed it into Cadoc's thigh. The man grunted with pain and his hand on Aki's face loosened. Aki drew in a ragged, shuddering breath before sinking the knife in again. Cadoc yelped this time and reached for the knife.

If he got a hold of it, Aki knew it was over. Bringing it up faster than Cadoc could react, Aki did the only thing he could think to do. He slashed the blade across Cadoc's exposed throat.

Warm blood splashed down on his face and Aki twisted his head out of the way, trying to squirm his way out from underneath Cadoc's body. Cadoc's hands flew to his throat. They pressed against it in a frantic effort to stem the flow of blood. A strange choking, gurgling sound came from him.

In the darkness, Aki could just make out his eyes, wide open with horror and the fear of dying. Aki shoved his weakening body away, off of him. Cadoc stumbled off the bed and fell with a crash against the wall.

Aki was on his feet before his mind caught up with what his body was doing, with what he'd done. The door was only a few feet away. He reached out a hand and took a step toward it. Help was beyond that door. He needed help. He needed someone. Anyone. But his body failed him, all of his strength deserting him. He sank to the floor against his bed.

There was a roaring in his ears. His heart hammered against his chest. He was heaving for every breath. Staring down at his blood covered hands, he knew they were trembling wildly. A curious moaning sound broke through the roar that filled his head. It was coming from him, he realized. And just as he came to that realization, the door to his room was thrown open and light flooded in, preventing him from seeing who stood beyond it.

"What...," the question faded off in a soft gasp.

Aki just sat, staring down at his hands still. They were so much worse to look at in the light.

Blood.

There was so much blood.

More than Aki had thought it was possible for one man to bleed. He stared and stared at his hands, at the bloody knife still clenched in the one. He heard a shuffling of feet, more gasps, more whispers, but still he stared.

His hands had killed a man.

And not just any man. His hands had killed the man responsible for his darkest moments, the man who had shown Aki that lust was not just reserved for the slave girls.

Cadoc was dead.

He repeated the words to himself silently. Cadoc was dead, because of him. Cadoc would never hurt another, would never force another in his bed.

Someone was kneeling in front of him. A hand touched his bloody one, the one still holding the knife. He flinched at the touch and the rhythm of his heart flared wildly out of control. His fingers were being pried off. He refused to let go, though.

"Give it here, courier," Captain Tyrrel said softly.

"He's dead," Aki whispered, but made no effort to release the knife. Captain Tyrrel continued to force his fingers from it. "I killed him."

Captain Tyrrel sighed. Aki heard it, but he didn't understand it. Was Captain Tyrrel annoyed that Aki had killed him? Did he not understand what the man wanted from Aki?

Aki finally dragged his eyes away from his hands, and as if that action freed his hands, he let go of the knife. He stared up at Captain Tyrrel and then past him. The prince and Gregory both stood in the doorway. Their faces were ghostly pale in the dancing light of the lamp Gregory held. Beyond them, he knew there were others, but he couldn't make them out.

"What happened?" Captain Tyrrel asked, and Aki turned his attention back to him. "Did he try to kill you?"

Aki shook his head.

"Then what was he in here for? Is there something of yours he wanted to steal?"

Aki shook his head again. He didn't want to tell anyone why Cadoc was in his room. Ever since Cadoc had first taken him to his room when Aki was eight, Aki had pretended those nights never happened. He couldn't bring himself to acknowledge that they were real now.

"Aki, tell me." It was the first time Captain Tyrrel had ever used his name.

His eyes dropped. He would never tell what Cadoc wanted from him. Not ever. No command in the world would induce him to confess.

When he looked back up at the captain, he knew the man had guessed. Aki glanced over the captain's shoulder to the others, hoping they hadn't. The prince still looked confused. He did not understand the baseness a man could achieve. But he saw understanding on both the captain and Gregory's faces. Understanding and something else - disgust, maybe? Aki had never been so humiliated in his life.

"Well, this is a disaster," Gregory murmured, and Aki was pretty sure the man hadn't wanted him to hear. He looked apologetic as soon as it became obvious that Aki had and tried to explain himself. "I just mean, this complicates things with our hosts. If I'm not mistaken, that's one of their... what do you call them?"

The controlled, distant part of him was starting to separate Aki from the horror that surrounded him, and he was surprised to hear his own, emotionless voice answering, "Clansmen."

"Yes, clansmen. What are they going to say when they find out that he is dead, killed by one of our own?"

"We'll tell them the truth, that he attacked one of ours first and the courier only killed him in defense. Surely that's acceptable here?" Captain Tyrrel studied Aki's face for the answer.

"Only if he drew blood first," Aki whispered.

A look passed between the captain and Gregory. Gregory nodded slightly and Captain Tyrrel turned back to Aki. He glanced at the knife he'd taken from Aki and then back at Aki.

"I'm sorry." He reached for Aki's arm, but Aki pulled away. "I have to."

"Not that one. They can't see that arm." It was the logical part of him speaking, the part that wasn't bothered by pain or humiliation or shock.

And it was that part of him that watched as Captain Tyrrel brought the knife up to his upper left arm and sliced through his shirt and into his flesh. He clamped his mouth shut and no sound escaped him as he watched blood bubble up from the wound. The captain had done it diagonally, making it look as if Cadoc had been aiming for his heart but had missed.

Aki stared at the growing stain on his sleeve and then at the body of Cadoc half sitting against the wall a few feet away and then at his own hands. He blinked several times and swallowed hard as icy fingers climbed up his throat. Then he threw up.

Captain Tyrrel could move very quickly when he wanted to. Now was one of those moments he chose to exercise that talent. He jumped back out of the way while Aki's stomach emptied itself onto the floor.

"Everybody out. Go back to your rooms," he ordered. When Aki was done, he turned back to him. "Now, call the Aruuken guard. Tell them he attacked you first, show them the wound, and pray they believe your story."

Chapter 10

FEVER.

That was the latest rumor. It flew from mouth to mouth, almost faster than the dreaded illness did. Karina crouched behind a barrel, listening as two women discussed it while waiting their turn to buy bread. From what they said, more than half the town had already succumbed to it. Karina knew that part at least was nothing more than rumor. She had seen the graves being dug outside of town. There were a lot, but definitely not half the town.

For not the first time, Karina wished she were back home with her mistress. It was safe there. Safe from fevers. Safe from vulgar men. Safe from thieves and pickpockets. Her mistress never allowed bad things to happen to her. If Karina fell ill, her mistress's own physician was there to take care of her.

The women moved on and Karina decided there was no more information to be gleaned from this hiding spot. She stood up, her hand gripping the edge of the barrel as a wave of dizziness sent the world spinning around her. One hand pressed to her head, she wandered down the main street.

There was no point in lingering in this town anymore. Her search wouldn't end until she crossed the great plains. She'd put together a skeletal plan to accomplish this, but today her head ached too badly to even think about beginning. It's what came from sleeping in any nook she could find, she thought. Last night was worse than most. It had rained all night and there wasn't a dry place to lay her head. Instead, she'd sheltered behind a stack of crates, the space cramped and full of puddles by the time dawn came.

There weren't many people out today. It was the fever. Everyone was afraid of it. They hid in their houses. Karina knew this because she'd caught glimpses of faces peering out the windows at those brave or foolish enough to walk the streets.

Houses that were already stricken with the illness hung a piece of red cloth outside their door as a warning. Karina usually gave those homes a wide berth but today she was too tired to care. She'd have to find a better place to sleep tonight, Karina told herself.

"Watch where you're going, girl," a woman's voice chided her.

Karina looked up and realized with horror that she'd nearly collided with the woman. "Forgive me, ma'am," she whispered, putting her hand on her head again. It didn't actually make the pain lessen at all, but her head felt like it was going to burst, and it was a strange sort of consolation to try to hold it together with her hands.

The woman started to move on, obviously in a great hurry. Everyone was in a hurry these days, Karina noted. No one wanted to be out in the streets where they could be exposed to the fever.

Why she did what she did, Karina would never know, but she called after the woman. Perhaps it was because the woman had a pleasant, kind looking face. Or perhaps Karina was so lost and miserable that she didn't care anymore. Whatever the reason, she was surprised when the woman turned and faced her again.

"What is it?"

Karina floundered. She wasn't sure what she was going to say. She only knew that she did not want to spend another night out on her own. Not with the ache that settled over her entire body and a chill from last night's rain that wouldn't go away.

"I don't have anywhere to sleep," she blurted out.

The woman raised her eyebrows as she studied Karina and Karina, in turn, studied the ground. She could never bear to meet anyone's eyes. Her mistress had taught her that it would attract the sort of attention that she wanted to avoid.

"You're ill," the woman said, her voice quiet enough that no one else could hear her.

"No, ma'am. Only very tired and cold from trying to sleep in the rain."

"Nonsense, child. You've got fever. I should know. I've seen it often enough."

Karina stepped back and stumbled, her hands gripping her head. She shook her head as a chill surged through her. "I can't be sick. I can't," she cried. "I haven't finished yet. What do I do? How do I make myself better?"

The woman stared at her in pity. "There's not much you can do."

Karina's eyes smarted. She brought her hands down to cover her face. "This can't be happening. It just can't. If I die, I'll never get back to her."

She stumbled away from the woman who had given her such cruel news. Her legs trembled under her as she tried to run through the streets to some corner where she could hide until this nightmare was over. People got out of her way as if she carried a sign before her announcing her illness.

"Wait!" The woman's voice caught up with her. "Wait, girl."

Karina tripped and fell onto her hands and knees. Every muscle in her body ached with weariness and instead of getting to her feet, she curled up on the ground and wrapped her arms tightly around herself. There was no warmth to be had, though, and the chill she'd had since last night made her shake convulsively. Tears slid out of her eyes as she lay there.

"Why did you run away from me like that?" The woman's voice came from just behind her shoulder and Karina felt a hand resting on her arm. "Come with me."

Karina staggered to her feet.

"I'll never forgive myself if I left you to fend for yourself in the streets. And there's no point in pretending it'll do any good to stay away from you. Norman and I have both already had it. So come along," the woman said, grabbing Karina by the arm and guiding her back the way she'd run.

"You haven't been sick long. Perhaps we've caught it soon enough to cure you."

Karina stared at the woman in wonder. In all her travels, starting in Jarle, she had never come across anyone who had shown such spontaneous kindness to her.

"Who are you?"

"You can call me Lydia." She stopped in front of a small house that had a red cloth tied across the top of the door. "Here we are. You'll be safe here...?"

It took Karina a moment to realize the woman was waiting for her to share her name. "Karina, ma'am. I don't have money."

"Did I say a word about money, Karina? You may stay as long as you need to."

Karina allowed Lydia to guide her inside and into a small room. There was a fireplace burning brightly that chased away the dampness of the autumn rains and a soft couch in front of it. Karina curled up on the couch and relaxed for the first time since she'd left her mistress's side.

Chapter 11

CONSIDERING IT WAS ONE OF their own leaders dead, Desmond thought the Aruukens handled the news with surprising calm. Indifference, almost. But even more surprising than that was the way Aki delivered the news. His voice was dead and his eyes even more so. There was no sign of the fear that he'd shown earlier. Only nothingness. Desmond found it a little unsettling to listen to.

Desmond remembered what they had first seen upon entering Aki's room. It was a sight he wasn't likely to forget soon. Aside from the shocking amount of blood, he had been most startled by the look in Aki's eyes. They were filled with such horror, such loathing that it frightened him a little. He could tell that even Captain Tyrrel was deeply disturbed by what he'd seen in that room. The captain's face was pinched with worry now as he sat beside Aki, following a conversation he couldn't actually understand.

It was still the middle of the night, much to Desmond's annoyance. They could just as easily discuss this in the morning and nothing would have changed.

When Aki had stumbled out of his room, bleeding from the wound Captain Tyrrel had given him, and summoned the Aruuken guard there had been a flurry of activity. The present clansmen were awakened and now Prince Desmond found himself sitting in the same room they'd met in earlier. With him was Captain Tyrrel, Gregory, Aki and two of the captain's soldiers. On the other side of the table, were the two remaining clansmen and the first Aruuken guard Aki had told.

So far, Aki had spoken only to the Aruuken men and hadn't bothered to translate. Desmond couldn't decide if he'd just forgotten to or if he felt there was no need to. It didn't matter. They all knew the story he was telling. Desmond searched the faces of the two clansmen. Gregory was right about one thing. If they didn't believe Aki, their entire party was in trouble. There was nothing diplomatic about killing. Even if it was justified.

The clansmen questioned Aki, speaking quickly, and frowning and glancing at each other often. It made Desmond nervous. He didn't care so much what happened to Aki, except that he was their only way to communicate with these people, but he cared a great deal about what it might mean for him and the rest of the party.

He turned his attention back to Aki as he answered their questions. The same dead, vacant expression. The same dull tone. Either the questions didn't bother him, or he was beyond caring. Desmond suspected the latter.

Aki started to say something else just then but the eldest clansman, the one Aki introduced earlier as Faramund, waved his hand and interrupted him. He gestured toward Aki's arm and Desmond realized that no one had bothered to bind up the wound Captain Tyrrel had given him. That explained the paleness of Aki's face. Part of it, at least. Aki had been plenty pale before the captain had cut his arm open. His sleeve was now completely soaked red.

Faramund sent the Aruuken guard out of the room with a few words and turned to his companion. While they spoke together, Aki leaned back in his chair and shut his eyes.

"What did they say?" Captain Tyrrel laid a hand on Aki's shoulder and turned him toward them.

"They believed me."

"That's good. That's really good." Gregory said, relief loosening his features.

Aki nodded, his eyes vacant as they met the captain's. Something passed between the two, a look Desmond couldn't decipher, didn't want to decipher. Desmond, watching Aki, couldn't help but wonder what it was like to be responsible for taking another life. For a moment, he understood why his father was always so intent on maintaining their peace.

Footsteps crossed the floor and Desmond looked up to find the guard returned, another man trailing behind him.

"Who is this, courier?"

"Just a doctor."

Desmond leaned forward in his chair, curious as the doctor went to work. His own life in the castle had not included many injuries at all. Captain Tyrrel helped Aki pull his arm out of its sleeve. He made to remove his shirt completely, but Aki shook his head weakly.

"I can't let them see that arm," he whispered, his voice faint.

"Why not?" Desmond spoke up for the first time. "You've said that twice now. What's the secret?"

"Tell you later, Your Highness."

Desmond scowled. He thought, under the circumstances, that his title would be dropped from conversation. He'd become quite tired of it. Besides, he didn't like being put off and he could tell that Aki had no interest in revealing his information later.

"There's no need for all of us to stay in here," Captain Tyrrel said. "Your Highness, you should return to your quarters and try to get some rest. Gregory, you too."

With a heavy sigh meant entirely for the captain, Desmond got to his feet. He was being dismissed. Gregory put a hand on his arm to draw him away as the doctor began stitching Aki's sliced arm closed again. Desmond fought down his own nausea at the sight and his reluctance to leave vanished. He gave one glance back at them as he left the room and noticed for the first time the scars that were just visible on Aki's shoulder and back - scars that could only have come from a whip.

Gregory followed him into his room.

"Your Highness, I think we'd best prepare the men to leave soon. Even if they believe our courier, this incident will only breed ill will with our hosts. He clearly has old enemies here and we don't want to linger long enough for more of them to reveal themselves."

"It's not a trap, do you think? He has betrayed Dival once before. Perhaps this was planned all along."

Gregory shook his head. "Your Highness, I've seen a lot in my many years. I think I can safely say that nothing that happened tonight was planned by our courier."

"We still have to search for the captives and find out who was behind the attack. I'm not going home to my father without succeeding."

"Then let us hope that they will not rescind their offer of help over this."

Although Desmond wasn't sure how long it would take, he was determined to still be awake when Aki and Captain Tyrrel returned to their rooms. He heard the murmur of their voices, or the captain's voice at least, as they came down the hallway sometime later. He waited even longer. Until there was no sound at all. Then he left his room and went to Aki's.

The door stood ajar, and Desmond pushed it open quietly. Inside, his back to him and bent over the basin of water, Aki was furiously scrubbing his hands, his arms, his face. Considering the fact that both the cloth in his hands and the water in the basin were now the color of blood, Desmond didn't think his continued efforts were going to produce a better result.

His eyes passed over the room, noting the attempts someone had made at cleaning up the mess. The body of the man Aki killed was gone and it was evident that efforts had been made to scrub the floor and the blankets had been stripped off the bed and replaced with clean ones. Still, the stains remained, and Desmond's stomach twisted at the memory of what had just taken place.

When it became clear that Aki remained unaware of his presence, Desmond coughed. There was no missing the terror in Aki's eyes as he spun around to face him. It faded instantly, replaced by the same dullness Desmond had seen before.

"It's later," Desmond said.

Aki looked vaguely puzzled.

"You said you'd tell me later why no one can see that arm. What are you hiding?"

Shaking his head tiredly, Aki held out his right arm. Desmond winced when he saw what Aki had been hiding. He wasn't sure what he'd been expecting. The symbols burned into Aki's skin definitely weren't it.

"Just these, Your Highness.   Because, despite everything Sasha has tried to do to change this country, they will always see a slave as nothing more than a slave. Because if they ever see these, they'll not listen to another word I say." Aki's voice was as monotone as before but there was a weariness that crept into as he spoke, a weariness that came from more than just a sleepless night. "I'm not hiding anything from you for the sake of treason, Your Highness. I'm hiding it so that we can get home in one piece."

Desmond looked away. Ashamed. He didn't want Aki to see that even now he distrusted him. "Did it hurt?"

It was a ridiculous question and Desmond wished he could cut his tongue out for having spoken so thoughtlessly. He didn't have his father's skill in guiding a conversation or saying just the right thing.

The slightly puzzled look returned to Aki's face, and he cocked his head as he stared at the prince. Desmond preferred that to the vacant expression he'd seen most of the night. "Of course, it hurt. They are burned on, Your Highness."

"How long have you had them?"

This time Aki's expression turned distant and wary. He turned away again, his steps unsteady as he crossed the room, and sat down on the bed without answering.

"Don't ignore me."

"Can we not have this conversation in the morning, Your Highness?"

Desmond opened his mouth to insist on an answer, but he realized just how white Aki still was. For the first time that night, it occurred to him that what was an inconvenience and irritation to him was a waking nightmare for the courier. He'd been attacked, killed a man, been injured by his own captain, and then had to answer questions about it all in the space of a couple of hours. He stopped himself from speaking the words he wanted to say. Instead, he gave a crisp nod and went for the door.

"Thank you, Your Highness."

Chapter 12

BACK AND FORTH HE WENT.

The room was small, and Aki was avoiding the side of the bed where Cadoc's body had fallen. Although it had been removed before he'd returned to the room, the smears of blood remained. His steps were quiet but restless, pacing the length of the room.

He was tired.

Not just tired. He was heavy. The thought of falling asleep in this room made him ill again. Every time he tried to shut his eyes, he saw Cadoc's leering face, saw blood running between his fingers as they pressed against his throat. The alternative was to just not close his eyes. Hence the pacing.

Outside the window, day was dawning. Aki paused in front of the window. From it, he could see the hunting spot Lars and he had spent many hours in. Above the peak of the mountain, gray clouds swirled threateningly, hiding the rising sun. There would be more rain. Soon it would be snow.

There was a knock on his door. Aki tensed and his breath caught in his throat at the sound of it. He didn't answer. He was not ready to face anyone again. Not yet. It was better if they thought he was just asleep. Another knock came, a little louder than the first. Then the door opened, and Captain Tyrrel stood just outside in the hallway, arms folded across his chest.

"I was just coming," Aki tried to explain.

"No, you weren't." Captain Tyrrel looked mildly annoyed for a moment. He looked around the room and his expression softened a little. "You didn't sleep at all, did you?"

"I'm fine."

"Didn't ask that. Guess it doesn't really matter anyway at this point. One of the clansmen, Faramund I think you said his name was, seems to want to talk to us. Think you can manage that this morning? Both Gregory and the prince are of the mind that we should leave as quickly as we can - with or without the clansmen's help. And judging by the looks we're getting this morning, I'm tempted to agree with them. Faramund might have believed your story, but some of his people aren't happy about it."

"It's me they're not happy with," Aki murmured. He sat on the edge of his bed, holding his head between his hands. "Give me just a few minutes. Then I'll say whatever you want me to say to Faramund."

"You'll remind him that his man attacked you first, that if he allows any reprisals, it will precipitate war with Dival, and that he still owes us help that he promised yesterday."

Aki looked up, an argument on the tip of his tongue. But then he just nodded.

"Is something wrong with all that?"

"No. Nothing." Aki stood up. "I'm ready."

Faramund was waiting, just as Captain Tyrrel had said. Agitation deepened the wrinkled map of his face as Aki approached. There were several others in the room with them this time, men Aki didn't recognize. Aki stiffened as he saw some of them whispering to each other at the sight of him. They made no effort to conceal the fact that he was the topic of their murmured conversations, nor did they attempt to hide their disapproval.

"Aki Gundarson," Faramund said loudly, drawing everyone's attention to him, "in light of last night's events, we have come to the agreement that it is best for you and your people to return as soon as possible to their own kingdom. We acknowledge that you were not the instigator of the attack," Faramund paused to look pointedly at some of the more surly members of the meeting, "and we promise you safe passage through our lands. It is our hope that the matter ends here. We still wish to maintain the peace we have enjoyed the last few years."

Aki repeated his words for his own people. Since it was what they wanted anyway, he didn't give it much thought. He watched Faramund's face as he translated, realizing just how worn it was. Faramund had never been like the other clansmen, vying for great honor in the raids, soaking their lives in the blood of their enemies. Faramund had always seen a better world than the one Aruuk created. Sasha had been wise to appoint him as chief councilman.

But he was old.

And Aki could see that the others, like wolves drawn to blood, were just waiting for their chance to assert their own power. And with that realization came the knowledge that Faramund's promise of safe passage was only good within sight of Illsen.

He glanced around at the others with more care. Bits and pieces came back to him. He knew some of the men. He knew the one who shared Cadoc's dark stare - his son and heir, Cristof. Cristof was a few years Aki's senior and although he had never demonstrated the same twisted desires his father had, he'd been cruel to Aki as a child.

"Ask him if they still intend to help," Gregory insisted.

It's not a good idea, Aki wanted to say. We should leave now before anything else bad can happen. But they had never shown much inclination to listen to his advice, so he kept it to himself.

Faramund looked pained when Aki put the question to him and there were a few whispers of disapproval from the others. Aki willed his face to remain impassive as Faramund answered, willed the blood not to drain away as he translated the answer to his companions.

"He says Cristof has already sent men out. If they find anything, they will come to us along the trail."

"Then we leave immediately and put this entire debacle behind us," Prince Desmond said.

"Yes. We leave now." Aki turned to the three men behind him and something in his face must have conveyed his urgency. Captain Tyrrel gave him a searching look and then disappeared to ready the men. And for once, Prince Desmond didn't find a reason to argue with him as they exited the room behind the captain.

An hour later, Aki stood beside Sky. One hand rubbed her neck as he leaned against her shoulder. All around him, the soldiers were readying their own mounts. There were eyes on them from every direction and none of them were friendly. Aki turned his head as footsteps came up behind him. His eyes widened with surprise as Faramund approached, holding a long bundle half hidden beneath his voluminous cloak.

"Aki Gundarson," he started, and Aki cringed inwardly at the name. Faramund always used it, and Aki hated it. Faramund glanced around, noticing the malevolent eyes on them. "You know you ride into a trap. Cristof sent his men off before I had a chance to counter them and as long as he swears they're acting in accordance with our promise, I cannot recall them. And I can send no one else out to help you. Our numbers have not been great since our defeat in the mountains and unrest here at home is too grave a danger for me to ignore. Push them. Make them move quickly or you will be caught. We do not want a war, Aki. Make them understand that."

Aki nodded, not sure what to say. Prince Desmond didn't listen to him. Nothing he said was going to change that. Faramund wasn't finished yet, though. He lifted the bundle he'd been hiding and held it out between them.

"I have kept these for many, many years, unbeknownst to our late Chief Gundar. They are yours by right, though. By birth." He pushed it into Aki's hands and then peeled back the cloth. Aki saw at once what was inside. The hilt of the sword was simple but beautifully crafted. "This belonged to your father. Your real father, Anton."

Aki swallowed hard and stared down at the sword with a different sort of interest. His fingers brushed the cool metal, running gently over the engraving on the pommel. He didn't even question how Faramund knew the truth of his birth. "My father's?"

"Yes. He gave his life for you. He would want you to have these now."

At a shout from the captain, Aki tied the bundle onto his saddle and turned to mount before a thought struck him. Looking over his shoulder at where Faramund still stood, he asked, "Is anything left from my mother?"

Faramund nodded. "There is a trinket in there. It belonged to your mother. She did not come to us as most slaves did but still, that was the only thing that was hers, that she was permitted to keep. She was..."

"What? What was she?"

"She was different. She saw herself as someone different. Always."

It made no sense to Aki. Seeing himself as someone different hadn't made him less of a slave, it had just made his enslavement harder to bear. There was too much else going on to give it enough thought, though.

"How many men did he send, Faramund?"

"A dozen at least. And I am quite certain they have no intention of looking for your captive people. If you are to find them, it will be by yourselves. Look near the border. I do not think they would have traveled very far into Aruuk for fear of being seen."

Pulling himself up onto Sky, he said a hasty goodbye and pushed his horse toward Captain Tyrrel's. He stood a better chance of convincing him to hurry than he did the prince. As it turned out, the captain didn't need any warning to sense the tension in the air and urge his men to make haste.

Aki waited until they were riding before confiding in the captain all that Faramund had warned him of.

"We'll move as quickly as we can and watch for an ambush. Otherwise, there's not much we can do. What did he give you? I saw him handing you something," there was suspicion in Captain Tyrrel's voice as he spoke.

Aki sighed and, pulling the bundle open, slid the sword in its scabbard out. He laid it across his legs so that Captain Tyrrel could see it clearly and noticed what he'd missed the first time. Bound with a piece of rough twine around the hilt of the sword was a ring. His mother's. That was what Faramund had been talking about. He forgot all about Captain Tyrrel. He forgot everything but this piece of his parents sitting in front of him. Letting his reins rest on Sky's neck, he untied the twine and held the ring. It was a signet ring, engraved with a symbol. Aki studied it, struck by how familiar the symbol was but unable to understand why. He couldn't recall having ever seen it before.

"That's a well-made weapon," Captain Tyrrel interrupted his thoughts. "Why'd he give it to you?"

"It was my father's." Aki slipped the ring into the pocket of his shirt and examined the sword for the first time. It was a short blade, not meant to hang at his side, but to strap onto his back. Aki had seen other men wear them but had never used such a weapon before.

"Your father? Gundar?"

"It's a long story." One I don't want to tell, Aki wanted to say.

Captain Tyrrel, to his astonishment, asked nothing more of him. Nodding toward the sword, he simply said, "Might as well put it on. It does you no good tucked beneath your saddlebags."

Aki did as the captain said, shifting a little in his saddle at the unfamiliar weight of it on his back. He reached up with his hand to get a feel for what it would be like to draw the sword. It would take getting used to. Aki didn't mind that thought, though. It would give him something else to keep him busy when he returned to Dival.

The captain set a brisk pace despite the mud and rain that came in bits and spurts throughout the day. Still, Aki's eyes darted about, taking in every rock, every tree, every crevice within the mountains that could possibly hide a man. They would come. There was never any doubt of that. And when they did, he was quite certain they would be coming for him. Sure, the others would be caught up in the trap as well. But he was the one they wanted. He was the one they would have been ordered to kill or worse, capture. Aki shuddered with the thought.

He could save the others.

If he just gave himself up to Cristof's men, they would likely let the rest go.

Aki hated himself for such a noble thought. He wanted to beat it out of his own head. If he was a better person, he would not hesitate. Sasha never hesitated. He remembered that night with Boris. When Sasha had thought his choice was between himself and Boris, he didn't hesitate. Aki always hesitated.

The clouds finally cleared off late in the evening and Captain Tyrrel ordered a halt. Aki wanted to keep going. He wanted to put as much distance between Illsen and them as possible. If it were possible, he would have kept riding all the way to the border and past it without stopping. Although he half thought it was just imagination running wild with him, he had seen men following them.

He saw the sense in stopping in this spot almost at once. It was a wide clearing with a sheer cliff rising up on one side. With their backs to that cliff, they could see anything that came towards them on all the other sides. Still, when the men not on guard went to bed for the night, Aki sat up.

His eyes burned from staring out at the darkness for some many hours but every time he closed them, the images returned. After a while he stood up and walked the perimeter of their camp. Captain Tyrrel was taking no chances. Half the men were on watch at a time. Aki passed each one as he moved silently around.

Morning came and he dragged himself to the horses. Sky's saddle was heavier than usual. The straps were more troublesome. His patience was in short supply. All around him, he felt the eyes of the others watching him. It had been easy in Illsen to pretend that the only ones who stared at him were the Aruukens. Here, he felt them. He could almost read their thoughts. It would have been better, he imagined them saying, if he hadn't killed Cadoc. If he'd just submitted the way he had as a child. If he'd just endured like he knew he could. They blamed him. And perhaps they were right.

"Aren't you going to eat?" Captain Tyrrel said over his shoulder as Aki fumbled through tying his bedroll onto his saddle.

"Not hungry."

"Really? Because you haven't eaten anything since night before last."

That was true. Every time he looked at food, he wanted to be sick all over again. He waved the captain's concern away.

"We should keep moving. Eat later." He thought about his hesitation yesterday and tried to make up for it now. "Maybe I should ride ahead and see if I can spot any of them."

"No," the captain answered flatly as if he could read Aki's mind. "We stay together."

Aki did his best not to look relieved.

When, several hours later, they rode through a particularly narrow part of the trail, Aki was not at all surprised to hear a shout echoing off the mountain sides. He was almost relieved to see the men burst from their hiding places and ran them down. It meant that the tension was over.

The tension, not the danger. Aki was right about one thing. They wanted him. Out of the dozen men who rode into their midst, three went straight for him.

Aki pulled his sword free just as they reached him. He caught the first across the arm. A fountain of blood erupted from the wound. The man yelled and fell onto the neck of his horse, his sword clattering to the ground. But there was no time to think. No time to watch his own handiwork. The other two pressed him. They pushed Sky toward a large rock. Aki saw the trap only a moment before his leg was pinned between the horse and rock. The next moment, he was clear of her back and standing on the rock.

It was a terrible position. Higher than everyone else and fully exposed. Worse, there was nothing but a cliff behind him. No retreat. No hiding. And both men were equally quick in jumping up after him. The only advantage he had was that the space was too narrow for both men to attack him at once.

A hot pain shot through his arm. Another came in his leg. He stumbled. Brought his sword up past the guard of the nearest attacker. It sank into the man's chest. Aki didn't waste time trying to pull it out. There was no time. He dodged the swing of the last man's sword, the air whistling in his ear as it missed him by only a few inches.

His plan was to jump off the rock. His wounded leg failed him though. It buckled under him, and he fell.

All he could see was the sky above him, and the looming face of the man who would kill him. There were shouts but they seemed distant. He saw the point of the blade descending and knocked it aside. He rolled away, trying to get to his feet. But then the body of his attacker slammed into him, pinning him to the ground.

The man was completely limp, and Aki could feel warmth spreading across his chest. But no pain. He had imagined being run through the chest would have hurt more.

"You have an awful habit of making people want to kill you, Aki," a familiar voice said from somewhere beyond his line of vision.

Chapter 13

THERE WAS A BENEFIT TO BEING royalty, Desmond decided. When the ambush started, he and Gregory were kept in the center, the soldiers forming up around them. Although he carried a sword, he had no need to use it. In fact, it quickly became apparent that most of the men attacking them weren't trying to kill them all. They were just keeping the soldiers away from Aki.

As the last of their attackers fell, Desmond heard Captain Tyrrel shout Aki's name. He turned to see the reason for the captain's shout. And he was horrified by what he saw - Aki on the ground, a sword above his head. The horror changed to confusion when another horseman leaped from his horse onto the rock and ran his sword through Aki's attacker.

Whoever this last rider was, he wasn't unknown to Aki. Desmond watched as he sheathed his sword, pulled the fallen body of their attacker off and held his hand out to help Aki up. Aki didn't stand. He allowed his rescuer to pull him up into a sitting position but made no effort to recover his feet. The other one knelt down in front of Aki. They were talking, Aki shaking his head at whatever the other had to say. And then the stranger was pulling part of Aki's shirt away to look at the fresh wound on his arm. It was the stranger's turn to shake his head. He got to his feet and when he offered his hand this time, Aki stood.

By the time Aki and the stranger had climbed down off the rock, the soldiers had left the tight cluster they had fought in and were examining the dead. Desmond did not move. He wasn't sure he had the power to move. It had all happened so quickly. From the moment the men had appeared to the moment the last one fell couldn't have been more than five minutes and yet twelve men had died in those five minutes. None of their own had fallen but a few were bleeding from wounds. Desmond wished he knew enough to see whether any were seriously injured or not.

"Who is this, courier?" Captain Tyrrel asked as Aki limped towards them, his arm draped over the shoulder of the other. The captain had his weapon ready as they got close, suspicion all over his face.

"He's not a threat, Captain," Aki answered, his voice taking on the same dull tone it had the night he killed Cadoc. "He's my brother, Lars."

Desmond scoffed. "That doesn't exactly assure me that he's not a threat."

Aki stared at him, and Desmond couldn't read the look in his eyes. Finally, Aki just gave a weary sigh and turned to the captain. "He has news for us. About the captives."

"Which I can actually tell you myself," Lars interrupted, and Desmond winced. He hadn't realized the Aruuken could understand him.

"You're wounded," Captain Tyrrel commented, gesturing towards Aki's arm first, then his leg. "Sit down somewhere so I can take care of it. And Lars can tell us his news at the same time."

Lars helped Aki to the base of a tree and set him down with his back against it. Captain Tyrrel retrieved one of his saddle bags and followed, with both Desmond and Gregory on his heels. As the captain went to work, first on Aki's arm and then his leg, Lars sat down cross legged beside his brother.

"So what is it you know?" Desmond asked, anxious now to take his mind off the recent skirmish. He carefully avoided watching the captain as he cleaned Aki's wounds. A single glance had made him queasy.

"I know there are people hiding in the mountains near the border. They have captives. I can only assume they are the same ones you are looking for."

"Who are they?" Desmond asked.

"Where are they?" Gregory said at the same time.

"I have no idea who they are. I've been keeping an eye on the border for Faramund and that's when I spotted them. I was actually on my way back to Illsen to tell him when I ran into you all, which turned out to be fortunate timing on my part. Whoever they are, they either don't mind being seen or they aren't from around here."

"Why do you say that?"

"Because they weren't hiding very well. You wouldn't have seen them coming up the main pass, but if you took one of the smaller ones, they're right there, pretty much out in the open."

"You'll take them to us," Desmond demanded.

Lars gave him an incredulous look and then laughed. "Not like that I won't."

Desmond's face reddened and he balled his hands into fists at his side.

"Will you help us find them?" Gregory rephrased the words before Desmond could speak again. "We would be most grateful for the help."

Lars raised his eyebrows and looked from Gregory to Desmond. He turned, grinning, to Aki and said something in Aruuken. Aki smiled briefly and then grimaced as the captain tightened the bandage on his leg. It was the first time Desmond could remember seeing the courier smile.

"I'll help, I suppose. But first," Lars stood up and walked over to the nearest body and turned it over with his foot to examine it, "tell me why Cadoc's men were attacking you."

"They're not Cadoc's anymore. They're Cristof's," Aki answered quietly before anyone else had the chance.

Lars' eyes narrowed as he studied Aki. He didn't say anything, just waited for someone to continue the explanation.

"It was me they were after," Aki said after a moment had passed and it was clear no one else planned on speaking.

"Why? Oh. You killed Cadoc. Didn't you?"

Their silence was the only answer Lars needed. A look passed between the brothers, some exchange of understanding. "He'll hunt you for the rest of his life or yours."

"I know."

Lars forced a smile onto his face and punched Aki lightly in his good arm. "Bet Faramund had something to say about all that. He's hated Cadoc for longer than we've been alive. How long did it take him to thank you?"

Aki started to shake his head, then stopped, frowning as he thought back over their last hours in Illsen. "Right when we left."

Desmond cleared his throat loudly to bring their attention back to him. "You are still able to ride, courier? Because I think it's high time we moved on."

Without waiting for an answer, Desmond got up and the others followed. He heard Aki whistle for his horse so that he wouldn't have to walk any more than necessary. The time they'd spent talking had been enough for the soldiers to bind up any wounds they had and regroup. Desmond surveyed the group from the back of his horse, impatient to move on.

As they made their way down the mountains, Desmond watched the courier and his brother from where he rode in the middle of the group. There was a tinge of jealousy inside him at their easy friendship. He watched as Aki pulled the sword on his back out of its sheath and handed it to Lars. Lars said something in return and Desmond wished he knew what it was because it made Aki laugh and a part of him thought they were making fun of him.

Desmond knew multitudes of people - from the highest noble to the servants who were employed at the castle. Yet for all those people, he had no real friends. And no brother. His sisters, all older than him, were poor substitutes in his own eyes. Charlotte was the closest to him in age, but they got along about as well as fire and water. Aki and Lars were closer to his age than any of the other men in the group and if Desmond had been anyone but the crown prince, he was pretty sure he would be up in front with them.

Or maybe not.

He hadn't gone out of his way to endear himself to anyone on this trip and most especially not Aki. They'd likely just laugh at him behind his back. That thought made his face hot. It made him want to ride up to them silently and listen in just to be sure and then he could be truly furious.

"We should stop for the night, Your Highness," Captain Tyrrel said, and Desmond jumped a little. He'd been so wrapped up in his own thoughts that he hadn't realized how low the sun was.

With a crisp nod that he hoped hid the fact that he hadn't been paying any attention to their surroundings, he pulled his horse up.

There was a solemn air about the camp that night. No one could quite forget the attack of just a few hours ago. It kept most of the men quiet as they ate. When it was time to set up a watch for the night, Aki volunteered and was quickly struck down by the captain.

"Oh, just let him. He's not going to sleep anyway," Desmond said peevishly. "He hasn't since he slit Cadoc's throat."

Aki didn't wait for the captain to argue. He picked himself up and limped off into the darkness. Desmond shifted uneasily as he felt Lars' gaze settle on him.

"Is that true?" Lars asked quietly after a moment.

Captain Tyrrel nodded.

"Get someone else to stand guard," Lars said this to the captain, completely ignoring Desmond. He got to his feet as well and disappeared. He was gone for a half hour at most and when he returned, he nodded at the captain. "He's asleep."

For a while, they just sat in silence, no one daring to ask what exactly Lars had done. Gregory finally tired of it and spoke. "You speak our language well for one who does not live in Dival."

Lars shrugged. "I've spent a while there. A winter when I was twelve and most of last year."

"We are most grateful for your help in this matter," Gregory reiterated, glancing pointedly at Desmond.

Taking the hint, Desmond said, "Yes, we would have had no idea where to look without you. Our guide had suggested that finding them in the mountains would be next to impossible. I'm glad you can prove him wrong."

Lars stared at him open-mouthed for a moment. Then for the second time that day, laughed at him. There was frustration and disbelief in the laugh. "Your guide has a name, and you seem to be forgetting that, as my brother, I don't feel quite the same animosity towards him as you clearly do. In the future, you'd do well to remember that. And I'm not doing this for you, I'm doing it for my brother."

They collectively looked in the direction Aki had disappeared in, and Lars shook his head. "Not that one. Sasha. Aki couldn't care less what happens to Aruuk. But Sasha sacrificed an awful lot to make sure there was peace and I'll see it kept if it's in my power to do so."

"Why would Aki care so little for his own people?" Desmond asked. It was the only safe thing he could think of saying.

"Not my story to tell. But you're an idiot for bringing him back here. There's a reason he chose to stay in Dival when Sasha gave him the choice."

"Do you have any idea who I am?" Desmond demanded through gritted teeth. No one, except his father, spoke so bluntly to him. And the captain, he remembered.

"Yes, I do, princeling," Lars answered pleasantly.

Desmond felt both Captain Tyrrel and Gregory tense beside him. He hoped one of them would speak up in his defense, but neither did. In fact, when he saw them out of the corner of his eye, he could have sworn they looked ready to laugh.

"You have no right to speak to me so," he finally managed to get out.

"Not so. You and I are equals, my friend. I was born to a sovereign and a free woman, same as you. So I could just as easily demand you tell me everything I want to hear. And last I checked, I'm doing you an enormous favor. One that I most certainly don't owe you."

Gregory coughed into his hand and mumbled something about how they should all turn in for the night so that they could get an early start in the morning. Lars winced at that.

"It won't be so early. Aki will not wake for many hours."

"What, exactly, did you do to him?" Captain Tyrrel asked, and Desmond was stunned to see a small smile on the man's lips. He hoped it was what happened to Aki that he found amusing and not the recent exchange between himself and Lars.

Lars looked apologetic for the first time. "I might have drugged him."

Chapter 14

"YOU DRUGGED ME?" AFTER TWO days of being told the same thing, Aki still couldn't convince himself of the truth.

"Yes, for the hundredth time, yes, Aki."

"Why?"

"If you'd just slept like a sane person I wouldn't have had to. What did you think, you could just go the rest of your life without sleep? Did you lose that much sleep when you tried to kill Halle?"

Aki's retort died in his mouth. He looked away.

"I'm sorry. I shouldn't have said that."

They rode in silence for a long while after that. Aki's eyes moved constantly, scanning the landscape around them as if expecting an attack at any second. They were close to the border, close to where Lars had spotted the raiding party and their captives. He insisted they would reach them within an hour or so.

"You know, it was really easy," Aki said softly. "Killing him, I mean. I wanted to do it. I wanted him to die. And those men that attacked me. I wanted to kill them too. And I did. It was so easy."

"Cadoc deserved to die. You know that better than anyone."

Aki didn't say anything more about it. Even to Lars there was a limit to what he could explain. He couldn't make him understand the darkness within himself, the reason he practiced so doggedly, pushing himself because he wanted there to be a day when he didn't have to be afraid of anyone. He couldn't tell him that his greatest achievement in all his efforts was learning to fear himself. To fear what he was capable of. What he was made of. The boy who shoved Halle off of a cliff was still buried within him. Aki wished he could reach deep within himself and tear that part of him out like a weed. But it was him.

"We're here," Lars said.

Aki stopped Sky alongside Lars and heard the others stop behind them. Captain Tyrrel, never far from his side, came abreast of them.

"You're sure?"

"Just through that defile." Lars pointed toward a narrow path cut behind two mountains. "If they're slavers..."

"We brought gold. I'd rather not lose any men in a fight. Wait here."

When Captain Tyrrel returned, it was with Gregory and two of his soldiers with him.

"We'll go in and bargain. I've told the others that if we're not out in half an hour, to come in after us. Lars, I'd prefer it if you stayed back as well. No need to risk both of you where one will do."

"Then I should be the one to go. Aki's wounded, three times over."

"It's fine, Lars. It's what they brought me along for anyway."

"You know, sometimes I think you're trying to get yourself killed," Lars said, shaking his head.

Aki knew from the moment they rode in that something was off. He just couldn't figure out what. The defile opened up into a pleasant little valley. A few tents were scattered about it and two or three fires were burning, the damp wood belching smoke into the air that would have given their position away to any mildly attentive passerby. On the far side, he could see the captives. A passing glance told him that they were all men and they were kept chained together. Milling around the makeshift camp were the raiders.

Aki understood Lars' assessment of them at once. This was no organized Aruuken raiding party. These men were rough and lawless. They reminded him of the men who roamed the streets in Karu. Although belonging to one of the wealthiest and most powerful women on the island had protected Aki from them, he'd seen them at work and they were men who knew no bounds, no authority other than violence.

One of the men separated himself immediately from the others and started toward them. Captain Tyrrel held his free hand up in a gesture of peace and Aki and the others mimicked him. Even so, several of the bandits held their weapons at the ready. Captain Tyrrel motioned for Aki to come up next to him.

"Tell them we're here to reclaim our people."

Aki did. "He says he's willing to ransom them. But we have to show him the gold first."

"We'll do no such thing." Captain Tyrrel glanced around the camp and seemed satisfied with what he saw. "Explain to him that the only way out of this valley is through the defile we just came through. We have enough men waiting on the other side to kill anyone who tries to leave. If they want the gold, they do it our way."

"And what is our way?"

"They send the captives out with two of their men. We'll hand the gold over then and only then."

Aki translated the words, watching the face of the leader as he did. The man rubbed his chin and looked from side to side at his companions. When he smiled, it sent a chill snaking down Aki's back. There was pure evil in his eyes as he agreed.

Too easy, a voice chanted in Aki's head, too easy.

No bandit or raider or thug would let their prize go without a fight. If it was money they wanted, they'd bargain for the most they could get. If it was blood, nothing would stop them from claiming it. It was all too easy, too quick.

He looked beyond the bandits and to the captives but that unsettled him more and he wasn't sure why. There was something he was missing. And none of the others even seemed bothered.

As they waited outside for the captives, Aki wrestled with whether or not to speak. It wasn't like Prince Desmond would listen to anything he said. But Captain

Tyrrel might. He spotted the captain waiting near the mouth of the defile and came to stand next to him.

"You don't think they're planning some sort of trick, do you?"

Captain Tyrrel's stern mouth pulled down at the corners as he thought about it. "It's possible, I suppose. It appeared to me, though, as if they were ill prepared to keep their captives. Winter's almost on us, and they aren't in a position to survive it right now. I think they're new to their business. And that's a good thing for us."

He added the last part as he caught sight of the first of the captives coming toward them.

Maybe he was right, Aki decided as the exchange took place without a hitch. The bandits exchanged a few greedy smiles amongst themselves as they took the gold and disappeared once more into their valley. Aki watched in bemusement as one of the captives broke free of the group and fell on his knees in front of Prince Desmond and Gregory, thanking them profusely over and over again. The other captives remained impassive, either unaware or unimpressed by the change in their fate.

With nothing better to do, Aki studied the man who was no longer on his knees but still in front of the prince. He was a younger man, in his early twenties at most, Aki thought, close to Prince Desmond's age. Despite their captivity of almost a month, Aki was surprised at how well cared for he looked.

Aki tensed when the man approached the captain and him. He took the captain's hand in his own and shook it enthusiastically and introduced himself as Tristan. "I owe you gentlemen my life. We had all but lost hope of any help coming. And to think that the king would care enough about our lives to send his own son to negotiate our release."

Aki bit his lip to keep from pointing out that the prince wasn't actually the one who negotiated their freedom. In fact, the prince hadn't done much of anything useful on this trip.

"We should move on." Captain Tyrrel pulled his hand free and started for their horses. In a quieter voice meant only for the prince and Gregory to hear, he said, "We won't be able to move as quickly with all these men on foot."

Aki was tightening Sky's girth when Lars approached him.

"This is as far as I'm going. I've still got to make it back to Illsen before the passes are closed off by snow."

Aki wasn't good with goodbyes. He never knew what to say. Apparently, Lars wasn't either because he stood fussing with his own horse without any real purpose.

"There's one more thing you should know. It's just a rumor, but I've heard it repeated a lot so there's probably some truth to it."

"What's that?"

"There's fever in Dorsten. If you can get that idiot prince of yours to listen, you'll bypass it completely."

Aki hid a smile at his words. "You shouldn't say that too loud."

With a shrug, Lars said, "I've already called him one to his face so it's not like he doesn't know what I think of him."

Around them, everyone else was mounting up. Aki hated the idea of riding off with them and leaving Lars behind, because the last few days with Lars had reminded him of just how lonely he was. He wasn't ready to return to that. Reluctantly, he swung up onto Sky's back and tied the lead rope of his second horse to her saddle.

"You shouldn't come back here, you know. Cristof won't forget."

"Neither will I."

Lars was on his own horse when the prince approached them.

"You're leaving?"

"I am. But I've a word of advice for you before I go, if you'd like to hear it," Lars said with a smile that dared the prince to ask.

Prince Desmond gave him a dark look then waved his hand for him to go on. With a grin, Lars did. "Arrogance won't make you many friends, but it'll make you a whole lot of enemies, Your Highness. And I think you are in desperate need of friends."

Chapter 15

"WOULD YOU LIKE TO HEAR a story, my pet?"

"Is it a happy one?"

"Oh no, my pet, it is not a happy one."

"Then I do not wish to hear it."

"Ah, but if you only hear the happy stories, you'll never learn the truth."

"What truth?"

"Listen well, my dear, and I shall tell you. Are you ready?"

"I suppose."

"Once upon a time, there was a princess."

"I love princesses."

"Shhh... This princess was beautiful and well loved by all around her. She had a brother who was several years older than her, but that did not prevent them from being the very best of friends. This princess loved nothing better than to be at her brother's side as he learned how to be a prince and, eventually, a king. There was war in the land, but the princess thought little of it for it was always kept far away from the castle, and her brother was never called upon to fight in it. They were safe, that prince and princess. Often, they spoke of what it would take to end the war. What it would take to make peace. The prince vowed that he would do whatever it took and the princess, because she wanted to make her brother happy, said the same."

"What was the war about?"

"What are all wars about, my dear? Ambitions, greed, gold, power. The princess hated these things. When she was but fifteen years old, her father, the king, sent his men out once more to make war. It was a terrible time. Their enemies had made an alliance and were ten times as strong as the armies of the king. His men returned defeated, vanquished. But the king did not make peace with his enemies. Instead, he sought to break their alliance with the people from the land of snow and ice and rock. He sent messages to their ruler, offering him many wonderful things.

"The princess spent that winter in happiness, with no idea of what was to come. For she was among the things promised to the ruler of that far away land. The ruler agreed and the king called his daughter to him to tell her the news. It did not matter how the princess wept and implored her father to change his mind. There would be a ship prepared to take, he told her. She would live as a queen in that far away land. People would listen and obey her. She would learn to love it there, learn to love their people like she loved her own.

"On the night before the princess was to be sent away, she found her way into her brother's chambers. On her knees she begged him to help her escape. He was kinder to her than her father, but in the end, his answer was the same. He reminded her gently of what they had promised when they were too young to understand the words - that they would do whatever it took to end the war. This was what it took, he told her. It was a sacrifice she had to make for her people. It was her duty to them as their princess.

"Betrayed by those she thought loved her most, the princess did indeed travel to that unknown land. There she was wed to a man whose heart was as cold and cruel as the land he ruled. There was no one there to love her and slowly the princess realized that she didn't need anyone's love anyway. She began to understand why men fought for power and ambition. She began to desire her own power.

"When she gave birth to a son, she held him in her arms and thought she could love again. But as the years passed, her son chose another over her, and it cost him his life. *Despair became the princess's constant companion. But she did not let it destroy her. She let it make her stronger. She learned how to use her despair, her anger, her pain to grow her power. And powerful she became.*

"*And for all those years, she never forgot how she came to be in that cold country. She never forgot her father or brother's words. She remembered them. And she planned one day to return and punish them for their words, for their betrayal.*"

"*Is that the end? What is the truth?*"

"*No, dear, but the end has yet to be written. The truth is this - when you give people the choice, they will always choose themselves. And love couldn't save the princess, only power could do that. Perhaps it shall be a happy ending, though, for the princess?*"

"*I hope so. She deserves a happy ending.*"

"*She does, indeed. She deserves a very happy ending. And what do you think would make her happy?*"

"*Finding someone who loved her?*"

"*Revenge. Revenge will make her very happy. And power.*"

"*But it's a better story if she finds someone who loves her.*"

"*It wouldn't be real, though. No one can love the princess anymore. She made sure of that.*"

"*Then it is a very sad story.*"

A very sad story indeed. Karina woke with the sadness still lingering in her mind. It made her limbs heavy and her thoughts slow. Such sadness. A princess who could not be loved anymore. A princess who only wanted revenge and power. Karina didn't like the story. She'd never liked it, not from the first time she'd heard, her head cradled on the lap of her mistress. But it was a good story. It reminded her of why she needed her mistress. Men were not to be trusted; she'd seen that often enough. People were selfish, she'd experienced their selfishness firsthand.

Despite the story though, there was a gentle hand washing her forehead with a cool, damp cloth. Karina thought maybe the woman who hovered above her was an exception to the truth of the story. She'd brought Karina into her home, knowing that fever raged through her body.

Maybe she'd never heard such a story and so didn't know the truth herself. Whatever the reason, Karina was glad to have been found by Lydia.

If only her eyes did not burn so at the light and her head didn't ache with the tiniest of movements. Karina shut her eyes against the pain and prayed it would be gone when she awoke again.

Chapter 16

THERE WAS A HEAVY LAYER OF frost on the ground when they woke that morning and Desmond was loath to crawl out from beneath his blankets. His breath hung in the air like a little cloud before his face. Putting on as many clothes as he'd brought with him, he finally left the relative warmth of his tent and stepped outside in the chilly morning air. At least the sky was clear, he thought.

Making a path straight to the nearest fire, he sat down and held his hands out over the flames to warm them. All around him the others prepared for the day's ride. Desmond thought about Lars' last words to him when they parted ways two days before. If it had been a little warmer out, he would have helped the others.

"You don't mind if I join you here, Your Highness?" Tristan lowered himself to the ground near Desmond, who shook his head. "Couldn't help but overhear you and the others talking last night. Your captain doesn't think you'll make it home before the snow falls."

"Captain Tyrrel always errs on the side of caution, Tristan."

"Ah, he's one of those sorts, is he? If you don't mind my asking, what are your plans for us, Your Highness?"

"I suppose I hadn't really made any plans," Desmond frowned as he spoke. "You're free to go to your homes whenever you like."

"Well, that's just the thing, Your Highness..."

"You can drop the titles when it's just you and me, Tristan." Desmond was heartily sick of it from everyone else, but Tristan didn't seem to do it with any malice.

"Of course. Hard to make friends when you're the prince, isn't it?" Tristan gave him a sympathetic smile.

"More than you know. Go on, though. What was it you were going to say?"

"Yes, well, you see, our homes were destroyed during the raid. Burnt to the ground. Even if we wanted to, there's no time to rebuild before the snow comes. And we're the sole survivors."

"How awful! Our path didn't take us past your village, and I can't say I'm sorry to miss seeing the carnage. You have no place to go now, do you?"

"Not really. I had a thought, listening to you all talk last night," Tristan stopped himself. His face broke into an embarrassed smile. "Never mind. It was a ridiculous idea. Completely impractical."

Desmond's curiosity was piqued. He leaned closer to Tristan and said in a lowered voice, "It's alright. Just tell me. I promise to take it seriously."

Tristan stalled for a moment, clearly debating whether to tell him or not. Desmond was pretty sure it was only because he was the prince and Tristan felt obligated to obey him that made him speak in the end.

"I heard your plan to winter in the castle in Dorsten. My thought was that, since we've nowhere else to go, we could perhaps stay there with you. In the servants' quarters, or the guardhouse, of course. I've been told only a small staff is kept on at that castle since it is no longer anyone's permanent residence. We'd stay out of the way and make ourselves useful."

The idea appealed to Desmond for no other reason than that Captain Tyrrel and Gregory would protest it. He wouldn't mind having Tristan there through the long winter months, either. He was near enough Desmond's age to be a friend and yet he treated Desmond with the deference due him - unlike Lars, whose words still gnawed at his pride.

"I'll consider it, certainly. Of course, there's always the chance that we'll make it home before winter."

That topic had been the source of a very intense discussion just the night before. For once, Gregory and Captain Tyrrel were at odds and Prince Desmond was caught between them, listening to two very logical sides, and faced with the knowledge that he would have to choose one of them.

Winter was coming, fast. And as early as it was arriving, it was likely to be a harsh one. Captain Tyrrel predicted snow within a week. That did not leave them enough time to reach home, not with the speed they were traveling at now with the freed captives. The castle was separated from the town enough that Gregory wasn't concerned about the fever if the rumor was true.

Captain Tyrrel argued that the rumors of fever in Dorsten were most likely true and that the risk of illness was greater than the risk of being caught out in the Void in a blizzard. He preferred the idea of freezing to death to slowly burning up with a fever.

Desmond agreed with both.

Mostly, he just agreed that he didn't want to risk his life to such an extent. There were more concerns than just those, as well. His father would be waiting for either his return or some news. Desmond could only imagine what would go through his father's mind if they did not return soon. He would think the worst. He might even try to send men out after them. And then there was the matter of getting enough supplies to see them across the Void again - something fever in Dorsten would make very difficult.

His only solution so far had been no solution at all. No decision would be made until there was no choice but to make a decision.

That day came all too quickly. They were within sight of the castle when the heavy clouds that had blocked out the sun all day finally released their burden of snow on the world beneath. Wind whipped the small, frozen flakes across the land. Desmond pulled his cloak around him tighter and decided he'd rather face fever than this.

The only relief the castle had to offer when they first rode across the heavy drawbridge and into the courtyard, was a break from the fierce wind. As Tristan had said before, the staff here consisted of only a small handful of people, made even smaller by fears of the fever. Without a stable hand present, Desmond handed his horse off to the nearest soldier and started inside. He paused in the open doorway and turned to search the courtyard.

"Courier," he called out. He watched Aki push through the others to stand in front of him.

"Your Highness?"

"Since it is obvious we will not make it across the Void before spring, I want to send word to my father. You'll be carrying it for me. I'll have a letter ready for you to take within an hour. Take whatever you need from the pack horses and be ready to leave by then."

A shadow passed over Aki's face but he answered, "Yes, Your Highness."

"Go on. You clearly want to say something."

"It's nothing, Your Highness."

It irritated Desmond after Aki had walked away again to not know what it was he wanted to say. Setting the matter aside, he turned his attention to penning a letter to his father. It took him a while to collect his thoughts enough to put them into words. What if Father would want him to return home immediately despite the winter? What if Father disapproved of his using the Aruuken's help? Desmond found himself questioning every decision he'd made since he left home and the result was a very terse note that stated little more than that the captives were safe, and he was unable to return immediately.

When he descended to the courtyard well over an hour later, Aki was waiting. So was Captain Tyrrel. They were deep in conversation but stopped the moment they spotted him.

"You will take this to the king as quickly as possible."

"You can't cross the Void in the winter, Your Highness," Captain Tyrrel spoke up. "He can't cross it."

"Actually, you can. Isn't that what his brother did? And I won't have my father worrying all winter."

Captain Tyrrel was going to say something else, but Aki took the sealed letter from Desmond's hand and tucked it safely into one of his saddle bags. Without a word, he stepped one foot into his stirrup and pulled himself up. Captain Tyrrel grabbed the reins of his horse and prevented Aki from riding straight out.

"If you're going to go, go around the town. It'll add some time, but if you catch the fever they have there, there's no hope for you on your own."

"Yes, Captain." Aki tugged at his reins, guiding his horse toward the gate, stopping along the way to grab the lead rope of a waiting packhorse that Tristan was patiently holding onto.

Desmond shivered and hurried inside before Aki was out of sight. Captain Tyrrel was right behind him, and Desmond could feel the disapproval rolling off him in waves. He was glad to find Tristan had followed them in as well. Tristan gave him an understanding smile and invited him to join him before one of the many fires they had lit. That was one decision Desmond didn't regret. It would have been an eternally long winter without the alleviation provided by Tristan and the others.

Chapter 17

SUSPICION.

Karina could see it all over their faces. And it was aimed at her. Her chest rose and fell rapidly as she tried to think of what she had done to arouse their suspicions. Norman and Lydia had been so kind to her, and Karina had kept herself as small as possible once she'd been well enough to think about it.

"Where are you from, Karina?" Lydia's voice was gentle, belying the distrust stamped on her face.

"Why do you ask?"

"Because you raved in another language when you were sick," Norman answered. "We could not understand a word you said. It sounded a bit like what our northern neighbors speak."

"It doesn't matter." Karina twisted her hands together in her lap. She caught a fistful of fabric from her skirt between them and bunched it up in her fists to keep them from shaking. She needed to lie. Just long enough to get away from here. She needed a plan. But she was still so tired, so weary from fighting off the fever. Her mind was still too muddled. Tears. Those always worked well. Her mistress had taught her the power of well-timed tears from a very young age, although her mistress never deigned to use that tool herself. Letting them pool in her eyes, letting her lower lip quiver as she looked up at the two people who had undoubtedly saved her life, she spoke, "My parents... they died. I didn't have anywhere else to go. If I'd stayed there, I'd have been turned out on the streets and... and awful things happen to the girls who live on the streets there. I couldn't... I couldn't bear..." She let the words hang unspoken in the air and covered her face with her hands.

A rustle of fabric told her Lydia was moving and she stiffened with surprise when she felt the woman's arms wrap around her. Laying her head on Lydia's shoulder she gave way to tears that could convince the hardest heart of her sincerity. For she had been absolutely sincere. Her parents were dead. If she'd lived on the streets in her hometown, awful things would have happened to her. It's why she needed to stay with her mistress.

"It's alright, Karina. We meant nothing by asking. It was curiosity, nothing more," Lydia murmured in her ear.

But Karina knew better. She'd seen the suspicion. The distrust. Her days with these kind people needed to come to an end before a more coherent story was required of her.

Two mornings later, she slipped out of the house before anyone else was up. It wasn't until she reached the main road that it occurred to her that she should have tried to steal some of their money. She was destitute without it.

It was time to leave the town behind, she decided, money or no money. Luck was with her that morning. She hadn't been wandering long at all when she overheard a conversation that made her heart leap. It wasn't a way across the great plains. That was too much to hope for as she watched the first flakes of snow begin to fall. But she had a way out of town, away from people who were growing suspicious of her and that would have to be sufficient for now.

She waited until the wagon was temporarily deserted, those in the process of loading it having gone back inside. Casting a quick glance around her to make sure no one was watching, Karina darted across the street and climbed into the back of the wagon. Almost full already, she crawled between pieces of furniture, chests, and a barrel. Slipping under a stack of blankets in the farthest corner, she had nothing to do but wait and stay quiet.

By the time the small family had finished their preparations, Karina was tired of the cramped position. The wagon moved forward with a lurch, and she bit her tongue to keep from making any sound. As the wagon rattled down the road, Karina tried to think of anything but her own discomfort. The unwitting family she was traveling with spoke little above her head and she guessed they were wrapped up too tightly against the cold. It was obvious why they were leaving town, going to live with relatives who were far enough away that they didn't have to worry about the fever.

She lost track of any sense of time, the stiffness in her bones growing worse by the minute. There was only one time that the monotony of the ride was broken up. Another traveler ran into them on the road and for a time they rode together. Karina heard the exchange that took place between the husband and the rider as they shared the road. The rider spoke with an accent that was terribly familiar to Karina.

After what seemed forever, the wagon came to a stop and Karina let out a grateful sigh of relief. Until she heard that they were only stopping for a midday meal. They offered to share with their traveling companion, but he was in a hurry and rode on without them. Karina listened as the hoofbeats of his horse grew fainter, fading into the distance.

The smell of fresh bread and cheese drove Karina mad with hunger. She should have stolen some food in town as well. Above her head, she could hear the small voices of very young children. To take her mind off her hunger, she tried to discern how many there were. Three, she decided after listening to their chatter for a few minutes. And not one of them older than seven or eight.

A thundering of hooves sent a thrill of terror through Karina. It was nothing, she whispered silently to herself. Just people in a hurry. A very big hurry.

Then the screaming started.

Chapter 18

HE HADN'T MADE IT FAR BEYOND the point where he'd left the small family to their meal, although a bend in the road and a small hill kept them out of sight. The road he was on took him far around the town and brought him close to the edge of the old Sar Forest. The dark line of trees was just a short sprint away.

Stephan had told him once about an old, mostly forgotten road that ran through the dense forest. Given what he'd heard from Sasha about crossing the great plains in the winter, Aki was seriously considering finding that old road. He'd have to make up his mind soon. If he meant to follow the road through the great plains, he'd need to cut across that direction before he'd gone much further.

A scream rent the quiet air behind him.

Followed by another and then another. A shout. The wild neigh of a horse in terror. Aki spun Sky around, dropping the lead rope of his pack horse at the same time. It took only the lightest pressure from him to send Ski racing across the open ground. He didn't stick to the road. He ran her straight up the small hill, stopping her just short of the crest, his feet hitting the ground before her own had stopped moving, jarring the wound still healing in his leg. He ignored the pain. Crouching in the long grass that thick on the hill, he made it the rest of the way to the top and froze.

The sight that met his eyes made his blood run cold.

A party of five or six men surrounded the wagon, half of them dismounted. Already laying in a pool of blood on the ground was the man and his wife. Aki couldn't see their three young sons.

Another shout reached his ears, and this time Aki could see the cause of it. One of the mounted men had reached into the back of the wagon and was dragging a girl out by her hair. A girl Aki hadn't even known was in the wagon. He didn't have time to consider that, though. Her screams filled the air, spurring Aki into action.

It took only a few seconds to retrieve his bow and arrows from Sky's saddle and return to his spot at the top of the hill. In those few seconds, the girl had been dragged, still screaming, her arms flailing wildly, completely free of the wagon. Now she stumbled alongside the man on the horse, her hair still caught up in his hand.

The grass gave him all the concealment he needed. A year ago, he wouldn't have been able to make the shot. Now, he drew the bowstring back with the tips of his fingers, feeling the painful strain of it down his wounded arm. He held it only for a moment. Letting out half a breath, he released the arrow. Another was knocked in its place before the first met its mark.

He drew back again.

Released again.

Another arrow.

And then another.

The girl collapsed to a heap as her captor fell forward onto the neck of his horse, an arrow protruding from his stomach. Aki willed her, whoever she was, to get up. To run. To get away before another took hold of her and galloped off. Two of the others were hit as well, but not dead. All of them were looking around, searching for the source of the arrows.

She was on her feet. Running straight toward him. Aki ducked down. He wasn't sure if she had seen him or not, but he wasn't ready to give away his position. One of the horsemen gave chase. Aki drew one last time. And released. This one missed the man entirely but struck his mount in the shoulder. The horse stumbled, pitched forward, its rider thrown clear as it went down. But the others had seen Aki now. He could see them pointing. Hear them yelling.

The girl was only a few feet away from him now. Her eyes were wild with fear as she ran. He held out his hand and she clutched it as they ran together toward Sky.

He was on Sky's back, pulling the girl up behind him and kicking the horse into action all at once. A single glance over his shoulder showed him two men were in pursuit. Another two were staggering around, wounded. One lay still where he fell and the last was putting a torch to the wagon still harnessed to the team of horses.

Sky flew across the ground. Aki steered her towards his placid pack horse, snatching the lead rope and yanking hard to pull the animal along after them. There would be no point in surviving this encounter if he lost all of his supplies. Fortunately, the pack horse was startled and broke into a gallop alongside them easily.

The girl's arms were wrapped so tightly around Aki that he struggled to draw breath and he could feel her shaking against his back. The hoofbeats behind them slowly fell back and Aki risked another look. Their pursuers were slowing down, giving up the chase. Aki didn't dare slow down. He kept Sky heading for the Sar Forest, the decision of which road to take now entirely out of his hands.

They passed beneath the tangle of trees and into the Sar Forest. Branches whipped in Aki's face, caught on his clothes, tore at his arms. He heard the girl gasp behind him, her arms tightening even further around his middle. Sky was forced to slow down, swerving to avoid the thick trunks of trees, picking her way over the uneven and treacherous ground. When the open ground was no longer in sight, Aki pulled her to a stop. Her sides were heaving, and her coat was flecked with lather.

"You can let go now," he said, half turning in the saddle.

And let go she did. As if he was fire. She threw herself off the horse, barely keeping on her feet. Staggering back, she pointed an accusing finger at him.

"You are one of them. I thought you were saving me, but you are not. You are one of them."

"What are you talking about? I did save you." Aki got down.

"No. You tricked me. The others are on their way now, are they not?" She backed up another step, tripped on a thick root, and fell back with a startled cry. "You sound just like them."

He stepped forward, reaching out a hand to help her up. She shrieked and scooted back away until she was up against a tree and could retreat no further.

"Stay away from me. I will not go with you. I will not do anything you want. I will not, ever. I would rather die."

Aki withdrew his proffered hand and shook his head. As long as he remained still, she made no move, so he studied her for a moment, trying to work out what she was saying. Her most outstanding feature was a veritable rat's nest of hair. It sprouted from her head in wild curls that were matted and frizzy with poor keeping. It added at least three inches to the size of her head all the way around, Aki was sure, and it resembled the color of dust. Strands of it hung over her face, concealing it from any thorough scrutiny but he could still see that her cheeks were sunken in, and dark shadows smudged the skin beneath her eyes. Her dress was in tatters and part of the shoulder of it was ripped away completely - probably by the man who'd dragged her from the wagon.

With a sigh, he sat down where he was, still watching her and fully aware that she was watching him from behind the tangle of hair. "If I was with the men who attacked you, do you really think I would have shot them?"

She didn't answer, just kept staring at him through lowered lashes.

"And if I was with those men, don't you think I would have taken you back to some sort of camp and not stopped in the middle of nowhere?"

Still no answer.

Aki shrugged and got to his feet. He didn't dare remove Sky's saddle or unload the pack horse, but he did loosen their girths and tie them to a nearby tree, leaving enough slack that they could paw through the thin layer of snow to get to the dried plants and leaves on the forest floor. There would be no fire, either. Pulling out the food he packed, Aki stared down at it with distaste. Hard bread and dried meat didn't make the most appetizing meal. He was hungry though, and the girl was clearly starving. He felt her eyes on him as he came toward her with the food in his hands. Breaking a loaf in half, he held it out to her.

"Is it poisoned?" she asked, taking it tentatively.

Aki stared at her for a moment, puzzling over the oddity of her question. Then he pulled it back and took a bite out of it. "If it is, then I guess I'm dying."

She clutched it in both her hands and hunched over as she brought it to her mouth. Aki thought she looked like a raccoon with the dark shadows around her eyes and holding her food that way. The picture made him smile.

"Are you laughing at me?" she asked through a mouthful of bread,

"No," Aki answered too quickly.

"But you were smiling?"

"I just thought of something funny."

"Was it about me?"

"I guess it was."

"Then you were laughing at me. You were just doing it on the inside so I would not know." She paused, taking the time to swallow several bites. "What did you think of?"

Aki didn't really feel like explaining. It would sound terrible out loud, he realized, but she was staring at him so intently that he knew she wouldn't leave him alone until he'd given a satisfactory answer. "It's just the way you were eating. Like this," he demonstrated, "it reminded me of the way a raccoon holds its food."

She blinked several times and turned away.

"What's your name?" Aki asked after several minutes of uncomfortable silence had passed.

She looked up and twisted her mouth to one side and then the other in contemplation as she thought about it. Finally, her gaze returned to him, and she said, "Irene."

"That's not your name," Aki said flatly.

"Yes, it is. How would you know it is not?"

"I sat here and watched you make it up. If you're going to lie about something, at least make it convincing. Like this. Ask me my name."

Her mouth twisted to the side again as she thought about it then she shrugged. "Alright, what is your name?"

"Roland," he said without missing a beat. "See, I didn't give you a chance to watch me come up with the lie."

"So, what is your name?"

"Aki."

"Is that true?"

"Yes. I don't have any reason to lie to you about my name."

"Ask me again."

Aki rolled his eyes. "What is your name?"

"Irene," she said it quickly, confidently this time.

Aki rolled his eyes again and threw his hands up. "But I already know that's not your name."

"It is my name."

"Fine, Not Irene. I'm going to keep moving for a few hours before it gets dark. Come if you want to."

He readied the horses and turned to find her standing directly behind him, watching in fascination as he tightened Sky's girth.

"Where were you heading?" he asked.

She screwed her face up and twisted a strand of hair around a finger. "I think I want to go to Bren."

"You think?"

She nodded, her eyes studying his face with a strange intensity.

"Well, you're lucky today, Not Irene. That's where I'm going. Are you still going to insist that I'm one of them or are you coming with me?" He mounted without waiting for an answer but held out his hand for her.

There was only the briefest hesitation before she took it and let him pull her up. She let him do all the work and Aki thought it was a good thing she was at least a head shorter than him and thin enough to blow away in a stiff breeze. Once behind him, her arms closed around his chest with their vice-like grip and he heard her breath catch in her throat.

"If you're coming with me, Not Irene, you're going to have to learn to hold on a little looser. You're going to suffocate me at this rate."

"I hate horses," she muttered in return. "Too big. Way too big."

Despite Aki's words, her grip did not loosen until they had been riding for at least an hour. By the time Aki felt the slack in her arms, he was pretty sure his ribs were already bruised beyond hope, and he was regretting having invited her along. Not that he could have just left her. Especially not with those men still on the loose.

After a while, he became aware of her shivering. It was getting dark anyway and he stopped the horses. She slid off and collapsed into a heap, her arms wrapped tightly around herself, her teeth chattering loud enough that he could plainly hear them.

"I think it's safe to say we haven't been followed," he said, as much to himself as to her. He'd listened carefully in the hours of silent riding and had heard nothing but the sounds of the forest around them. "But I'm not risking a fire. You'll have to put something else on."

"I do not have anything else."

"Yes, I am aware of that." Aki tossed her the last of his clothes that he'd packed. "Change into these."

"Out here? In front of..."

"Me? No, I'm going to take the horses down to that creek to water them. There are plenty of big trees for you to hide behind. And there is no one else here except the wild animals. Unless you'd rather freeze to death, Not Irene."

"That is not my name."

"No, and what you said your name was earlier isn't actually your name. I thought we'd already established that. So, you can either tell me your real name, or I can just keep calling you Not Irene."

He grabbed both horses by their bridles and led them some distance to the creek he'd noticed earlier. While they drank their fill, Aki filled up his own canteens. He'd kept a sharp lookout all afternoon for any sign of the road Stephan had once told him of. So far, there had been no sign of it. Maybe it had been abandoned for too many years now. Or maybe it was not as much of a road in the first place as Stephan made it sound like.

When he was sure several minutes had gone by, he picked his way back through the woods to where the girl waited for him. She was sitting against a tree, looking quite ill at ease in her new garments and staring dejectedly at the torn remnants of her dress.

"I am still cold," she whispered at last.

He tossed her a blanket and divided up more food. He'd have to hunt along the way. When he'd packed, he wasn't planning on feeding a second person - especially not one who was half starved.

"You should get some sleep. We have a long road ahead of us."

The girl looked around them, taking in every shadow. She gathered herself up into a tight ball against the tree as if trying to disappear into its brown trunk entirely. It wasn't until many minutes passed that Aki noticed her relax and drift off into sleep.

Chapter 19

THE SUN WAS SHINING BRIGHTLY when Aki jerked awake, suddenly conscious of something being amiss. The first thing he noticed was how late in the morning it was. He'd meant to leave again at dawn, but, having spent half the night up watching for any sign of an attack, he'd overslept by a few hours. The second, and much more disturbing thing that came to his attention, was the fact that he was alone. Alone, with the pack horse. Neither Sky nor his strange and evasive traveling companion were anywhere to be seen.

Leaping to his feet, Aki bundled up the blanket he'd used and secured it with his things. It took a few moments to rearrange his packs so that he could ride as well, and he chafed at the wasted time. Impatience made his hands clumsy.

The pack horse had no saddle or reins, but it was a docile beast and Aki jumped onto his back anyway.

A light layer of snow had fallen overnight, and in the fine white powder, Sky's hoofprints were clearly visible. She hadn't broken a walk. That didn't come as too much of a surprise considering how terrified the girl had been the day before just to be up on a horse. It made him wonder how she'd found the courage to try to run away on one by herself. He kicked the pack horse into a trot, hoping that they hadn't left too many hours before.

His haste was rewarded only a short time later. A soft nicker came from up ahead and he spurred his mount on a little faster. There were still too many trees and bushes in the way to see them, but he closed the distance quickly.

When he did spot them, Aki was torn between laughing and yelling at her. She was a comical figure alone on the horse, hunched over Sky's neck, her fingers clutching her mane, and her legs held rigidly out away from the horse's body. Aki was irritated enough to prove a point to the girl and hopefully ensure she never tried such a thing again.

Bringing two fingers to his lips, he whistled a signal. Sky spun around so fast that the girl tipped sideways off of the mare and landed with a yelp on the ground. Sliding off the pack horse, he scratched Sky's forehead as she came to a stop in front of him.

The girl sat where she fell. Beneath the tangle of hair, he could see she was blinking fast, her face betraying the pain of her fall. He didn't want to care. She'd stolen his horse and out here, that could very well have spelled death for him. Still, he couldn't help but remember the time Oscar and the others at the academy had set him up to be thrown off a horse. Besides, he understood why she'd done it. If he'd been in her position, he would likely have done the same.

He walked toward her. The closer he got the more obvious it became that she was fighting back tears. Her chest rose and fell rapidly, and her bare hands gripped the ground on either side of her. He crouched down in front of her.

"Don't ever try to steal my things again," Aki said quietly.

She promptly burst into the tears she'd been holding back.

He didn't want to feel sorry for her. He wanted to be angry. He was angry. Down to his very core, he was angry. Angry at her, angry at being stuck out here in the cold while everyone else got to stay safely behind, angry at the way everyone treated him, angry at how lonely he was. He wanted to yell and fume and scold. But he couldn't. Because the person he wanted to yell and fume and scold the most was himself. There was no one who hated him more than he hated himself most of the time. And sitting here, watching her cry in front of him, his self-loathing plunged to whole new depths. He'd done a cruel thing calling Sky back like that, knowing that she would respond too quickly for Not Irene to stay on, wanting her to respond too quickly for the girl to stay on. He could have easily just caught up to her.

The deed was done, though, and he didn't know how to undo it. He wasn't good at making things right. He'd barely managed to patch things up enough with Halle the year before and that was after nearly dying.

"Enough," he said at last, his voice harsh although he didn't mean it to be. "Are you coming with me or not?"

Wiping away the last of her tears, she stared up at him in bewilderment. "You will still take me?"

"I can't very well just leave you out here. You'll die. But I'm in a hurry to get back so I'd rather we not play this game of chase every time I wake up. You'd never make it on your own anyway."

She was still uncertain when she took his hand and let him pull her up behind him but at least her grip around him was not as tight.

More snow fell during the day but inside the forest it did not cover the ground so densely. Aki thought they were far enough away from where the bandits had attacked to risk riding along the edge of the forest so he steered Sky back toward where he knew the great plains were, even if he couldn't see them. His strange companion remained silent behind him and after several hours, Aki was bored.

"So, where are you from?" he asked to break up the monotony. Although she spoke Divalian well and without an accent, he'd noticed the way she enunciated each syllable with great care as if afraid she might say it wrong.

She stiffened behind him. "Why do you ask?"

"No particular reason, I suppose. Just tired of listening to the birds."

"Where are you from?"

"Originally, Aruuk. But I live in Dival, in Bren now."

"You sound like them. Like the ones from Aruuk."

It was Aki that tensed this time. It was the same thing she'd said to him when he first spoke to her. He sounded just like them.

"Who? Who do I sound like?" He kept his voice even, afraid of frightening her into silence.

"The men who attacked us. They had the same accent."

"What?"

She flinched at the tone of his voice, but Aki didn't care anymore. The alarm her words sent through him took away his ability to think of anything else. She didn't say any more about it and Aki didn't either. He thought about what she'd said, what it meant, what it could possibly mean. His mind went back to their mission in the mountains, to the bandits who let their captives go way too easily. The uneasiness he'd felt then returned, magnified tenfold.

It wasn't until they stopped for the night that the girl spoke again. Aki had been watching her while she chewed on a piece of bread, her face twisted up as she thought about something.

"What is 'the courier'?"

Aki froze, his hand halfway to his mouth. "What?"

"Those men. The ones you sound like. They kept saying the same thing over and over again. They were asking the man and woman before they killed them. 'Where is the courier? Where is the courier?' It was all they said. And the man and woman, they did not know. It made the men angry. It is why they killed their sons first, before they killed them."

Aki stood up and staggered away. He was going to be sick. Waves of cold nausea rolled over him. He gripped the nearest tree to steady himself and stared out into the growing darkness. They were dead, because of him. More people dead, because of him. All because he'd given in to his loneliness and had ridden alongside people who didn't know him and didn't judge him. He'd enjoyed the companionship he'd briefly shared with them on the road. And they were dead now because of it. If he'd just kept to himself, they would still be alive. His hands were shaking. His entire body was shaking. The taste of bile was in his throat.

If it was him they were looking for, they wouldn't have just stopped.

"Get up," he turned back to the girl who was watching him curiously. "Get up," he repeated, urgency lacing his words. "We have to go. We have to get away from here."

Sky picked her own way through the darkening forest and Aki let her. As long as they moved in the right direction. He'd learned from Master Wehr how to use the stars as a map, and he was glad of the clear skies tonight. They guided him through the woods. The girl's arms were completely slack around him, her weight resting on his back, and he was sure she'd fallen asleep. He wanted to yell at her to stay awake, to be ready to hold on if they had to sprint away at a moment's notice. But he bit his tongue because he knew that she needed to sleep at some point. He'd need to sleep at some point. He just wasn't sure when he would feel safe enough to do that.

When the moon was starting its descent, Sky stumbled into a ditch of sorts. The jolt woke the girl and she and Aki both got down.

"Are we there yet?" she asked, yawning and wrapping her arms around herself.

"No. Not even close." Aki walked along the ditch, trying to find its end. "But I think we might have just found the road."

Daylight showed that he was right. It was a sunken lane, wildly overgrown and Aki thought if they'd tried to find it in summer when the trees were full of leaves, they would have been hopelessly lost. Even without leaves concealing it, it was hard enough to find. Branches hung over like a spindly arch and Aki had to bend over Sky's neck more than once to avoid being snagged by them.

A sharp cry of pain came from the girl once and he stopped Sky. Twisting his head around to get a look at her, he stifled a frustrated groan. A knotted-up strand of her hair was tangled in an overhanging branch. She reached up to pull it free, but it stuck fast.

"You'll have to cut it," Aki said, withdrawing a small knife from his sleeve.

"I do not want to."

Aki didn't wait to hear any more of her argument. He cut the strand free and then, swinging his leg over Sky's neck, jumped to the ground. While he undid the clasp of his cloak, she stared at him with a mixture of anger and fear. Aki couldn't quite interpret the expression, but he motioned for her to get down as well. She obeyed. He handed her the cloak.

"Pull the hood up over your hair so it doesn't get caught anymore." When she looked ready to protest, he added, "Or we can just cut it all off."

She put the cloak on.

When he started talking to her again it wasn't because he was interested in anything she had to say. His eyes were growing heavier by the second and he found himself drifting closer and closer to sleep. So, he talked instead.

"What are you going to do when you get to Bren?"

"I am going to meet someone."

"Are they your family?"

"I have no family."

"Why were you hiding in that wagon?"

"I did not want them to know I was there."

When he decided that she wasn't going to give him satisfactory answers, he changed tactics. He repeated some of the more interesting history lessons he'd learned from Master Wehr and told her the story of how Sasha had crossed the great plains in the deepest part of winter. She listened without response and Aki thought he might as well be talking to himself. It didn't matter. He was really just doing it to stay awake.

For four more days they traveled. Aki kept their stops brief, only sleeping for three or four hours each night while his companion became very adept at sleeping in the saddle. She didn't complain to him, but he caught her muttering under her breath a few times and assumed she was just keeping it to herself. The food he'd packed ran out and he resorted to hunting as they traveled, although, since he'd used so many arrows rescuing the girl, he had to be careful.

When the forest finally began to thin out in front of them and Aki caught sight of the small town of Soble in the distance, he felt some of the tension of the last few days evaporate out of him. They were now within the old borders of Dival. The roads here were well traveled and an attack was far less likely. And there were places for him to stay. They would not have to sleep out in the open anymore.

"Is that Bren?" The girl's voice in his ear interrupted his daydreaming of a warm bed and food that didn't taste like leather or wood.

"No."

"How much farther is it?"

"Two days."

She was only silent for a moment. "Can you teach me?"

"Teach you what?"

"How to make a horse move and go the right direction."

"Why? So you can steal my horse more successfully?"

"No," she seemed offended by the reminder, "I just think it would be something I want to know."

Because there was a town within sight, Aki was in a better mood than he'd been since he'd left Bren almost a month before. And because he was feeling a bit generous, he agreed. He helped her down. It took only a moment to rearrange his dwindled supplies on the pack horse so that he could ride him instead.

"Hold onto her like this," he demonstrated, grabbing the reins along with a fistful of Sky's mane in his hand, "put your left foot in the stirrup and..."

"I think I know that part. I have watched you do it many times."

He stepped away and with a sweep of his arm gestured for her to try. It was clumsy and she looked more like she was climbing a pile of rocks, but she made it into the saddle. Aki suppressed a laugh and helped guide her other foot into its stirrup before getting on the other horse.

"You can't sit like that. If she stops or turns suddenly, you'll fall right off the front of her."

"Like I did before?"

"Yes, like then."

As they rode toward Soble, he continued to give her instructions and she tried to listen and he tried not to laugh. When they entered town, he guided them toward an inn. He held out a hand to help her down and tied the horses up to the hitching post.

"It is a lot of work to ride," she said as she followed him inside.

"Not once you've done it for a while. Most of the time I don't even have to think about it. I just do it."

"I would like to try again, I think. I would like to be good at it."

"You have a long way to go before you're good at it."

Chapter 20

IS THIS BREN?"

She asked every time they saw a town in the distance. Aki didn't have to twist around anymore to see her. She rode on Sky alone while he continued to use the pack horse. After two days, she still leaned forward stiffly, her hands never far from Sky's mane.

"Sit up straight. You'll fall off if she stops."

"Is it?" she repeated, straightening for a moment before tipping forward again.

"Yes, Not Irene, this is Bren. You can tell, because it's the only town we've been to so far that has its very own royal castle."

"Dorsten had a castle."

"Yes, but it's almost never used. Not since the union."

"What is the union?"

"Once, a really long time ago, Dorsten and Dival were one country. Then the king died and left it equally to his twin sons. They split it into two countries and fought for years and years because they both thought they deserved a bigger part. After both sons died and after a bit more fighting between them, they eventually decided to become one country again." At least, that was the story Master Wehr had told him. The union had been a result of Sasha's warning and the work of King Darien. It laid to rest more than fifty years of conflict.

"But if they spent so many years fighting, how do they get along now?"

Aki shrugged. That wasn't part of the story.

It was snowing again when they finally entered Bren, passing the first few houses. They had only ridden a little way in when the girl pulled Sky up and started to slide off. She did it with little grace or finesse, simply leaning to the side and pulling her leg down after her. No matter how many times Aki had shown her, she just couldn't seem to manage anything better.

"What are you doing"

"This is Bren. This was where you said you would take me."

Aki glanced around, half expecting someone to be standing nearby waiting for the strange girl, but no one even seemed to notice either of their presence. Most people had their heads down, in a hurry to finish whatever errand brought them out into the cold and snow and return to the warmth of their homes.

"So, what exactly are you going to do?"

"Look. I have to find someone."

Aki raised a bemused eyebrow. She seemed confident, though, and he had his own task, so he didn't linger to watch her disappear into the streets of Bren.

He needed nothing other than his courier's jacket to get him through the front gate of the castle. Snow muffled the sound of his horses' hooves on the stone courtyard as he rode in. Aki reached into a saddlebag to retrieve the letter from Prince Desmond before allowing a stable hand to hurry the horses off to the shelter of the castle stables. When his hand found the paper, he frowned and pulled it free. There wasn't one letter, but two.

Both were sealed shut and addressed to the king, but only one bore the prince's seal. The second one was unfamiliar to him, and he knew all the seals of the noblemen. It was a wolf's head, stamped into the red wax. The handwriting was soft, flowing, a graceful flourish adorning each letter. It was a woman's, not a man's. He thought of the signet ring from his mother, but the symbols were not the same. Aki put both in his pocket.

The guard at the door recognized him. Most people in the castle did and that wasn't such a good thing. Quite a number of them remembered him only for the time he'd spent working off his indenture. Still, it meant few questions when he arrived. After stating that he carried a message for the king, he was escorted to the entrance of the council room.

"Weapons," his escort, a very bored looking young man, reminded him and Aki went through the tedious process of disarming himself, handing his weapons over to a guard. He wasn't the only one required to do so and he regularly had to remind himself of that. It was a precaution that had nothing to do with past actions. Aside from his guards, very few were allowed to be armed in the presence of the king.

Aki did not anticipate the presence of the entire council. When the door was opened to admit him, he paused, his mind going back to the only other time he'd seen them all together - the day he was tried for treason and sentenced. He could take comfort in the fact that, at least this time, there was no audience aside from the council members.

The hum of conversation died away the moment his presence was noticed, and all eyes were on him as he crossed the room to stand before King Darien. Their stares were heavy, slowing his steps and Aki couldn't shrug them off. It was more than the usual weight of accusation. There was something else, something he was missing. Quite a few in the room seemed shocked by his presence.

"From Prince Desmond, Your Majesty," Aki held out only the one letter, still not fully decided on what to do with the other. It felt more and more like a hot coal in his pocket. He could be punished for carrying an unauthorized missive, and Aki was pretty sure that any infraction on his part would be the end of his career. He'd already been given a second chance. However, it was addressed to the king and if the king discovered he was carrying it and hadn't given it to him, Aki was certain that would also mean trouble. If he'd been alone with the king, he wouldn't have worried quite as much. King Darien had always given him the chance to explain himself. Some of the council members were not so generous. He tried not to look in Baron Orlander's direction.

King Darien leaned forward and took the letter from his hand. "You came alone? All the way from Dorsten?"

"I left the prince and his men in Dorsten," Aki answered carefully, not wanting to mention that he'd traveled most of the way with a strange girl who was burdened with the purpose of finding someone she didn't know in Bren but also wishing to avoid an outright lie to the king.

The king noticed his evasion and studied him a moment before breaking the seal open and turning his attention to his son's words. He finished only a few seconds later with an exasperated sigh and tossed the letter onto the table. Aki could see from where he was standing how little was written.

"My son seems to have forgotten the importance of communicating clearly and thoroughly. Perhaps you'll be able to fill in the details he's missed. All he mentions here is that the captives are safe, and he is wintering in the castle of Dorsten. Please elaborate for us. Who was to blame? Should we consider our treaty with Aruuk dissolved? Were any men lost? Why did he choose to remain in Dorsten rather than come straight here?"

Aki took a moment to collect his thoughts. He wasn't used to having to address so many people at once and, having been in the warmth for a few minutes, he now found himself fighting off the urge to fall asleep on his feet.

"The Aruuken government had no knowledge of the raid and offered us their help in finding the captives. The prince was able to negotiate their release without a fight, so we didn't lose anyone. But..." Aki stopped himself, biting his lip. The thought that had been nagging him since they'd found the raiding party and captives came to mind now. Coupled with what had happened on the road home, it became an even bigger puzzle. Or maybe it was two different puzzles and he just happened to be tangled up in both of them.

"What?" Baron Orlander spoke up from Aki's side. "What are you not telling us, courier?"

Aki looked at King Darien who gestured for him to speak. There wasn't a good way to say it. It was only his opinion and few people thought much of that, but Aki didn't dare deny the king. "Something wasn't right about it all, I don't think."

"What do you mean?"

"Well...," Aki felt the unwavering attention of every member on him now and swallowed hard before continuing, "they... it was almost like they wanted to be found. A raiding party can disappear for months into the mountains, but they were barely off the trail. And it was too easy. We went in and they just handed them over to us, no fight, no bargaining." Now that he was giving voice to it, Aki realized what had bothered him most about the entire affair, the thing that had made it unsettling and unrealistic. "And the captives - they were all men. No women, no children. Just men. No raiding party ever takes just men. Men don't make easy slaves. And they weren't afraid. They weren't anxious or worried about what might happen to them. They weren't even glad to be released. It was like they knew they weren't in any real danger."

"Just because they hadn't stooped to your level of cowardice hardly means they weren't afraid, does it?" Baron Orlander's voice was sharp.

Aki clenched his teeth as blood rushed to his face. He didn't wait for anyone to say another word. He didn't wait to be dismissed. Turning on his heel, he simply walked out of the room. The guards at the door even opened it for him.

Once it shut behind him, Aki realized what he'd just done and what a terrible mistake it was. He'd left the king's presence without permission. He hadn't even told them everything. His breath came fast as he sought a place to sit down. Maybe he should go back in and apologize. Or just go back to the academy and wait for someone to find him. Once sitting on a bench in the hallway, though, he couldn't make himself get up and do either of those things.

While he sat with his face in his hands waiting, footsteps approached, and someone coughed into their hand above his head. Aki looked up and found himself staring at one of the king's attendants.

"You're to come with me," the man said.

Aki tried to decipher the extent of the king's wrath based off of his attendant's expression, but the man was schooled in the art of keeping his face neutral and closed. Aki exhaled deeply and got to his feet. It was his own fault. He'd been a coward and it shouldn't bother him so much to be called one. But he also knew what he was talking about when it came to captives and slaves. Better than anyone in that council room, except, of course, Hamo.

And he knew he was right.

The room he was led to was familiar to Aki. It was the same one he'd been brought to when he finally revealed Kezi and Jasper and Halle's plan. The attendant bade him sit and left without another word.

It was quiet in the room. Peaceful. A small fire kept it warm and comfortable, and no voices could be heard beyond the walls. It smelled of wood and books and warm wax from the candles burning in sconces on the walls. Aki leaned forward and rested his arms on the desk. After a few minutes went by, he laid his head on his arms and shut his eyes to rest them a little. He'd pushed himself hard on his trip from Dorsten to Bren and he was beginning to truly feel it.

There was a hand on his shoulder. A voice in his ear. Aki drew in a deep, sleepy breath and sat up, blinking. It was hours later. He didn't know how he knew that, but he did. He turned, searching for the one who woke him and found himself staring up at King Darien.

"I presume I can blame exhaustion for such poor judgment and behavior on your part."

Aki scrambled to his feet, and then grasped the edge of the desk to steady himself as it made his head spin. An apology was already in his mouth when he noticed the faint smile on the king's face. Then he wasn't sure what to say.

"Although I'd love to say Baron Orlander regrets his words, that would be a lie," King Darien continued. "He is a blunt man, not one to mince words much. It makes him valuable on my council, but it can make him difficult to be around. And forgiveness is not one of his stronger merits."

Since Aki was still rubbing the sleep from his eyes and yawning, he didn't answer. He didn't know what to say anyway. When the king sat down on the far side of the desk and motioned for him to resume his seat, Aki did so gratefully. It was only then that he realized the king was not alone. Hamo had accompanied him and took a seat near Aki.

"I'm sorry I kept you waiting so long. That was not my intention. However, despite the baron's opinion, your words gave us much to discuss. Hamo agreed entirely with your perception and since the two of you are the only ones I have who share any experience in that area, I'm inclined to believe you. Am I correct in understanding that you believe the entire affair was set up?"

"I guess that's what I was saying. It just seemed off, the whole thing. And there's more."

"Oh? Perhaps you should have stayed around long enough to finish." King Darien's reproach was gentle but unmistakable and Aki looked down.

"What else happened, Aki?" Hamo asked quietly.

There wouldn't be a better time to explain, and he preferred to tell just the two of them to the entire council. There also wasn't an easy way to tell his news.

"I killed one of their leaders," he blurted out and was rewarded by a stunned and speechless audience of two. He went on to explain their time in Illsen, leaving out the more sordid details regarding Cadoc's intentions. From there, he recounted the ambush, Lars' timely appearance and help, and their negotiations to free the captives.

"Is that all?" King Darien asked.

"Not really, no. Prince Desmond was afraid of being caught in the great plains when the snow came so he decided, like I told you earlier, to stay in Dorsten with the rest of the men. However, they've had fever in the town so when he sent me to take word to you, I took the long way around. I shared the road for a couple of hours with a family who was moving out of town to escape fever. They stopped and I kept going, but I hadn't gone far before I heard them being attacked. By the time I made it back, the entire family had been killed but there was a girl who'd stowed away in their wagon, and she was alive still. I killed and wounded some of the men with arrows and she and I made it into the old Sar Forest."

"Who were the men who attacked? Thieves?"

Aki shook his head. "They put a torch to the wagon with all the belongings in it. Besides, the girl told me they kept asking the same thing over and over again. 'Where's the courier?' They were looking for me, I think."

King Darien exchanged a troubled look with Hamo. Aki pretended not to notice.

"She also said that they sounded like me."

"Sounded like you?" King Darien asked, his face puzzled.

"Their accent. She meant their accent."

"I see. And who was this girl?"

Aki shrugged. "I have no idea."

"What happened after you made it to the forest with her?"

"I brought her with me. She would have died on her own and she said she wanted to go to Bren. I'm sorry. I didn't know what else to do with her. If I shouldn't have..."

"She's here?"

"Somewhere here. She disappeared pretty much as soon as we made it into town. Said she was looking for someone."

King Darien stood up and went to the window. For a long time, he remained there, silent and lost in thought. When he faced them again, Aki was struck by how much the king had aged in the last year. Concern deepened wrinkles that hadn't been there a year ago. His hair was more gray than brown. He returned to his chair with a heavy sigh and laid his folded hands on the desk.

"Aki, although you had no way of knowing this," he started, "You have brought us the first news we've had from beyond the Void in over a month. I've been expecting other couriers, but none have come. I've sent some, and none have returned. The last one to arrive was the man who brought word of the attack. Not only have we had no couriers, but there has also been no travel from that province to ours since then. It's as if they no longer exist. Putting together everything you've told us with that fact paints a very disturbing picture. I do wish you'd have stayed in the council room long enough to tell everyone. You'll have to do it tomorrow. And you'll have to answer, thoroughly, any questions they may have for you."

"I understand. I'm sorry, Your Majesty."

Another look passed between the king and Hamo. This time Aki didn't bother to pretend to not see it. He looked from one to the other. And then they were both watching him. He shifted in his seat and tried to keep his hands still in his lap. For the first time he got the sense that he hadn't been brought to this room to explain himself, but so that the king could explain something to him. He would be having this conversation regardless of how things had gone in the council room. His suspicion was confirmed a moment later when the king spoke again.

"There's something I need to tell you, Aki. And I will apologize now because perhaps I should have told you right away. It seemed right at the time to wait."

"It's something to do with my sentence, isn't it?" Aki interrupted, suddenly remembering Captain Tyrrel's words to the prince.

"Yes. There was some debate as to what your sentence would be, but there was one thing that the council was unanimous on - your actions, if not your motives, were treasonous."

Aki stole a glance at Hamo. He'd never spoken to the man about that day, partly because he didn't want to know what Hamo really thought of him. Hamo wasn't looking at him now.

"By our laws, a traitor's life is forfeit. Even the king can't pardon that crime."

"But I wasn't sentenced to die." Aki looked from one to the other again, an awful idea coming to life in his mind. "Was I?"

"No. You weren't sentenced to die. There's more than one way to take a life. And there is a way for traitors to live. But never fully free."

"I'm bound in service to you for the rest of my life," he said, not even asking. He already knew it was true. He stared down at his hands, unwilling to meet either of their gazes.

"Yes. That was the only way for your life to be spared. You can live, but you'll never have all your own choices again. It means that while you are free to come and go as you please, you will always be available for me to use in whatever way I see fit."

Aki said nothing. Somehow, he'd known something like this was coming. What the captain had said had only confirmed it. It was his training for the last year that had raised his suspicions. None of that made the news any easier to swallow.

"Perhaps I ought to have told you right away. We... I wanted you to heal first, though."

"I've been healed for months," Aki looked up, suddenly angry.

"Aki, he's not talking about your body," Hamo said softly.

"What do you mean? I'm fine. I've been fine. I was healed enough for you to put me to work."

"How many times did you go home this past year?"

"Just once, when Stephan...," Aki couldn't go on. He'd been so busy that he'd been able to push the loss away. Now wasn't a good time to bring it up.

"Were you offered any other chances to visit home?"

"Yes. A few."

"But you didn't take any of them?"

"I didn't want to go home. I wanted to stay busy."

"And what do you do in your free time?"

"I... I study, or train."

"With the others?"

"No. By myself, mostly, or at the barracks because Colin told me to."

Both men fell silent, watching him, letting the truth sink in. Aki set his jaw and looked up to meet the king's eyes. He tried to reel in the anger that pulsed through him. He hated them for this. Hated their pity, the way they tried to take the sting out of his punishment. Hated that, in spite of everything he'd done, they still cared.

"So, what does it mean? I have to do whatever you want me to, don't I?"

"Something like that. Aki, it was honestly my intention to leave you to pursue your training as a courier. That would have been service enough for me. However, there are things afoot that may require me to use you for something beyond just carrying messages. Both Colin and Atticus have shared with me that you have talents beyond riding a horse. I'm sure you've noticed that your training has been somewhat different than the others."

"What happens if I don't obey?"

"Quite simply, you die. Any breach in your bond will result in the traditional sentence of traitors."

"Is that why you came to see me? The night before my trial. You came to see if I was worth you trying to save, didn't you?"

King Darien nodded and leaned forward, laying his arms on the desk. "How angry are you with me?"

It was a dangerous question. Aki was boiling over with anger, but he couldn't direct it at the king. Not when the king was the only reason he hadn't faced execution. It was anger at himself, really.

"Can I go now?" he asked, unable to think of a good answer for the king's question and feeling as if there suddenly wasn't enough air in the room to breathe.

King Darien smiled sadly and nodded. "You may. I'm sure you're still quite tired from your journey. I am sorry, Aki. If it were up to me, this isn't how it would go. And perhaps we are wrong about everything, and you will be able to continue as just a courier."

Aki started for the door, but the king stopped him.

"I'll need you here again tomorrow. And if you happen to see that girl again, we'd like to speak with her as well."

Mention of the girl made Aki remember the second letter still in his pocket. Too angry to care anymore, he pulled it out and tossed it onto the desk before the king.

"I have no idea where it came from or who put it in my bag, but this was with the prince's letter."

King Darien took one look at the handwriting on the outside and paled. He whispered something too softly for Aki to hear. He didn't pick the letter up, only stared at it.

"Go," he said at last.

Chapter 21

WHATEVER WAS IN THE LETTER, King Darien was still troubled when the morning came, and Aki was once again in front of the council.

This time, he was given a seat but that just reminded him even more of his trial - especially since he'd done nothing but answer questions and explain himself since he first came in. Neither the king nor Hamo asked him anything. Apparently, he'd been detailed enough last night. Aki thought the king might go the entire meeting without speaking once.

Just when he thought it was over, King Darien addressed him. "The letter you gave me yesterday evening, I'm quite curious about where it came from. Do you recall if, at any time, there was an opportunity for someone to have access to your horse? An opportunity for someone to slip it inside your bag?"

Aki didn't have to think hard at all about that. The only questionable person he'd been around was Not Irene. And she'd had the perfect opportunity.

"The girl I told you about. She did try to steal my horse the first night. It would have been easy enough to do then."

The king acknowledged his words with a distracted nod and then dismissed everyone. Aki was the first to his feet, bolting toward the door before anyone could stop him and ask him any more questions.

"Aki," King Darien's voice arrested his feet, calling him back into the room.

"Your Majesty?"

"Would you know the girl again on sight?"

"Yes." There was no way he could not know that fountain of hair.

"We need to speak with her. Find her. Bring her here."

"What if she doesn't want to come?" Aki asked uneasily. Although he'd only spoken to the king a handful of times, there was something in his tone now that gave him cause to hesitate. He wondered for the hundredth time what could possibly have been in that letter and who had sent it.

"Then find her and tell the nearest guard. I need to know if she had anything to do with that letter."

"Yes, Your Majesty."

King Darien managed a tight smile, so unlike any expression Aki had seen on him before. "You do not have to fear for her. We're not barbarians. She will not be hurt. But I need to speak with her."

"I'll find her, Your Majesty. Although, it might take a few days. Am I still to go to Master Wehr's?"

"Yes, yes. But when you are free, look for her." Aki realized that this was the first time he'd ever seen the king flustered, panicked almost.

They were vague orders at best. Aki reclaimed his weapons before leaving the castle and struck out into the streets of Bren. He wandered back to where he'd first left her but found no sign of her. Not that he was really expecting to. She could be anywhere now, perhaps no longer even in Bren. She'd been evasive when he asked her anything about herself, either lying outright and obviously or ignoring his inquiries entirely.

Master Wehr's was not so far from that spot. Aki kept up a careful scrutiny of every alleyway and corner as he made his way to his instructor's. He only passed a handful of people along his way, most well bundled against the cold and snow. His own face was nearly obscured by his hood and scarf.

The door opened almost at once when he knocked as if Master Wehr had been standing there waiting for him.

"You made it back." There was genuine relief in the old man's voice as he pulled Aki inside and shut out the cold behind him. "We've not had anyone come from the northern province in a month. A whole month. Not a word. People were beginning to fear the worst."

"Were you worried about me, Master Wehr?" Aki asked as Master Wehr urged him to take off his cloak and jacket beneath. The man hurried him to a chair in front of the fire, an honor Aki almost never received. His usual spot was the high stool by the window.

"I'm an old man. Worry is one of the few things I still get to enjoy in this life. Come, come. A month away. You must have a story to tell."

Aki repeated the same story he'd told the king and Hamo and the council, although he was far more comfortable telling Master Wehr. His instructor's face went through many expressions. Shock, horror, sadness, relief. And, although Aki missed it, a hint of pride. By the end, though, only worry lined his face, deepened his gaze.

"That is troubling news, indeed. Most troubling." He muttered a few words under his breath, then brightened forcibly. "It is good to know the many hours of training you've done with Colin and at the barracks have paid off."

"Did I miss much while I was gone?" Aki asked, glad to have the chance to enjoy an ordinary conversation rather than simply feeding information to an audience.

"I'm afraid our time has been far less eventful than yours, not that I can complain about that." Master Wehr narrowed his eyes and studied Aki. "You've spoken to the king, haven't you?"

It was as if the door was opened, and a gust of wind allowed in to steal away the warmth of the room. Aki's answer was stiff. "About my real sentence? Yes. You knew."

Master Wehr nodded. "We were told not to say a word to you at the time. The king thought it best to give you time to mend. I think in his mind he rather hoped to never have to impose such a bond on you. Unfortunately, I believe circumstances may make that desire impossible for him to fulfill."

"I'm mended," Aki said with irritation. "Why does everyone think I'm not?"

Rather than answering, Master Wehr leaned forward and, before Aki could pull away, gently pushed the sleeve up on his right arm. Past the brands that Aki hated the sight of. Aki did not resist. He just hung his head. He knew exactly what Master Wehr was showing him, for he'd put them there himself. Scratched them out late at night, adding the last two names just the night before when he could not sleep.

"Because you still hate yourself for surviving," Master Wehr's answer came at last. "Otherwise, why would you carve the names of the dead on your skin."

"It's not like that," he said feebly.

"Isn't it? Tell me honestly, Aki, did you not put them there because you feel that in some small way, they own you too?"

"Dagmar's dead because I survived. If I'd given up or if she'd been just a few hours later, she'd still be alive. Nothing anyone does to me, no service, no sentence, will ever wipe away that debt. Never. My parents...," Aki stopped. He couldn't even speak of his parents. He wanted so badly to understand what it was they saw in their infant son that made death a worthy option. "Those people I met on the road, they're dead because of me. I survived because of their deaths." Aki twisted away, pulling his sleeve back over the crudely written names. "Tell me, really, why should the king spare my life when I'm the reason so many have died?"

"On a purely practical level because you are useful. And obedience comes easily to you, even if loyalty does not. You could be the king's weapon should trouble with our northern neighbors ever arise. You don't even know your own potential, Aki."

"We're at peace with Aruuk."

"Peace is fragile. Half the council wished to declare war over the raid. Had they prevailed, our peace would have been shattered and whether Aruuk was responsible or not, war would have been waged and innumerable lives lost. And the very circumstances surrounding your sentencing were brought about by people from Aruuk and Karu. The king knew that it was likely not the last time he would face a threat from them."

"So, the only reason I'm alive is because I'm useful."

"I didn't say that." Master Wehr sighed and leaned forward to set another log on the fire. "King Darien is a good man. A just king. His greatest flaw, according to some at least, is the extent of his compassion, especially and inexplicably when it comes to the sons of Gundar. I think, more than anything, King Darien saw a half dead boy locked away in his tower prison because he'd been too afraid to speak out and he didn't have the heart to end that boy's life while there was still so much of it yet to be lived."

"I should go," Aki choked the words out, desperate now to end this conversation.

"If you're going to keep a tally of the dead," Master Wehr went on as if he hadn't spoken, "then you should keep one of the living, too. Not on your body. That's scarred enough. But maybe it's time you started looking to a different list. You can't raise the dead, Aki. But you cannot always grieve for them either. You ask why we thought you were not ready? These names are the reason. These scars. You haven't yet forgiven yourself for still being alive."

"You don't understand."

"Perhaps not. There is much about your life I do not understand. But I think I do. Tell me what I've said that's a lie. You need to start living again. That would be a better way to honor the dead than marring yourself further."

Aki said nothing. He stared down at the now covered marks, seeing in his mind the names he'd written there - Anton, Mother, Dagmar, and the most recent, Jory and Lisbeth. Without a thought, he brought a finger up and traced them through the fabric of his sleeve, remembering the pain he'd put himself through to get each and every letter, the pain he knew he deserved.

Too agitated to sit any longer, Aki paced the small space.

"If it bothers you so much, you can always choose the alternative," Master Wehr said after a space of a few minutes when the only sound to be heard was Aki's restless footsteps on the wood floor.

"I don't get a choice. That's the entire point of it. My life belongs to the king. How is that any different than being a slave?" Aki ran a frustrated hand through his hair and stopped in front of the window. He took a deep breath, trying to stem the anger he hadn't dared show the king. Master Wehr didn't deserve it. Not even King Darien deserved it.

"You always have a choice, Aki. It's mindless obedience that makes a slave and the king will never ask that of you."

"Do I? Serve him any way he asks or die? That's not a choice. Who would ever choose death?" He turned around and faced Master Wehr. "No one would be that much of a fool."

"Your parents did," Master Wehr answered softly.

Aki's face crumpled as the words sank in. His anger pulled back but only so that it could drown him in itself a moment later. He found himself gripping the desk to keep himself steady. Shaking his head, he tried several times to speak but the words did not want to form. When they did come out, Aki spoke from the very deepest, darkest part of him, the part that craved the pain of carving names into his arm, the part that drove him to train until he was ready to drop in exhaustion, the part that he never showed anyone.

"My parents were fools, then. Better that they had lived. They might have done some good then."

"To value another's life before one's own is not foolishness, Aki, it is love - of the very highest kind."

The door shut hard enough to jar the walls of the house, but Aki didn't pause. Cold wind bit at his face. Clumps of snow disintegrated when he gave them a savage kick. There was only one place he had in mind. Only one place where he could turn the anger into something useful, into something controllable.

The weapons room was cold and empty when he entered. But Aki wasn't looking for company anyway. He drew his sword and attacked the first post with a vengeance. The metal rang dull against the wood and bit deep. Hours would have to be dedicated to the sharpening of his blade when he was through, but Aki didn't care. When it became tiresome, he pulled out his father's sword, keeping it in his left hand while his right wielded his own. He'd never tried it before but Captain Tyrrel always made him practice with his left hand as much as his right so he wasn't as clumsy as he would have been a year ago.

For an hour, the only sound that could be heard was the clang and thud of his swords and his own ragged breathing. For an hour, Aki was in absolute control of everything. He could focus every thought, every sense into the post before him. With a final lunge, he embedded both blades into the hardened wood and stopped.

Sweat trickled down his face, his arms. Safely alone, he dared to roll his sleeves up past his elbows. For a few minutes he just stood, bent to catch his breath, his hands resting on his knees. When it slowed, when his pulse wasn't pounding in his head anymore, he pulled his father's sword free. He'd been so preoccupied with getting to Bren alive that not once had he pulled it out and looked at it since leaving Dorsten. Now, he ran a light finger down the length of the blade.

His father.

Those words were supposed to mean something. They were supposed to evoke something - respect, love, something. A fool, he'd just called him. A fool for choosing death instead of obedience. He wondered if Anton had ever used the sword to kill another man. And if he had, what he'd felt doing it. Had his father stared in shock at the blood he'd shed? Or become ill at the horror of it? Did his father hate Gundar and everything he stood for? Was keeping his son alive just another step in a rebellion against the Chief? Or perhaps his father was hungry for the power of the Chief and that was why he refused to yield to it.

Sitting down on the dirt floor, not caring that it was cold or filthy, Aki pulled out of his pocket the ring. He'd looked at this even less, not even showing it to Lars. Rubbing it between his thumb and forefinger, he let the light catch the sapphire stones set on either side of the signet. There was nothing sinister in the symbol. Nothing but a simple tree, devoid of leaves and two letters intertwined in the branches - HB.

Then Aki made a dreadful mistake.

He thought of Stephan and Alina. The only two people in his life who had ever truly acted like parents. It opened a pit inside him, yawning and cavernous. And he ached to feel its emptiness. Out of that void came only one coherent thought.

He missed Stephan.

He missed the man who had taken him in and given him a home when he was nothing, who had spared him the misery of returning to Aruuk, who had taught him most of what was worth knowing. There was nothing, absolutely nothing, he would rather do in that moment then go home and talk to Stephan. Not the stilted conversations they had managed from time to time in the last year, but the way he'd spoken to him before, when there was no barrier of distrust and betrayal.

Aki pressed his clenched fists over his eyes, fighting the grief he had not allowed himself before. Not a sound escaped him.

"Aki?" a voice reached him through the fog of his grief, "Are you alright?"

There stood Felix.

Aki was on his feet in an instant, the sword that had been balanced across his lap clattering to the floor, his hands scrambling to push his sleeves back down over the scars on his arms before Felix's eyes wandered down to them.

He looked away. There was no way to know how long Felix had been standing there watching without asking and Aki had barely said five words to him in the past year. Normally when he saw Felix coming, he would run the other way.

"I'm fine. I was just leaving."

"No, you weren't." Felix bent down and retrieved his fallen sword. Instead of handing it straight to Aki, he looked it over. "This is new. And very well made. Where'd you get it?"

"It was my father's." Aki held out his hand expectantly.

"I am sorry for your loss, Aki. Stephan was a very good man. My father respected him greatly."

"Yes, he was."

They stood facing one another in silence. Aki let his hand drop and slid both into his pockets. Felix studied the sword again. When they did speak again it was simultaneous.

"I should go," Aki said.

And Felix said at the same time, "We all heard the news."

Felix stopped and gave him a sheepish smile. "You don't have to leave every time you see me. It's not like I'm going to do anything to you."

"I wasn't. I...," Aki stopped. He didn't have a good excuse. Then again, he hadn't most of the year and that hadn't stopped him from hiding away in his room.

"You know, we've all heard what happened up north. About getting the captives back and the attack. And what happened to you, of course." Felix finally remembered the sword he was holding and held it out for Aki to take. "Did you meet your father there?"

Aki groaned internally. It would have been easier if he'd lied about where the sword came from. But, after last year's debacle, he was trying hard to avoid such dishonesty. Felix had no inkling of his complicated and miserable past. His question was asked out of polite interest and nothing more.

"My father's dead. It was someone who knew him that kept the sword and gave it to me."

"I'm sorry. How did he die?"

Felix was only asking because it was the courteous thing to do. Aki could tell he was as uncomfortable with the turn in the conversation as Aki was, although for very different reasons.

"My grandfather killed him," Aki answered.

The answer took Felix by surprise, but he did a good job of concealing it quickly. He also did a good job of carrying the conversation in a new, although equally uncomfortable, direction. "Is it true you killed someone in Aruuk?"

"Yes."

"I thought it was. Some of the others, they...," Felix stopped and looked distressed.

"They what?"

"I don't believe them, Aki. At least, I don't want to believe them."

"They what?" Aki repeated.

"Some of the others think that, well, that you're a spy. For Aruuk, I mean. They think that's why you're the only courier who has come back from the northern province for more than a month. Not just the only courier, the only person. They think you're the enemy."

"Are we enemies with Aruuk?"

"Well, they did attack one of our mountain villages. And then they ambushed your party in the mountains. The king hasn't declared anything yet, but most everyone believes that come spring, we'll be at war."

Aki's heart raced at the word. At what it would mean, not just for everyone he knew here in Dival but for Lars and Faramund in Aruuk.

Chapter 22

THERE WAS A CERTAIN AMOUNT of boredom that Desmond actually enjoyed. Back home in Bren, he often indulged himself in that luxurious boredom. But that had been when he had servants to bring him food when he desired it and comfortable rooms to lounge in and the prospect of entertainment to look forward to whenever the boredom became too tedious.

Here in Dorsten, there were none of those things. The miniscule staff that had been kept on hand had steadily shrunk since they arrived. Either the fever itself, or fear of the fever had robbed him of his servants. And the provisions that were kept on hand were old, mostly stale or tough, and without a real chef to bring them to delicious life. Most of the castle was cold. The men were crowded into just a handful of rooms to conserve both their workload and their fuel.

His only relief in the mundane was Tristan. Desmond couldn't thank the man enough for the brilliance of his suggestion to stay with the prince and his party. If it weren't for Tristan, Desmond would have had nothing to do but walk the battlements alone and watch Captain Tyrrel drill his men.

"That's why I could never have made soldiering my life," Tristan said from where he stood next to Desmond. In the courtyard beneath the window they were sharing, Captain Tyrrel was once again drilling his men. "Imagine being forced awake every morning with nothing to look forward to but this." He mocked a shiver.

Desmond laughed. "I might have liked it if I wasn't the crown prince. Father would never let me do anything of the sort, though."

"You, Desmond?" Tristan choked on a laugh. "Pardon me, but you would never have been a soldier. That would have required you to give up your comforts."

Desmond had to concede that this was true. He wasn't used to being contradicted, though. Usually when he said such things, and he said them often, everyone's reaction would be something about what a wonderful soldier he would have made if he were ever given the chance. They said the same words if he mentioned he'd prefer to be a blacksmith or a sailor or a merchant. Inevitably he would be the best at whatever he wished he could do. Coming from Tristan, he appreciated the candor.

"The captain wishes I would give up a few comforts. You know he asks me every day to come down and get some sword practice in?"

"I can see he's most effective in his request."

"Oh, not at all. What's the use of practicing 'til my arm feels as if it'll fall off. That's what the soldiers are here for. Besides, my father would never take us into war. He values peace over everything."

"It has made for a prosperous time for his kingdom," Tristan pointed out quietly.

"Yes, yes. Trust me, I know. He regularly tells me as much. You know, at times, I believe him. But...," Desmond stopped. He wasn't used to openly contradicting his father to anyone.

"But you're not so sure right now?"

"Exactly. I mean, I know the courier said that Aruuk wasn't involved in the first attack, but who's to say he wasn't lying, covering for them? And the ambush on the trail? That was most certainly Aruuk. Even Aki couldn't deny that."

"Hmm." Tristan crossed his arms over his chest. "Do you really think your father won't see that as an act of war? I presume you explained the entire affair to him in the letter you sent off with that courier."

"Of course I did," Desmond snapped.

The truth was, that he tried his best not to think of that. What he'd written could hardly qualify as a letter. It was barely two sentences. And there was, of course, the possibility that Aki had never reached Bren. Captain Tyrrel reminded him of that often and Desmond avoided thinking about that possibility. It meant Father was waiting at home, desperately worried, and there was nothing he could do about it.

"Well, however the king sees it, I'm sure he'll do what's best for the kingdom." Then he added quietly, to himself, "At least, he'll do what's best for his native half."

Desmond heard the words. He suspected Tristan wanted him to hear the words. "You think my father favors one half of the kingdom over the other? Those are dangerous words to say to me, friend or no friend."

"Forgive me. I shouldn't have said that."

Giving up on watching the soldiers in the courtyard below, Desmond threw himself down in a soft, stuffed chair before the fire. A few minutes went by before his curiosity overcame his filial respect.

"What made you say that?"

"I'd rather not elaborate if it's such a dangerous topic, no offense. I've found I rather like having my head attached to my shoulders."

Desmond chuckled and waved a hand to dismiss his concerns. "I don't believe my father has actually ever had a man executed for disagreeing with him. Now my grandfather, that's a different story. So, please, humor me. You might even convince me that you're right."

Despite Desmond's reassurance, Tristan looked ill at ease. Rather than joining the prince by the fire he remained looking out the window, his fingers drumming a nervous rhythm on its sill.

"It's not entirely my opinion, just so you know. Just things I've heard from time to time."

"What sort of things?"

"Well, for instance, I'm sure you are aware of the Aruuken Chief's son that your father pardoned after the battle in the mountain pass?"

"Of course."

"You know, he was sentenced to die here for participating in a raid that killed quite a few of our people, destroyed three different villages. And it was the king's own man who stole him out of prison before his execution."

"He had good reason to pardon Sasha Gundarson. He saved both our lands with his warning."

"Ah, yes. Forever remembered as the hero. If only we all could be so brave and valuable."

Desmond grimaced at the bitterness in Tristan's voice. "You think my father should have executed him after that, despite the service he rendered us?"

Tristan took a moment to consider the question. "Perhaps not. But a full pardon? And no consequence for the man who broke him out of our prison? People died, Desmond. Those villages are lost forever."

Put like that, Desmond couldn't deny the truth of Tristan's words. It made him think of Aki and his own sentence. And thinking of him reminded him of the note he'd sent to his father and made him wonder once again if it had even reached him.

Tristan mistook his silence for anger. "I'm sorry. I should have kept my thoughts to myself. King Darien has brought about the longest peace we've known in generations and that is no small feat. Who cares if he shows a bit of favoritism now and then?"

"He's brought about peace because he absolutely refuses to go to war."

Chapter 23

"THAT'S HER," AKI SAID. "THAT'S the girl who came with me, the one King Darien wants to talk to."

Colin followed his eyes to where the girl sat near the gate of the castle. It was the last place Aki thought she would be, yet there she was and not making the slightest effort to hide or blend in. To any observant bystander, it was obvious she was fixated on the castle entrance.

"You're sure?"

"I'm sure." Aki couldn't forget that wild tangle of hair. Besides, she was still wearing his clothes that he had given her.

"I'll go in and let him know. See if you can keep her here."

Before Aki could point out that the chances of her running from him were probably higher than the chances of her staying and talking with him were, Colin was gone, walking toward the castle without so much as a glance in Not Irene's direction.

She was studying the castle so intently that she was quite oblivious to Aki's approach a moment later. Sitting on a barrel, one ankle resting on the opposite knee and her cheek squashed up with the fist she was using to support her head, she looked as thin and ragged as the first time Aki had laid eyes on her. Thinner and more ragged, perhaps. And that gave him an idea. Feeling in his pocket to make sure he had a few coins, he spoke.

"Hungry, Not Irene?"

She jumped and let out a tiny squeal before recovering her composure.

"Why would you think I am hungry?"

Aki looked her over and shrugged. "Possibly it was how skinny you are that gave it away. Have you found who you're looking for?" Anything to keep her here and not running away, which she was obviously considering doing. She was eyeing the open space of the road.

"If I had, I do not think I would still be in Bren. But..."

Aki jumped up on the barrel next to her. He looked at her out of the corner of his eye and followed her gaze back to the castle gate. "You think they're in there?"

Not Irene bit her lip, one finger furiously twirling a strand of hair around it. "They might be. Or they might not. I do not know."

"And I thought I was good at keeping secrets," Aki muttered under his breath.

"What?"

"Nothing."

She turned to look at him, tilting her head far to one side. "I have seen you go in there many times since we came here. Are you friends with the people who live in there?"

Aki laughed a bit bitterly. "No. I think I can safely say I'm not friends with anyone in there. How long have you been sitting out here, anyway?"

"Several days."

A bit miffed at having missed seeing her when he was coming and going and instead spending long hours wandering through town trying to find her, Aki fell silent. His feet kicked the side of the barrel, making a hollow sound.

"If you are not friends with anyone in there, why are you always there?"

"Because of my job."

"What is your job?"

Aki was spared from answering when Colin reappeared. To Aki's shock and bewilderment, he had a woman at his side, her arm hooked comfortably through his. Her face wasn't really visible between her hood and scarf, but her eyes were bright and laughing as they crossed the street towards Aki and Not Irene. Aki sensed Not Irene stiffening beside him, but she didn't run.

Ignoring him almost entirely, the woman smiled at Not Irene and held out a gloved hand. "You must be Aki's friend," she said, her voice warm. "Colin and I were just going to find something hot to eat. How would you like to come with us?"

Aki couldn't understand why her offer of food was less offensive than his, but Not Irene didn't hesitate to take the woman's proffered hand and jump down to the ground. The woman drew her close and draped half her cloak over Not Irene's shoulders, shielding her from the worst of the cold as they walked, Colin and Aki falling in step behind them.

Although some distance from the castle, the tavern the woman led them to was not one of the seedier ones in Bren. It was well lit inside, sconces lining the walls and lamps on each table, and a giant hearth with a blazing fire kept the room warm. It was only midday and there were only a few others inside, so it was easy enough to find a table far enough away from anyone else to prevent eavesdropping.

Aki slid into his seat just as the woman was saying to Not Irene, "You really must try their mutton roast. They serve it better than anyone else in Bren."

A few minutes later, Aki had to agree with her.

"My goodness, I've forgotten to introduce myself," the woman exclaimed when Not Irene had finally eaten enough to slow down between bites. "I'm Charlotte and this is Colin, and, of course, you know Aki."

"Your name really is Aki?" Not Irene looked up at him sharply.

Aki mumbled an affirmative answer through a mouthful of food.

"And I'm afraid Aki's quite forgotten his manners as well. He never told us your name," Charlotte went on.

Not Irene glared at him then, although Aki wasn't sure why. Charlotte was expectantly watching her, waiting for a name. And Not Irene was clearly unsure of what to do. She looked at all three of them. She twisted her mouth to one side and then the other and pulled a strand of hair away from the rest to wrap around her finger.

"I cannot tell you my name," she said at last.

"Whyever not?"

"Not with him around," Not Irene pointed straight at Aki. Then, nodding as if she reached a decision with herself, she added, "You may call me Irene."

"But that is not your name?"

Not Irene glanced one last time at Aki before shaking her head.

"Very well, Irene, is there anything else you cannot say in front of him?"

Her eyes darting from Aki to Charlotte, she nodded.

"Perhaps it would be better if you two moved to a different table while Irene and I talk," Charlotte suggested in a way that made Aki very sure it wasn't actually a suggestion but a command.

Talking was something Charlotte was very good at, apparently. She and Irene spent an entire hour alone at their table and more often than not it was Charlotte doing the talking. Aki didn't bother to pretend that he wasn't watching them. There wasn't much else to do since Colin had promptly set his feet up on the opposite chair, leaned back, and shut his eyes. Aki wanted to sleep as well after the run they'd made through the previous night.

But he couldn't. Not here. Not when his mind was whirling with trying to decipher what Not Irene was hiding. Definitely not while he was wondering what her real name was and why she couldn't tell him, only him. And so instead, he watched them. Watched Charlotte as she spoke with her hands and her face because he couldn't hear her voice. Her hands never stopped moving while she talked. Not Irene, on the other hand, only fidgeted, looking down at her empty plate mostly and stealing glances at Aki from time to time. Aki tried to figure out what those glances meant because they certainly meant something. There was a little bit of suspicion in them, a little bit of curiosity, a little bit of hurt. None of which made any sense to Aki.

Finally, they both got up. Aki elbowed Colin to wake him up just as they came over and sat down. He didn't want to be the first to break the silence, but curiosity was driving him mad.

"So did she tell you her real name?" he finally asked Charlotte.

Charlotte pursed her lips and nodded. "She most certainly did. But," she looked from Colin to Aki meaningfully, "I've promised not to tell anyone else. So don't bother asking as I've no intention of breaking my promise."

Colin shrugged, accepting her words but Aki found himself glaring at Not Irene and watching her shrink away from that glare.

"She means nothing by it, Aki. It's just safest for her," Charlotte said, looking between them with amusement.

"Did you find out what you needed to know?" Colin asked.

"Oh, I did. We," Charlotte paused and smiled, her eyes sparkling with amusement, "negotiated an exchange of sorts."

"An exchange?"

"Yes, Aki. An exchange of information. Irene needed answers to her own questions, and I was able to give them to her. And she had answers to questions I had. I think, between the two of us, we've come a long way in finding the truth."

As easy as that. Aki let out a breath. All the tension, all the uneasiness, all the unanswered questions laid to rest as easy as that. He jerked when a hand touched his arm and looked up to find Not Irene's fingers tracing the scarlet band on the sleeve of his jacket. She pulled away when she noticed him looking but her narrowed eyes darted between him and Colin.

"What does it mean?" she asked. "Why are you always dressed the same when I see you?"

"It's our uniform, you could say," Colin answered. "It tells everyone we're the king's couriers."

"Couriers?" Not Irene's eyes opened wide, and she stared at Aki as her mind made the connection. "Couriers? 'Where is the courier?' They were talking about you. You were the one they were looking for."

"I think so."

"But... but you sound like them? You sounded just like them."

"That doesn't mean I am one of them."

"You did not tell me that you were the one they were looking for."

"You didn't need to know."

"I'm sure Aki had his reasons for not telling you, Irene. Now, if it's alright, I'd like to talk to my friends alone for a bit. Just follow my instructions and you'll be able to see him," Charlotte said, interrupting them.

Irene studied Aki once more and then turned to Charlotte. "You cannot be his friend. You live in the castle, and he said no one there is his friend."

"Did he? Then I'm afraid he doesn't know a friend when he sees one," Charlotte said, an odd tightness in her voice as she watched Aki watching the table in front of him.

Aki's face flushed hotly. He hated being talked about like he wasn't there. Absolutely hated it. It reminded him of... well, of every time in his life he wanted to forget. By the time he looked up again, Not Irene was long gone, and it was only Charlotte and Colin sitting with him and they were both watching him.

"You don't really know who I am, do you?" Charlotte asked him, giving him a funny look, the amused sparkle back in her eyes.

"Is your name not really Charlotte?" Aki didn't even attempt to conceal his annoyance.

"Oh, it is."

She was smiling, her hand covering her mouth. Trying not to laugh. So was Colin. Aki was missing something, he realized.

"My father took quite a gamble sparing you last year. Some of his councilmen disagreed most vehemently with that decision. They preferred the idea of watching you hang."

"Charlotte?" Aki said her name to himself, frowning. Then the frown gave way to confusion, then shock, then finally horror and disbelief. "Princess Charlotte? You're the king's daughter?"

"Yes. Although you really should keep your voice down," Charlotte answered blandly. "I don't want everyone here knowing that. Father thought it would go better if I talked to Irene and if we did it somewhere a little less imposing then the castle."

Aki looked back down at the table, still a little pale and shaken. He had never seen the princess. He only knew of her because of the plot to kidnap her the year before, the plot he was arrested and sentenced for being an accomplice of. He exhaled heavily and forced his eyes up.

"You must hate me."

Charlotte didn't say anything right away and that was answer enough for Aki. "Should I?"

"I wouldn't think you'd have to ask that question."

"Oh, I don't know. Treachery's the curse of royalty. There's always plans and schemes, and more plans after that. No one is ever satisfied. If one person's happy, another's plotting your demise. Live with it long enough and you either end up hating everyone or accepting that people are just that - people, human, prone to mistakes and failures and getting back up again. We're not above mistakes, ourselves, you know."

"You're not like your brother at all," he said. Which, when he thought about it, probably wasn't the best thing to say. But Charlotte and Colin both started laughing and the princess had an infectious laugh, one Aki couldn't resist entirely so he found himself smiling a little.

"I should hope not. My brother's a bit of an idiot. Not to mention hot headed. Des takes a bit more after our grandfather than he does our father - although, he means well, and I have my doubts about my grandfather." Charlotte gave him a long, hard stare, all trace of amusement now erased. "You were wrong when you told Irene you had no friends at the castle. Very wrong. You live only because of such friends and one day, likely soon, you will be called upon to pay that debt. My father gambled much to spare you, risking the wrath of some of his closest advisors and powerful men. Do not make him lose that gamble."

"Since that would mean choosing my own death, I think I can safely say I won't."

"Oh, Aki, you have no idea what's coming. It will be much more than you that dies if Father fails against this threat, if you fail him. It will be the end of our peace. The peace my father has worked so hard to attain. The peace your brother Sasha worked for."

Aki glanced sideways at Colin, wondering if he knew what the princess was talking about, wondering if he was supposed to know. Charlotte caught the look and read his question. She laughed again. "Don't worry. Colin is discreet about what he knows." She and Colin exchanged an unreadable look. "Colin is very discreet and very loyal to the family. Now, Colin and I must be off. The next time we meet, Aki, it must be for the first time, do you understand?"

Still dumbfounded and trying to piece together her earlier words, Aki gave her a mute nod.

Chapter 24

WITHOUT TURNING AROUND, Desmond could sense Captain Tyrrel wanted to speak. And whatever he wanted to say wasn't going to be pleasant. As winter crept by, they engaged in these conversations with growing frequency. And it wasn't just Captain Tyrrel. Desmond had heard the mutterings and murmurings of the men beneath him. He'd caught their whispered complaints and criticisms.

Still, standing before the feeble fire, his hands clasped together behind his back, Desmond was in no hurry to encourage his captain to speak.

"Your Highness."

That was the irritating thing about Captain Tyrrel, Desmond thought. He didn't need to be encouraged to speak. If he had something to say, he was going to say it, regardless of the willingness of his audience. And Desmond was most unwilling. He didn't answer. He didn't even turn around and acknowledge that the man had spoken.

"Your Highness, might I suggest you summon together all the men we rescued in the mountains?"

Desmond spun around at his words, too late to conceal his surprise. At least they weren't starting in on the same old argument.

"Why would I ever do such a thing?"

"Because, if you ever bothered to leave your rooms, you would notice, as the rest of us have, that there appear to be more men here then there should be."

Desmond waved his hand for the captain to go on.

"We recovered exactly twenty-two men from the raiding party, did we not?"

"I believe that is correct," Desmond answered, annoyed that the captain was making him answer at all.

"Yet, it appears as if we have more than twenty-two now staying with us here for the winter."

"How did you come to that conclusion?"

"We've been here for weeks. Long enough for me to know those men by sight. So, when I saw two men in the stables caring for the horses that I did not recognize, I spoke with my men. They have all noticed the same discrepancy."

"That's preposterous. Where would they have come from? And where would they all have been hiding?"

Captain Tyrrel pressed his lips together in a hard line. He took a deep breath before answering and Desmond knew that his answer was probably going to make him, the prince, sound like a fool. "Your Highness, this is a castle. A castle with many rooms, most of which we have not even entered since coming here. Do you not think it possible for them to be using those rooms?"

"Possible, yes. Likely, no. Where would they have come from and what purpose would they be serving?"

"Why don't you ask your friend, Tristan, and see what he knows."

Desmond started pacing before the fire. He twisted the ring on his finger round and round. Captain Tyrrel stood unmoving, just watching him. Desmond knew the man would not leave him alone until he received a satisfactory answer.

"I'll speak with Tristan the next time I see him," Desmond conceded at last, pausing to stare into the fire once more. It was weak, barely enough to warm the few feet in front of it. He missed the roaring fires that burned in the hearths at home. Here, they were conserving the fuel they had. Captain Tyrrel sent men out to get more in between storms, but that was no easy task and they remained in short supply.

"I'm glad you said that, Your Highness." Captain Tyrrel crossed the room to the door and had it open before Desmond realized what he was doing. "Come, Tristan, the prince would like to speak with you."

"Alone, Captain. I would like to speak with him alone," Desmond added, desperate to regain control of the situation.

"Yes, Your Highness."

Desmond watched the captain as he walked, his back rigid with disapproval, out the door, passing Tristan coming in. Desmond released a breath and sat down in a chair near the fire, holding his hands out to warm them.

"Why does he always make me sound like a child when he speaks to me? No one else does that."

Tristan laughed. "That is one of his greatest talents, isn't it? Although, lately, every time I see him, I get the sense he'd like to rip my head off. He's not a friendly man, is he?"

"He's Father's man, though. Loyal. Father would never consider replacing him. You know, he has this crazy idea that there are more men living here than we brought with us?"

Tristan laughed again and this time, Desmond joined him. "And where would these mysterious men be coming from? He has every entrance to this place guarded night and day. Not that we should laugh at him. I mean, he is just trying to keep you safe. It must be quite a burden to guard the only heir to the crown."

"Yes, and I'm sure now he'll double his drills with his men. At least it gives them something to do." Desmond sighed a bit wistfully. "What I wouldn't give to be home right now."

"You think your courier made it through to your father?"

"I hope so. I'd half expected to find word from my father when we first returned from the mountains, but perhaps he didn't feel I needed it."

"He did trust you enough to be in charge of that mission."

"He did, didn't he?" Desmond got up and wandered toward the window. Snow was falling again. It was so heavy that he could not make out the battlements or the town beyond. It muffled all the sound from the courtyard below and piled high against the windowpanes. "I cannot wait until this lets up and we can go home."

"I've been thinking about that. I have no idea what the others' plans are, but, if you don't mind of course, I think I'd like to accompany you to Bren. There's nothing really that keeps me here. And from what I've heard, there are plenty of opportunities for work in Bren for someone like me."

"Even if I did mind, you'd be free to. You need no one's permission to move from one part of the kingdom to another."

Chapter 25

AKI HEARD FOOTSTEPS HURRYING to catch up with him and turned to find Oscar half running, tugging his horse along into a jog, down the darkening street. Knowing that Oscar would only run faster if he tried to avoid him, Aki stopped and waited. Oscar fell into step beside him a little out of breath.

"What are you doing tonight?" Oscar asked. "No. Wait. I know. You're practicing or studying. All by yourself, of course, since Captain Tyrrel's no longer at the barracks."

Since he'd stolen the words right out of Aki's mouth, Aki decided there wasn't a need for him to answer. He continued walking toward the entrance of the academy.

"Wait up a minute, would you?" Oscar called after him.

Aki slowed his steps, not so much because Oscar asked him to but because of the figure he just noticed leaning against the wall of the academy, near the entrance. Oscar caught up with him again and noticed the waiting person as well. In the gathering darkness, his face was nothing but shadows. Aki knew him anyway.

"You should come out with me tonight," Oscar kept talking as if there was no one waiting. "It'll be more fun than sitting in your room all night. And I'll practice with you when we get back."

They were only a few feet from the entrance now. The person pushed himself off the wall and took an unsteady step forward.

"Aki." There was a slight slur in his voice as he spoke.

"Halle." Aki stopped and folded his arms across his chest. "What are you doing here? Why haven't you gone home?"

"That's a good question," Halle answered in a heavy accent. "Turns out my sentence was a little more complicated than Sasha let on at first."

"So was mine," Aki muttered. Without looking, he could tell Oscar was watching the two of them with intense curiosity.

Halle let out a short, harsh laugh. It died away. He slumped back against the wall, his face falling. "I can't go home."

"That's unfortunate."

"Unfortunate? That's it? That's all you can say?" Halle was apparently unbothered by Oscar's presence. "It's bad enough they work me like a slave for a year. Then they tell me I'm not allowed to leave. I have to stay here, in this hole of a town, scraping by on whatever I can and spending every night locked away because I'm too dangerous to send away."

Aki forgot that Oscar was standing there, too. If he'd remembered, he would have kept his mouth shut. "You kept me in a cage, paraded me in front of your crew, tortured and starved me and left me to their mercy. I don't feel sorry for you."

He heard a sound from Oscar behind him and regretted his words immediately. He started for the gate again, but Halle peeled himself off the wall and stepped in front of him.

"You have something of mine. Remember? You promised you'd give my knives back."

"Fine. Just wait out here."

"I can't actually have them back," Halle said. "If I so much as touch a weapon, I'm to die. Or so I'm told, every single day by the horrid little man who has to keep track of me. And let me tell you, that horrid little man is quite creative. He tells me a new way he'll kill me every morning when he lets me out for the day. Father would have been proud to make his acquaintance."

"Then what are you doing here?"

At that, Halle dropped his head and his shoulders slumped. He didn't say anything, just stood there with the same dejected posture that had been his since he was a child. And Aki knew why he was there. He hated the reason. Hated that Halle had no one else he could turn to. But Lars was gone, and Sasha was a full day's travel away.

"What is it you want, Halle?"

"You know, they said I could get work during the day. Earn a living. But no one wants...," Halle stopped, gathering his pride, and forcing his head up. "Never mind. I should go."

He started to limp away, and Aki tried not to watch. Watching him would be a mistake, he knew. The same mistake as he'd made a year ago, watching some of the other prisoners as they tormented Halle. Still, he turned his head enough to see him and caught Oscar's eye.

"He could come with us, if you want," Oscar said, shrugging. "Although, I could see why you wouldn't want him to."

"I didn't say I was going with you."

Oscar looked once at Halle's receding figure and then back to Aki. He had the gall to grin. "You're coming. And so is he. Just let me put my horse up."

Aki hesitated a moment longer as Oscar walked inside. Then, as he ran a few steps down the road, he called out, "Halle, wait."

Halle stopped and turned around slowly. Waiting. Pride battling against hope and pleading on his face. Aki stopped in front of him.

"Oscar and I were just going out to get something to eat. You can come, I guess. If you want."

"I suppose I wouldn't mind."

Aki suggested returning to the same place he'd gone with Colin, Charlotte, and Not Irene mostly so that they would avoid any of his old familiar places - the places he avoided like the plague. And there was a small part of him that thought he might see Not Irene hovering around the place. He was curious about the conversation she'd had with the princess, although, knowing her reticence to speak to him before, it wasn't likely she'd confide any of it in him now. He hadn't seen her since that day and winter was now nearing its end. Nor had he heard anything from the castle in all these weeks. It was as if the whole matter had been dropped and him with it. It ought to have been a relief, but instead, he couldn't help but think it was the quiet before a storm.

When their food was placed in front of them, Aki tried to ignore the hunger with which Halle attacked his. It reminded him of his own time at Halle's mercy and made a very ugly desire to snatch the food away from his brother rise up inside of him. It made him want to force Halle to beg from him, to throw himself on Aki's mercy for once. It was no more than he deserved. Then he thought of Dagmar. Thinking of her always tore him in two. He reeled in his anger. Shoved it down where it couldn't come out again.

Oscar, however, made no such efforts. He stared open mouthed at Halle as he shoveled food into his mouth, barely giving himself space to breathe in between bites.

"When's the last time you've eaten?" he finally asked.

"Days," Halle mumbled.

"Better slow down then, or you'll make yourself sick," Aki said. "Trust me. I've done it before."

Halle at least paused long enough to wince at Aki's tone. He avoided Aki's eyes and went back to eating.

"Father's worried, you know," Oscar said after a long moment. "Couriers haven't always been coming back. He says that the king hasn't heard from several of his noblemen since before winter."

"Could just be the weather," Aki said. It was the excuse everyone in Bren made when he overheard their worried conversations. Just the weather, always the weather. He shifted a little, remembering the words of the men who attacked the wagon, the men who had been looking for him.

"Maybe. Father doesn't think so, though. And he's not the only one. He says I should train to fight harder. He says I need to be able to defend myself better. Which, of course, I was hoping you could help me with."

"What makes you think I'd be any good at that?"

"Come on, Aki. Everyone knows you spend your free time doing nothing else. It's not like any of the rest of us get to train with the king's guard. Besides, Felix said the rumors of what happened up north were true. He said you fought and killed someone."

Aki dropped his fork and Halle snorted. "Who?"

"I don't want to talk about it."

"Sorry," Oscar said. "Forget I mentioned that part. You will help me, though, won't you? You don't have the captain to train with, at least not until spring. And I can help you with code reading."

"Who did you kill?" Halle insisted.

Aki flashed a glare in his direction. "Cadoc."

Halle's eyes went wide, and his food was momentarily forgotten. "Cadoc? The clansmen from Yassil? The one who used to make you..."

"Yes, that one," Aki interrupted Halle before he could blurt out what it was Cadoc used to make him do.

"You killed him?"

"Yes."

"Cristof won't forget," Halle said, echoing Lars' earlier warning. "He'll..."

"I know. I know, Halle." Aki pushed away from the table. "I'm done here."

He walked out without waiting for the other two and was a little surprised to find that they had both followed him out into the street. Halle didn't bother saying anything at all. He just limped away in the direction of the castle. Oscar trailed along behind him.

"You'll still practice with me tonight?"

"Yes."

"Good. Then maybe Father will stop pestering me about it."

Chapter 26

SPRING CAME SOFTLY, PUSHING back winter little by little. It first showed itself in a breath of warm air. Then in the melting snow that turned into piles of slush and then into muddy puddles. Then in the tiny blades of green that pushed their way through the mud, the crocuses that opened their blooms even before the last of the snow melted.

Karina stooped in front of a cluster of the small flowers and brushed her fingers against the silky petals. Purple, white and yellow added a splash of much needed color against the grays and browns that winter was leaving behind. Plucking one free from its stem, she brought it up to her nose to smell it. Where she lived with her mistress, crocuses didn't grow. She missed her home, with its beautiful courtyard full of flowers and its marbled halls and luxuriant rugs.

Soon, she could go home. Soon. Home. The words were a chant in her head, a melody in her heart. She had done what her mistress desired of her. She had found the missing son, even if he'd been less than enthusiastic at being found. Now that spring was here, the harbor would be teeming with ships coming and going. It would be easy to get home then.

With thoughts of home dancing through her mind, Karina paid little attention to those she passed as she neared the harbor. The sea beckoned her. It was her way home. She rolled the stem of the plucked flower back and forth between her fingers, her eyes not on the road. She missed the tall, broad-shouldered man who stepped out in front of her, his face half hidden in by an enormous beard. As his shadow fell over her, Karina started and stepped back. Only a half-step. She knew him.

"Change of plans, Miss Karina," the man said, his voice deep but soft, inaudible to those who were nearby. He held up a sealed letter, the imprint of a wolf's head clear in the red wax, the loose, flowing letters easily recognized by Karina. "Come with me and I'll explain."

Chapter 27

THE PATTER OF RAIN ON THE windowpanes woke Desmond. Pushing off his covers, he was pleasantly surprised to find the room didn't have quite the same chill as it did most mornings. He padded across the room and pulled open the curtain. A gray world, full of fog and distorted by the rivulets of water running down the glass, greeted him. And Desmond smiled to see it.

Aside from a few deep mounds here and there, not a bit of snow was left. Winter was done and the road home was open before him. In the gray courtyard below him, he could see a handful of men hurrying, heads bent, about their work. It was time to speak to Gregory and Captain Tyrrel, Desmond decided.

Dressing in haste and with little care, Desmond left his room in search of the two men. Captain Tyrrel was the easiest to find. Desmond wondered sometimes if that man ever slept. Despite the early hour, Desmond guessed that the captain had been up for some time already. He was watching a group of men gathered around one of the large dining tables. None of them were his soldiers and Desmond assumed the captain was still pursuing his suspicions that there were more people sharing the castle with them than the ones they brought.

"Good morning, Your Highness," Captain Tyrrel said in greeting. "What brings you out of bed so early?"

Desmond fought hard not to respond to the quip. "The rain. Now that the snow is gone, we can begin making preparations for our return."

"The Void will be nothing but mud and muck for a good long while. Even the road. Best to wait until the rain stops and it has a chance to dry out a bit."

"Captain...,"

"I agree with the prince, Captain," Gregory said, coming up behind them. He studied the men gathered in front of them with distaste. "The sooner we put this place behind us, the better."

"You'd prefer sleeping out in the rain to having a solid roof over your head?"

"I'd prefer to return to Dival."

"This is part of Dival," Captain Tyrrel said, arching his eyebrows as he studied Gregory.

"You know what I mean, Captain. Calling them the same country doesn't actually make them the same."

"My father would not be happy to hear you speak like that."

"Forgive me, Your Highness, but your father is well aware of my position on the matter. I do not keep secrets from my king."

Desmond sighed. He'd heard enough arguments between the two men that winter to last him a lifetime. It was a wonder they hadn't strangled each other through the long, dreary months. There hadn't been anything better to do.

"Have the men prepare to return, Captain. My father will no doubt be anxiously looking for my return and I don't want to keep him waiting."

It was the wrong thing to say. Desmond felt the captain stiffen next to him, sensed another lecture coming.

Instead of a lecture that Desmond had already heard a thousand times, Captain Tyrrel only said, "Let's just hope the courier survived both the fever and winter and reached your father with news of our delay."

That was almost worse than the usual rant the captain gave him. Desmond didn't want to think about the courier possibly lying dead somewhere between here and Bren all because of him. It would have been wise to keep silent, but wisdom was not something Desmond was often accused of.

"From what I've heard of him, he's too hard to kill so I'm sure he made it. And if he didn't, it's no great loss to us. My father has other, more reliable couriers."

Captain Tyrrel spun around then, cold fury written all over his face and Desmond retreated a step.

"You hold the lives of those around you very cheap, Your Highness. You would do well to consider the price others may put upon your own."

"Is that a threat, Captain?" Gregory asked.

Desmond was glad the council man had the power to speak. He did not. For the first time in his life, Desmond looked at his father's captain with fear. But Captain Tyrrel didn't waste a glance on Gregory. He stepped closer to Desmond.

"I am sworn to protect your life with my own. Every soldier here is sworn to protect your life with their own. It would be a comfort to all of us if you did not take our lives so flippantly."

"But the courier..."

Captain Tyrrel slapped a hand to his forehead and stormed away. Turning before he reached the end of the short hallway, he called back, "Pray the day never comes, Your Highness, when you have no one but your friends to rely on. Because you have precious few of those."

The words so closely echoed what Lars had said to him that day in the mountains that Desmond recoiled. Pulling himself together, he said to Gregory, "Spread the word. We leave at the end of the week." Then he retreated back up to his room, slamming the door shut behind him.

When he was king, Captain Tyrrel would be one of the first men to be replaced. Yes, he would demote him as well, strip him of his command, probably even throw him out of the guard completely. When he was king, he wouldn't have to tolerate such disrespect, such condescension by men who thought themselves to be wiser only because they were older. When he was king...

Desmond stopped his pacing as a knock came on his door.

"Go away," he called out.

"It's Tristan," came the muffled response.

"Fine. Come in."

Tristan slipped inside as if he wished to avoid being seen entering.

"How does your father tolerate that man?"

"He's loyal."

Tristan raised his eyebrows and folded his arms across his chest. "I would never have guessed."

"To Father," Desmond clarified. "Besides, I don't think he ever speaks to Father like that. He's never spoken to me like that. Except..." Desmond didn't want to continue. Except for on the road in the Void, after Desmond had attempted to get the courier to fight with him. The captain had turned Desmond into a fool after that. In front of everyone.

"Perhaps I should stay back here. I wouldn't want to be the cause of any more... trouble between you two."

Desmond waved his concern away. "I'd like it better if you came." He smiled. "Perhaps, some day, when I'm king and I've sent him off, you can be my captain."

"I'm afraid I don't have the necessary skills for that, although I would be quite happy to serve you."

"I wonder if I can convince Father to give you a position in the castle back in Bren" Desmond mused aloud.

"It would be an honor, certainly. But don't go through all that trouble for me. I'm good with my hands and I have no doubt I'll find work in Bren." Tristan lifted the latch on the door. "Perhaps I should go offer my help making preparations for our departure. It's the least the others and I can do after all you and your men have done for us."

Desmond went to the window after Tristan left. The mist from the rain had cleared a little. Down in the courtyard, Captain Tyrrel was drilling his men. Always drilling. Desmond watched until he noticed the captain's stare fixed on him.

Chapter 28

FINISHED," AKI SAID, LAYING a paper on the desk
in front of Master Wehr.

"Already?"

Aki nodded.

"You're getting faster. Good. Very good." Master Wehr
picked up the paper, reading it. He glanced up at Aki and
his gaze sharpened. "Where'd you get that?"

Aki followed his gaze to the ring that now hung around
his neck in place of his old talisman that Halle had taken
from him. He usually kept it hidden beneath his shirt, but
he'd had the habit of pulling the talisman out and rubbing
it between his thumb and forefinger anytime he was deep
in thought and apparently the habit had carried itself over
to the ring. He slipped it under his shirt now and pulled
the collar up close around his throat, hiding the scar that
remained there.

"It was given to me when I was in Aruuk. It's supposed
to have belonged to my mother."

"May I see it?"

Aki hesitated. He'd shown his father's sword off to
several people already but somehow the ring was a more
intimate thing. He couldn't really say why. Perhaps
because he had far more in common with his slave mother
than his father. Reluctantly, his hand closed around it but
before he could pull it out again, Master Wehr stopped
him.

"Never mind. It's yours to keep private if you like."

"Are you sure?"

"Of course I'm sure. I was merely curious about the insignia on it. It was," Master Wehr looked away, not meeting Aki's eyes, "unfamiliar to me."

Surprised, Aki stood in front of his desk a little longer. It wasn't the first time that Master Wehr had withheld some information from him. In fact, it had been happening more and more as the winter months wore on. There had been whispers, rumors, more whispers. Meetings at the castle, papers that crossed Master Wehr's desk that he spirited away to some hiding place, days of Master Wehr muttering to himself. And from it all, Aki had been completely and carefully excluded. But he wasn't just withholding information just now.

He was lying.

Aki was as sure of that as he was sure the sun rose in the east. Master Wehr hadn't been curious because he didn't recognize the symbol, but because he did.

"I'll see you tomorrow, I guess," Aki finally said when it became obvious that Master Wehr would disclose nothing more.

"Actually, you won't."

"What?"

"You're to go home." Aki bristled and Master Wehr added, "King's orders, not my suggestion."

"For how long?"

"Until you are sent for. A week, most likely. He," Master Wehr hesitated again, "he has need of you when you return."

Aki was halfway out the door when Master Wehr stopped him with a hand on his shoulder. The touch made him flinch and he turned to find his old instructor's face etched in sorrow.

"What is it? Have I done something wrong?"

"No. Nothing wrong. I'm afraid, Aki...," Master Wehr patted his arm and for once Aki didn't pull away from the touch. "I'm afraid that... Never mind. You've come a long way, Aki. A very long way."

And with that, Master Wehr turned and disappeared back into the house. Aki couldn't help but feel like it was a sort of goodbye. A goodbye he wasn't at all prepared for. A goodbye that screamed of finality. It left him hollow. He wandered through the streets of Bren, finding himself drawn, for the first time in over a year, to the sea.

The harbor was still almost deserted, in spite of weeks of spring weather. It was a phenomenon that Master Wehr found disturbing in light of other events. Aki made his way past the docks to the small stretch of sandy shoreline that separated the piers from the rocky cliffs. There was no one else there and Aki spent a few minutes pacing up and down, skipping pebbles into the waves.

For most of the winter he'd been able to forget about the strange letter he'd delivered to the king, and the events that had taken place in Aruuk and on the road back. But now, not so much. He couldn't help but think that everyone around him knew exactly what was going on, but he was being deliberately kept in the dark.

He heard someone coming up behind him on the sand and turned to find Halle standing not far off.

"What do you want, Halle?" He expected an ambiguous request for food or liquor. That accounted for almost every single one of their brief conversations through the winter.

"To go home," Halle answered, catching Aki by surprise.

Aki shook his head. "Still don't feel sorry for you."

"I wasn't asking you to." Halle sat down in the sand, stretching his legs out in front of him. "So much for Mother and her mad schemes."

"What does your mother have to do with anything?"

Halle laughed his brittle laugh. "You don't honestly think it was my idea to steal away the princess, do you?" He looked at Aki. "You do."

Aki shrugged. Did it matter whose idea it was? It didn't change the blame put on him. He started back up the beach.

"I'll be gone for at least a week, so you'll have to find someone else to beg off of," he called after him.

"They don't want us here, you know. They don't want me or you or even Sasha. I've heard them."

Aki stopped walking. "Who doesn't?"

"The people. They talk in front of me as if I'm not there. I hear all sorts of things. They hate us."

It was nothing Aki hadn't heard before. There had been all sorts of whispers after word of the raid in Dorsten had leaked out, followed by rumors of the attack on the party the king had sent. He'd seen the dark looks some of the townspeople had cast his direction.

Still, Halle's words bothered him. They bothered him as he packed up a few things late that night and they bothered him more when he rode alone for hours on his way home. It wasn't until the familiar house was visible that he was able to put the bothersome thoughts aside.

It was early evening as he came up the drive. From the outside, Aki could easily imagine Stephan in the barn working. It made the ache of knowing he was gone even deeper.

Alina was nowhere to be found inside the house. Aki put his things in his room and wandered back outside. He spotted her kneeling with her back to him in the small garden she kept behind the house.

"Alina," he called out softly, trying not to startle her.

"Aki," Alina exclaimed, turning to face him with a warm smile, "you're home."

The words were a blanket of warmth against the cold, a reminder that in the great, chaotic scheme of the world around him he had a place to call home. Aki sank to the ground beside her, not caring how dirty it made his clothes.

"What are you planting?"

"Potatoes and onions," Alina answered.

"I can help."

"Nonsense. You've ridden all day. They can wait until the morning if they must."

Aki laughed a little. "Riding was all I did today. I'm not that tired."

He helped her finish, savoring the rich smell of the soil and the feel of it against his hands. During the first three years he'd spent with Alina and Stephan, gardening was one of the few chores outside the barn that he truly enjoyed. And Alina didn't detract from the pleasantness of the moment by demanding troublesome explanations or pestering him with questions. They worked in companionable silence, and it wasn't until they were back in the house that they broke it.

"How long will you be staying?" Alina asked him as she cut open a still steaming loaf of bread. She kept her voice casual, but Aki could hear the worry that she left unspoken and it occurred to him that she knew of his sentence as well.

"I don't know for sure. A week, most likely, or so I was told. I'm sorry, Alina. I should have tried to come home sooner."

She ran her hand lightly through his hair and he tried not to flinch at the touch. "No matter. You're here now and I'll enjoy it for as long as we have."

"You know, don't you? About my bond of service to the king?"

Alina nodded. "Sasha told us when he came home after your trial. And he told us that it was not to be spoken of until the king decided. It was an awful secret to keep and, to be honest, I didn't think I'd be able to do it. But you never came home. For a whole year, we didn't see you except when we went to visit in Bren and, as much as I hated that, it did make it a little easier to not say anything." She watched him as he busied himself with tending the fire in the hearth. "Are you angry about it?"

"Yes." He sat back on the ground, brushing bark and splinters of wood off his hands and onto his trousers. "No. I... want to be. I just wanted to be free, to decide things for myself. But I suppose I had a chance at that, and I messed it up about as badly as I could, so maybe I don't deserve to be free. It is easier to just follow everything someone else tells you to do."

"I'm sure the king would never ask you to do something wrong. And I hope he would never use that to put you in great danger. He is a good king. He'd never abuse that sort of power over anyone."

"King Darien might not abuse it, but he won't be king forever and I don't think I'd like to serve Desmond. At least, not right now."

Alina laughed. "I've heard stories about the prince."

"They are more than stories," Aki assured her. "Lars called him an idiot, and I don't think he's wrong."

"Tell me about it. About all of it."

Aki did. It was the same story he'd told King Darien and Hamo, and then Master Wehr, but he told it lightly this time, skimming over the parts he knew would bother Alina, brushing past the parts that still bothered him.

Alina was good at hearing what he didn't say, though, and by the time he was done he knew she understood most of what was left unspoken.

"I'm glad you killed that man," she said when he finished speaking.

Aki raised an eyebrow and turned to get a good look at her face. With a shake of his head, he half laughed. "You're the first person to say that."

"That doesn't make it any less true. He deserved his death."

Aki stirred the fire again. He leaned back and his hand traveled to his neck, pulling his mother's ring out from its hiding place. The gold was warm from resting against his skin as he rolled it between his fingers.

"That was your mother's?"

"Faramund says it was."

"You don't believe him?"

"I don't know. I guess so. It's just... I never knew of a slave that was allowed to keep something like this. But he did say she was different, the way she came to them was different. I can't see a reason for him lying to me. I don't know."

"And the sword was your father's?"

"Yes." Aki had already shown her that. "It even has his name engraved on the scabbard, so it was most definitely his."

"Stephan would have loved to see it," Alina said quietly, a slight catch in her voice at his name.

"I wish I could have shown him."

Late into the night, they talked. And when Aki lay on his bed in the darkness afterwards, the rumors of trouble and unrest seemed like a bad dream, far removed from the comfortable reality here.

For a week, he kept himself busy, helping Alina. There was more planting to do. There were repairs needed to the house. And there were others to see. He wandered over to Sasha's late in the afternoon a few days after his arrival. Ophelia answered his knock, a baby in her arms.

"Come in." Ophelia stepped aside and gestured for him to enter. "It's been so long since you've come home."

"I missed a lot, didn't I?" Aki asked, his eyes on the infant's face. "What's their name?"

"This," Ophelia shifted the baby and pulled the blanket away a little, "is little Boris. Here, you can hold him if you'd like."

"I've never held a baby. I don't really know how."

Ophelia laughed. "You and Sasha both. I promise he won't fall apart if you touch him."

Aki let her place little Boris in his arms and didn't move. He felt about as comfortable holding him as Not Irene had riding a horse. He smiled to himself at the comparison.

"Sasha will be home soon. You'll stay until then, won't you? He'd hate to miss you."

Aki nodded, too afraid to speak and wake the sleeping baby in his arms. Ophelia, meanwhile, was moving around the house, making all manner of noise without the slightest concern and Boris didn't so much as flinch. Still holding himself rigid, Aki dared to move to a seat.

"Have you been back long? With all the rumors that have been flying around - couriers not coming back and those sorts of things - we've all been worried sick about you."

"Just a few days. I'll be going back soon."

"Are things really as bad as people say? Father says that barely any ships have come in since the weather cleared."

Aki had almost forgotten that Hamo would have told everyone here what was going on. He filled in the details that he knew, which weren't many since he'd been left in the dark most of the winter. By then, Sasha was home, and they talked of everything but the gathering shadows.

When Colin knocked on his door early in the morning a few days later, Aki wasn't ready. Dread weighed heavily on him as he packed up his few things. He couldn't quite manage a smile when he allowed Alina to pull him close. And she couldn't quite, either.

"Come home when you can," she whispered.

And he wanted to promise her that he would. That everything would be alright. That he would be back before she'd had a chance to really miss him. But it was a lie he couldn't tell because he could see she already knew the truth.

Colin didn't say much during the day as they rode back. He set a very brisk pace, pushing the horses harder than usual so that they arrived in the early afternoon instead of the evening.

With Bren in sight, Colin said, "The prince has returned."

Aki wanted to ask him for more but one look at Colin's face told him that the man would not elaborate. They did not speak again until they were outside the academy.

"Put your horse and your things up, then come to the castle. King Darien's expecting you," Colin said before riding away.

He was halfway through taking Sky's tack off when Oscar found him.

"You haven't heard the news, have you?" Aki shook his head and Oscar, his face more solemn than Aki had ever seen it, went on, "Felix is gone."

"What?" Aki dropped the saddle onto its hook.

"He went out with his instructor right before you left. They were only supposed to be gone for two days. They never came back."

"They might have just been delayed...," Aki said, scrambling for some reason, some excuse good enough to keep them from returning.

But Oscar was already shaking his head. "The prince is back. They found bodies on the road. Couriers, travelers. They haven't been getting lost or delayed, Aki, someone's been killing them."

The world pitched violently beneath his feet and Aki gasped for breath. He shut his eyes, gripping the stable wall beside him. All he could think of was that day on the road, the day he'd saved Not Irene, the day he'd seen an entire family murdered. "Where's the courier?" Not Irene had heard them say. He'd thought it was just him. That they were only looking for him.

It was worse than that, so much worse. And now, Felix had been caught up in it. Felix, who had tried so hard to forgive him, who tried not to believe what the others said about him.

"Were any of the bodies..."

"No. No one's found him or his instructor."

"I have to go. I have to..." Aki stumbled away, walking toward the castle because that was the only clear thought he could form.

The very air inside the castle spoke of worry and uneasiness. Aki could sense it the moment he stepped inside. He could see it on the faces of every servant, guard, and attendant he passed.

Prince Desmond stood in the hallway just outside the door he was led to and eyed him with dark suspicion as his escort curtly reminded him to remove his weapons. Aki went through the process of disarming himself in a daze. Beyond the plain wooden door lay his fate, a debt the princess had called it, and Aki was not ready to meet it.

Chapter 29

DESMOND TOOK HIS SEAT NEAR his father, conscious of the stares of the other council members. His own eyes were drawn to his father. In the months he was gone, the king seemed to have aged years. Desmond's arrival the three days earlier had done nothing to assuage the deep lines of worry that furrowed his father's brow. In fact, the few words that had passed between them in private had been sharp. Father was deeply unsettled by events and the news that Desmond had returned with had only added to the burden.

Their ride through the Void had turned into a macabre nightmare, the road littered in spots with the bodies of men, women, and children. Most were left where they fell, cut down by swords or knives. Then there were the couriers. They had been searched, some of them mutilated, whatever missives they were carrying lost to the hands of their killers. Desmond tried to shut the grisly scenes out of his mind as whispers flew around the room.

It was Aruuk, some said.

Dorsten, others insisted.

And in the very middle of all the whispers and rumors sat the courier he'd sent back, the only one to make it from the northern province to Bren in almost six months. Aki kept his head down, not meeting the malevolent glares of some, most particularly Baron Orlander. Desmond couldn't blame the baron. The man's own son was one of those missing. And they now all understood what missing meant.

King Darien called their meeting to order once more. It was the second time they'd met that day and Desmond wondered what more there was to discuss. The answer was obvious. Call up the army. Stamp out whatever group was responsible - whether it was a band of rebellious citizens or a group of foreigner saboteurs. Restore the order and peace they'd enjoyed for the past several years.

But the look on Father's face told him that there was something more, something deeper, something more sinister than just a band of rogues intent on breaking down the web of communication the country ran on. So, when Father called the meeting to order, Desmond leaned forward, intent on what happened next. And not at all prepared for it.

"Aki Turston," the king's voice rang out in the now silent room. Desmond watched as Aki's head snapped up. "It has come to my attention that the plot against my daughter more than a year ago was only the preliminary step in a much larger scheme. Who else was involved?"

Aki's face fell into confusion, and he shook his head. "No one else that I know of."

"No one else? You spoke to the conspirators. You were aware of their plans. Did you, at no time, hear any name, any country mentioned? Who provided the money? The ship?"

"I do not know, Your Majesty. I told you everything that I knew."

A murmur rippled through the room. Desmond turned just in time to see Baron Orlander stand.

"This, Your Majesty, is what you get for your leniency. He lies even now. Ask him to explain how he alone, out of a dozen couriers, was able to make the journey between the province of Dorsten and here. Ask him why he was sent on his own in the first place when he is not yet cleared to ride alone."

The king didn't have to repeat any of the baron's words. He just turned to Aki, the questions burning in his eyes. Aki met his gaze, his face still clouded in confusion, but Desmond could see fear there as well. And then Aki locked eyes with him and Desmond looked away.

"I was sent alone on the prince's orders, Your Majesty. I told you that when I first arrived."

"And why would my son send you, knowing full well that you were not qualified to make any solo run?"

"You would have to ask him that, Your Majesty."

Desmond felt the shift in attention from the courier to himself. He straightened in his chair and drew in a sharp breath. Across the room, Gregory caught his eye and gave a slight shake of his head. Desmond only took a moment to puzzle over its meaning before cold realization washed over him. If Captain Tyrrel were in the room, Desmond wouldn't have dreamed of it. But Captain Tyrrel was not.

"I didn't send him," Desmond said, heat flaring up inside his chest as Aki turned to him in horror. He cleared his throat and said again, "I didn't send him. He saw the letter I had started, took it, and rode off before anyone knew what he was doing."

"Is that so?"

"Yes, Father, it is. Gregory can confirm it," Desmond answered, hoping he'd read Gregory's expression correctly. A tiny exhale escaped him when the councilman solemnly nodded his confirmation.

"Now that we've cleared that matter up, Aki Turston, please explain to us again how you made it across and no one else did?"

Aki had to try twice before he got the words out and even then, there was a catch in them. "I took the lost road in the Sar."

"And how did you know about this lost road?"

"Stephan told me about it once. It was the same road he used to take as a spy into Dorsten."

"And why did you choose that road?"

"Because there was an attack. The men chased us in there and it seemed safer to travel that way."

"Men who had managed to catch and kill every other person who tried to cross?" This came from Baron Orlander.

Aki looked down at his hands, his fingers locked so tightly together that Desmond could see they were turning white. When he raised his head again, Desmond was startled to find the same hard, dead expression on his face that he had worn the night he killed Cadoc.

"I know you have no reason to believe what I say, but this is the truth. At no time was I in league with the men who attacked us on the road. I knew nothing of the fate of the other couriers until I was told today, right before coming here."

His voice was the same hard, dead voice as that night, too. The only thing that still seemed alive were his eyes and Desmond shuddered at the hatred in them. That was what Aki's control was hiding. The control Desmond had envied so much. Aki had hated Cadoc. Hated him enough to kill him without hesitation. And now, he hated the prince. Desmond shrank back against his chair a little, conscious all at once of the enemy he'd just made.

"You expect us to believe anything you say?" Baron Orlander asked.

"No. I expect that you'll have me executed now."

Voices filled the room, everyone talking at the same time. Everyone except Desmond, Aki, and the king. Desmond watched his father watch Aki. And he almost took back his lie. The look of devastation, of anguish on his father's face was unlike anything Desmond had seen before. After minutes had dragged by, King Darien raised his hand to silence the room.

"We did not come here today to conduct a trial. Although, there will undoubtedly be one." He gestured toward one of the guards at the door. "Remove him, please, so that we can discuss our next step in confidence."

Aki didn't resist or even hesitate. Before the guard even reached him, he was out of his chair and on his way to the door. Captain Tyrrel's words whipped across Desmond's mind like a lash, and he winced visibly at the internal rebuke. What would the captain say if he knew what Desmond had done? If he knew that Desmond had just sold Aki's life to protect his... what? Not his own life. Father wouldn't execute him for sending Aki. He wouldn't have done anything more than reprimand him. His pride. Aki was going to die to protect his pride. At least, that's what Captain Tyrrel would say.

He hardly paid any attention to the rest of the meeting. Couldn't really pay attention. His mind was tossing itself back and forth between telling his father the truth or leaving things as they were. In the midst of the turmoil a question arose. Why didn't Aki even try to argue against him? He hadn't said one word to accuse the prince of lying. That bothered Desmond more than he could have imagined.

The meeting wore on and Desmond felt an ache beginning in his head. Nothing was being decided. And everything was. No one knew who was responsible. Everyone had a guess. Desmond's head was spinning with it all.

It was late evening before everyone came to the conclusion that the first step was to gather more information. Although, how that information was to be obtained, no one had a clear idea. With the harbor still near empty and fewer couriers returning, there was little to be known of what happened outside of Bren. In the meantime, King Darien would send Captain Tyrrel with a sizable force of men into the Void in the hopes of hunting down those responsible for the string of killings.

When the room emptied for the night, Desmond started for his own room. Already his thoughts were on the hot bath and soft bed awaiting him. When he heard his father behind him, his footsteps slowed, and he waited.

"Come with me. There's more I wish to speak of with you tonight."

"Can it not wait until the morning?"

"It cannot," his father answered with irritation.

Desmond mumbled under his breath about the ridiculousness of late-night meetings, but he followed his father. They stopped in front of one of the smaller meeting rooms and his father motioned for him to wait outside.

Slouching against the wall in the hallway a few feet from the door, Desmond could hear the raised voice of his father. The temptation to put his ear against the door to catch the words was held in check only by the guards standing in front. Minutes went by. The only voice he heard was his father's. Desmond tapped the wall behind him with his fingers and shifted his weight from one foot to the other.

The door was thrown open, its handle slamming against the wall with force. Desmond stepped away from the wall and found himself face to face with Aki. Whatever mastery the courier had shown in the council room was slipping fast. His face was white. His eyes furious with accusation. Desmond stepped back as Aki snatched the bundle of his weapons from the guard. Guilt clawed at Desmond, and he wanted to look away, but something needed to be said. At the very least, he wanted to know why Aki hadn't even bothered denying the prince's lie.

"Courier...,"

"Don't. Don't speak to me," Aki ground out between clenched teeth. Desmond was reminded once more of the night in Illsen. Of what Aki had done to the man there. Without another word, Aki stalked off.

Desmond waited until he was out of sight. He waited until he regained his own composure. Promising himself that he would explain the truth to Father now that it was just the two of them, he entered.

The words on his lips fell apart when he saw his father. King Darien sat at the table, his head bowed in his hands. Desmond crept forward; his footsteps noiseless as he crossed the threshold.

"Father?"

"You lied." King Darien raised his head. "In front of my entire council, you lied."

So much for telling Father the truth, Desmond thought. Instead, he bristled at the accusation.

"He's not to be trusted, Father. Anyone can see that."

"Nor are you, apparently."

Desmond dropped into a chair and crossed his arms. "Well, if you knew it was a lie, why didn't you say so out there?"

"How could I discredit my son in front of the very men he will one day lead? You forced me to choose. Do you understand that? You forced me to choose between you and him."

Desmond was on his feet again, sending his chair flying behind him. It clattered against the wall. "I understand that you would do anything to keep the peace. That's why you didn't say anything. Because you knew what it would start if you tried to defend him. All you care about is your precious peace. It doesn't matter that people are dying or..."

"Don't you dare say that. You have no idea what I've just had to do. The sacrifices I've made, that I've had to ask others to make."

"If it bothers you so much, I'll just tell everyone the truth."

"No. No, you cannot. Not now."

"Why not? I'll just say it was a mistake and we can let the whole thing blow over. You can save Aki again because that's more important to you than anything else."

"Does it truly not bother you that you threw his life away for your own pride?" King Darien's eyes searched Desmond's. Then he shook his head. "I do not have the luxury of choosing any one person over the needs of the kingdom. Aki will face the consequences of your lie because the people are afraid, and they need someone to blame. Thanks to you, they now have that. And you, you will live with that for the rest of your life and perhaps you will begin to understand what it costs to keep our precious peace. Now, go. I want to be alone."

Chapter 30

THERE WAS A DESPERATE PLEADING in his ear. A voice begging him to wake up. But Aki couldn't remember falling asleep. He reached out an arm to shove the person away, but a hand caught it and shook him.

"Aki, please."

Aki forced his eyes open. A dull sense of dread hung over him, smothering him. He was in trouble. More trouble. Bits and pieces of the day before came filtering back to him through his sleep ridden mind. A face. The prince's face. The prince who lied about him just to cover his own mistake.

"Aki, come on. You have to help me."

Aki squinted through the darkness, although he didn't need to see a face to know whose hand rested on his arm. Coming fully awake, he grabbed the knife he kept under his pillow and sat up, bringing its tip just beneath the chin of the room's only other occupant.

"What are you doing, Halle?"

"You have to help me, Aki. They're going to kill me," Halle choked out against the pressure of the knife.

"What? Who? What are you talking about?" Aki pulled the knife away.

"The king. He's gone. And they're saying I did it."

Aki was on his feet, knocking Halle away. He raced for his window, peering outside into the dark streets. A soft rain was falling, and everything was glistening wet but

166

quiet. No cries of alarm could be heard. Turning back to Halle, Aki ran a hand through his disheveled hair.

"Are you drunk? Nothing's going on. And how did you get in here anyway?"

Halle sat down on the floor, his hands opening and closing and opening again. "I'm not drunk, Aki. I overheard them. When I was going back to the castle for the night. I overheard two of them. One of them was the new friend of the prince. He told the other that tonight was the night. That they were to take the king. That they were going to blame me. I didn't know what to do. Aki, they'll kill me if they think it was me. You have to help me get away from here."

"I don't have to help you do anything," Aki said, but he was already lacing up his boots.

Outside, a cry was taken up, faint but growing stronger. Aki heard it first.

"The king is gone."

"The king is gone."

Blood fled Aki's face. He shook his head slightly in disbelief. A hand wandered to the ring at his neck, fingering it as he stared at Halle.

"They're going to kill me," Halle pleaded. "They'll kill you too."

And Aki knew it was true.

Prince Desmond would blame him at once. Baron Orlander, too. Probably most of the council. After yesterday, after his final conversation with the king... Pieces of the puzzle slipped jarringly into place. He was doomed if he stayed.

"Let's go," he said, snatching up the saddlebags he'd packed late the night before.

Sky was saddled in moments, as well as another horse Aki selected from the academy's stable. As they left the academy behind them, the cry of alarm was carrying through the light drizzle. From mouth to mouth the words flew and grew. There were accusations in the air now, too.

Aki pulled his hood farther over his head. He kept his face down and spurred Sky into a gallop, trusting Halle to do the same. They rode past people just waking up, past people ignoring the rain to venture outside and share the dreadful news.

Bren fell away behind them and as the cries faded, Aki dared a glance over his shoulder. He would never see it again. Because of a prince and his lie. Because of a king who had disappeared. Because of the letter in his pocket that burned against his chest. Because of a promise he'd had no choice but to make.

He swiped an arm across his face. It was just rain. Nothing more than rain running down his face. But as Sky's hooves beat a rhythm across the ground, an ache bigger than any he'd ever known splintered his insides. His eyes blurred and he could not see the road ahead of him.

"Stop," Halle gasped from beside him. "Who's that?"

Only then did Aki manage to blink the moisture from his eyes and look ahead. Huddled in the grass beside the road, sat a small figure with wild hair. She looked up at them as they raced towards her, her face barely visible in the gray dawn and mist of rain.

"Not Irene?"

"Aki? You are running away?" Her face lit up with hope.

"What are you doing out here?"

"Running away. Charlotte, she told me to. She saw me last night and she told me something terrible was going to happen and that I was in danger and needed to leave."

Aki glanced back through the grayness. He could hear nothing but the rain. No pursuit. But that didn't mean they weren't coming. He glanced at Halle who lifted one shoulder in a halfhearted shrug. Holding out his hand, he pulled Not Irene up behind him.

They left the road behind them. They ran until the horses could not run any more, and then they walked, then ran again. Only once did they stop, late in the night and deep in a woods.

Aki slipped away from the other two for a few minutes then and neither of them asked him where he went when he returned. They were too weary to even comment on where the other two horses he brought back with him came from. As Aki hurried to switch the saddles to the fresh horses, both Halle and the girl stood together watching him.

By the next sundown, Aki guided them into the Sar Forest. He found the old road, but left it almost at once, pushing deeper and deeper into the dense foliage. At last, after he almost fell out of his saddle asleep, Aki stopped. The other two didn't question him. Halle slid down, stumbled a few feet away to a clear spot in the ground and laid down. The girl was already half asleep when Aki helped her down.

Aki wanted to just drop to the ground and fall asleep himself, but he forced himself to tie the horses up and switch the saddles once more to the first two so that they would be ready to run at a moment's notice. Then and only then did he allow himself to sleep, his last conscious thought wondering how he managed to find himself on the run with the two most useless people in the world.

Chapter 31

"THE KING IS GONE, YOUR Highness."

Those were the words that dragged Desmond back into the waking world. The voice came from the other side of his bedroom door, accompanied by another series of thumping knocks against the wood. Desmond stood so quickly his head spun and it took him a moment to disentangle himself from his blankets.

"Your Highness?" The voice came again, urgent and loud. It was the voice of Captain Tyrrel.

"I'm coming," Desmond called back.

A few moments later and fully dressed, he threw the door open and was met with an array of people waiting just outside. Captain Tyrrel was the foremost one and the only one whose face showed any semblance of calm and order. Desmond pulled him inside the room and shut the door in the faces of everyone else. Whatever was going on, he wasn't ready to deal with them yet. Better to start with just the captain.

"What's this about, Captain?"

"Your father is gone."

"Dead?" Desmond's throat constricted over the word. His mind went immediately back to their last conversation. That wasn't how he wanted to leave things, with his father thinking so poorly of him.

"No. Missing. We've searched the entire castle already and he's nowhere to be found."

"Send men out. Search the town. Search every house if you have to."

"Already done. My men are out there now."

"No one leaves until he's found. Close off the roads leading out of town. And the harbor." Desmond paced, beating a fist against the palm of his other hand. "This has something to do with the attacks, with...," he paused as a thought crossed his racing mind. "Find the courier. Find Aki and bring him to me at once."

"You don't think..."

"He was one of the last people to speak to the king last night, Captain. And he had reason to want the king removed."

Captain Tyrrel's eyes narrowed as Desmond spoke and Desmond felt heat rushing to his face as he remembered the day before and the lie he'd told. The lie that fueled Aki's anger the night before. Even he hadn't imagined Aki would do something so drastic, so treacherous and bold.

"I will send men to the academy right away, Your Highness."

"Yes, do that." Desmond stopped his pacing, his back to the captain, as the news sank fully in, as the weight of responsibility settled fully over him. In a whisper, he asked the silence, "What do I do?"

"What you were raised to do, Your Highness. Rule. Speak to the council. Restore some degree of order," Captain Tyrrel answered him. "You don't have the luxury of hiding in your room and speaking only to those you choose."

Desmond nodded. "The council, yes. I'll speak with them. I'll speak with them. Yes. And you'll find the king. You'll find my father."

"I will do everything in my power to see him returned."

"Yes, yes."

He took a deep breath, then another, steadying himself, bracing himself for what awaited him beyond the closed door. If only he had Aki's self-control, his ability to hide a myriad of thoughts and emotions behind a stone wall of indifference. He'd never desired that more than he did now as the captain drew the door open and Desmond faced his people.

There was an eerie silence in the hallways of the castle. Servants and attendants still went about their work, but with hurried steps and nervous glances. Most of the guard was out searching the town. And inside the council room, the silence was unbearable. Desmond quailed at the sight of every eye on him as the door was opened before him.

"Desmond?"

"Tristan," Desmond turned in relief to find his friend standing there.

Tristan twisted his hands together and glanced from Desmond to the full and waiting council room. "I don't want to interrupt anything important, but I heard what happened and thought..."

"Come in with me," Desmond said, not waiting for him to finish. "I'd like you to."

"It's not my place."

"Everything's in chaos this morning so it doesn't matter."

"The others won't..."

"It doesn't matter," Desmond said. "Please, Tristan?"

Even with the presence of someone he knew to be on his side, Desmond wanted to slink out of the room again and hide away. Everyone was looking at him. Everyone. And not the way they would look at a prince. It was the way they looked at someone they wanted answers from, someone they expected to know what to do, what orders to give. The problem was, Desmond had no idea.

Wild thoughts darted around inside his head, keeping pace with the racing of his heart. Not one of them was coherent. Not one of them worthy of being put into words and yet all these people stared at him, waiting for him to speak.

"Just tell them what you know," Tristan whispered in his ear, and it felt like a roar.

Desmond cleared his throat and swallowed. Tightened each hand into a fist and then uncurled his fingers.

"I'm sure," he started, but his voice was too quiet to be heard by even those standing nearest him, so he tried again. Louder. Tried to imitate his father's confidence. "I'm sure you've all been made aware of the king's disappearance. I have already ordered the guard to close off all the roads and the harbor leading out of Bren while they search for him."

"Was there anything in the king's quarters that might enlighten us as to who is responsible?"

"How was he removed from the castle?"

"Was there a struggle?"

"Did any of the guards notice anyone unusual last night?"

"Was Aruuk involved?"

"Was it Dorsten?"

The questions came.

And came.

And came.

Hammering at Desmond, bombarding him on every side. He turned to address one only to be met by another. And he didn't know the answers to any of them. There were those who didn't voice questions as well. Those whose eyes asked their questions for them, and Desmond didn't know which way to look.

"Enough!"

The single word, echoing across the room, was a wave of water on the burning fire of everyone's curiosity. Desmond knew it wasn't his own voice that spoke, although it was the word he wanted spoken. Looking across the entire length of the room to the open doorway, he saw Captain Tyrrel.

Alone.

The captain made his way forward. That he had news was obvious. What that news was, Desmond could only guess. Captain Tyrrel's face revealed nothing. It could have been carved out of marble for all it told Desmond.

"What have you found, Captain?" Desmond asked before he was halfway across the room.

"Aki Turston is no longer in Bren, Your Highness."

"What?" Desmond fell back into his chair.

"Nor is his brother, Halle Gundarson. Apparently, they both left sometime during the night or early morning."

"What?" Desmond repeated. "Where did he go?"

"I don't know."

Desmond rubbed his hand over his face. It made sense. That was why he'd sent the captain to find him in the first place. But the captain's news still shook him. He should have seen something like this coming. Father should have seen this coming. Maybe he had, Desmond realized. Maybe that was why he'd been so tense, so worried. He hadn't trusted Desmond enough to trust him with any of that, though. Anger seeped into his shock. With a start, Desmond remembered that everyone in the room was still looking to him to say something.

"Find him. Alive. There are questions we need to ask him. He wouldn't have run if he wasn't involved somehow."

"He wouldn't be doing anything alone," Baron Orlander spoke up. "With everything we know, don't you think it's safe to say that Aruuk is behind this? First, they attack a village in Dorsten, then set up an ambush against you and the men who went with you. They are most likely the ones killing off couriers and keeping the northern province isolated."

"We don't have proof..."

"If we wait for proof, we'll have lost the opportunity to respond. King Darien has long taken a very lenient view of our northern neighbors in an effort to establish peace between us. Perhaps it's time to try something different."

"Are you suggesting we declare war on them? Based merely off of your suspicions?" Gregory asked.

Desmond straightened and drew in a sharp breath at the suggestion. War was the one thing his father had spent most of his reign trying to prevent.

He felt Tristan lean in close to whisper. "Your father granted citizenship and protection to many from that country, did he not?"

Desmond gave him a slight nod, curious of what Tristan might say next.

"Is it possible that they have infiltrated the country through such means? Perhaps the raid and the ambush were just precursors to a much more devious and far-reaching plan? This may be a plan that has been in the making for many years."

"You're right," Desmond said out loud, causing everyone to stop talking and look at him again.

"Who is, Your Highness?" Gregory asked.

Desmond waited a moment to answer, putting the words together carefully in his mind. Captain Tyrrel said that he needed to lead. To restore order. So that's what he would do. He needed the council's permission to go to war, but he didn't need their permission to make the kingdom safe.

"Until we find out otherwise," he began, his voice finding strength with each word he spoke, "we will treat this as a threat from Aruuk. For many years, the king has offered our country as a home to those who wished to leave Aruuk. According to the courier, Aki Turston, the men perpetrating the attacks in Dorsten and in the Void appeared to be from Aruuk. With this last move, a move that could only have been orchestrated by people living here among us, I think our next steps are clear. For the safety of our people, we need to eliminate the possibility of more attacks such as this."

He had everyone's undivided attention. In most of their eyes, he could read agreement, approval. That was all he needed. A few dissenting voices would not be enough to override him.

"Captain Tyrrel," he addressed the man in a voice loud enough to be heard by all.

"Your Highness?"

"You will be responsible for collecting and relocating any and all Aruukens who have made their home here. I want them separated from our people, contained, and watched."

"Your Highness, that is not possible."

"Isn't it? Every foreigner who makes their citizenship here is registered, are they not? Simply use those registers. That is part of why we have them."

"And where are we to put them? That is a considerable amount of people."

Desmond hadn't thought of that. He frowned and the pause gave his council members time to speak.

"You cannot issue an order like that, Your Highness." Desmond turned to see that it was Hamo who'd spoken. "Those people are citizens, the same as the rest of us, whether they were born here or not. You cannot assume them all guilty just because of shared origin."

"I would expect you to think so," Desmond answered. "After all, you've become very close to some of them, including the one who is right now a fugitive."

"He's not assuming guilt, Hamo. He's simply taking precautions against further attacks," Baron Orlander said.

"Exactly," Desmond said. "It's just a way for us to keep an eye out for possible infiltrators, spies, saboteurs. Once we've sorted all this out, everything can go back to the way it was before."

"What about the old border forts we passed coming here?" Tristan whispered in his ear again. "They were empty and well suited for housing large numbers of people. Why not put them to use?"

It was a good idea. Desmond was glad he'd insisted on Tristan coming in here with him. There was no need to mention it now in front of the council, though. He would work out the details of it all later with Captain Tyrrel.

"You still can't issue such orders, Your Highness. You are not the king," Hamo insisted.

"Then put it to a vote. What I'm proposing is for everyone's safety, not just ours but also the Aruukens who live here. How long do you think it will take once word of this leaks out for people to take reprisals?"

"They would only be doing it because they've been convinced to see their neighbors as their enemies. This solves nothing."

"Then what do you suggest?"

"I suggest we follow the plan your father agreed to yesterday. Hunt down those who are actually responsible instead of wasting our time rounding up innocent people."

"You only insist on their innocence because of your attachment to them," Baron Orlander interjected. "Anyone can see that. Next you would tell us to let Aki Turston go. That he couldn't possibly have any part of this."

Hamo shook his head. "If he ran, he had reason to. By all means, find him and find out why."

Desmond knew, before they voted, that he'd won. Too many of the faces in the room mirrored his own feelings for him to lose. Baron Orlander was the first and loudest to side with him. Only a few dared not to. Despite the worry that gnawed at him over his father's disappearance, there was a giddy satisfaction in watching his own word become law.

Chapter 32

AKI TOSSED THE CARCASSES OF two rabbits onto the ground in front of the fire and then sat down to clean and dress them. Another day of moving through the Sar Forest without any sign of pursuit had passed. Another night spent wondering what had gone so wrong in such a short time. At least he'd been awake enough when they stopped in the evening to set up snares. They would be going hungry again if he hadn't.

Halle and Irene were still asleep, kept warm by the fire he'd built. When they woke up, they would eat the food he provided. Aki was tempted to saddle Sky and ride away on his own, leaving the two of them to fend for themselves. If it was just Halle, he would have already been gone.

Halfway through gutting the first carcass, Irene joined him by the fire. She didn't make any noise as she walked across the ground and Aki would never have noticed her if it weren't for the way she stared at him. He glanced over to find her only a couple of feet away, her knees drawn up in front of her, a tangle of hair falling in front of her face, shielding her from the same scrutiny he had to endure from her. She'd been like that since they left. Always staring, always watching as if she were waiting for him to do something.

"I don't suppose you can help with this?" Aki asked, more to break off her ceaseless staring than because he actually expected her help. She hadn't lifted a finger to help when he brought her to Bren.

She shook her head, sending the veil of matted hair in front of her face swaying back and forth. "I do not know how."

"What do you know how to do?"

She took a moment to think about it, her face screwed up and a finger twisting a loose curl. "I can sing."

"Yes, I can see how that's very useful. Perhaps you can sing a song that will make everything go back to the way it was before this mess."

"You are making fun of me. That is rude, is it not?"

Aki shrugged. "I guess so."

"I cannot do many things. I never learned. It is not fair of you to make fun of me for that."

"What's not fair is that I'm running for my life when I've done absolutely nothing wrong. Besides, just because you weren't taught before doesn't mean you can't still learn."

"I do not want you to teach me."

"And why's that?" Aki reached out to stir up the fire and set skewers of rabbit meat over the flames.

"You are not very good at teaching."

Aki was surprised to find himself laughing. It wasn't the response Irene wanted. At least, that's what Aki guessed when her face pinched into a frown. She scooted a little closer to the fire and didn't tear her eyes off the sizzling chunks of meat for several minutes.

"Why are you running away?" Irene asked after several minutes.

He couldn't stop the anger that flashed across his face. "Because there are a lot of people who want to believe I'm guilty."

"Of what?"

"Conspiring against the king. Having something to do with his disappearance." And, of course, there was the lie Prince Desmond told about him. That had only deepened everyone's suspicions. If he ever saw the prince again...

Irene peered at him more closely. "Is that the only reason you left?"

Aki nodded, staring into the fire.

Halle stirred and sat up. No doubt awakened by the aroma of food, Aki thought, annoyed. Halle scooted closer to the fire; his eyes locked onto the meat roasting above it as if he could devour it just by looking at it.

"Hungry?" Aki asked him wryly.

Halle ignored his tone and reached out to lift a stick of meat off the fire. He tried to pull a chunk of meat off the skewer but jerked his fingers away with a hiss of pain. He stuck those fingers in his mouth and held them there for a minute.

"Where are we going?" Halle asked after the meat had cooled enough for them all to eat.

Aki looked up to find both of them looking at him, waiting for him to answer. They hadn't questioned anything he'd done in the last three days but now that they were able to slow down a little, Aki expected Halle to reassert himself. Apparently, Halle was content to follow this time.

"North. We... I need to go north. You can go wherever you want."

Halle snorted. "You'd like it if we did that, wouldn't you? No. If I'm running, I'm going all the way to Aruuk. It's the only place where I'll be safe."

Irene was still watching him, her gaze boring into him. Aki stood up abruptly and went to saddle the horses. The grueling pace they'd kept up for the last three days was wearing on the animals. Aki rubbed Sky's neck as his other hand fumbled with a buckle. They would have to slow down today. The horses needed it. He needed it.

Little sunlight reached them as they rode through the day, moving further and further north. As the ground grew more rugged, with steep rises and deep ravines, all covered in thick trees and dense brush, Aki decided that they would just have to risk riding closer to the great plains. Halle either didn't notice the subtle shift in their direction, or just didn't care. When Aki turned his horse, Halle followed.

Aki was half asleep when he felt Irene tug on his sleeve. "What's that?"

He followed her finger to a patch of bright sunlight just up ahead. The ground sloped down towards it and as they got closer, the trees and bushes thinned out.

"Just a clearing," Aki answered.

They came to the edge of the trees and found a small, grassy meadow. A creek ran through it and since the sun was going down Aki decided it was as good a place as any to stop for the night. He led the horses toward the water while the other two sat down at the edge of the clearing. Crouching down, he splashed some of the cool water on his face.

"Aki," Halle called softly from across the short distance, his voice strained.

Aki didn't bother answering. If Halle wanted to talk to him, the least he could do was walk over to him.

"Aki," Halle called again, his voice more insistent.

"What?" Aki stood up and turned around.

His heart stopped.

Halle and Irene were no longer sitting against the trees. And they were no longer alone. A man stood behind each of them, holding them in place. Halle's captor had a knife pressed to his throat. Aki's first thought was that the king's men had found them. By the time his heart started beating again, he knew they couldn't be. They wore no uniform. Aki's hand was on his sword before he realized it was moving.

"I wouldn't do that if I were you," a man said, stepping out from behind a tree. His voice was heavy with an Aruuken accent. "Not unless you want your friend to die." He gestured toward Halle. Halle's captor tightened his hold on Halle and pressed the knife a little deeper against his skin.

"He's not really my friend," Aki answered, his fingers still closing around the hilt of his sword.

"Aki?" Halle's voice cracked.

Even if he didn't care what happened to Halle, there were at least a dozen men just inside the trees. He couldn't hope to fight all of them. He released his sword and let his hand drop, empty, to his side.

"What do you want with us?" he called, trying to keep his voice as confident and nonchalant as he could.

"I think I should be the one asking the questions."

The man waved him towards the group. As Aki started forward, the leader snapped his fingers, and three others left the shelter of the trees. Two of them grabbed the horses from Aki and the third reached for his weapons. Aki stood still as the man removed both his swords and the knives that were visible. When the man stepped away, Aki made a mental note of the ones he had left behind. One inside his boot and another in his sleeve. Not that they would be of any use to him against these odds.

The leader clapped his hands together and the others came out of the trees as well. Aki realized his earlier assessment was off. There were about twenty men, all heavily armed. By some prearrangement, the men started setting up a camp in the clearing. Aki was grabbed by the arm and guided to where Halle and Irene were. He knew what would happen next even before he saw the leader approaching with several pieces of rope in his hands.

Tied to a tree, Aki watched as the camp took shape. When not speaking to their captives, the men spoke in Aruuken. Aki tried to look like he wasn't listening to every word he could catch. Halle, tied to the tree next to him, didn't attempt to pretend. His eyes darted about, following first one of their captors and then another. Aki couldn't see Irene from where he sat but so far, the men seemed content to leave her alone.

"Do you think they'll feed us?" Halle whispered to him when their captors sat down to eat sometime later.

Aki tried to shrug but with his hands tied behind him it wasn't very successful.

Whether the leader noticed their exchange or not, Aki couldn't tell. He wiped his hands off on his trousers, said a few quiet words to four of the others and waved them toward Aki and Halle.

The leader was seated on an overturned log near the fire. Freed from the ropes that held them to the trees, Aki and Halle were led to the space in front of him. Aki heard Halle gasp and turned in time to see him shoved to his knees and held down by his two captors.

"Sit, please," the leader gestured Aki to another upturned log.

Aki wasn't given a chance to decide whether to obey the request or not. The man on either side of him pushed him down onto the log. It was only then that he noticed the sword laying across the lap of the man in front of him. His father's sword. The man followed his gaze to it and smiled, tapping his fingers on the scabbard.

"Let's see, where shall we begin? Introductions would be a good place, don't you think?"

Aki watched his face, trying to guess whether he wanted an actual answer or if he simply liked to hear himself speak. He decided on the latter and remained silent.

"My men call me Ritter. You'll understand, I'm sure, if that's the only name I'll give you. It's not often we get travelers coming through these woods. In fact, you three would be the first since we've taken up residence. Who are you?"

That was a question Aki had not yet decided how to answer. By this time, their names were likely to be plastered all over the kingdom, possibly with the offer of a reward if found. Then too was the fact that these men were clearly either from Aruuk or Karu, and he didn't really want them knowing who they were in that case either. The brands on his arm grew heavy beneath his sleeve. The man had but to catch a glimpse of them and Aki could be in far worse trouble than if the king's men had found him. It didn't help that everything about Ritter's demeanor reminded Aki of Cadoc.

Before he made up his mind, Ritter gave a flick of his wrist. Halle started to yell but it was broken off in a gurgle and splash of water. Aki looked over and noticed what he'd missed before. A large bucket of water had been placed on the ground in front of Halle, and Halle's head was now held down inside it. Halle fought wildly, but his hands were tied behind him still and it was useless.

Aki looked from Halle to Ritter. The leader didn't even bother to glance at Halle.

"Who are you?" he repeated, his voice calm and patient.

"We're fugitives of the crown," Aki finally answered.

Another flick of Ritter's wrist and Halle was let up, spluttering and coughing. Water streamed down his hair and face, soaking the entire front of him. He sent a baleful glare in Aki and Ritter's direction as he spit out water.

"You shouldn't use him like that. I told you he's not my friend. I don't care what happens to him."

"Perhaps not," Ritter admitted, "but you look like a decent person. And decent people don't need to be friends with someone to try to save them. After all, you did answer my question." A satisfied smile flickered across Ritter's face. "Although, you really only told me why you are out here and not who you are. So, let's try this one more time."

Aki heard Halle's grunt of pain as the fist of one of the men caught him squarely in the stomach. Before he could draw in another breath, his head was under water again. Aki bit down on his lip to keep from protesting. It was Halle. He really didn't care what happened to him. He made himself think of what Halle had done to him to keep himself from caring now because there was no way he was telling this man who they really were. Ritter watched him. He watched Ritter. Beside them, Halle thrashed and fought but never got his head above water.

"Perhaps you were telling the truth," Ritter said, still watching him, still smiling in a way that reminded Aki very much of a cat toying with its prey. "But..."

Halle's efforts were slowing, getting weaker. Aki lowered his head and tried to ignore his own racing heart and the sick feeling in his gut. Think of Halle's branding, he told himself. But it wasn't working. Halle went limp, slumping against his captors' grip. Ritter motioned for them to pull him out. When they let go of him, he fell over unconscious onto the grass.

"Wake him up," Ritter ordered his men in Aruuken.

Aki wasn't sure kicking someone repeatedly in the stomach and chest was the best way to revive a person. After a series of such blows, however, Halle began gagging and coughing up water. Aki turned away. Ritter waited only until Halle's eyes fluttered open and then the whole process was started over.

It was harder to ignore Halle's renewed, frantic efforts this time. Sweat beaded on Aki's forehead as he sat under Ritter's scrutiny, and he had to work to keep his own breathing steady. Held in place behind his back, his hands were clenched into tight fists. He didn't care.

"You're more stubborn than I imagined, but I have all night. He doesn't," Ritter gestured to where Halle's movements were already weakening.

"I told you; I don't really care what happens to him."

Ritter just smiled pleasantly. Aki shifted uneasily beneath that smile. Ritter knew. He knew that Aki was bothered. When Halle was pulled out of the water unconscious a second time and subjected to the same rough awakening, Aki couldn't help but wince at the sound of each kick. He knew exactly how much that would hurt in the coming days.

"Aki?" Halle managed to gasp out this time between coughs, his desperate eyes meeting Aki's just as he was hauled back up onto his knees in front of the bucket. "Please?"

Aki hated himself. He didn't want to tell the truth, and he couldn't think of a good enough lie. And all the while, Halle fought and fought to get his head up out of the water.

He didn't care.

He didn't care.

He didn't care.

"Who are you? Why are you running from the crown?" Ritter repeated.

He did... care.

"Alright. Enough. Just let him up and I'll tell you," Aki blurted out. "We're running because King Darien is missing and the people in Bren blame us."

Halle lay panting in the grass by the time Aki finished speaking. Ritter smiled in satisfaction and triumph. Aki wanted to tear the smile off his face.

"And where are you going?" Ritter asked.

Aki hesitated and Ritter waved a hand at the men standing over Halle. Before they got him up, though, Aki was shaking his head. "Wait. I'm answering. We're going north."

"Not good enough."

Halle writhed against his captors' grasp, a whimper escaping him as his head was forced toward the water once more.

"We don't actually know where we're going. Just north, as far from here as we can get. Probably Aruuk. We haven't planned anything beyond that."

Ritter leaned back, stretching his legs out in front of him on the ground. "Well, now, it appears you aren't quite so heartless as you wanted me to believe. And since you're feeling so talkative now," Ritter lifted the sword that was laying across his knees and examined it, "where did you get this?"

"What?"

Ritter sighed and Halle was back under water before Aki could blink. "This is getting tiresome, don't you think?

Let's make this very simple. I ask you a question. You answer that question. You don't respond with your own. I really thought you would have figured that out by this time. Now, where did you get this sword?"

"It was given to me," Aki answered. Still Halle was not released. Ritter nodded for him to go on. "It was my father's."

"Perfect, it seems you're finally beginning to understand how this works. Although, it was still a bit too long for him again, I'm afraid."

Ritter was right. Halle lay limp and unmoving on the grass once more. Aki cringed as the men set about waking him up for a third time.

"Where's the ring?"

"The ring?" Aki asked, then saw Ritter's hand raised to signal the men holding Halle. "No. No, wait. I'll answer you, just, what ring?"

"You had a ring you carried with you as well. Where is it?"

"I don't have it anymore."

Ritter's eyebrows shot up and he gave a meaningful glance in Halle's direction. By the hoarse fits of coughing that were coming from there, Aki assumed he was awake again.

"It's the truth, Ritter. I lost it sometime while we were riding through here. It must have got caught on a branch. I noticed it missing last night."

Shaking his head, Ritter got lazily to his feet and motioned Aki to do the same. He made a sign to someone standing behind Aki and Aki felt a pair of hands work the knots that bound his own. His arms dropped to his side with relief, and he took turns rubbing the sore spots left behind on his wrists.

"Take off your shirt."

Aki bit his tongue before he let slip another questioning exclamation. Stripping in front of this man was the last thing he wanted to do but...

Halle was being forced toward the water again and Aki found his hands already working to pull his shirt off.

Ritter studied him in a way that Aki found horribly familiar and discomforting. The man turned Aki around in a slow circle so that he could see Aki's back by the light of the fire. When he turned Aki to face him again, he grabbed Aki's hair and forced his head back enough to see the scar the noose he'd been sentenced to die in a year ago had left. Then a callous finger traced the fainter marks that Halle had cut across his chest. It took every bit of Aki's control not to flinch at the touch. Finally, Ritter reached for his right arm. Pulling it towards him, he examined the two brands and the names.

"Didn't say anything about these," Ritter ran a thumb over the names, "but otherwise, you're the one we were told to look out for. You were supposed to have that ring, though. She'll be furious that you don't." Aki yanked his arm back and Ritter let him with a short laugh. "I meant no offense to you."

He was halfway through putting his shirt back on when the question came to him. "Who's she?"

"You'll find out soon enough."

"And how did she know to tell you to look for me? I didn't even know I was coming this way three days ago."

"Oh, she didn't know. But, well, there's been an awful lot of talk in Dival these days. Rumors and accusations and all manner of speculation. She just told all of us that if by chance we ran into you, we weren't to kill you."

Chapter 33

IT WAS EARLY EVENING WHEN Captain Tyrrel knocked on the door. It was answered by a young woman with a baby in her arms.

"Can I help you?" she asked.

Captain Tyrrel hated this. He'd delegated most of this work to inferiors. But this was one stop that he trusted only himself to make. The young woman was still waiting, a slight crease forming on her brow.

"Ophelia Gundarson?"

"Yes. Is there something I can help you with?"

"I'm here to speak with your husband, Sasha Gundarson."

"He's not home yet." She looked past him, to the soldiers waiting outside. "You can come in and wait, if you like."

"Do you know where I can find him?"

"He was going to stop at my grandmother's to help her, I think."

"Alina Turston's?"

Ophelia nodded. "Is there something wrong, Captain?"

She wasn't asking about the rumors that surrounded the king's disappearance, Captain Tyrrel knew. She was asking about her husband. And Captain Tyrrel didn't have the courage to tell her.

"Nothing at all. I just need to ask him some questions."

It didn't take more than a cursory glance to know that she didn't believe him. The baby in her arms started fussing as if it, too, could sense the current of trouble that was rushing through the kingdom and coming to rest on this very doorstep. Captain Tyrrel couldn't bear the sound of it and backed away from the door.

"I'll look for him there," he told her.

He had to go to Alina's anyway. It wasn't just to get away from the worry that radiated from Sasha's young wife. The same worry that had the kingdom shackled. As he rode the short distance to his next stop, Captain Tyrrel tried to prepare the words he needed to speak in his mind.

When Alina opened the door, there was none of the surprise or uncertainty that had been on Ophelia's face. She stepped aside to let him in.

"Is Sasha here?" he asked before crossing the threshold.

"He's in the barn."

Captain Tyrrel turned to the soldiers who rode with them and gestured them toward the barn. Then he entered the house. Alina led him into the sitting room. He waited until she was seated, her hands folded in her lap. And then he waited some more. One look at Alina told him she would not speak until he did.

"I'm here about Aki."

"I know."

"You've seen him?"

"I have not seen him since Colin came for him several days ago."

It was a lie if ever Captain Tyrrel heard one. And he had no desire to extract the truth.

"You have heard..."

"I have heard what others think. Please do not ask me to agree with them."

"And what do you think?"

Alina gave him a stony stare. "Does it matter what I think? My son is being hunted for a crime he had no hand in committing. And your men are right now arresting my granddaughter's husband for the crime of being born Aruuken. Are you going to arrest me as well?"

"Of course not. I simply need you to tell me anything you can that would help us."

"Help you carry out the prince's mad orders? I have nothing to tell."

"Alina, I understand that you want to protect Aki. But it's my job to protect this kingdom. He must be found."

"Then do your job, Captain."

"He was here."

"I told you; I have not seen him in days."

"You're lying."

"You have proof of that?"

Captain Tyrrel threw his hands up in frustration. "Alina, think. Where is he going to run? Aruuk? I saw what it was like for him there. You know better than I do that he would never go back there. And if he does not leave the kingdom, he will be caught. Maybe not today or tomorrow, but eventually. He can't live forever running. The prince has put a price on his head. He'll be hunted by anyone and everyone, who will do who knows what to him when they find him. Wouldn't it be better if I reached him first? I can at the very least ensure that no harm comes to him until he is given a fair trial."

He could see that Alina was at least considering his words. He could see her reasoning through them. And he saw the moment she made up her mind.

"I have not seen him, Captain," she repeated with steel in her voice.

"Captain?" One of the soldiers leaned inside the still open door and Captain Tyrrel turned to face the man. "We have him, sir, and he's asked to speak with you. Also, there are horses missing from the stable."

"Bring him in," Captain Tyrrel said. Turning to Alina, he asked, "How long have they been missing?"

"They're not missing, Captain. As you no doubt know, my husband passed some months ago, leaving me this entire farm to care for. I have sold off some of the stock since then, including two or three of the horses."

With a sigh, Captain Tyrrel gave up. They were alone only a moment longer before the soldier returned leading someone who could only be Sasha. Aside from being a little pale, he did not appear to be in any way intimidated by the situation. Captain Tyrrel straightened, readying himself for the protestation he was certain he would hear.

"Am I at least allowed to say goodbye?" Sasha asked, surprising him.

"I'm afraid not. We must return immediately."

"But Phelie doesn't even know..."

"I've already spoken to your wife. She knows. Alina, forgive our intrusion," he said, starting for the door when his eyes lit on something. The ring. The same ring he'd seen Aki slip into his pocket the day they left Illsen. The ring that was given to him by the elderly councilman. It lay on the windowsill, the sapphire stones catching the last light of the day. He snatched it up and held it in front of Alina's face. "He left this with you, didn't you? Why?"

Alina looked at the ring. She looked at Sasha. Then she met Captain Tyrrel's eyes and he read the resolve in them before she spoke. "He left in such a hurry with Colin that he forgot it."

Chapter 34

A HEADACHE THROBBED AGAINST his temples as Desmond shut the door softly behind him. All he wanted was a moment's peace. All day, for the last three days, he'd been hounded by a host of people needing directions, orders, information. Council meetings swallowed whole hours of time.

Trapping himself in one of his father's favorite rooms now, Desmond sank into the soft chair and caught his head between his hands. The room was one of the smaller ones in the castle. It was cozy and smelled of wood and books and warm wax. On the cluttered desk before him lay stacks of papers, unfinished work his father had left behind. Desmond had no intention of picking any of them up at the moment. This was the last room he'd seen his father in, where they'd argued. The last room Aki had met with his father. Desmond shut his eyes and tried to remember if he had actually caught any of the words that the king had spoken to Aki that night.

When that failed, his eyes wandered over the desk. A map lay spread across the tops of several papers and Desmond leaned forward, resting his elbows on the desk, to get a better look. The map was an old one. Very old. Its edges were frayed and worn and there were spots where the ink had rubbed off altogether. It showed Dorsten and Dival, with the boundary lines marked between them, and beyond them, Aruuk and the small, scattered kingdoms that had not yet been overtaken by the Aruukens.

Desmond lifted the map up to look more closely at it and a small piece of paper that he hadn't noticed before fluttered to the floor. Setting the map aside, Desmond bent to retrieve it. It was a letter, addressed to his father and written in a beautiful, flowing hand that ended each word with a flourish. Desmond turned to face the fire and opened it.

In the yellow glow of the fire, color slowly drained itself out of Desmond's face. After a few minutes, the paper slid out of his slack hands and drifted to the ground again. Desmond didn't seem to notice. He stared and stared at the empty space in front of him as if he could still see the words.

Then he snapped out of his stupor. Throwing the door open, he called out to the nearest person, "Bring me Tristan. And the princess Charlotte. Bring them to me at once."

Desmond found himself out of breath. The room had lost its coziness. It had traded it for a suffocating heaviness. He pulled the collar of his shirt open a little and paced restlessly until the door opened.

Instead of Tristan or Charlotte, he found himself face to face with Captain Tyrrel. And the look on the captain's face made Desmond think the man was contemplating murder.

"Tell me you have him, Captain."

"If by him, you mean Aki, then no. There has not been so much as a whisper about his whereabouts. It's as if he and that brother of his, Halle, have vanished into thin air. I do have something that you will no doubt find interesting."

"I'm not sure I want it, then, Captain. I feel as if I've had my share of interesting things in the last few days."

"I personally questioned Alina Turston, Your Highness. She denies having seen him since he ran away, but I found this in her home." Captain Tyrrel held out the ring he'd taken from Alina's.

"What is that?" Desmond held out his hand and the captain dropped it into his palm. He held it up to examine it. "What possible use is this?"

Captain Tyrrel explained what he knew of how the ring came into Aki's possession.

"It's a signet ring, but I don't recognize the seal. Who do you suppose it belongs to?"

"I have no idea, Your Highness. It may merely be coincidence and have nothing to do with any of this."

"Why do you always do that, Captain? Why do you always try to think of a way to keep him innocent?"

Captain Tyrrel hesitated.

"Well? I asked you something, didn't I?"

"Because, Your Highness, some of this just doesn't add up. I know you have most of the council convinced that he set us up in Aruuk but... but what happened that night," Captain Tyrrel shook his head, "I don't think you really understand. There was nothing set up about that on his part."

"If he were innocent, why would he run?"

"Wouldn't you have?"

Desmond hung his head. The words he spoke in the council room haunted his memory. The words that condemned Aki whether the king had disappeared that night or not. Perhaps Aki had left Bren hours before. Perhaps he'd only run because he knew he was doomed if he didn't. But Desmond couldn't even entertain that thought without admitting to Captain Tyrrel that he'd lied, and that was something he'd never do. Holding the ring up once more, he asked, "Who do you think might know this?"

Captain Tyrrel considered for a moment. "Atticus Wehr. He knows every sign and seal for the last seventy years at least. And from countries outside of ours. Ask him. If he doesn't know it, I doubt anyone would."

"Thank you, Captain. I think you should continue your search for Aki and Halle towards the north."

"Why's that? Have you heard something?"

"This," Desmond picked the letter up and tossed it back down. "A letter my father received some time ago. A letter stating that there is rumored to be an heir in Dorsten, an heir who has a greater claim to Dorsten than either my father or me. I would imagine this letter has some bearing on recent events."

"A northern heir? But the old Dorstenian king never had any children. That was why it was passed to Lord Bayner instead. And I believe he died without children as well. It is a trick, Your Highness. It can be nothing more than a trick."

Desmond wanted to believe that. But then he read the letter again and there were so many things in it he didn't understand. So many more pieces to add to the puzzle. And, he scowled as he realized, there was a second page to the letter that he did not have. Nor did a thorough search of his father's desk reveal it. There was a name on that missing page, Desmond was sure of it. And someone didn't want him to see it.

If there really were a possible successor in the north, then he, Desmond, Crown Prince of the newly united kingdom of Dival, was no longer the undisputed heir.

Chapter 35

I'VE MADE MY TENT AVAILABLE to you for the night, miss," Ritter said, offering a hand to Irene. "It won't do for a young lady to sleep out in the open. Although, in return for my hospitality, I must remind you that any trouble on your part will end badly for your friends here."

Aki was too weary to even respond to the threat. Slumped against the same tree and half laying on his shoulder, Halle continued to cough and spit out water. He hadn't said a single word since Ritter decided Aki's interrogation was over. Irene glanced down at where they sat as she got to her feet. Behind the veil of her hair, Aki saw confusion in her eyes as she looked first at him and then at Halle. She also hadn't said a word since the entire ordeal.

Ritter returned a few minutes later and stared down at them, his hands once more holding a length of rope.

"Your friend cannot run anywhere tonight."

Aki glanced toward Halle and knew Ritter spoke the truth. Halle could barely hold his own head up.

"And despite your words earlier, I do not think you will leave either him or the girl behind."

Again, Ritter spoke the truth. Aki remained silent, though, waiting to see what Ritter was getting to.

"I could tie you to the tree for the rest of the night and not lose a moment's sleep over it. But I don't think that's necessary. Do you understand that if you cause us any trouble tonight, it will be your friends that pay for it?"

Aki nodded to show he understood. Satisfied, Ritter returned to his spot by the fire. Aside from its light, which Aki and Halle were seated close enough to be caught in, it was dark out. Aki shifted, trying to find a more comfortable position. His hands had been tied behind him again. Apparently, Ritter didn't trust them with too much freedom. The leader was right about one thing, though. Aki wasn't going anywhere by himself. He'd stayed with Halle and Irene too long to just abandon them now.

Halle moaned softly as Aki moved, his head lolling back against the tree before coming to rest once more on Aki's shoulder. Aki wanted to shrug him off as another fit of coughing and retching took hold of him. Halle had coughed up more water than was in the bucket, Aki thought. But he couldn't bring himself to do it, not when he knew from personal experience the extent of Halle's pain, and so Halle continued to lean against him. When the coughing fit ended and Halle grew quiet again, Aki shut his eyes and tried to sleep.

"Aki?"

Halle's voice dragged him out of a semi-sleep sometime later. Aki murmured a response, slowly growing conscious of Halle's shivering against him. The night was cool, and Halle's clothes were soaked. Aki was shivering a little, too.

"Aki?" Halle repeated, his voice raspy and raw.

"What do you want?"

"Did you plan on killing Cadoc?"

Aki yawned and frowned in the darkness. There was too little of the fire left to see much but a quick glance sufficed to show that Ritter hadn't left them unguarded. "It's the middle of the night. Why are you asking about that now?"

"I... I just wanted to know... I wanted to know if you're still planning on killing me."

"I'm not going to kill you."

"But you almost let him do it for you."

Aki didn't know how to answer that. He couldn't deny it. A minute more of waiting and Halle would have been dead. The darkness inside of him had wanted it. The same darkness that had thrilled at watching Cadoc die. But he hadn't given in to it. He had fought it back, at least this time.

"I'm not going to kill you, Halle," he repeated with a little more strength in the words than before.

"Then why'd you let them hurt me so bad?"

Aki almost laughed, except he was far too tired. Halle couldn't stay meek for long, no matter how close to death he came. Then he grew sober. He couldn't very well deny that accusation either. Ritter had kept asking him questions, questions Aki was even more reluctant to answer, and Halle had paid the price for that reluctance in savage beatings and countless minutes under water. There hadn't been any satisfaction in watching it, though. No, no satisfaction at all. Because, like it or not, he was stuck out here with Halle. With everyone else intent on hunting him down and accusing him of something he hadn't done, Halle was, unbelievably, on his side. The only one really on his side.

"I'm sorry," he murmured after a long silence, surprised to realize that he actually meant it. "Try to get some sleep, Halle."

Halle didn't sleep. Between the pain and the cold, he never did anything more than doze off for a few minutes at a time.

Aki tried and failed to ignore him, the same as he tried and failed to ignore the onslaught of questions that flooded his mind. Ritter's words refused to leave him alone. Someone had told them to look for him. Someone who knew all the scars that marked him. And someone who must have known enough about the last year and a half to guess that Aki's position in Bren would be untenable. The gnawing pangs of hunger inside him didn't help. Irene had been offered food while Aki was questioned, but either their captors forgot or just didn't care about feeding him and Halle when the ordeal was over.

When sunlight first scattered the darkness, Aki forced himself to sit up a little and look around the place. Halle groaned as Aki's movements jarred his aching body. Only a few of the men were stirring yet and most of them were putting their efforts toward a new fire. Ritter was among the men up and when he saw Aki awake and watching he made his way over.

Crouching down in front of them, he grabbed Halle's face and tipped it up. "You look terrible," he commented cheerfully. Halle let out a tiny, frightened whimper and tried to pull away. Ritter grabbed Aki by the arm and pulled him to his feet. Halle, his support so suddenly gone, fell over completely but Ritter didn't seem to take notice. "Come. We need to talk."

Not again, Aki groaned silently as he allowed himself to be guided toward the fire. At least this time Halle was left behind. Ritter invited him to sit, and Aki knew he had no choice but to obey. There were a whole host of questions he wanted to ask the man, but so far Ritter had been very closed about sharing. All Aki had been able to find out the previous night was that someone, a woman, had given orders to all of the men responsible for killing travelers between Dorsten and Dival that he was to be spared. No mention had been made of whether those orders extended to Halle and Irene. Nor did they say anything about why he was to be spared.

"You're anxious to be on your way, no doubt, so I'll make this quick."

"Wait? You're letting me go?"

"Why would we keep you? She had hoped you would find your way to the north. And I've no intention of stopping you. I only needed to be sure you were the right one."

"Then why am I still tied?"

Ritter laughed and motioned to one of the men nearby to untie Aki's hands. Aki rubbed his wrists by turns, the skin tingling with the rush of blood returning.

"What about the others?"

"We'll kill them," Ritter answered. There was nothing malicious or personal in his words or tone. It was just a fact.

"No. If you can let me go, you can let them go." He saw that Ritter was going to object and didn't give him a chance. "We're enemies of the crown. Doesn't that put us on the same side?"

Ritter considered for a moment then shrugged. "But if you run into any other groups, they might not be quite so easy to convince."

"I'm willing to take that chance."

"Then you'll be wanting these back, won't you?" Ritter held out the weapons they'd taken from him the prior evening.

Their horses were already prepared for them by the time breakfast was cooked. As hungry as Aki was, he barely touched his food. There was simply too much else that demanded his attention. He was still puzzling over who had given the orders to let him pass unharmed. Obviously, it was the same person who had organized the bands of men responsible for killing anyone who tried to travel from Dorsten to Dival. With all of that, riding north suddenly didn't seem so desirable. Not that he was left with many choices.

"We'll meet again, I'm sure," Ritter said as they mounted up.

Aki bit his tongue to keep from saying that he sincerely hoped not. Halle, already on his horse, refused to even look up. Aside from their brief conversation in the night, he'd remained silent. Aki reached out a hand to help Irene up behind him, but Ritter was already there lifting her.

"If you stay this deep in the forest, you're not likely to run into any other parties."

Tugging Sky's reins free from the man who'd brought her over to him, Aki started to ride away but Ritter called after him, "Remember, we're on the same side. Don't make me regret letting all of you go."

"I wouldn't dream of it," Aki answered without bothering to look back.

As they rode on, the forest closed in around them again and there were times when it felt as if the three of them were alone in the world. Aki supposed that was better than running into the king's guard or more roving bands of killers working for a mysterious woman.

He turned his head to watch Halle riding behind him. Halle was hunched over, only one hand holding his reins. His other arm, he hugged against himself. He flinched with every step his horse took and Aki worried that they wouldn't make it far before he needed to stop. More than any of that though, he was silent. Not a word of complaint escaped him. No muttering about how hungry he was or how he hated riding all day or how it wasn't fair that he had to run away.

Once again, neither Halle nor Irene questioned or protested when he suggested they stop for the night. Aki watched Halle limp a safe distance from the horses and collapse onto the ground before turning his attention to taking care of the horses.

"I think I can help you with that." Irene's voice took him by surprise. She stood right at his elbow, watching him loosen the saddle from Sky's back. "I have watched you do it many times now and I think I could do it too."

"Go ahead," Aki stepped away.

Irene's fingers worked quickly, undoing the buckles and knots.

"Did I do it right?" she turned to ask him when she was done.

"You did."

Irene smiled for the first time that Aki could recall. It flashed across her face and was gone in a moment. She started on Halle's horse.

"Is he going to be alright?" she whispered.

"He'll be fine. They didn't do anything to him that'll kill him. He just isn't used to being in that much pain."

"I thought you hated him. I thought you wanted him dead."

Aki shrugged. "Not enough, I guess."

"I do not understand you. Why do you go through all the trouble of taking us with you?"

"I don't know if you've noticed or not, but you wouldn't have made it far on your own. Unless, of course, you were planning on singing your way to wherever it is we're going."

"That is what I mean. You would go much faster alone, so why bother with us?"

Aki had asked himself that question since he'd ridden out of Bren with Halle, of all people, at his side. He didn't have any better of an answer now than he did then. He just shook his head.

"Do you know where you are going?"

"I'll make you a deal. You tell me your real name and I'll answer your question."

Irene frowned and stared down at her hands. "I cannot tell you."

"Why not? You could tell Charlotte."

200

"It is better if I do not. You keep secrets, no? You kept it secret that you went to see someone before we left."

"How did you know?"

"Before you went, you were just angry. But when you came back, you were sad."

Aki turned away and decided it was a good time to start a fire. It was Alina he'd seen that night. For only a moment or two, but he couldn't bear the thought of leaving her without a word. Besides, there were things that he needed to leave with her for safekeeping. But he hadn't thought that either Halle or Irene was paying enough attention to notice much of anything that night.

"Now you are angry, again," Irene said, once more just beside him.

"I'm not. I just don't understand how telling me your name is so different from telling anyone else."

Irene picked up a stick that was lying on the ground beside her. She poked at the small fire Aki was fanning to life.

"I know where we can go. Someplace safe. Someplace no one will look for us."

"Oh?"

"I," she paused, her face twisting up the way it did when she was thinking hard, "I found it, when I was in Dorsten."

"You're lying again."

Irene shook her head. "It is safe. I promise."

Aki rocked back onto his heels and considered her. And then he laughed. He laughed until he couldn't breathe. "Why not?" he said, still laughing. "Why not? Why shouldn't I trust the girl who can't even tell me her real name? What else could possibly go wrong that hasn't already?"

Chapter 36

THE OPEN COUNTRY AFTER SO many days inside the Sar Forest left Aki feeling almost naked. He'd grown so used to the dimness of the forest, to the close air and the concealment of the trees that it was like leaving an old friend behind. The sun was bright against his eyes, and it took several minutes for them to readjust to the unfiltered light.

"Where to, Irene?" he turned his head to ask her.

"See that mountain?"

He followed the direction of her pointing finger and nodded. It was impossible to miss. Closer than any of the others that rose up along the horizon, its peak looked as if a giant ax had cut away the right half. The left side sloped steeply to its point only to end abruptly in a sheer cliff.

"Keep moving straight toward it and we will reach it."

"And just how long is it going to take?" Aki held a hand up to shield his eyes as he studied the sun. They only had a few hours left before it went down.

"I do not know. A few hours?"

"Can you ride any faster?" Aki asked over his shoulder.

"No," came Halle's sullen response.

"Come on, Halle, it's been days. You're getting better."

Halle mumbled an answer and Aki chose to assume he agreed. He spurred his horse into a canter, tugging Sky and the other spare horse along after him. He didn't bother to see if Halle sped up or not. Since they'd left Ritter and his men behind, Halle's mood had deteriorated steadily. He barely spoke. Barely ate. Looked over his shoulder constantly. The oddest part was that he seemed reluctant to get to wherever they were going, which made no sense since he didn't actually know where they were going. He drug his feet in the morning, keeping them from starting early. He kept his horse at a walk. Aki's sympathy had run itself out.

It was hours before the mountain appeared to get any closer and by then the sun was setting. They'd switched horses once through the afternoon and Aki pushed them once more into a canter. Irene tugged on his shirt and pointed ahead. In the distance, just barely visible in the rays of the dying sun, he could make out the outline of a building.

They approached it shortly after dark. Even then, Aki could see it was both sprawling and impressive. And familiar. Aki pulled his horse to a stop in front of the wide, columned veranda. Not a single light showed in any of the windows. Ivy grew up the columns and some of the walls.

"This is it?"

Irene nodded, slipping down. "No one lives here anymore. They have not for at least five years."

"How do you know?"

"I asked. There is a town more than an hour away. That was where I heard about it."

"It looks deserted enough. I suppose we might as well stay the night at least."

Aki led the horses to the back of the house, looking for a stable to put them in. There were a few out-buildings scattered around. All of them were in some sort of disarray and neglect. Broken boards, doors that had fallen loose from their hinges, paddock fences that were knocked over. The stable was easy to locate and was one of the few that still had doors that shut fully. By unspoken agreement, Halle and Irene followed him inside and Irene helped him care for the horses.

Then they made their way into the house. Aki winced as the front door emitted a squeal that was sure to be heard as far off as the town Irene had spoken of. Inside, he groped his way forward in the darkness, tripping over objects that he could not identify.

"I don't like this place," Halle muttered just behind Aki.

Aki nodded, the motion lost in the darkness. His hand found a wall and he followed it. Coming to a doorway, he ran his hand higher up the wall, searching for a lamp or candle. He was rewarded a moment later as his fingers closed around a dusty candle. Whispering for the others to stay still for a minute, he searched inside his saddle bag until he found his flint.

The darkness scattered in the fresh light of the single flame, and so did several rodents, running squealing and chittering to their holes and hiding places. Irene gave a small yelp at the sight and Aki felt her fingers digging into the skin of his arm.

"You know they're running from us, right?" he whispered. A whisper felt right, even though it was clear no one had entered this house in some time.

Just in front of them stood a grand staircase. Aki started up it and the others followed.

There was a balcony at the top, overlooking the main entrance, and opposite that were several doors. Aki pulled them open one by one to reveal mostly bedrooms. There was a small room at the end that appeared to have been used as an office of sorts and another room that was piled up with an assortment of furniture, rugs, chests, and a host of other unidentifiable items.

In the very back of the room, propped against a wardrobe and made prominent by the circle of light the candle shed on it was a large painting of a young woman. Stacks of old, worn books sat on a table just in front of it. And over everything lay a thick powdering of dust.

He was halfway out of the room again when Irene said, "I wonder who she was."

"Who?" Aki asked, thinking about the woman Ritter had mentioned and wondering if Irene was doing the same.

"The girl in the picture."

"Oh, her. Probably just the lady of the house. Or a daughter, maybe."

"She looked so happy."

"It's a painting. I think it's part of an artist's job to make everyone look happy."

"Maybe. I still wonder who she was. Or who anyone was that lived here."

"I'd like to know why no one lives here," Halle said.

Aki agreed with him. He was far more curious to know why the place was abandoned than to know who had occupied it at one time.

They picked the bedroom that seemed the least disturbing to sleep in. There was a distinctly feminine touch beneath the layers of dust but more importantly, there were thick, heavy curtains that were drawn over the windows, shielding them from any prying eyes. Aki found a few more candles and lit them as well.

Too wound up to sleep, he wandered around the room, examining the things that had been left behind. There was a wardrobe in one corner, full of old, moth-eaten dresses that would only have been worn by someone in the highest ranks of nobility. There was a dresser that contained more everyday clothes. There was the bed, of course, large and soft and with cobwebs stretching between the massive posts. Then there was a small table and mirror. Aki stopped in front of it. A comb, a few faded hair ribbons, a set of lace gloves lay scattered across the top. And a leather-bound book, its pages yellow with age. An inkpot, long ago dried up, stood beside it.

Aki picked the book up and flipped it open. A few pages came loose from their binding. Only the first half of it had been written in, with a neat, tight handwriting that slanted smoothly across each page. Dates were written in between passages. It was a journal, Aki realized. Something Master Wehr had encouraged him to keep. Master Wehr insisted it was not only a good way to practice his writing, but also beneficial for keeping track of events that tended to be forgotten. Aki hadn't wasted his time on it.

"What did you find?" Irene stood behind him on her toes, trying to see over his shoulder.

"Just this," he held it up. "It's a journal. Probably belonged to whoever stayed in this room."

"You should read it out loud for us. Perhaps it will tell us why no one lives here anymore," Halle spoke up from where he'd already made himself comfortable in the bed.

"It is a sad story," Irene said.

Aki turned to study her. There was distance in her expression, and she wasn't looking at him or even the journal anymore.

"How would you know?"

"I told you; I asked the people in the town. They told me it was a sad story."

Aki and Halle both looked at her expectantly, but she shook her head. "They did not actually tell me the story. They did not like to speak of it, they said."

Aki set the journal down again. "If it's that sad, I don't think I want to read it."

For the first time in over a week, Aki fell asleep with a real roof over his head. It was a fitful sleep though. There was something about the house that made him uneasy. Perhaps it was just its emptiness or the signs of a life that used to exist inside it. Or it had something to do with how familiar it looked as they rode up. Whatever it was, he did not fall into a deep sleep until well after midnight.

He woke up again to Halle's insistent shaking.

"What is it?"

"Irene's gone."

"What?" Aki sat up.

"She's been gone for at least a couple of hours."

He was out of bed in an instant, his eyes searching the room. There was no sign of Irene anywhere. A faint light shone through a crack between the curtains, and he realized that it was very early in the morning. That meant she'd left while it was still night.

"Maybe she just couldn't sleep and went exploring," he said, as much to himself as to Halle.

Halle didn't respond and he didn't look at all convinced. In fact, Aki stopped thinking about Irene at all when he looked at Halle. He looked like he was ready to be sick and refused to meet Aki's eyes. Aki didn't have the patience for it. Not this morning. He started for the door.

"I'm going to look around and see if I can find her."

Halle nodded, still avoiding his eyes. "I'll stay here in case she comes back."

In the light of the morning, Aki looked in each room as he passed them but saw no sign that Irene had been in them or was in them now. He went downstairs to continue his search. The entrance hall was full of overturned furniture which must have been what they were tripping over the night before, he realized. A door led into a dining room. Empty. The next, a small sitting room. Also empty.

The third door was cracked open already and when he pushed it all the way back, he found himself staring into a great hall. And in the center of it was...

"Irene?"

Only, she wasn't the Irene he'd met running for her life towards him, with her wild hair and tattered clothes. She was clean. New, neat clothes replaced her old, worn ones. Her tangled curls were braided back. And for the first time, Aki got a good look at her face. There were tears in her eyes, spilling in little tracks down her cheeks.

"I am so sorry, Aki. I had to."

"What have you done?" Aki didn't recognize his own voice, cold with fury.

"She will not hurt you. I promise she will not."

"What have you done?" he repeated.

"I had to, Aki. I did not have a choice."

Aki took a step toward her, his fingers curling into fists at his side.

"Oh, don't be so hard on her, Aki," a woman's cool voice arrested him from behind. "It really isn't her fault."

Everything went red around him. Aki heard the roaring of his own pulse as if he were standing outside himself. He heard his own voice, shaken and horrified, whisper, "Mara."

"Yes, we meet again, Aki," Mara said, stepping around in front of him. "It seems as if we cannot stay away from each other."

The sight of her robbed him of breath. His chest rose and fell in rapid successions, heaving for air. His fingers closed around the hilt of his sword, the metal cool and calming against the wild rhythm that coursed through his body.

"I wouldn't think about that if I were you."

Footsteps hurried up behind him and Aki's weapons were gone before he could wrap his head around what was happening.

"Thank you, Sebastian," Mara said.

Aki turned and found himself staring into the face of the very man responsible for breaking him in as a slave in Mara's salt mines, the man who had dragged him at the end of rope for miles every day. His hand crept to his throat, to the old scar there. He swallowed hard. Shut his eyes against the onslaught of memories. The feel of the coarse rope on his throat, the panic as his breath was stolen from him, the pain. Pain and more pain, unending pain at the hands of these people. A choking sound escaped him, and he turned back to face Mara.

Her gaze settled over him, pulling him apart from the inside out the way it always did. She saw his fear, his loneliness, his own self-loathing, more clearly than any other did. It was her power; to read people so thoroughly that they were nothing but an open book for her own study and amusement. And as her eyes wandered over him, taking in every secret he'd ever had, a smile spread across her face.

"Still so afraid, Aki? Karina did not lie. I have no plans to hurt you. I simply wish to talk."

Karina. Aki frowned at the name. He knew it. Remembered it in some dark recess of his mind. He looked past Mara, and it all came flooding back. Now that he could see her face, now that she was standing, slinking behind Mara, he knew her. He knew why she would not tell him her name. Anger battled against fear as she shrank away from his recognition.

"Karina," he spat out her name with all the distaste he'd accumulated years before.

"I am sorry, Aki," she sobbed it this time, shook her head and hid her face behind her hands. "I did not want to do it."

"Enough, Karina. It doesn't matter whether you wanted to or not. It only matters that you did." Mara shooed her away with her hand and swept across the room to the long meeting table that was the centerpiece of the room. "Come, Aki. Sit."

Aki came and he sat. Because he couldn't disobey Mara. It was as ingrained in him as walking, as much a part of his life as breathing. His heart was still thudding against his ribs as she sat opposite him.

"Leave us, Karina."

Karina nearly tripped over herself in her haste to leave them behind.

Aki fought the urge to squirm under her continued study. His hands, hidden from her view by the table, opened and closed and opened and closed, the repetition almost effective in steadying him. He opened his mouth to speak but remembered how Mara felt about slaves speaking out of turn. And then he remembered that he wasn't her slave anymore but decided he still didn't want to risk it.

That's when he noticed the portrait hanging on the wall over her head and he knew why the house was so familiar. He saw the seal etched on the wall beneath it and not even Mara's presence could override the icy fingers of realization that crawled up inside his mind.

It was a simple tree, devoid of leaves. Two letters intertwined within its branches - *HB*.

Chapter 37

SUNLIGHT GLINTED OFF THE BLUE stones as Desmond tossed the ring in the air and then caught it again. Up it went again, only to return to the palm of his hand.

"Your Highness, Atticus Wehr is here," an attendant stuck his head through the doorway to say.

"Show him in." Desmond swept his feet off the desk where he'd had them propped up and set the ring down on the newly emptied space. The door opened fully in front of him, and he waved the old man in. "Come in. Sit. There's something I need to speak with you about."

Atticus walked briskly despite his cane. He lowered himself into the empty chair. "I was wondering when you'd get around to questioning me."

Desmond let out a bemused laugh. "Why would you assume that?"

"Well, let's see, Your Highness, you've sent your captain to question Alina Turston, did you not? And to arrest Sasha Gundarson and bring him here for you to interrogate. It only makes sense that, as his instructor, you would also wish to question me."

"Yes, well. That's not exactly why I sent for you. Although, if you know anything about where Aki can be..."

"I do not. I have not seen him since the king sent him home for a week."

"And you wouldn't lie to me, would you?"

"I would not."

"My father trusted you greatly. I hope I can do the same."

"I trusted your father greatly. I hope you are worthy of the same trust," Atticus replied.

Anger flashed across Desmond's features, and he took a moment to leash it. He tapped the ring in front of him with a finger and then slid it across the desk. "What can you tell me of this?"

Atticus Wehr did not bother to conceal his expression. Shock, sorrow, and disappointment confused Desmond as he watched the old man. Atticus picked it up almost gently and rolled it between his fingers.

"Have you found him then?" he asked softly. "What have you done with him?"

"No, we haven't found him. Captain Tyrrel found that at Alina's. She insisted he left it behind when Colin brought him back," Desmond said. He noticed that Atticus was still turning the ring over in his hand. "You've seen it before, haven't you?"

Atticus nodded. "The ring. And that symbol. He never took it off, though. It surprises me that he left it behind."

"I'm quite certain he didn't do it by accident. Alina was lying about that. But never mind that. Where's the symbol from? Captain Tyrrel thought you might know. You've been around longer than any other couriers and you served in the great war."

"Your Highness," Atticus sighed, "this sign belongs to the now dead house of Bayner."

Desmond exhaled sharply and took the ring back from Atticus. The bare tree had the letters HB intertwined among its branches. House of Bayner. It made no sense. But then, neither did most of the other recent events. This was just another drop in the sea of confusion that Desmond was already drowning in. He looked up to find Atticus equally confused.

"It doesn't make sense," he was saying, echoing the words Desmond was thinking. "Perhaps he was mistaken."

"What? Who?"

"Aki told me it was his mother's. But if it belongs to the house of Bayner, it can't be. Lord Bayner died without an heir."

Unless he didn't. Desmond couldn't help but think of the letter, the incomplete letter, he'd found on his father's desk. A northern heir, it had promised, one with a much stronger claim to Dorsten.

"Perhaps he lied to you about it. Made it seem like its only value to him was in sentiment. Perhaps he carried it for some other purpose. It was given to him by one of the Aruuken leaders, or so Captain Tyrrel says."

Atticus was shaking his head before Desmond even finished speaking. "To him, it was his mother's. He believed that."

It made Desmond's head pound to think of it all. He opened the drawer at his side and pulled out the half of the letter that he had. So far, he'd shown it to no one but Captain Tyrrel, who would take its secret with him to the grave if Desmond told him to. He didn't know if he wanted to ever show it to anyone else. There was the wild hope that by keeping its news to himself, he could control it. He could quell any rumors of a rival before they even really began. But keeping secrets was a lonely business and Desmond wanted to share the knowledge and worry with someone.

Wordlessly, he passed it across to Atticus and got up to pace while the old man read it.

"What do you make of it?" he asked when Atticus set it down again.

"I don't see how it could possibly be true. The writer claims to know for a fact that such an heir exists. They claim there is unrest in Dorsten, which we have no way of knowing or not since no couriers aside from Aki have returned. They claim there have been skirmishes between Aruuk and Dorsten that have been unmet by the king. It all seems like a rather elaborate trap."

It was a relief to have someone come to the same conclusion as he himself had drawn after reading the letter.

"Except for one thing," Atticus continued, cutting Desmond's relief short.

"What's that?"

"The king is truly gone. Which means that this is not just a collaboration of idle threats meant to scare you."

"It was written to my father, not me. I found it among his things and there's at least a page missing, I'm sure."

"Ah, yes, it does seem to be unfinished. In fact, it seems as if the writer intends to reveal the identity of this long-lost heir. I wish the other half had not gone missing. It would have been quite enlightening to know."

It would have been more than just quite enlightening, Desmond thought. It would have given him some hint, some idea of where to go from here, some clue as to who he faced. All the letter did for him now was point him in the vague direction of north. Dorsten. The province that was one time the bitter enemy of Dival. And Aruuk, of course. Dorsten had made alliances with Aruuk in the past. Desmond had heard stories of the devastating battles that ensued for Dival. Thousands of men lost, whole armies sent reeling back to where they came from. Before their crushing defeat in the mountain pass, Aruuk had been a formidable opponent.

Slowly the pieces were coming together. Drawn into place by tidbits of information that continued to turn up. The letter, the ring, his father's disappearance, they were all connected. A web of conspiracy that he was trapped right in the middle of. And somewhere out there the spinner of this web continued to work, several steps ahead of him.

Atticus Wehr was too lost in his own thoughts to notice Desmond's prolonged silence. Desmond watched as the old man picked the ring back up and studied it. He must have felt Desmond's gaze on him because he looked up and smiled sadly.

"He was to be my last, you know. I've grown too old for all this, but I wanted to give him another chance. He was always stronger than he knew, and I thought, maybe, one day he would... Never mind. You've no time to listen to the sentimental ramblings of an old man, I'm sure."

Desmond wasn't sure what to say. Captain Tyrrel and he had argued about Aki more than once, but not because the captain cared at all for the courier. Atticus was the first person he'd spoken to who was truly a friend of Aki. Not counting Lars, of course. Desmond tried very hard not to think about Lars because it always made him angry.

"I don't mind," Desmond said with a rueful smile. "I'd rather listen to the ramblings of an old man than the complaints and criticisms of everyone else, I think."

"You're in a hard place, Your Highness. It is no easy thing to fill the place of one's father."

It was in such sharp contrast to the badgering and complaining and arguing that took place between him and everyone else that Desmond was caught off guard and he didn't know what to say for the second time in just a few moments. Atticus got to his feet.

"If you trust me enough, Your Highness, I would like to be the one who holds onto this," Atticus said, holding the ring out between them.

"Of course. And, if you learn of anything that might help us understand, you will come straight to me?"

"You have my word."

If he'd had his way Desmond would have remained alone the rest of the afternoon. There had been people clamoring for his attention constantly for days now and solitude was a rare commodity. He wondered how his father ever tolerated it. Desmond just lost his temper. He'd even taken to avoiding Tristan, snatching up the few moments of peace and quiet that he could at every chance. But as he sat with his head once more in his hands, soft footsteps crossed the room.

"Just wait outside. I'll speak with you in a moment," he said, not raising his head.

"Unfortunately, this is my home as much as it is yours."

"Oh, it's you, Lotte."

"Yes, just me." She drew up a chair beside him.

"How's Mother?"

"As well as she can be, under the circumstances. You know, rather than asking me every time you see me, you could just go see her yourself. She's almost as worried about you as she is about Father."

Desmond shook his head. "It never ends, Lotte. There's always someone waiting to see me. I don't know how Father ever learned to put up with it."

Charlotte didn't say anything. She looked over the desk and plucked up the letter that was lying there. Desmond opened his mouth to tell her not to, but realized it was useless. Charlotte would read it just to spite him, then. A few moments of perusal and she set it down again.

"Father kept secrets, you know," she commented.

"What's that supposed to mean?"

Charlotte pursed her lips, carefully considering her words before she answered. "I mean that, I think there's a story behind this letter. Doesn't it seem awfully personal to you? Like whoever wrote it knew him."

"I hadn't really thought of that. But it does."

"The question then would be who."

Turning over every memory, every story he'd ever heard, in his mind, Desmond couldn't think of anyone. He rubbed a tired hand over his face and leaned back with a groan.

"It's hopeless. Whoever this is has clearly been planning their move for ages and I can barely keep my head above water, so to speak."

He looked to his sister when she made no answer and saw at once that she wanted to say something he wouldn't want to hear. Her lips were pressed into a thin line and her eyebrows were drawn together as if in a scowl. He knew the look well. Whatever came out of her mouth next wasn't going to be pleasant.

"I don't envy you your place, Des. But you can't make everyone your enemy and you can't listen only to those who say what you want to hear. The entire purpose of the council is to bring balance to the king's power."

"And what would you know about it?" he scoffed.

"I may never be a king, Desmond," she answered coolly, "but that doesn't mean I don't understand these things. And I understand that a king has absolute power until he doesn't." He started to shake his head, but she wasn't finished yet. "You need friends, Des. You need allies. You need people on your side. Even the ones who think a bit differently than you."

His mind went immediately back to the cold mountainside where Lars had said the same in so many words. Then Captain Tyrrel had echoed the sentiment months later in the Dorstenian castle. And what had he done with their words? He'd turned around and lied to save his own reputation. He'd made an enemy. One who wasn't likely to forget.

Aki might have had a hand in the king's disappearance, but Desmond had given him a reason to be.

Chapter 38

IT COULD NOT BE.

Of all the people in the world, why did it have to be him?

Aki's attention was so riveted on what he saw on the wall that he did not notice anything else.

"Fascinating, isn't it?" Mara's voice broke into his thoughts. "Finally seeing all the pieces coming together."

He tore his eyes away from the portrait and the symbol beneath it.

"For years it bothered me - Gundar's insistence on keeping you alive. It certainly wasn't because he felt honor bound to keep a promise to a slave girl. And you were never worth enough as a slave to justify it. It simply made no sense. Until just a few months ago."

She was up, gliding back and forth on the far side of the table. Stopping in front of the portrait, she turned to examine it. With her back now to him, Aki released his breath slowly, trying to collect the scattered remnants of his mind.

"You seemed to recognize this just a few moments ago?" Mara faced him again, her eyes expectant.

She wanted him to answer and, reluctant as he was, Aki felt her unspoken demand dragging the words from him. "I've been here."

"Go on."

"It's Lord Bayner's estate, isn't it?"

"Yes. Or it was Lord Bayner's," she said, running a finger across the portrait that wiped away a line of dust and revealed the vibrancy of the colors beneath it. She brushed away the dust in disgust and waved at Aki to keep going.

"We stayed here, when Gundar brought Lars and I with him to find Sasha."

"Yes, yes. To search for Sasha. Tell me, Aki," she turned to him, her dark eyes strangely wild with delight, "did Gundar have any other plans then?"

Aki recoiled a little from the change that had come over Mara. There was excitement dancing across her face, a smile that was all the more cruel for its sincerity. She was thoroughly enjoying whatever revelation she was about to bring into his life. And he'd never liked anything that Mara enjoyed.

"No," he answered in a small voice.

"Oh, but he did. Such big plans. And Lord Bayner at the very heart of those plans. I'd say it's a pity Sasha killed the two of them, but really it only means that I have the opportunity to succeed where they failed."

"Boris killed Gundar," he corrected, not thinking, and winced as her hand raked across his face. He brought his own hand up over the spot, covering it, and glared at her.

"You know better," was all she needed to say. "You have the ring with you?"

He shook his head.

"What? Karina told me you wore it always."

"Karina lied. I lost it." He told her the same story he'd told Ritter, silently thanking whatever voice in his head had whispered to him to leave the ring behind with Alina that night. If he'd known the significance of that trinket, he would likely have buried it in a hole in the ground deep in the forest where no one would ever find it.

Mara's eyes narrowed and her lips drew together in a disapproving frown. Minutes went by as she stared at him, trying to read the truth in his words or detect the lie. Aki lowered his head the way he always had when she looked him over like that.

"Well, I suppose we'll make do without it. At least I still have the letters."

He wanted to ask but his stinging face reminded him of why he shouldn't. His head still down, he heard a chair scrape against the floor as she pulled it out and sat on it. A warm hand touched his face and lifted it up and Aki swallowed back the revulsion that always came from her touch. Gentle, and yet so violating, a corruption of anything and everything good. He didn't fear it so much as he hated it, hated the way it turned him into nothing but a plaything for her amusement.

"Come now, Aki, for once we are on the same side," she said softly. "Have you not guessed it already?"

"Guessed what?" he managed to choke out, fighting against the burning desire to retreat as far from her as he could get.

"Gundar did not keep you alive because of a promise he made. He kept you alive because he needed you. He needed your birthright." She leaned back again, and Aki let out a shuddering breath. "It took me so long to figure it out. In fact, it was not until last summer that I came across the letters between him and Lord Bayner."

"My birthright?"

Aki looked past her, at the symbol on the wall and the stern, thin face of the man painted above it. He remembered why the symbol looked familiar to him before. He'd seen it and not just here when he stayed with Gundar and Lars.

It had been only a few days after he'd returned to Stephan's at the end of his sentence. Hamo had come across him that day, sitting behind Stephan's barn, his sleeve rolled up as he scratched Dagmar's name into his arm. Aki hadn't been quick enough to cover the brands when he heard Hamo approach. The man hadn't said anything right away. He'd just sat down beside Aki and showed him the brand on his own arm.

"They're just marks," Hamo had said at last.

"So are letters, but they still mean something."

"True. But they don't change who you are. Are you alright?"

Aki had shrugged. "Stephan doesn't understand."

He'd expected to receive a lecture about how Stephan understood more than he thought he did. Instead, Hamo had laughed. "No. Stephan definitely doesn't understand," he'd said. "But it will get better, Aki."

That was where he'd seen the symbol. Burned into Hamo's arm just like the ones on his own.

"Yes, your birthright." Mara paused and seemed to be waiting for him to make some connection, to come to some conclusion. Aki shook his head to show he didn't understand, and Mara sighed. "The old king of Dorsten died childless. The throne was passed to his closest advisor and the most powerful nobleman in the kingdom. Lord Bayner. In theory, rule was to be passed down to his descendants."

"He didn't have any," Aki murmured. Master Wehr had taught him this part of their history. How Lord Bayner was deposed after Aruuk's defeat in the mountain, how he'd left no living heir behind and so the people of Dorsten had agreed to a union with Dival, making King Darien their king as well.

Mara gave a bitter laugh and his head snapped up. All the excitement from a few moments ago was gone now and in its place was a pain so raw that Aki almost pitied her. Almost.

"Oh, he had one. Her people forgot about her just as my people forgot about me. Look around this place, Aki. Whose room do you think you slept in last night? Lord Bayner incurred Gundar's wrath when he failed to deliver a group of slaves to him that he'd promised. In an attempt to appease him, he offered his only daughter in marriage to the Chief."

Aki thought about the portrait they'd seen last night, tucked away in a storage room and covered in dust. He thought about the way she'd looked, smiling and carefree. Happy, Karina had called her. It made him ache a little to think of what she must have gone through in Aruuk, to think of how little she had to smile about there. Chief Gundar's wives were better than slaves, but not much. Unless, of course, they were the favorite one, like Mara had been for most of the time he'd known her.

"He never made her his wife," Mara continued and jolted Aki out of his reverie. "He was still too furious with Lord Bayner when she arrived. He declared her a slave and put her in with the others. I don't believe he wasted another thought on her after that until Anton did something that pleased him particularly well."

At the name of his father, Aki froze, and his stomach turned. Mara noted the change in him and gave him a knowing smile.

"Yes, she was Anton's slave girl. Your mother."

"My mother," Aki whispered. He raised his eyes again to the face of the man on the wall, the man Sasha had killed. He was the grandson of that man. A bloodthirsty tyrant on one side and a corrupt, conniving nobleman on the other. "What was her name?"

"It's not important," Mara said. She got up now and came around to his side of the table. "What's important is that I finally know why Gundar wouldn't end your life. He never just had one plan. Never. He wanted to take Dorsten by force, but he knew he might be defeated. You were his second plan. A puppet heir. And one with blood ties to the royal family of Dival."

"What?" Aki's head was already swimming.

"Oh, he didn't tell you, did he? My dear, foolish brother. Thought he could keep you safe by keeping you ignorant." She sat down in the chair right next to him. Refusing to turn and look at her, he picked at an invisible speck of dirt on his trousers. "We're on the same side here, Aki. Those people in Dival don't want you. Prince Desmond despises and hunts you down. When disaster struck, you were the first one they blamed. You have no place to go. No one left you can turn to. You came running here because you wanted answers."

"What do you want, Mara?" he asked miserably.

Her next words rattled him to his core. "I want you to join me. I want you to serve me."

"You don't own me anymore."

"But I don't need to. I am offering everything you ever wanted," she said softly, grabbing his hand in hers. He kept his hand limp. "I can make you ruler of these lands. All you have to do is serve me. It's already yours by birthright - all of this," she gestured to the estate around them, "is yours by birth. We can help each other."

Before she was done speaking, he was pulling away, shaking his head. He started to his feet, but hands shoved him back into the chair. He'd forgotten all about Sebastian.

"Let him go, Sebastian," Mara said. "It doesn't matter if he runs now. He'll come back to me."

"No. No, I won't. I don't want to have anything to do with your plans. I just want..."

"To go home? You can't. My spies have already told me all about what happened in Bren. You have a price on your head. Besides, I've already informed the young prince of his rival. He fears the threat you bring to his rule."

"But I don't," Aki cried. "I don't want to rule anything."

"It's a pity Prince Desmond won't see it that way. I've made sure it's your name he hears, and he'll execute you the first chance he gets. They've always prided themselves on being so much better than Aruuk, but they won't let a rival live, either." She got up and started walking out of the room. When she had reached the doorway, she turned around, a small leather-bound book in her hand. "Besides, what you desire most is to learn more of your mother. And I have her journal right here. You will come back to me, Aki. When you realize just how cruel the rest of the world is, you'll come back to me."

Chapter 39

MARA DIDN'T LEAVE. Aki sat, frozen, for what felt like hours and still she didn't leave. But she didn't come back in the room either. Voices drifted in from another part of the house, but Aki made no effort to hear them. His weapons lay on the table in front of him where Sebastian had returned them. He couldn't even find the strength to put them on. A fog had settled over him and he couldn't find his way out of it.

Outside, the sun climbed steadily and still he hadn't moved. All his recent hunger and exhaustion were forgotten in the haze of Mara's revelation. From time to time, he was aware of being watched but he couldn't bring himself to care enough to find out by whom. He suspected it was Karina, only because he'd caught the sound of Mara and Halle's voices coming from a different room and subtlety wasn't exactly Sebastian's way. He stared and stared at the face of his grandfather, not sure what he was looking for but sure that he wasn't finding it. It was a cold painting of the man, meant to show his power and nothing more.

Sasha hated Lord Bayner. Hamo hated Lord Bayner. Everyone Aki knew hated Lord Bayner. And he was Lord Bayner's own grandson, the heir to his house and estate, and, according to Mara, the heir to his power.

Aki shook his head even though there was no one there to see his silent denial. He had to go on. Somehow, he had to get himself up out of this chair and move on. There was a promise he had not yet fulfilled. A task yet unfinished.

He picked up the first knife off the table and slid it into its sheath on his belt. Then he grabbed the second one and slid it in its place on his thigh. He did the same for two more knives. His long sword came next. And last of all he picked up his father's, ran a finger down the blade that he kept razor sharp, and slid it into its scabbard with a soft thud.

Without making a sound, he got to his feet. His footsteps were light as he crossed the floor, testing each board before putting any weight on it. Mara might have said to let him go, but Aki did not trust Mara. He made his way to a door in the back of the room and found himself in a kitchen. Here, at last, he remembered his hunger. The kitchen, however, was barren and had been for a long time. Mice scurried out of his way in indignant haste as he hurried through to a back door put in place for servants to bring goods into the house without interrupting the business of the house. It led out behind the sprawling house with a path straight to the stables.

He was halfway through saddling Sky when he realized he wasn't alone anymore. In one motion, he had his short sword free and had spun around to face who he could only assume was Sebastian sent to retrieve him. The sword was arcing through the air before he realized it was Karina. She threw her hands up and let out a frightened cry. Aki stopped his weapon mid swing.

"If she expects me to come back just because you ask me, she's wrong," he said, sheathing the sword again.

"She did not send me."

"Then go. Get out."

Karina wrung her hands and blinked back tears, but she didn't move.

"I said get out. I don't want to see you," Aki half yelled.

"I am sorry, Aki. I did not want to do it. I was not supposed to run into you."

"Well, I wish I would have known that. I could have just kept riding and left you to those men. Next time, I will." He pulled the girth tight and led Sky toward the door.

"Why do you hate me so much?"

He stopped walking. "Why do you think, Karina? You just betrayed me to her. You were a part of all of this. For all I know, you are the one who stuck that letter in my bag."

"But you have always hated me."

Which was true. He always had. From the first time he really met her, he'd disliked her. She had been Gundar's gift to Mara, given around the same time that Aki was assigned to her for work. Aki had never understood what Mara was so furious about, but Gundar gave her Karina to pacify that anger and from that day forward, Karina had been Mara's pet, her favorite. Although she was only five, she never slept in the slave children's quarters again. Mara kept her in her own rooms every night, sparing her from suffering the vices of the many men who came and went in the Chief's house.

Aki hadn't been so fortunate. He'd caught Cadoc's eye and learned firsthand the depth of that man's debauched passions. The first night, he hadn't known what was happening until Cadoc had him stripped and lying on Cadoc's bed. The second, he'd lingered in Mara's rooms until she'd grown annoyed with him and ordered him gone. That's when he'd asked her. Begged her to let him stay with her for just one night.

She had laughed and said, "But I don't need you. I already have Karina."

"Please?" he had dared to ask a second time.

She'd hit him. Hard. Hit him three times and then she'd knelt and cupped his face in her suddenly gentle hands. "I cannot protect you, boy, not from what Gundar has already agreed to. He will only allow me one, and it must be Karina." And with that, she'd sent him into Cadoc's waiting arms. He'd never asked again. He'd suffered, night after night, while Karina remained safe.

None of that fit into words that he would ever speak. Rather than answer Karina's question, he mounted Sky and spurred her into a run.

Wind tore past him as the horse galloped beneath him, carrying him farther and farther away from Lord Bayner's deserted estate. He didn't know where he was going. It didn't really matter. He just had to get away. After days and days of dragging Halle and Karina with him, holding himself to a pace they could manage, the freedom of being alone grew and swelled inside him. The mountains grew closer, the familiar strength and silence of them calling to him for once. These mountains were still part of Dorsten. He could get lost in them forever and live a life far away from the schemes of everyone else.

When the ground began sloping upward to meet the mountains, Aki slowed down. He twisted around but Lord Bayner's estate was no longer in sight. For one moment, he allowed himself to relax. He was free. More free than he had ever been in his life. No one knew of his promise to hold him to it and Aki was ready to throw it away in exchange for this newfound freedom.

A cloud of dust was moving towards him and the moment was gone. He had nothing left but that promise. To keep it was his only way home. To keep it, he knew where he had to go, although he dreaded it more than anything in the world.

The cloud of dust got bigger, and Aki turned Sky around to watch its approach. It was close enough now that he could see the horse and rider that caused it. Even though the rider's face was obscured by distance, Aki was pretty sure he knew who it was. Mara would never really let him go. She might lengthen the leash, but there was always a leash. And she was always the one holding it.

Sebastian stopped a safe distance from him and for a time they just stared at one another. Finally, Aki shook his head. "I'm not coming back. We're not on the same side, no matter what she says."

"She didn't send me to bring you back."

"Oh?"

"She sent me to keep you alive."

Aki cocked his head and smiled at the strangeness of it all. "Considering that she ordered me executed almost two years ago, I'm not sure I really believe that."

"That was before she knew who you were. It serves her purpose now to keep you alive."

"How convenient, then, that I didn't die when she wanted me to. You can go back to her and tell her that I've managed better without her help than with it."

"You know I cannot."

Aki shrugged. He didn't really expect Sebastian to disobey Mara. He was one of her most trusted overseers for a reason, after all. Aki touched his throat at the thought and swallowed, remembering the feel of the rough rope against his skin, the way it rubbed and chafed with every step Sebastian had dragged from him. Sending Sebastian after him was exactly the sort of thing Mara would think of. He wasn't there just to keep Aki alive; he was there to remind him of just how low she could bring Aki through him.

A spark of irritation took hold of him, and Aki started moving forward again. If Sebastian's orders were simply to remain with him and make sure he stayed alive, Aki could spend the rest of the summer wandering aimlessly around the mountains. Sebastian was content to follow him at a distance.

When night came and Aki was forced to stop, Sebastian continued to maintain that distance. He was as aloof as a protector as he had been as an overseer, but Aki couldn't complain. Without the burden of carrying on a conversation with the man, he was left with more than enough time and silence to sort through his turbulent thoughts.

He replayed everything Mara had said. Although he wanted to deny the truth of her tale, some voice in his head whispered that she did not lie. He thought about the journal, the journal Karina must have taken to Mara when she left him and Halle the night before.

With a pang of regret, Aki realized Mara was right. There was nothing in the world he wanted more than to see what was written in that journal. To read the words of his mother and know her in even that small way. Knowing that it was there, beyond his reach but there, tore him open on the inside and made him ache. Staring into the flames of the fire he'd built as darkness shut everything else out, it was all he could think about.

Branches snapped and broke as Sebastian approached from the darkness beyond Aki's fire. Without turning his head, Aki slid a hand to his knife.

"What do you want?"

"I brought food," Sebastian answered.

Aki's grip on his knife relaxed. He turned to watch Sebastian come forward and sit down, careful to keep the fire between him and Aki.

"You are hungry, aren't you? You left in such a hurry that you didn't take anything with you."

"I left Bren in that big of a hurry too and I've managed to survive this long."

Sebastian shifted, moving a little further back, well out of Aki's reach. Aki raised a questioning eyebrow but didn't comment. He caught the bundle Sebastian tossed over the flames. As much as he wanted to refuse, he hadn't eaten all day and he hadn't taken the time to hunt for anything on his way up. He was hungry.

Aki was in no hurry to go to sleep with Sebastian sitting right across from him. Sebastian seemed just as reluctant. As the fire slowly died between them, Sebastian had moved even further back and watched Aki's every move as if he were waiting for something. It dawned on Aki that there was a look of apprehension in the man's eyes.

"Are you worried about something?" he finally asked over the dying embers of the fire.

Sebastian frowned at the question. His gaze wandered over Aki and lingered on the weapons he carried and that's when Aki realized it. Sebastian was unarmed. The man was no soldier. He was used to overseeing unarmed slaves.

"You're afraid I might kill you?"

"Halle seemed to think it likely. You have reason to want me dead."

Aki shook his head but took his time considering before answering. There was a grim laugh in his voice. "You know, despite everything you did to me, you weren't the worst overseer I ever had. There're a few people who come a little higher on my list of ones I hate."

"I'm not sure that reassures me. No one else on that list happens to be around."

Shrugging, Aki lay back, staring up at the stars. There was a part of him that wondered if Sebastian's worries were closer to the truth than he wanted to admit.

Chapter 40

D UST, BLOOD, AND GRIME COATED the rider who entered Bren in the early hours just before dawn. Few were awake to see his arrival as his weary horse plodded through the streets, its head drooping with each step it took. He rode straight up the road to the gate of the castle where the guards accosted him, and a flurry of activity greeted his arrival. A stable hand led his horse away. An attendant was sent racing to the prince's room.

Not a night had passed since his father's disappearance that Desmond had been able to sleep uninterrupted. Tonight was no different. A fist pounded on his door, rattling it against its frame. Desmond lingered beneath his blankets for a few seconds, savoring the comfort of being alone. When a second set of footsteps came marching down the hall, he knew he could delay no longer. He recognized the steps as belonging to Captain Tyrrel. As he dressed, he tried to guess what news they might be waiting to deliver to him. It was a dying hope that they had found Aki. There'd been no word or sign of him since that night.

"I hope this is news that couldn't wait until the morning," he said as soon as the door was cracked open enough for him to see them waiting in the hallway.

"Your Highness, one of the couriers has returned."

"What? Where is he? What news did he bring? Take me to him at once. I want to see him immediately."

Desmond tried to read the gravity of the courier's news by the rigid posture of Captain Tyrrel as he led the way down the hallway. There was little to be discerned there, though. Captain Tyrrel looked just about the same as he always did.

"He's waiting in here, Your Highness," Captain Tyrrel stepped aside to let Desmond through the door.

"Have you already heard what he's had to say?"

"Only some."

"Then come in with me," Desmond said, trying hard to keep the plea out of his voice. He needed the captain's steadiness, and he hated that he did.

Inside the room, Desmond couldn't conceal his shock at the courier's appearance. His skin was barely visible beneath the layer of dust and blood that had dried to it. His clothes were torn in several places and reddish-brown stains corresponded with the tears. He was slumped in a chair near the fire, his legs sprawled out before him. Someone had already thought to bring food and drink for him.

"What happened?" Desmond asked.

"We were attacked. On the road. Half a dozen men, maybe more. We didn't stand a chance."

Desmond glanced at Captain Tyrrel. The captain's lips pressed together, and he drew in a sharp breath. Desmond turned back to the courier, whose head was falling forward, his chin resting on his chest. There was a letter held loosely in the man's hand and Desmond reached forward to pull it out. The action roused the man.

"Your Highness, I saw them. They're burning towns. The north's in chaos. They only kept me alive to send that to you," the man said, waving a feeble hand in the direction of the letter now in Desmond's. "They wanted you to know what they're doing. They're trying to draw you out."

Desmond's insides turned to ice at the man's words. He stared down at the sealed letter in his hands. Afraid to open it. Afraid not to. The seal, stamped in blood red wax, was a wolf's head. He'd never seen it before. As he stared at it, Desmond realized the letter was trembling in his hand. No, that wasn't quite right. His hand was trembling holding the letter.

"Your Highness?" Captain Tyrrel's voice reached out to him. "We need to know what it says."

"Yes. Yes, I'm getting to it."

"If you'd like…"

Desmond broke open the seal before he could change his mind. It was a single page, written in the flowing hand of whoever had written his father first. His fingers clutched the paper tighter and tighter the more he read, until it was crumpling in his grasp. In the silence that surrounded him, he could almost believe his heart had stopped altogether. Even when he'd reached the end, he continued to stare at the words now swimming before him.

"Your Highness?" Captain Tyrrel said.

He couldn't repeat what the letter said. Not out loud. The words were too much. He handed it over to the captain and groped his way on wobbling knees to a chair, sure that his face was bloodless.

"It can't be. It can't be," he murmured over and over.

The door to the room slammed open and Baron Orlander stood framed inside the doorway. Anguish and hope fought against each other on his face as he saw the courier.

"Where is he? Where's Felix?"

The courier shielded his eyes with a hand. Baron Orlander was across the room before Desmond had fully registered what he was asking. He caught hold of the front of the courier and shook him.

"Where is he? What have those animals done to my son?"

Then Desmond realized what the baron sought. His son, his youngest, was among the couriers missing. And the man in front of him could only have been his instructor.

"Dead. He's dead," the courier answered, his voice cracking. He turned away from them, his shoulders shaking and his hands hiding his face from their eyes.

Desmond looked away, ashamed for the man. Baron Orlander, his face frozen in despair, stepped in front of him.

"Call up the army. You must call up the army."

Desmond nodded, unable to form a sentence. He ought to say something. Ought to offer some words of comfort and solace. It's what his father would do. But Desmond was not his father and the difference had never been more glaring than it was now. Instead of comfort, Desmond wanted to offer the baron his own anger. It was flooding him, drowning him.

Captain Tyrrel cleared his throat and both Desmond and Baron Orlander turned their attention to him. He held the letter up.

"We need to talk about this. Now."

None of the council members had left since the king's disappearance. Every day they met, anxious for word of the king. Now, Desmond stood in front of them, the sky still dark outside the windows, prepared to give them just that.

"You will please do the honor of reading this aloud for us," he said, handing the letter to Gregory.

Gregory was slow to his feet, his eyes scanning the page he had not yet seen. When he held out a hand for silence, it was unnecessary. Not a sound could be heard in the room. There was a collective holding of breath as Gregory's voice intoned the words of their enemy.

"To my dear nephew and prince, Desmond," he ran his tongue over his lips before continuing. "You, no doubt, have many questions that you seek the answers to. Chief among them, I'm sure, is the question of your father's departure. Never fear. He is alive, for now.

"There are many things I wish to explain to you in person and I'm sure we will meet someday very soon. One piece of information cannot wait until that day, though. Two pieces, really. The first is that the unrest I warned your father, my brother, of several months ago is both real and growing. The people of the northern province have waited long enough for the aid of their southern king and have found his care to be wanting.

"Which brings me to my last bit of news. Dorsten fell under the control of my brother, Darien, when it was claimed that there was no living heir of Lord Bayner's to take his place when he was deposed. That claim is no longer recognized as true. I have presented to the people of Dorsten an heir. One who not only is a direct descendant of Lord Bayner himself, but who shares the blood of your own royal family. Aki Gundarson, known to you by the name Turston, is that heir. His relation to the late Chief Gundar of Aruuk makes him ideal in facing this new threat from Aruuk, which my brother seemed wholly inadequate to do.

"We shall meet again soon, my nephew, although I doubt very much that your father will survive until that meeting."

Gregory sat down in the hush that followed his reading. Even though Desmond knew exactly what the letter said, its words still felt like a punch.

"Who wrote it? Is there any name signed to it?"

"Mara," Gregory answered, "just Mara."

"Who knew that my father had a sister? Did anyone or is this just some story to drag us into a trap?" Desmond demanded when he'd had the chance to collect his thoughts.

For a long moment, no one answered him. It was the eldest councilman, a white-haired man by the name of Rainier, who finally stood to answer. "Your Highness, King Darien did indeed have a sister. And her name was Mara. It was believed she died many years ago of a fever that killed many in Bren. It seems inconceivable that she not only still lives but has remained in hiding from her own countrymen since that time."

"But it is possible? She did, at one time, exist?"

"She did, Your Highness. Mention of her is likely to be found in the royal archives and records. She was several years younger than your father, but she lived here in Bren until her sixteenth year."

"Thank you," Desmond said.

"Your Highness, you must call up the army," Baron Orlander spoke up. His face was shadowed with grief and anger, his eyes bloodshot, but there wasn't the slightest hesitation or catch in his voice as he spoke. "This letter as good as declares war on us. She's threatening to overturn your rule with Aki Turston at her side."

"It's not my rule."

"Your Highness, it's as good as yours. Your father is clearly held by this woman, his own sister apparently. We cannot waste time hoping she has a change of heart and returns him. The traitor made it all the way north. No doubt, he had her protection. With him and his claim, she can start a full-scale rebellion."

"It still takes the vote of the council," Desmond pointed out. All he wanted at the moment was to disappear himself, to run away and never come back.

"I'm sure the council will support any decision you make," Gregory said. "They've killed enough of our people. It's time to end this, Your Highness. Anyone who says otherwise is just as much of a traitor as Aki Turston, in my opinion."

There were a few looks of dark suspicion that traveled around the room, most coming to rest eventually on Hamo. Desmond could see that he was going to say something. He'd avoided the man as much as was possible since he'd had Sasha arrested but he couldn't very well leave the room now.

"You should call up the army, Your Highness. But you should also find out whether or not this is a trap. Her letter seems very intent on drawing us out into the open. We would be fools to walk right into it. We would also be fools to believe everything she says."

"Please tell me you are not trying to defend the traitor," Baron Orlander said, heat in his face.

"Not at all. Despite my personal feelings toward him, everything does, in fact, point to his direct involvement. But where's the proof that he is what she says he is? As far as we know, Lord Bayner died childless. She has given us no reason to trust her."

But there was that ring, Desmond thought. The ring that belonged to the house of Bayner. Aki had claimed it was his mother's. Atticus Wehr believed him. Desmond did not. How easy it would be for someone to get a hold of such a trinket and use it to claim power and prestige that they had no right to. And Aki was nothing if not very skilled at hiding the truth.

There was no dissent in the vote. Desmond had never witnessed such a thing and it was a little terrifying. After that, orders flew around the castle and beyond.

It would take two weeks, at least, to gather the army. That's what Captain Tyrrel told Desmond when the prince, his impatience swelling with every passing day, demanded to know why they hadn't marched yet.

However, it was three full weeks before Captain Tyrrel approached him to say that all was ready. Despite the captain's protest, Desmond's horse was ready and waiting in the courtyard with the rest of the guards' that day.

They rode for the old border, just on the edge of the Void, where the rest of the army was assembled. Desmond's breath caught in his throat at the sight of the fully gathered army. Never had he seen the full might of the Divalian army in one place.

Baron Orlander was there, riding out to greet them as they drew close. News of his son's death still left a heavy mark on the man. The expression on his face reminded Desmond a bit of the one on his own mother's. He'd visited her in her rooms only hours before he'd set out. The same lost look haunted her eyes the same as the eyes of the baron. Desmond thought of his promise to her. A foolish, hopeful promise. A promise that he would find his father and bring him home.

"We've set up a tent for you for the night, Your Highness. We plan to move first thing in the morning," the baron explained as they rode through the men. Desmond cast a somewhat longing look in the direction of the old border fort nearby. Baron Orlander noticed. "We would've turned it into quarters for you, but it's housing the Aruuken men you ordered rounded up right now."

"Of course." Desmond nodded, remembering. A wise move on his part, he thought. There was no telling how many more incidents the act had spared them from, no telling how many of those locked away were in league with their enemies.

"I've sent a scouting party out into the Void to see if they can find any sign of the men who have been working in there to keep the road closed."

"Very good. When do you expect them to return?"

"By tonight."

Desmond tried to make himself comfortable inside his tent that night. He knew it was far more luxurious than what anyone else had, but that could take away the fact that he was sleeping on the ground with only a thin wall of cloth to separate him from the outdoors.

He tossed and turned for some time, kept awake by more than just his discomfort. The men Baron Orlander had sent ahead hadn't returned yet. Eventually, none of that was enough to keep him awake.

It was with heavy, sleep laden eyes that he greeted the next morning. Dew left him and everything else in the tent with him damp. But he quickly forgot about it when Captain Tyrrel stuck his head inside the tent flap, his face grim with news.

"You need to come out here now."

Desmond was still rubbing his eyes when he followed Captain Tyrrel out. Baron Orlander was already there and several other men, all gathered around something on the ground. Desmond stepped closer then clamped a hand over his mouth to keep from being ill. Lying on the ground was a man - or what was left of a man, anyway. To Desmond's horror, the man was still alive. A doctor bent over him but even Desmond, with his inexperience, knew the man's efforts were wasted.

"He's the only one who came back. Dragged in by his horse," Baron Orlander said quietly.

"Who did this to you?" Captain Tyrrel knelt on the ground beside him.

"Aruukens," the man croaked out.

"Not Dorstenians?"

"They fight together."

"That's not possible," Desmond said his thoughts aloud. "Aruuk was burning through Dorsten. Why do they fight together now?"

"They said, their lost heir unites them."

Desmond grabbed his head between his hands as he walked away. It was too much. Too much to wrap his mind around. Aki wasn't the kind of person to unite anyone. At least, not the Aki that Desmond had met. But perhaps that was all an act too. Another part of the ruse that bought him enough trust to infiltrate.

Desmond remembered again the night in Illsen, the night everyone insisted could not have been an act on Aki's part. They were wrong. Clearly, everyone was wrong about that. Captain Tyrrel claimed Cadoc meant to harm Aki, but what if he was the only Aruuken who stood in Aki's way? A burning flame of hatred kindled inside him, feeding wildly on all that had gone wrong in these last months.

He stopped walking. The old border fort stood just in front of him. Inside it were men who no longer belonged in Dival. How many of them were conspirators? How many of them were part of this plan to bring Dival to her knees?

"Your Highness, we must prepare to move," Captain Tyrrel said, coming up behind him.

Desmond turned to find both him and Baron Orlander standing there, waiting. Waiting for him to give an order, make a move. He looked back at the wooden fort, its walls too high for him to see inside.

"Bring one of them out here," he said quietly. "I don't care who, just bring one of them to me."

"Your Highness, whatever you're thinking...," Captain Tyrrel started to say after he'd sent two men off to obey the prince's command.

"Whatever I'm thinking? You have no idea what I'm thinking. But I'll explain it to you. We are preparing to march across the Void and face our enemies. I will not leave our homes at risk while we are gone."

He stopped speaking when the two men returned, leading a third between them. Desmond looked the third one over, pleased to see the fear that was already forming in the young man's eyes.

"Now, Captain, have your men set fire to the fort."

"What?"

"I said, fire the fort, Captain. Burn it. I want it destroyed."

"You cannot..."

"You obey me," Desmond yelled. "I give the commands here, not you. And I said to burn it. Now burn it."

It wasn't the captain that followed his orders. It was Baron Orlander. It was the soldiers the baron commanded. Desmond watched as torches were brought. He watched as the flames sputtered and smoked and then caught on the dry wood. He watched as they climbed higher, licking the walls with orange tongues. He watched as the cries of those inside began.

"Shoot down any who try to escape," he turned to Baron Orlander and ordered. "And bring me a horse."

When a horse stood ready beside him, he faced the Aruuken still standing between two of his soldiers. The young man's face was white, his eyes riveted to the macabre scene before them.

"You will ride north, and you will tell your people what has happened here. Tell them this is what will happen to all our enemies. Every ambush, every attack will be met with retaliation such as this. You will find Aki Turston or Gundarson or whatever name he is going by right now and you will tell him that this is what he can expect from me and if he wishes to spare any of his people, he will turn himself over to us immediately. Do you think you can manage that?"

The man, mute with horror, simply stared in anguish at the inferno. He made no sign that he'd even heard the prince speak. But when he was shoved toward the horse and made to mount it, he turned at last to Desmond and spoke, "I will never forget what you've done today."

Which was exactly what Desmond intended.

Chapter 41

THE TOWN IN FRONT OF HIM was bigger than most they'd seen in the last three weeks. Silence hung over most of the empty streets as Aki guided Sky through them. Some of the towns they'd passed through had been burnt specters of the turmoil that gripped the land. He half expected this town to be the same but as they rode through the eerie quiet it was broken every now and then by the sound of a distant voice.

The voice became distinct as they approached the center of the town. A crowd had gathered there in the large open space that usually housed the open-air market. Their backs were to Aki and Sebastian as they came near. Standing on the back of a wagon so that he was well above the crowd, a man was speaking.

Aki dismounted and left Sky standing in a side street, mostly hidden from view. Sebastian did the same without question.

In the last three weeks, Aki had found himself rather impressed by the man's almost unlimited patience and composure. He couldn't help but admire it a little, really. Aki had gone out of his way to choose the most circuitous routes from one town to the next so that most of their time was wasted in aimless wandering. At no time did Aki give any hint as to where he was going or why. Yet, Sebastian never complained. He never questioned. He just tagged along behind him, speaking rarely and usually only when Aki spoke first.

Three weeks, and Aki had pieced together a slightly more coherent picture of what Mara was doing. He'd seen firsthand the chaos she'd unleashed on the unsuspecting towns and villages that dotted the countryside. The land was rife with rumors ranging from the reasonable to the unbelievable. But one rumor had cropped up with growing frequency and belief. Word was spreading of a possible heir, an alternative to the Divalian crown and a bridge between Dorsten and Aruuk.

"Do you know what they call us over there?" The man on the wagon bed gestured toward the south, his voice carrying well over the crowd. "They call us the paupers province. We're nothing but dirt beneath their feet. The only reason they wanted a union between us was so that they could use our land and our lives for a barrier between them and Aruuk."

Aki slouched against a building, blending in with the rest of those assembled. Mara had done a thorough job cultivating these people, he realized. She'd turned her power into reading whole nations and using that knowledge to stir up their anger.

It didn't matter that Aruuken raiders had reduced parts of the land to charred rubble. What mattered was that King Darien ignored them. It didn't matter that she'd eliminated any communication between the two parts of the kingdom. What mattered was that no word of support had reached them. It didn't matter that Lord Bayner was deposed by the Dorstenians themselves. It only mattered that Mara had promised them someone different, someone who belonged to them.

There was a smattering of applause and agreement throughout the assemblage, enough to let Aki know that people were listening. Pushing himself off the wall, he returned to Sky. It was time to make a decision. He wasn't likely to hear anything new by wandering from town to town and the burden of his promise grew heavier with every passing day. It was time to keep it.

They were following along the base of the mountain range, the town no longer in sight.

"She has the king, doesn't she?" Aki asked, not bothering to look over his shoulder at Sebastian.

"She does. And believe it or not, it was his choice to come."

"I'm sure," Aki muttered. "As much as it was my choice to get dragged behind you for days."

Sebastian made a sound Aki hadn't heard from him before, a short bark of laughter. "You did choose that."

Turning his head enough to glare at his former overseer, Aki rested his hand on his sword meaningfully. Sebastian stopped his horse.

"You're not going to kill me. If you were, you'd have already done it."

"Maybe I just let myself forget how strongly I dislike you and what you did to me?"

"See, that's the part I have a hard time believing." Sebastian started his horse forward again. "You don't seem like the kind of person to forget that sort of thing. That's why you've been dragging this out for as long as you can."

Aki raised an eyebrow and found himself half smiling. It disappeared with a shake of his head. Without another word, he prodded Sky forward. Once again, Sebastian only followed. He asked no questions, but this time Aki suspected the man already knew his destination. It was the last place he wanted to go. The only place left he could go to.

When the castle of Dorsten became visible in the distance, Aki slowed his horse and waited for Sebastian to come up beside him.

"Why do you serve her?"

Sebastian looked taken back by his abrupt question. "Work with her is good. She knows how to take care of those who are faithful to her."

"Would you do anything she told you to?"

"Yes," Sebastian answered without hesitation.

"Even if you disagreed with her or didn't want to?"

This time Sebastian took a moment to consider. "Yes."

"Let's get this over with, I suppose."

Dread wrapped itself around his chest, making every breath difficult as he closed the distance to the castle's front gate. His lips were dry no matter how many times he wet them and the reins in his hands were damp with sweat. He was coming back to her, just like she said he would. But she'd woven her trap so carefully, so intricately that there really was no other place for him to go. Especially if she'd spoken the truth about informing Prince Desmond of who he really was. Desmond would not cease until he was hunted down and killed.

Thinking of Prince Desmond reminded him of why he'd run in the first place and brought all the rage of that moment surging to the surface, drowning out the trepidation that made his heart flutter and skip inside his chest. It was Prince Desmond who'd left him no choice but to run. Mara was merely using that to her great advantage. She probably had a scheme already in place just in case he hadn't showed up in Dorsten.

Once at the gate, Sebastian took the lead and Aki let him. He wasn't sure he could speak right now, anyway. And he knew he couldn't bring himself to ask for Mara. There were two men guarding the gate, both dressed in all black. They weren't soldiers. Not real ones, anyway. They slouched against the stone wall, chatting, until Sebastian was pulling his horse to a stop right in front of them. With a casual glance over Sebastian and Aki, they waved them through.

Aki wasn't sure what sort of reception he expected. Mara was unpredictable, a fact that had seen him into more trouble than he cared to remember. He decided his odds of being locked away in the dungeon were equal to her greeting him like she actually planned to work together.

A man hurried across the stone courtyard, also dressed in black, and whispered a few words to Sebastian. Sebastian nodded and kept walking. Aki followed him. Through a door and up a narrow stone staircase that spiraled as it went up, then down a hallway past several doors. Sebastian stopped in front of one of them and opened it, revealing a large and, to Aki's surprise, comfortable looking bedroom.

"You're to wait here until Mara sends for you. There's a bath and a change of clothes for you."

"Are you locking me in?"

"No. Mara does not think that is necessary. She will take you to see your king once you've had the chance to clean up."

"And I'm supposed to believe that?"

"You did come here willingly, Aki. And there aren't many other places that are safe for you to go."

Aki hated the truth in Sebastian's words. He stepped inside the room and then stood waiting until Sebastian shut the door and walked away. When he was certain the man was gone, he lifted the latch and opened it again.

So, Sebastian wasn't lying about that.

The hallway was silent and empty, an invitation to explore written all over it. Aki stood just outside his door, the fingers of one hand tangled in his hair as he considered the opportunity. Just to the far end of the hallway, he told himself as he took a step in that direction. His feet made no noise on the stone floor as he covered the length of the hall. There were just more doors. Lots and lots of doors, all of them identical. All of them probably just leading to bedrooms such as his.

Glad that he'd left his own door ajar so that he knew which one it was, Aki hurried back into his room. The stone walls trapped cooler air inside, keeping the room from getting too hot. Its sole window overlooked the courtyard below, effectively preventing him from escaping unseen through that avenue. It didn't matter. Escape was the last thing on his mind.

It was more than an hour later before a rap sounded on his door. Aki, dressed in clothes that were entirely black but designed to fit his weapons comfortably, was ready for it.

"Well, I guess you decided the fugitive life wasn't for you after all," Halle said from where he leaned against the door frame. "Come on, Mother's waiting."

There was an extra layer to Halle's sullenness as he led the way. Aki wasn't sure it was aimed at him, but that seemed to be a good guess. Halle led the way with as much speed as his limp allowed him and Aki's head was spinning with all the turns they'd taken by the time they descended a different staircase and Halle stopped in front of a set of massive double doors.

"Go on. She's in there."

"Aren't you coming too?"

Halle let out a snort. "She doesn't want me. After all, I'm not the lost heir. I'm just dead weight he happened to bring along."

Aki started to open the door, but Halle wasn't finished speaking yet. Aki sensed he'd been waiting the last three weeks for just this moment.

"You know, she gave orders to all her people to let you through unharmed if you came north. Do you think she gave those same orders for me, her own son?"

Aki already knew that she hadn't. He already knew that Ritter had been planning on killing Halle and Karina.

"If you hadn't convinced that wretched man to let me go, he'd have killed me. How hard would it have been for her to give orders for me too?"

His hand still resting on the door handle, Aki shifted from one foot to the other. He wasn't sure what to say. Pity didn't come easily for Halle, but he was right. Mara hadn't bothered to put any safeguards in place for the return of her only son.

"Better get in there. You know how much she hates being kept waiting."

What waited beyond the doors could only have been the throne room. Aki had never been in that room in King Darien's castle. A vaulted ceiling soared above his head, held up by columns and arches. Rich tapestries adorned the walls in between windows that were taller than him. At the far end of the room a dais held three seats. The middle one was clearly the throne. It was grander than the other two, raised a step higher, and occupied by Mara herself at the moment.

Everything echoed in the vast room, from the doors shutting behind him to the gasp of amazement that escaped his lips. Each step he took rang out as he started forward.

"Come, come, Aki. You've arrived just in time," Mara said, her voice soft yet carrying across the distance with ease.

She wasn't alone. Sebastian stood off to one side. Someone stood in front of her. Aki followed her gestured command to climb the short set of stairs and sit down in the seat next to her. From there, Aki could see that it was a young man standing before her, disheveled and distraught. His clothes showed signs of hard travel with mud and dust changing them to a nondescript shade of brown. His hands held a cap that he twisted around and around.

"Aki, this is Finn. He's come to us with a very interesting story. One that has particular bearing on you. Finn, will you please tell us just this once more."

Finn looked up at Aki with something betwixt awe and despair. "You're Aki Gundarson?"

Aki looked to Mara before he could stop himself. She gave him a slight nod. "Yes, I am."

"Prince Desmond said to find you. He told me to deliver a message to you."

"A message that pertains to the story I just asked you to share, correct?" Mara asked, giving Finn a cold smile by way of encouragement.

"Yes, of course. The prince... he," Finn let out a deep, shaking breath and twisted the cap in his hands into a tight ball, "he, uh, well, he blamed you for his father, the king, disappearing," he gave a nod in Aki's direction, "and, he sent out his men to round up all of us. Anyone who had come from Aruuk and made their home in Dival. He had us all arrested. Said it was for our own good, to keep us safe from reprisals from the people. They separated us, the men from the women and children and locked us away in one of their empty border forts. We thought that was the end of the matter. That he'd keep us there until things quieted down and then we'd be allowed to get back to our lives. Then, one day, the army showed up. They camped right outside the fort. We could hear them out there, everyday getting bigger. More men coming. Then the prince showed up. We couldn't see him from inside the fort, of course. But we heard rumors from the guards."

Finn stared down at the cap in his hands, swallowing several times as his jaw worked back and forth.

"Go on, Finn. He needs to hear it all. He needs to hear it from you."

"The next morning... I don't know what happened. I really don't. All I know is that two soldiers came in and just grabbed me. Dragged me outside without saying a word. And there was the prince, just waiting for them. He didn't say anything to me. He just... he just told his men to set fire to the fort. Told them to burn it to the ground and to shoot anyone who tried to escape. And they did it. They did everything he said. All those men. They were screaming inside. I heard them. And he just stood there and watched the whole thing. Then he put me on a horse and sent me here to tell you."

"And what was the message he wanted you to give to Aki Gundarson?"

Finn drew himself up tall, his hands finally still as they gripped the cap. He looked straight at Aki and Aki fought to keep his own eyes up. "He said, 'Tell Aki Gundarson that this is what I will do to his people and that if he wishes to spare any of them, he will turn himself over immediately.' That's the message he gave me. To turn yourself over to him if you want it to end."

"Thank you, Finn. Your plight will not be forgotten. Nor will the lives of all those poor, innocent people. They will be avenged. I have arranged a place for you here and hope that you will continue at our side in these coming days. We have need of every man we can get, and I think you will want your chance to repay the wrongs wrought by the prince."

Finn nodded, bowed, first to Mara and then to Aki.

"Is it true you are the lost heir everyone speaks of?"

Aki didn't need to look at Mara this time. She had left him with only one answer he could give. "It's true."

"Prince Desmond fears you."

Which was the last thing Aki wanted to hear. Mara was so many moves ahead of everyone else that he didn't see a way out of this trap she'd made for him. Any way he turned, she was already prepared for.

Chapter 42

BEFORE I ALLOW YOU TO SEE my brother, I think it's important we come to an understanding."

Aki sat unmoving as Mara stood and paced the length of the dais. Her voluminous skirt swished with every stride, brushing against his legs when she passed him. It was so unlike the way she dressed in Aruuk or even in Karu. He could almost imagine a crown already resting on her head. He was pretty sure she could too.

"I knew it was only a matter of time before you came to me. Like it or not, Aki, life has brought us together once more. And this time, we both have something to offer one another. I can give you the protection you need and you, you can fill the need I have created in this land, the need for a leader."

"Mara, how am I supposed to lead anyone?"

"You misunderstand, Aki. We work together. You will sit in this seat," she gestured toward the one she had only moments ago vacated, "but I will be at your right hand, and I will be the one to guide you."

And there was her leash.

"I'm to be your puppet then?"

"A puppet with power and prestige and comforts beyond anything you've ever known. It's a long way up for a half-bred slave born traitor. You will never have to fear for your life again. And fear is all you will know if you leave these walls."

A golden leash, but still a leash.

But it was death to go home. Death to keep running.

Aki leaned forward, letting his elbows dig into the soft spot above his knees. He pressed the palms of his hands together to keep them still. Inside, he was still reeling from the news Finn had just delivered. Outside, he was trying to match Mara's cool detachment. It was the only chance he had to keep himself from crawling entirely beneath her thumb. His only defense against her control.

"You know what I'm saying is true. Or you wouldn't have come running back to me in the first place. Face it, Aki, you were never raised to make even your own decisions, let alone the decisions of an entire country."

"Then why do you need me at all? Why don't you just march in with your army and claim all this power for your own?"

Mara laughed. Its brittle sound reverberated off the walls and Aki grimaced at the coldness in it. "There is so much you don't understand. For one thing, Aruuk, Dorsten and Dival all share one important and ridiculous likeness. Thrones are patriarchal. They pass only to male heirs. The people of Dorsten would never allow a woman to sit in power. They'd sooner crawl back to Dival than suffer that."

"If you overthrow them, why would that matter?"

"You misunderstand my desire. I wish for the power to rule, yes. But I do not wish to be hated. Hated leaders are assassinated." Mara stopped her pacing and sank into the throne, her hands smoothing down the many folds of her dress. "But you, I've already made the people love you."

"They don't know me."

"They don't need to. I've sold them a story, an idea of you. In their minds, you are the embodiment of all their suffering. You are their savior. You are a survivor who has won despite everything," she said. She leaned toward him, an earnestness in her face that wasn't entirely insincere.

"And have you told them how I survived? Did you mention that my parents were murdered so that I could live or that you traded Dagmar's life for mine?"

Mara recoiled as if he'd burnt her. A look of hurt crossed her face.

"You didn't," he answered his own questions wryly. "I guess those don't make a very good story."

At that, Mara smiled. "Now you begin to understand. I do believe it's time you met my brother. He has such an interesting story to tell you."

There was a door behind the dais, hidden by a scarlet and gold tapestry, that led to a small, secluded chamber. The walls of the room were made of thin wood paneling, allowing anyone who was inside it to hear all that took place in the throne room. Mara pulled the heavy cloth back and slid the paneled door to the side. Aki tried to see over her shoulder as he followed her into the space. There was a low couch that ran the length of the far wall and two other chairs angled to face it. Sebastian must have left the throne room without his noticing because he sat in one of the chairs. And on the couch... Aki caught his breath and stiffened.

"Your Majesty?"

"Not here, I'm afraid," Mara said, sweeping forward and settling herself on the other end of the couch. "Leave us, Sebastian. Our family would like some time alone."

Aki stood frozen in place, forcing Sebastian to step around him to exit the room. "I don't understand. What are you talking about?"

"Shall you tell him, Darien, or shall I? I must admit, I was surprised to find you hadn't already broken the news to him. It must have been an awful secret to keep. And so utterly useless. Here he is, despite his ignorance."

"Tell me what? What secret?" Aki wished he could keep his voice from rising.

"About who you really are, of course."

Aki stepped back a little, as if to distance himself from whatever Mara was going to say next, his face darkening with suspicion. "You've already told me who my mother was. What more is there to know?"

Mara was laughing again, but there was nothing bitter in this laughter, just pure, wicked delight. "I told you right before you ran away from me that you shared royal blood as well. If you'd stayed, I would have explained everything. No matter. I shall tell you now since my brother seems disinclined to. I told you about how your mother was a peace offering to Chief Gundar. So was I. But unlike your mother, Gundar did actually take me as a wife. Do you have any idea how miserable it was? When I first arrived

in Aruuk, I couldn't speak to or understand anyone.
Gundar was a cruel husband, but he liked me better when
I gave him a son."

Aki found his way to a chair and sank down in it. He
knew where the story was going. He wanted to stop it, to
cut it off before Mara could speak the words. But he didn't
dare interrupt her.

"As Anton grew up, he was Gundar's favorite. Clever,
strong, ambitious. Everything the Chief of Aruuk could
want in a successor. Anton pleased him once. He
uncovered a plot against Gundar's life and Gundar
rewarded him. With your mother, as I'm sure you've
guessed. If Anton had been anyone else, it would have
been fine. But Anton let the girl talk. Let her fill his head
with all sorts of ideas about how different life could be. He
listened to her so much that when she begged for your life,
he couldn't deny her."

His hands found their way over his ears, blocking out
the sound of her voice, blocking out the meaning of her
words. Everything she'd ever done to him, she'd done
knowing that he was her own grandson. It made it all so
much worse.

"Enough," he cried out, not caring that Mara was still
speaking. "You were my grandmother? You were awful to
me. You ordered me killed. How? What kind of person
are you?"

If she could have struck him dead with her glare alone,
Mara would have. Any other time the look would have
quailed him but instead he turned to King Darien.

"And you knew. You knew. I was punished for the rest
of my life for concealing the truth, but you couldn't take
the time to tell me we were related? How was that any
different?"

"Leave us, Mara," Darien spoke for the first time, his
quiet voice in sharp contrast to Aki's.

As if there weren't enough surprises already, Aki
watched as Mara acquiesced without question. "As you
wish. Perhaps the truth from you a little sooner might
have helped, though, brother."

The deafening silence that reigned in the room after her
departure was thick with all the words Aki still wanted to
speak. If Mara's revelations at Lord Bayner's estate were

unexpected, this was earth-shattering. Thoughts frayed apart inside his mind before he could really latch onto them. The sensation that the room was spinning around him forced his head into his hands.

"Aki."

His eyes still shielded by his hands, Aki shook his head. There was nothing he wanted to hear from anyone right now. There weren't words that could sort through everything that was churning inside his head and make sense of it.

"Aki, look at me."

He dragged his head up from his hands and met the king's eyes.

"When Sasha first came with his warning of an Aruuken attack, I thought that perhaps he was my sister's son. It made sense given the fact that he came to us the way he did. I could have been very proud to call him family. And later, when Boris fell into our hands after the battle, I wondered if perhaps he was my nephew. I pitied him even when I knew he was no relation of mine."

"I'm sure it was very disappointing to find out that it was me," Aki snapped, a little surprised at himself for the anger he couldn't hold back. "I understand why you'd want to keep it a secret."

"I did not know of our relationship until you brought that strange letter at the start of the winter. I had hoped that by keeping your identity secret, it would keep you safe. Uninvolved. I was wrong. For that, I am truly sorry."

It wasn't enough. None of their reasons or excuses were enough. He'd been used. He was still nothing more than a plaything, a piece in the games of people who wielded more power than he did. He was tired of it. So very tired.

"But it was not a disappointment to discover the truth, no matter what you think."

"Yes, who wouldn't want a traitor and a coward in their family?"

"A coward would have run that night. I gave you the choice, yet here you are. For your own sake, I almost wish you had run. But for the sake of the kingdom..."

"The kingdom that wants me dead? And that locked innocent people inside a building and burned them alive? I'm not sure I'm really interested in helping that kingdom."

"There is nothing I can say that could possibly excuse the actions of my son."

"Forgive me, Your Majesty, but all I want right now is to see him dead."

Whatever Darien might have said next, Aki missed it. He was already out the door, standing back in the cavernous throne room, his chest heaving, and his breath ragged and shaking. Mara stood there, watching him, watching his reaction. No doubt she'd heard every word that passed between them. Which explained her willingness to leave the room when she did. Aki passed her without a glance and had nearly reached the double doors that led out of the throne room when she called after him.

"Sasha would have been inside that fort."

Because that was all he needed. As if his entire world wasn't already caving in on top of him, she needed to remind him of just how much he was losing. A choked sound escaped him as he left the room, echoing off its high arching ceilings and stone walls. He fled back to the privacy of his room.

Aki was content to spend hours in the secluded space, trapping himself in with his thoughts. Twice there was a knock on his door and both times he ignored it. As the dying rays of the sun shone through his window, he pulled out his smallest knife and toyed with it in his hands.

"I'm sorry," he whispered into the emptiness, not sure who exactly he meant it for - Sasha, who was dead now, Ophelia and the baby he'd left behind, Master Wehr who would have stopped his next move. Probably all three, he decided as he rolled his sleeve up. With gritted teeth he made the first mark, scratched the first letter of Sasha's name. Another life lost because of him. He ought to have just stayed in Bren, faced whatever punishment Desmond and the council saw fit to bestow on him, and then perhaps Desmond would not have felt the need to take out his wrath on so many innocent people. He winced with each cut. And when it was done, he sat for a long time staring at the lines of blood that rose up.

He didn't hear the door open and close. It wasn't until he heard soft, measured footsteps crossing the floor that he looked up to find Mara coming towards him. He turned away, yanking the sleeve of his shirt down to hide what he'd done. The bed shifted as she sat on its edge.

"Whatever differences we've had, Aki, there is one thing we agree on. And that is that Sasha did not deserve to die. He spared the lives of both myself and Halle when he could just as easily have done otherwise. I could not have foreseen what happened. I had always thought he was such a hero to them that he was untouchable. Apparently, Prince Desmond no longer recognizes those who are truly on his side."

"What do you want, Mara?" Aki turned miserably to her.

"At this moment? Nothing but to tell you that your grief is not yours alone. And to give you this. I told you I would if you came to me, and I always keep my promises. You know that." She held out the leather-bound journal that had once belonged to his mother.

"I haven't agreed to anything."

"I know. But, still, it belongs to you."

Mara set it down on the space of bed between them and stood. Aki reached out and picked the journal up with a great deal more care than he had handled it with in Lord Bayner's house. His hands were reverent as he laid it on his lap.

"I'll do it. I'll do whatever you need me to, Mara. If it stops Desmond, I'll do it."

Mara smiled in victory and laid a hand on his face. He flinched, pulling away from her.

"We'll do great things together, grandson."

Aki wanted to be sick as Mara swept out of the room. It wasn't right. None of this was right. He shouldn't be at Mara's side. He shouldn't be agreeing to her schemes. He shouldn't be mourning the loss of one of the few people who cared about him, the first person to ever show him kindness. Everything was upside down and turned inside out and he didn't know how to make it all make sense again. Even the ever-present burden of the promise he'd left home with lay dormant and quiet inside him. The only thing he did know was that Desmond was at the heart of it all. And Desmond needed to die. He needed to pay for the monstrous deed he'd done.

Chapter 43

DESMOND STOOD ALONE ON THE top of a rise. Before him, behind him, and on either side of him, the Void stretched on; a great, desolate plain that bore silent witness to years of war and death. His father had ended that war. There was a poetic irony in Desmond starting it over - all for the sake of his now missing father.

Wind whined and whistled across the vast expanse of nothingness. Desmond hated that wind when he crossed before. Now, the wind seemed to be his only companion. It was ridiculous, really. He was surrounded by the entire army of Dival, and Desmond had never been more alone. It wasn't that the others wouldn't speak to him. It was the way they did it. It was the clipped, terse sentences Captain Tyrrel spoke to him. It was the bitter, nagging words of Baron Orlander. It was the soft, nervous advances of Tristan. And it was the words he'd heard attached to his own name - monster, barbaric, cruel, merciless.

His hands clasped behind him, Desmond surveyed the Void in front of the army now. Despite Baron Orlander's decimated scouting party, they had now traveled two days into the great plains and had seen no sign of the enemy. Nothing but swaying grass and incessant wind. He despised that wind. It seemed to carry with it the screams of those inside the burning fort. For two days, he'd listened to it as it followed them. The sound of it made it impossible for him to close his eyes at night without seeing the wild flames devouring the wooden walls and all life within them.

"We're ready to move, Your Highness," Captain Tyrrel said from just behind him.

Desmond spun around, startled that he hadn't heard the captain's approach. He gave him a single nod.

That was it. That was the extent of conversation he would have with Captain Tyrrel until they stopped for the night. Desmond found his horse and, avoiding the eyes of the unfortunate man holding it in place, mounted up.

It was all Aki's fault, really. Aki and Desmond's own newly discovered aunt, Mara. He still couldn't quite get used to the idea that such a person existed. And why hadn't Father ever mentioned her? There must have been a scandal of sorts. That was the only thing Desmond could conclude.

The day passed the same as the previous two, as unchanging as the landscape around them. Tomorrow would be equally dull. And the day after that and the after that. It made Desmond ill to think about. Because after enough of those dull, tedious days, they would reach their destination. And once they reached their destination...

Desmond wasn't entirely sure. Would there be an army waiting for them? Would they try to negotiate? Would his father still be alive by then? All the answers he sought lay at the end of their journey.

Chapter 44

AKI DREW IN A DEEP BREATH.

He picked up the journal.

For two days, it had done nothing but lay on the little table next to his bed. For two days, he promised himself he would open it just as soon as he had time. For two days, he lied.

Mara made few demands on his time just yet. She said it wasn't the right time for him to show himself to the people and Aki couldn't argue with that. In his mind, it would never be the right time. Instead, he'd spent his days wandering around the castle, exploring its many rooms. After the precipitous events that led him to this place, he felt vaguely vacant just waiting, waiting, waiting.

He ran his hand over the aged, cracked leather. Just like he'd done the previous two nights. For seventeen years, he'd lived thanks to the woman who wrote this book that now rested in his hands. For seventeen years, he hadn't even had a clue as to who she really was. Now with answers sitting at his fingertips, Aki couldn't quite break the spell that kept them still. To open the book was to know. It was to say goodbye to every idea he'd ever had about his mother. It was to learn the truth and dispel the dreams.

After seventeen years of waiting, Aki thought he would have torn it open the very second it was placed in his grasp. But it was like jumping off a precipice. He could stand at the brink forever and nothing changed. As soon as his feet left the ground, it was beyond his control.

There were enough other things out of his control right now.

Still, longing was eating away at an ever-growing hole in his heart.

He opened the journal.

He opened the picture of words his mother had left behind.

The candle by his bed burned down to a nub. Aki replaced it and kept reading. Page after page written in a tight, tidy hand. He devoured them all. Some were nothing but the mindless ramblings of a girl coming of age. Others mused on the antics of people she watched around her, her words often scathing in their humor and mocking. His mother thought very little of the noblemen and courtiers she was raised with. Without fail, though, each entry ended the same.

"The good thing about today was..."

He came to the last entry she'd made.

"Father's been in an awful mood all day. He's yelled at pretty much everyone who's crossed his path and he curses the Divalians every chance he gets. He won't say what happened, but I've heard rumors from Norman. Divalian spies have interfered with his attempt to negotiate the use of the Aruuken army. I can't say I'm particularly sorry to hear it. The last time the Aruukens came through here, most of us girls had to stay locked away until they left again. From what I could see of them, they were every bit the picture of murdering barbarians that Grandmother used to tell stories about.

"Perhaps I should try to think a little differently about them. Father has reached an agreement with their Chief. He's arranged for me to marry him. He says it's the only way to keep the Aruukens from turning on us. I wish it weren't. I've never even met the Chief and from everything that Father has said, he's not an easy man to get along with. But I suppose if it keeps the peace and protects our people, there's not much sense in arguing it.

Father will only say 'royal blood means royal burden' and even if we aren't really part of the royal family, people do look up to us to keep them safe.

"The good thing about today was that, even if I'm scared out of my mind at traveling all the way to Aruuk to marry a man I've never met, I'm also a little, tiny bit excited. Not many girls get to travel and meet new people and see new places. I should count myself fortunate to enjoy that privilege. And who knows? Maybe I'll get there, and I'll love it and then I'll look back on this and laugh at how childish and frightened I was!"

The pages after that were empty. His mother, for a reason he would never know, chose not to take her journal with her. It had remained behind, a written testament to a life that was deemed worthless in the frozen heart of the mountains. The words left Aki hollow. They made his eyes burn and his insides twist. She'd tried so hard to look forward to it. Her innocence and naivety screamed up from the pages.

He started to shut it when he realized that there was a loose piece of paper stuffed in the back of it. A piece of paper he was quite certain hadn't been there when he'd picked it up in Lord Bayner's house. He pulled it out and unfolded it.

Right away he recognized his mother's hand, although it was sloppier now as if she'd written in haste. Aki wasn't sure he wanted to read any further. He wasn't sure he wanted to know what happened after, but he knew he'd never sleep again if he didn't read it now.

"Hope's such an insane thing. Yet here I am, absolutely wild with it. Why? Because you're here in my arms and just the sight of you makes my heart so happy I think it will burst. Anton's just as bad. He can hardly take his eyes off of you, although he's too scared to actually hold you. We're leaving now that you're here. Faramund has been as kind as anyone I've ever known, and he's promised to get us aboard a ship. I don't even care where it takes us, just so long as it takes us far, far away from this place. I'd live in a cave if it meant you were safe. All this fuss for you and you don't even know how special you

are! But you are so very special. You're my son. But more than that you're living proof that our people can know peace. You're proof that we get to come back from the darkness. I've never known a night yet that the dawn couldn't chase away. You're the dawn to a very dark night, indeed. And that's why I have hope. I don't know what difference Anton and I could possibly make, but we're running away from here and we're going to raise you right and make a difference for you at least. And perhaps you'll go on and make a difference in someone else's life. Because, really, this is just the beginning. I can't wait to get to know you. I wonder if you'll look more like me or Anton? You'll be strong like Anton, of course. Perhaps you'll talk as much as I do. It won't matter because I will love you. Always."

Swiping the back of his hand over his eyes, Aki lay back on his bed, the paper clutched to his chest. The last of the second candle sputtered out, leaving him in complete darkness but he didn't mind. The darkness was good to hide in. He stared up at the ceiling he couldn't see and tried to bring to mind the portrait tucked away in the storage room at Lord Bayner's estate. The smiling girl who always looked for the good in every day, who had somehow, despite everything, managed to snag a bit of happiness in her life. That was his mother.

He must have fallen asleep eventually because he found himself waking up to a pale-yellow beam of sunlight pouring through the window. The last paper still lay beneath his hand on his chest and, sitting up, Aki folded it with solemn care and put it inside his pocket. He couldn't carry the entire journal with him but that last page, the one that was really nothing more than a letter to him, that he would never part with.

Downstairs, Mara was already in the throne room. It was one of the only places Aki ever saw her and she always seemed quite at ease in its grandeur. She was speaking to a man when he entered and at first, Aki thought it was Finn again. She waved the man off and as he turned to leave Aki saw that it wasn't Finn, but an older man, probably from the town that lay below the castle.

"Fools," Mara murmured as he approached her. "They think they do not need my protection."

Aki didn't speak. After yesterday, he wasn't really sure what there was to say anyway. Did he even want to ask her why she'd been so cruel to him, knowing that he was her own son's child? Besides, speaking out of turn with Mara was never a good idea and he could tell by her face that there was more she wished to say.

"After all I've done for these people, they still have the nerve to ask me to move my men out of the town. As if their presence was the source of all their problems." She paused and frowned down at her hands that were resting idle in her lap. A slow smile pushed it away. "No matter, though. Ritter and his men will return soon and then they shall see just how much they need my protection."

"What do you mean?" Aki asked, wary of the satisfaction in her smile.

"What I mean, Aki, is that sometimes, as a leader, you must create a problem to show people that you are the only one who can fix it. How do you think I've managed as much as I have already?"

"You're going to have Ritter and his men attack the town just so you can prove you were right?" Aki asked, not masking his horror. "What then? The men you have here will ride in and save the day?"

"Exactly. See, you are already beginning to understand. You're more like me than you want to admit."

"But what about the people?"

"Some of them will be lost, no doubt, but the others will understand that they need me, that I'm on their side. It's an unfortunate but necessary evil."

Shaking his head, Aki wondered again how it was that he'd ended up sitting at her side. Just the nearness of her now made him cringe. If it weren't for that promise... Aki sighed. He wasn't even sure how to keep that promise now.

"What was her name?"

Mara arched her eyebrows and looked him over coolly. "I had hoped that by giving you her writings, you'd stop pining over her. You act like any of that actually matters. And it doesn't. All that matters was the family she was born into, not what kind of person she was or what she did. It doesn't do a thing to change who you are."

"I just want to know her name," Aki said, a hint of meekness creeping back into his voice. "I won't ask another thing about her if you'll tell me."

"It was Sybil. Her name was Sybil Bayner. Now, enough of this."

"What are you going to do with King Darien?"

"Stop calling him that. He gave up his throne when he agreed to come to me and try to settle things. Nothing will happen to him that the people don't want."

"And can I talk to him again?"

"Plotting against me already, Aki?"

Aki shook his head. "There's no point in that. I'd never win. And I have nowhere else to go. Cristof wants me dead in Aruuk and Desmond wants me dead in Dival. At least here, I get to stay alive."

"I'm glad you see the truth. You may speak with him now if you like. Sebastian can take you to see him."

Aki ran through the words that were churning in his mind, trying to put them into clear thoughts. As angry as he'd been the day before, his brief conversation with the king didn't result in anything worthwhile. Aki had a million questions he wanted to ask the man, but there wouldn't be enough time for that.

The room Sebastian led him to was almost identical to his own. It also faced the courtyard and that was what the king was watching when Aki entered alone. He was tempted to see if Sebastian was waiting with his ear to the door outside, listening for any hint of Aki's disloyalty to Mara.

"Why did you come to her? You had to have known it wouldn't end well."

Darien didn't turn around to answer. His hands resting on the stone ledge beneath the windowpane, he continued to stare out at the courtyard below. "I hoped that I could settle the past with my sister without dragging an entire country into the mess. I hoped that she would still be the same sister who left so many years ago."

Since he couldn't imagine Mara being anything other than what he'd always known her as, Aki asked, "And what was she then?"

"A better person than this. We both wanted peace. When our father made the arrangement for her to marry the Chief of Aruuk, I thought it brought us one step closer. She hated the idea from the beginning. She begged me to help her run away so she wouldn't have to go. I didn't."

"That's what this is all about?"

"Our father was so ashamed of having to use her to buy peace that he kept the entire affair hidden. Only a few ever knew what really happened to her. Most of the kingdom believed she died of fever. I think that has more to do with how she is now. She was forgotten."

Touching the letter in his pocket, Aki remembered the words of his own mother - royal blood means royal burden. Mara and Sybil could have been friends for all they had in common. Yet, they were such different people.

"You should have just helped her run away. Gundar didn't need another wife."

Darien's laugh was so similar to Mara's in its bitterness that Aki recoiled a little. "Here's the thing about being the king, Aki. We don't get to choose individuals. Not for love. Or hate. We choose our kingdom - its needs, its benefits. None of our decisions can be made personal. And yet the irony of it is, that the moment we stop seeing our people as individuals, we become tyrants. Monsters. Men without heart or conscience. It's an impossibly hard balance, but I've tried to do the best I could. In the end, I suppose it does not matter."

Aki thought about the king's words for a moment and a question came to mind. Almost afraid of the answer, he asked, "When you spared my life, was that solely a choice that would benefit the kingdom?"

Darien turned away from the window to answer. "No. And yes. I've indulged myself a few times in the past years, usually to the chagrin of my council. However, you could serve a purpose as well, so it was a bit of both. It was not hard to guess that the attempt on my daughter was only the beginning. You were too valuable a tool to lose. But, to answer your real question, I did not want you to die."

Aki accepted the answer with a nod as Darien turned back to the window. "Do you have any idea how she came to be in possession of this castle?"

"No. I hadn't given it much thought, I guess."

"It seems you were right when you warned us that something was amiss about the raid last autumn. If only we had acted on your warning sooner. Desmond's the reason she has it already. He invited all the men that were rescued to winter here as well. They never left."

It was almost a relief to hear that it was someone else's fault that something bad happened, but Aki couldn't even harbor a thought about Desmond without going hot all over at the memory of what he'd done.

"You haven't forgotten your promise, have you?"

Aki shook his head.

"This won't end with me alive..."

"She wouldn't kill you," Aki said, the words hollow because he knew from experience that Mara could and would do anything she wanted. And family relations made no difference.

"Aki, you and I both know that's not true." He paused and let out a heavy sigh. "I knew what might happen when I chose to come. If it's the price that must be paid to right past wrongs, then so be it. But I won't hold you to the promise you made me that night. I know what it will cost you. There's still time for you to change your mind."

There was freedom in those words. Like the freedom he'd had for those three weeks wandering around the countryside of Dorsten. And like that freedom, he knew it could never be his.

Chapter 45

AKI STARED DOWN AT HIS PLATE of food, trying to ignore everyone else in the room. There weren't many to ignore. Just Mara, Halle, Karina, and Finn. Finn was an unusual addition to their mealtimes. Mara insisted Aki take his meals with them and he couldn't refuse. The others were doing much the same as he was, pretending that they were alone. Everyone, except Mara, who seemed to thrive on the oppressive silence and awkward glances. At least, she was unfazed by the atmosphere.

Mara set her cup down with a clunk, picked up her napkin and dabbed her lips with it, and spoke, "Finn, there is something I would like to speak with you about when we are finished here."

Finn choked on the bite in his mouth in his haste to agree with her. Halle, across from Aki, looked up long enough to roll his eyes and Aki smothered a rare smile.

"Karina, you should show Aki around. There's so much of the castle he hasn't had a chance to see yet and it would be such a shame for him to not even know his own home."

"Yes, Mara," Karina answered. Worry wrinkled the skin around her eyes as her gaze darted to Aki and then back to her own plate.

For the rest of the silent meal, she kept at it. A minute didn't pass when Aki didn't feel her quick, apprehensive gaze on him. It was the same look she'd had when he was bringing her and Halle north only a month before. She'd been hiding who she was then. Aki couldn't think of what she could possibly be hiding now. Perhaps she just knew that he still despised her for what she'd done.

"Where would you like to see?" she asked, eyes downcast when they were left alone with Halle a few minutes later.

Aki shrugged, pushing himself away from the table. Mara didn't seem to be aware of the fact that he'd done quite a bit of exploring on his own. He'd already shown himself any part of the castle he was interested in seeing.

"Well, I know where I want to see," Halle said.

"And where's that?" Aki asked.

"The only place I haven't seen yet. The dungeons."

"Why would you want to see them? I could probably describe them without going down there."

"I heard a rumor and I want to see if it's true."

It had been Aki's plan to go straight to Darien's room when he was done here, but he couldn't risk Mara's anger. Karina was still watching him warily as he stood to go. He followed her and Halle out of the room. King Darien would just have to wait a little while he humored Mara's demands.

The dungeon lived up to every picture Aki had ever conjured up about such a place. A musty, fetid odor hung thick in the air down there. Moisture clung to the stone walls. There was a steady staccato of dripping water. In the faltering light of the lamp Aki carried, rats and spiders scuttled back into the darkness. Along the narrow hallway, heavy wooden doors bound with great strips of iron hung at intervals.

"This is almost as bad as Father's," Halle commented from his spot just behind Aki.

"I wouldn't know. I was never down in his. When were you?"

"After I tried to kill Sasha on his first night back, he had them take me there."

"You tried to kill Sasha?" Aki's voice broke a little over the name.

"It was another one of Mother's brilliant ideas. I didn't even come close."

"And he didn't have you executed?"

"Obviously not." Halle's voice dropped to a whisper. "I can't believe Desmond killed him. I mean, I sort of understand why he doesn't like you or I, but Sasha?"

"He'll pay for it," Aki murmured.

"Like Cadoc?"

Aki didn't answer. Not because he didn't have an answer but because he caught Karina's eyes. She hadn't said a word the entire time they'd been down here. Now she looked away, a guilty flush creeping up her cheeks. Aki decided it was one of her many oddities that he was destined never to understand.

"Turn down that way," Halle ordered from behind.

Aki held the lamp at arm's length, squinting to search the dark recesses of the tunnel Halle was pointing them towards. It sloped downward and the floor was worn away, making the middle of it the deepest part. He couldn't see any doors along it.

"What is it?"

"The rumor I was telling you about. Come on."

Aki turned around, a bemused smile on his face. For the first time that he could remember, Halle sounded excited. He ought to have been suspicious, he supposed. But after their time running together, the feeling just wouldn't come.

"I don't know what's down there," Karina said. "Mara wanted me to show you around the places I know."

"Yes, and you always do exactly what she says."

"So do you, Aki."

"Come on. Let's find out." Halle gave Aki a shove on the shoulder and Aki started down it.

The floor was slippery, and Aki realized there was a thin stream of water running down the middle of it. He stepped to the side and the footing was a little improved. The sound of trickling water followed them. The ceiling, never more than a few inches above their heads, began to close in on them, getting lower and lower the further in they went.

"What is this supposed to be?" Aki asked when he was forced into a crouch.

"It can't be much farther."

"What can't be?"

Halle didn't answer. Aki just felt his hand on his shoulder, pushing him forward again. The lantern in his hand swung and danced with every crawling step forward. The darkness beyond its illumination was deeper than any Aki had ever seen. Karina stifled a whimper behind them, and Aki couldn't help but feel a little bad about dragging her into this. And she had no choice but to follow them now since he held their only source of light.

The air grew close and humid, a deep, earthy scent filling Aki's nose. The trickle of water had grown as well so that the stream was now at least a foot wide as it flowed downward. At last, Aki caught a glimpse of something ahead. He stretched his arm out, extending the light of his lantern as far as it would go. It revealed a rusted grate and utter blackness beyond.

"This is what you wanted to see?"

Halle pushed his shoulder down to see past him in the cramped space.

"Keep going," he ordered.

Aki sighed but crawled forward. The nearer he got, the more the grate became visible. The sound of the stream changed. Somewhere up ahead, water was falling some distance down onto rocks, its splashing echoing off the walls of a large, invisible space. The grate itself was half buried in debris that had flowed down with the thin stream and become stuck on the iron bars.

When Aki was close enough to touch it, Halle leaned over his shoulder again and said, "See if you can push it open."

It took several tries before Aki felt anything give, not because the grate was incredibly strong but because the space was too cramped to find much leverage against the iron bars. Hinges at the top, rusty and creaking, swung the grate out away from them.

"Now see what's beyond it." The thrill in Halle's voice was unmistakable.

Aki lifted the lantern through the opening to reveal a vast cavern. He stuck his head through the opening and noticed a narrow ledge running off to the left side. Otherwise, it was a sheer drop down into nothingness. Although he could hear water striking rocks far below them, the light of his lantern was not strong enough to reach the bottom, however far down it was.

"Can we go out there?"

"There's a ledge that's big enough to walk on, I think. But it's a long way down if one of us falls." Aki turned to Halle, his eyes saying what his mouth wouldn't. He didn't need to remind Halle of the last time the two of them were on a narrow ledge and one of them fell. Halle still limped from that day.

Halle met his eyes. "I guess we'll just have to be very careful."

"I don't really want to go," Karina spoke up.

Halle and Aki both ignored her as Aki inched his way through the opening and off to the side. It wasn't as narrow as he first thought. There were at least a couple of feet and it widened almost immediately. The air was cool but without the dankness that smothered the dungeon. Aside from the smell of earth, water and rock, it was clean.

"Keep going," Halle prodded when Aki paused to hold the lantern up in an effort to get a better look.

The light bounced off of gray and red rock walls and revealed a ceiling only a few feet above their heads. He kept going.

It was impossible to tell time down here, but after they'd gone some distance, far enough that the miniscule waterfall that came from the grate was no longer audible, Aki stopped to look around once more. Although the drop off was still as sheer as ever, it had narrowed. The chasm was now only a few feet across, and another ledge ran along its far side. He could probably jump across to it if he wanted to.

A little further on and the chasm closed entirely, the two paths joining and leading into a tunnel. It was a short tunnel that opened into a wide, low cave that resembled a room. Here, the light of the lantern was sufficient to illuminate the entirety of the enclosed space. More tunnels branched off the room.

"I wonder how far under the mountain we are," Halle said as he walked around the room, examining the rock walls and peering down the darkened passages.

"How did you even know about this?"

"I've been bored out of my mind, Aki. All Mother ever does is talk about what a great scheme she's got now and she obviously prefers your company to mine these days."

"So how did you find out about this?"

"I was digging around in the library the other day. Couldn't read most of the books there, of course. But I found the building prints for the castle stashed away beneath a great big stack of really old looking papers. I don't believe anyone's looked at them in years and years. Anyway, whoever built the place knew about this and marked it."

"And you waited until now to come find out if it was real?"

"Well, I wasn't about to go off exploring by myself. That'd be dangerous," Halle said, turning to grin at Aki. "It's incredible, isn't it?"

And despite everything, Aki found himself smiling back. "It is. I wonder if it goes all the way to the other side of the mountain."

"That, I don't know. The building prints only showed this end of it."

"We should go back," Karina said.

Aki almost forgot that she was with them. She hadn't said a word since they stepped out onto the ledge. He turned to look at her now and found her crouched on the floor, her arms wrapped around her knees, her face ghastly white in the uncertain light of the lantern. And there it was again, the guilt that flickered in her eyes. It was just because she'd betrayed him to Mara at Lord Bayner's, Aki assured himself. She'd been wary of him ever since.

Part of him wanted to keep exploring, both out of spite to Karina and genuine curiosity. But he hadn't come all the way to Dorsten to explore. He needed to speak to King Darien again and he needed to figure out what to do next.

"We have been gone a while," he conceded, starting back the way they came in. "But, Halle, we should come down here again when we have more time."

Picking their way back, Aki guessed that they had been down there for at least a couple of hours. That worried him. If Mara had wondered at their long absence and started searching for them... He didn't want her finding out about the tunnel or the cave under the mountain. He suspected Halle didn't either since he'd waited until she was going to be busy before suggesting their exploration. Of course, Karina was probably going to run off and tell her the first chance she got.

At last, they stood back in the dungeon hall that had led them there. Aki stretched his arms, glad to leave the confined space behind.

Voices echoed from another passageway, one they hadn't gone down earlier, as they neared the exit to the dungeon. Aki stopped short, Halle walking straight into him from behind. One of the voices was Mara's.

"What's Mother doing down here?" Halle muttered in his ear.

Aki started forward again, hurrying towards the stairs that led up and out, hoping to reach them before Mara and whoever was with her rounded the corner and ran into them.

It was too late.

He saw their light first, growing stronger by the second. And then Mara came into view. She paused mid stride when she caught sight of the three of them. Anger, then suspicion flashed across her face before she masked it.

"Oh, there you all are. When I said show him around, Karina, I didn't exactly mean down here," her voice bounced off the walls with practiced boredom, but Aki heard the unspoken irritation in her words. "Come, then, now that you're done, we have much to discuss."

Mara started toward the stairs. Aki gasped and dropped his head as the man who'd been speaking with her came into view as well. Cristof. She had Cristof here. Down here in the dungeon. It didn't make sense. It didn't make any sense. He heard the whisper of steel as a knife was withdrawn from its sheath and looked up to see Cristof, his face twisted and red, coming toward him.

"Not now, Cristof," Mara's voice halted the man. "He had every right to kill your father and if you can't accept that, you'll join Ritter's men today."

Although Cristof didn't argue, he shoved Aki hard in the shoulder as he stepped past and leaned in to whisper, "This isn't over, yet. And she won't always be around to protect you."

The warmth of the summer sun wrapped around them as they left the cold dungeon behind. Aki glanced up at the window he knew looked into King Darien's room. A heavy curtain was drawn across it, probably to block out the very heat he was savoring at the moment.

"Can I speak to Darien again?"

Mara stopped walking. She turned around, a frown tugging her lips down at the corners. She studied and picked at her fingernails. "I'm afraid that won't be possible, Aki."

"Why not? I've already told you I'm not plotting anything with him."

"Yes, well, that's just it, isn't it? You lie so well and so often that I can't really believe you. So, I've taken care of the problem myself."

Aki felt like they were back in the dungeon, he was so cold at her words. A shiver ran through him, and his stomach twisted at the realization of what she was saying. "No. No, you couldn't have. You couldn't have. No."

He was stepping away from her, shaking his head, the words tumbling through his mind and out of his mouth before he could contain them. "You killed him, didn't you? How could you? He was your brother. How could you kill your own brother?"

"Enough, Aki."

Mara's words dammed the flow of words up. Even without wanting to, he obeyed her.

"You've no right to lecture me about him being my brother. You're the one who shoved yours off a cliff. Besides, you killed him," she went on. "He was executed by your hand this morning as a warning to Prince Desmond."

"But I didn't. I wouldn't. That's a lie."

"So it is. But it is the story I've already sent to Desmond, and I fear he shall believe it."

"Why?" Aki choked that single word out.

"Because," Mara stepped closer to him, close enough to take his face in her hand, "secretly, I think you still thought you had a way back. That if you could just rescue him and take him back to his people, that they would forgive you. And I couldn't have that. I need you to be mine. Completely. No other schemes. No other allies. Just all

271

mine. That's why he had to die. That's why you had to be the one to kill him. In time, the truth might come out, but it won't matter then. Because it's only ever the first story people here that matters."

"Who did it?"

"Well, I knew your attachment to him was too strong, despite the lies he told you. Finn, however, was a different story. Not only did he not share your attachment, but he's absolutely eaten up with his need for revenge on Desmond. It worked out perfectly."

Aki jerked away from her hand. His eyes fell on Karina. Guilty Karina.

"You knew. Of course, you did. You knew all along."

She didn't need to answer him for him to see the truth of it in her eyes. She knew exactly why Mara wanted him distracted. He stumbled back toward the gate. Mara's guards moved to stop him, but she waved them away.

"Where are you planning on going, Aki? Desmond will kill you the first chance he gets and if you run from me, Cristof will come after you."

He wanted to run. Through the gate and into the mountains. He wanted to run and run and never stop running until the burning pain inside of him sputtered out, until he drowned it in exhaustion. Instead, he drew himself up, forced his face into a mask every bit as impenetrable as Mara's, threw his arms out to the side in complete indifference and said, "Where would I go? You have me, Mara. I'm all yours. I just want to see something other than stone walls for a bit."

He walked through the gate unopposed.

Chapter 46

EVERYWHERE HE TURNED, PEOPLE were staring at him with furtive eyes. Aki was thankful for the thin scarf that was pulled up over the lower half of his face. Mara insisted on all her men wearing them when they were out in the town. She said it kept them anonymous, faceless to the crowds of people they mingled with.

Aki wouldn't have pulled his on, except faceless was just what he wanted to be right now. Dressed in the all black that the rest of Mara's men wore as well, he wasn't anyone in particular as he leaned against the side of a building trying to weave together the scattered fragments of his thoughts. He was oblivious to the fact that he was, at that moment, the only one of Mara's men in town.

He had another name to scratch onto his arm.

Another death to record.

Another debt.

He tried to remember Master Wehr's words, but they were distant now, spoken in a different lifetime, to a different Aki. His list of living wasn't very long now, anyway. Sasha's death had taken most of it with him. Darien's put another dent in it. Alina was still there, but who knew what she thought of him now. He hadn't been able to explain anything to her - just handed her his ring and a letter and told her to keep the letter, especially, safe. Master Wehr probably hated him now. Would hate him more when word was spread that he was the king's murderer.

He hated himself. He should have done something, anything to get Darien to leave. If only he'd known about the tunnel sooner, maybe he could have...

But he didn't. He hadn't. All the wishing, and regretting, and scheming in the world couldn't raise the dead.

He wanted to lie down and give up. It would be easier. And there probably wasn't a person alive who wouldn't agree that things would be better if he simply died. Mara would lose her pawn; Desmond would lose his rival and enemy. And Aki? Aki would lose this awful burden that dragged him down, down, down.

Shutting his eyes, it was like he was there, back at that abyss in the mountain, staring into its dark mouth. All he had to do was step off. There was no knowing just how far he would fall into that black nothingness. But once the choice was made, there was no going back. He felt as if his entire life had been racing toward this precipice. And no one was here now to tell him what to do.

A cry came from far away. A shout, a scream. The roar of flames. Shattering glass. More cries. Enough to fill the air.

Fingers of apprehension ran up his spine. Aki's eyes flew open. From the far end of town, the sounds blended into a crescendo of horror. Savagery mingled with terror into a dissonant melody that sang through air that was filling with plumes of smoke.

His back left the wall, and his feet carried him a few steps forward out into the middle of the street. The town was on fire. And it was coming toward him. In the thickening haze of smoke, people ran, their cries shrill. Aki watched, transfixed, as behind the fleeing townspeople, he saw the band of men with their weapons brandished. Ritter's men.

Mara struck yet again.

Aki watched as Ritter's men scattered through the streets, chasing down the townspeople. He knew Mara's plan. He knew she was going to allow Ritter's men to do their worst before staging a rescue. It didn't take much to imagine what their worst was. Aki turned away, unable to watch. Not when he knew that the entire thing was just for Mara's show, just for Mara's benefit. It was time to get out of there unless he wanted to be drawn further into the game that Mara was playing.

He turned into a side street that was still empty and free of the fire that was ravaging the lower end of the town.

"Aki," a voice called after him. A voice he recognized.

Karina stood in the mouth of the alley, her back to the inferno raging through the town. She must have followed him. He turned away in disgust. She was Mara's creature, obedient to her no matter what it was.

"Wait, Aki," Karina called out again. "I did not want to do it."

"You never want to, but you always do. You do anything and everything she says," he said, still walking away.

Footsteps pounded behind him as she ran to catch up. Her breath was heavy as she came up behind him. Aki kept walking. He didn't stop as he heard several others running toward them as well. It wasn't until Karina shrieked his name that he turned again.

They hadn't gone unnoticed by Ritter's men. Three or four were already in the alley and two of them had hold of Karina but none were coming toward him. Aki didn't have time to wonder at that. Karina screamed his name again. Her hands scrambled for a hold along the wall as they dragged her backwards.

"Help me," she cried out.

Instead, he kept walking.

"Aki," he could hear the tears in her voice, the panic, "wait. Don't leave me."

He rounded the corner out of sight, but her cries still followed him. He stopped, a hand on the wall beside him to steady himself. She was no longer crying his name or any other coherent words, but she wasn't silent either.

Aki tried to shake away the knowledge of what would likely happen to her. Mara had protected her for her entire life, but Mara wasn't around now. And right now, in this moment, he wanted her to suffer. She deserved it. Didn't she?

He was walking again. The haze in the air filling his mind as well. He was walking and the cool touch of metal in his hand steadied him. Her screams were fading.

Everything was fading, back into some recess of his mind. There was a man in front of Aki. And then he was gone. A startled look crossing his face a second before he sank to the ground, clutching his chest. Another man's face filled Aki's vision, but he disappeared like the first. All around him, there were dead and dying.

He saw her then. Still crying, still struggling. Her clothes torn; her face red from her crying. He wasn't sure why he came back. He wasn't sure of anything at all, except that all around him, death and destruction reigned supreme. And in all that chaos he had a purpose, a task towards which he could bend all his restless anger.

There was a man between them, his back to Aki. He never saw what hit him. And then she was looking up at him, her eyes widening in horror. Fear. She was afraid of him. He felt the realization sink in as if it belonged to another person. All around him, the fire continued its blazing, Ritter's men continued their pillaging, the townspeople continued their noisome flight. But none of it came close to them.

He had her by the wrist, dragging her after him. Still she cried.

There was a shift in the air, a moment when Aki realized Mara had sent her men from the castle. The final act of her charade was beginning. And he was still caught in the middle of it. Behind him, Karina stumbled and tried to pull away from him. He kept walking, his grip on her arm iron. People parted before them, but Aki couldn't say whether it was his own sword that cleared the way or some other unseen thing.

They were inside the castle walls before the haze that held him bound slowly faded. Karina was still staring at him in mortal terror, and he looked down to see the bloody sword still clenched in his fist. He was aware of stinging pain in a dozen different places. There were slices in his clothes. He was breathing hard. His fingers loosened their hold on her arm, and she fled.

He just stood there, in the courtyard, trying to piece together what had just happened. But his mind was a red blank. All he knew was that people died. Men died all around him. Men died because of him. The same illness that had clutched him after Cadoc's death threatened him now. He swallowed and drew in a deep breath. Above his head, looking out from one of the large upper windows, was Mara. Aki met her gaze, aware all of a sudden that it was her men he'd killed. And equally and startlingly aware in the same moment that he did not care.

All afternoon, he expected Sebastian to beat down his door and haul him in front of Mara. But, although he heard Mara's men return from the town, he heard no footsteps come down his hallway. All afternoon he waited for the fear of Mara's wrath that he was sure would come. But that fear was as absent as Sebastian.

At their supper table that night, Mara was as regally distant and cool as ever. Karina avoided his eyes and even a few hours hadn't been enough to conceal her swollen, red eyes. A bruise was darkening beneath one of them and there was a cut on her lip. Her hair, that had been badly mauled, was braided afresh. Halle, alone, appeared completely oblivious to the afternoon's events.

It wasn't until he was on his feet, ready to leave and retire for the night, that Mara said the words he'd been dreading. She set her spoon down, rested her elbows on the table and leaned her chin onto her folded hands.

In a soft voice, she began, "You made quite an impression in town today. I was unaware of just how much you've improved since your time in Aruuk. Ritter tells me he lost half a dozen men, at least, just to you. What a brave performance for the lost heir! If I'd known you were that desperate for action, I would have let you lead the rescue."

"I wasn't exactly counting," Aki said, his eyes darting toward Karina. Her head was bowed, and she was staring into her bowl of soup as if it were the most interesting thing she'd seen all day.

"Oh, I'm not upset. I think it's a wonderful story to spread. Not only have you rid the kingdom of the king who stood in your way, but you fought on behalf of the innocent and lowly people of Dorsten. What a hero that will make you in their eyes!"

There was so much Aki wanted to say. So many words simmering inside him, waiting to be let out.

But not to Mara.

Never to Mara.

He really was hers and he'd played right into her hands once again. Even without trying to, he fit the role she'd written for him.

It took him hours to fall asleep. Hours of tossing and turning, getting up and pacing, reading snippets of his mother's journal. He pulled her letter out of his pocket last of all. Unfolded it carefully and read it over and over until the words seared themselves into his heart and mind. He'd always thought he had more in common with her than his father.

But perhaps he was wrong.

She was good. Her goodness rose up off the pages and came to life; it was so strong. She thought that it was possible to come back from darkness. But all he knew was that he was teetering on the edge of a terrible darkness. All he knew was a voice in his head whispering, always whispering, for him to take that final, plunging step. And from that, he knew there was no coming back. There was that abyss, opened at his feet. He'd inched a little closer to it today.

Finally, he couldn't stay awake any longer. His sleep was full of troubling dreams. In them, he was back on that mountainside from so many years ago, but it wasn't Halle's hand he was holding, it wasn't Halle's frightened, begging eyes he was looking into. It was his own. And although he could hear the roar of the waterfall nearby, it was a voice that worked its way into his consciousness - a voice that whispered his name. Over and over. Begging him for something. And there was a hand on his shoulder, warm and trembling.

"Aki."

He jerked awake, his hand moving for the knife under his pillow. His other hand closed around the wrist of the person kneeling on his bed beside him. A frightened whimper escaped them.

"It's just me," she whispered.

"Karina?" His hand released the knife, and he rubbed his eyes. He remembered that he was angry with her. "What are you doing in here?"

She was quiet for a moment and when she spoke there was a tremor in her voice. "Mara sent me. She said I had to thank you for saving me today. She said you would want this."

Aki propped himself up on his elbow and noticed what Karina was wearing. Even in the darkness, he could see that it was nothing but a sheer nightgown. Her hands were already at the laces near her throat, untying them, pulling the thin nightgown open.

"What are you doing, Karina?" he repeated, although he knew exactly what she was doing.

"Mara said you only saved me because you wanted me for yourself."

He sat up, hot all over. Karina's eyes, visible in the moonlight that filled the room, followed his every move. They were wide with childish apprehension. Aki couldn't deny the desire that filled him. It was a desire to strip that childish innocence right out of her. He despised her. He despised everything that Mara had made her into. He despised how sheltered Mara had kept her, shielding her from all the vile things that took place within the walls of Chief Gundar's home.

His hand was on hers, pushing them out of the way, feeling their warmth. Feeling the shiver that ran through her at his touch. His eyes met hers and he noticed her apprehension had morphed into something else. Fear. Fear of him, because he wasn't bothering to hide how much he wanted her to hurt for all the times he'd been hurt. She read it all on his face. Every dark, base thought he had in that moment.

He hated her.

He hated himself.

And there was that darkness before him. It called to him now. Sang his name. Beckoned him to take that final step.

The darkness had no bottom, no limit. He was afraid of who he would be, of what he would become. Always, there was that fear, holding him back, pulling him away from the edge. The fear that whispered to him in the voice of every good and decent person he'd ever learned to care about. It told him that only monsters lived in that darkness. Men without souls. Men like Cadoc. Like Gundar.

There was no coming back from it. None.

He dropped his hand and looked away. Ashamed... angry. Pushing her away, he got up and went to the window. The moon was nearly full, its silver light cool and distant.

"Did I do something wrong?" Karina's soft whisper followed him.

"Yes," he answered, his voice harsh. "You're worth more than this, Karina."

He turned to find her watching him, her narrow face screwed up in confusion at his words.

"You don't want me, then?"

Aki slapped a hand to his forehead at her naivety. "Even if I did, this isn't right."

"But Mara said..."

"Mara lies. All the time. She doesn't care what happens to you or me or anyone just so long as she gets her way."

Karina recoiled a little and a finger caught a strand of hair and began twisting it around and around. "She cares about me. If it weren't for her..."

"Karina," he sat on the edge of the bed, saying each word carefully, "she sent you in here for me to rape. That's how much she cares."

She blinked back tears then and he grabbed his own hair in his hands in frustration. He wondered just what Mara was trying to accomplish by this whole affair. She never acted without purpose.

And as he sat there, watching Karina hold back her crying, realization crept over him like ice. Mara needed him to step off the edge. She knew. She'd always known, since the day he'd tried to kill Halle, that he had it in him. And it wasn't enough to drag him along as a reluctant accomplice. She wanted an ally. Mara didn't want him to be able to come back.

"Stop crying. Nothing's even happened," he said when he couldn't stand to watch her anymore. "Go on. Go back to your room."

"Please don't make me go. If you do, she'll think I've done something wrong. And she was already so angry with me for going into town after you today."

Aki hesitated, considering her words. "Why did you follow me into town?"

Karina pulled his blankets up over her shoulders and leaned back against the headboard, coiling into herself as if she hadn't just offered to share his bed with him. "I wanted to tell you I did not know exactly what she was doing. She did not tell me. All she told me was that you would be upset by it."

"Would it have changed anything? You still do whatever she tells you to. She could have told that she was planning on murder, and you still would have gone along with it."

"You do everything she wants, too."

"No. I don't. If I did, we wouldn't be talking right now, would we?"

Karina bit her lip and looked away. The finger that twisted a strand of hair worked furiously. "I was going to tell you. But you and Halle were so...," she paused, looking at him again with a bit of disbelief in her eyes, "you both were actually happy down there exploring. It would have ruined it to know."

"Karina," he burst out in a frustrated whisper, "Mara was committing murder up here. It should have been ruined. It wasn't even that important."

She shrank further, pulling herself into a tight ball up against the headboard. Afraid of him, again. "I told you I did not know what she was planning, Aki."

Leaning back beside her, Aki sighed. "It doesn't matter now, anyway. He's dead. And everyone believes I killed him."

There wasn't anything left to say because he was right. Nothing mattered anymore. Darien was dead. Mara was spreading the lie that Aki had ended his life. And Aki was stuck in her web, unable to escape.

He tipped his head back and shut his eyes. It wasn't sleep he wanted. He forced his memory to wander back to the only time in his life when everything was perfect - those three years he'd spent with Stephan and Alina before he'd ruined everything.

How he wished Stephan was here now to tell him what to do. Stephan always knew. No matter how hard it was, he knew the answers and what to do. He tried to think of what Stephan would say to him now. What direction he would give. But all he could think of was the grim disappointment that Aki had grown accustomed to seeing after his return from Karu.

"She has one like you," Karina whispered, interrupting his thoughts.

"What?"

"Down in the dungeon, the part we did not go in, she has one like you."

"What do you mean, 'like me'?"

"He is also a courier. That is what you are, right?"

Not anymore, his mind whispered. Not ever again. "Yes," he said aloud. "Why does she have him?"

Karina shrugged. Aki felt the gesture in the darkness. "Every day she goes down to see him with Cristof. Or sometimes, she is with Sebastian. I think he has something she wants or knows something she wants to know."

The codes. It had to be. Aki sat straight up and faced Karina. "Do you know who he is?"

There were so many couriers missing, most of whom he never knew. Most of whom had been killed, their bodies dotting the road across the great plains.

"I have only seen him once, but I have heard him scream when Mara and Cristof are in there. Mara never lets me come inside when she is talking to him. I think his name is Felix."

Chapter 47

YOUR HIGHNESS..."

"Leave me."

Desmond's voice shook as he spoke. His hands shook as they held the letter. That letter, written in such a lovely flowing hand, that cold letter which Desmond couldn't quite make himself believe. The words defied the gentle script, callous, cruel words that seared his eyes. His father was dead.

Dead. Dead. Dead.

The words formed a morbid chant. The finality of that word. The hopelessness of it. Desmond wanted to shred the letter into a thousand pieces and burn each one. But that couldn't change that single word. Dead. His father, the king, was dead. He wanted to tear his hair out with grief and rage, but that could change anything, either.

And then there was that cruel, cruel phrase. That wretched condemnation "in retaliation of those who were murdered on the order of the Crown Prince..."

In retaliation for what he'd ordered. The massacre he'd commanded. He hadn't meant for this to happen, though. He hadn't meant for his father to pay the price for that moment of angry indulgence.

There was more. So much more in that letter. It curdled his blood to read the words, "Aki Gundarson both suggested and carried out the execution."

Outside his tent, the wind kept up its mournful song. They were moving so slowly. Inching their way across the

Void with maddening sluggishness. Armies moved slower than men, he was learning. But he didn't have the patience for it. Every day that slipped by was another day lost. It both mattered and didn't all at once. It was too late to save his father, but not too late to put down this rebellion. Not too late to kill Aki. To make him pay for all the chaos he'd unleashed on the kingdom. And Desmond would make him pay.

"Your Highness?" Captain Tyrrel spoke from beyond the tent walls.

"Get the men ready to move, Captain."

He was not at all prepared for Captain Tyrrel to throw open the door of the tent and enter instead. Before he could hide it, the captain's eyes lighted upon the letter in his trembling hands.

"It's about him, isn't it?"

"Yes," Desmond answered, his voice only just audible. "He's dead. Aki's killed him because of..." No. He couldn't even speak the reason. He already knew well how the captain felt about his actions at the old border fort.

"Because you burned his people alive," Captain Tyrrel supplied.

"You won't say a word about this outside of this tent," Desmond snapped. "I can't afford to have the men thinking I'm the one to blame for his death. It's Aki's fault. All of this is his fault. My father should have killed him when he had the chance."

"You do understand that this sister of the king, Mara, is the one behind all of this, don't you? Even if Aki was dead, she would still be a threat and probably the greater threat."

"Stop trying to defend him," Desmond yelled, then checked himself. The tent was nothing but fabric between him and everyone else. It offered nothing for privacy of sound. "He ran for a reason. And he's the one who...," Desmond stopped, afraid to go on, afraid of what would happen if he did.

"I'm not trying to defend him. I'm merely suggesting that we don't turn all our attention solely on him. He hasn't acted alone. And whatever vengeance you want cannot take precedence over the kingdom. Kings don't get to make personal choices, Your Highness, and that's exactly what you are now."

Desmond turned away. His hands crumpled the letter and he let it fall. All his life, he'd been preparing for this day. Only, this wasn't how it was supposed to come. This wasn't how it was supposed to happen.

"I'm not like my father," he murmured.

"No. You never have been. But that does not change the responsibility you now bear."

"And what responsibility is that?"

"If you'd take my advice, Your Highness, finish this business, but don't waste the entire kingdom on personal revenge."

Personal revenge was all he really wanted, though. It was all that mattered.

Chapter 48

MARA SAT AT THE HEAD OF THE table, triumph on her face as Aki came in. Karina had left his room only two hours before and Aki was content to let Mara think what she wanted. It was a distraction he needed. Sometime between Karina's revelation and morning, he recovered enough from his shock at her words to let no sign of them now show on his face. He couldn't afford to care.

Not now.

Kings didn't get to choose individuals. That's what Darien had said. They chose the kingdom's needs first. Well, he wasn't a king, but he didn't get to choose individuals now either. Even if he had the opportunity, he couldn't risk helping Felix.

That didn't mean he couldn't at least see him, confirm that it really was his fellow apprentice.

When he was finished eating, Aki slipped back up to his room. The window that overlooked the courtyard offered him a perfect view of when Mara and Cristof entered the dungeon. He pulled a chair up to the window and sat down to wait.

Footsteps came down the hall and stopped in front of his door. Aki tried to guess who it was before they knocked.

Instead of knocking, though, they just opened the door. Halle stepped inside. Without any encouragement from

Aki, he drew up a second chair and threw himself down in it. He followed Aki's gaze out the window.

"Waiting for something?"

"No."

Halle gave him a disbelieving stare. He crossed his arms over his chest and propped his feet up on the stone window ledge, tipping his chair on its back legs. "She's going too far."

"Mara?"

Halle nodded. "I mean, she's always planned and schemed. But all this? There's just too much."

"It'll work, though. She's thought of everything."

"Even of you." Halle gave him an odd look. "I can't believe you're going along with all this."

"What else am I supposed to do, Halle?"

Halle started to say something, but Aki held up a hand to silence him. Mara was crossing the courtyard, Cristof two steps behind her. He jumped out of his chair and was halfway to the door before Halle said, "You were waiting for something."

Aki stopped.

"You're planning something, aren't you?"

"No. I just need to see something for myself."

He left it at that and hurried down into the courtyard. No one moved to stop him as he opened the door into the dungeon. It was hard to imagine that it was only a day ago that they'd found the tunnel.

It wasn't hard to find where Mara and Cristof had gone. There was only one passage, running off to the side, that was lit up at regular intervals by torches mounted in brackets to the wall. And he could hear the sounds that traveled down that passageway to where he stood. Sounds of pain that were all too familiar.

There wasn't any need to creep up on them and Aki had no intention of hiding. He walked down the passage until he came to a door that was ajar. Beyond it, Mara's voice, low and cool, murmured. Aki couldn't understand what she was saying, but he could picture how she was saying it. A feeble cry of pain followed her voice and Aki stepped into the room.

Even though he was facing away from the door and half blocked by Mara, there was no mistaking Felix. Aki knew he ought to turn around, ought to walk away before he witnessed anything more. He couldn't afford to care.

But he lingered.

"You know, all of this can end whenever you choose," Mara said. "All we need is for you to write down the courier codes for us."

Aki waited to hear Felix say something, to deny that he even knew what she was talking about. Instead, there was complete silence aside from Felix's harsh, labored breathing. From where he stood, Aki could see that Felix was chained between two pillars and Cristof was in front of him, facing him. But he couldn't see what was in Cristof's hands. He didn't really need to. He watched as a spasm of pain jerked Felix's body away from something.

"If it's just the codes you want, Mara, I can give you those," he heard himself say.

Cristof stopped whatever he was doing, and Mara turned around. There was a brief flash of annoyance across her face and then she smiled.

"Can you now? And how would you know them?"

Karina must not have told her, he realized. "I was training as a courier with him. I know everything he does."

Mara eyed him, her lips pursed as she weighed his words. She made up her mind in a moment and waved at him to follow her around to the table that stood in front of Felix and Cristof. As he got close, Aki could see not only an assortment of metal instruments of torture but also a stack of papers, messages and letters stolen from the couriers her men had been killing.

"Aki?" Felix's voice was weak, broken. "You're with them? I didn't..."

Mara's hand caught him across the face, throwing his head back with the force of it. "If you can't speak and give us the codes, then you don't get to talk now." She turned toward Aki, suspicion all over her face. "You know him? Is that why you're offering your help?"

"Just because I know him doesn't mean I want to help him. But it sounds like you're just wasting time down here. If you want to know what those say, I can tell you now."

She was still suspicious, but she gestured toward the table. "Go ahead then. Prove to me you're telling the truth. It's so hard to tell with you."

He avoided Felix's eyes as he picked up the one on top. It took him a few moments, but he read it out for Mara.

"You know, Aki, there are times when I think you're really with me." She turned to Felix, lifting his face up with a gentle hand. Felix's breath quickened at her touch and he tried to pull away, but the chains held him too tight, gave him too little space to retreat. She contemplated his bloodied face with mild interest. "You, on the other hand, are completely useless to me now. And I don't like keeping useless things around. Perhaps if you'd worked with me..."

She let the silence finish the thought for her as she continued to study Felix, turning his head from side to side as if examining a piece of work. Aki tensed beside her, pretending to keep his eyes on another letter. If he spoke out again, it would only make matters worse. If he didn't speak up...

"Cristof," Mara said, coming to a quick decision, "I don't suppose he needs the use of his hands anymore, does he?"

Cristof didn't answer, only smiled in a way that made him look just like Cadoc.

"Break them," she said, still holding Felix's face up. She ran her thumb over a swollen, bloody cheek, but her eyes were on Aki now, waiting for any reaction that she could pounce on. "I don't believe he needs his eyes anymore, either. Blind him. Let that be the price he pays for not giving me what I want."

A choked cry escaped Felix's lips and Mara let his head drop. It was a few more seconds before she'd satisfied herself that Aki wasn't going to speak out. He felt her stare but kept his eyes down on the paper in front of him. The marks were swimming in his vision now.

"Desmond's army draws near, Aki. And I do believe Baron Orlander rides at his side. Lord of his cavalry, if I'm not mistaken. I had considered offering my worthless captive to him for a ransom if he'd cooperated with me, but... How do you think the Baron would like to receive a gift from us? A gift in the form of his son's head. I think he'd find that quite disheartening."

Aki quelled the sick feeling that formed a pit in his stomach before raising his eyes. If he let Mara see that it mattered... It was too late. He knew what she was going to say next.

"I let you out of executing the king, Aki. I think it's high time you prove yourself, not only to me, but to the people you'll be leading. You will execute our uncooperative friend here," she patted Felix's flinching cheek gently, "first thing in the morning. And then I think it will finally be time for your people to meet you."

The voice that answered her was calm, detached. It was a voice that came from the part of Aki that shut out all of the bad. It said, "Yes, Mara. I'll do it."

"Good. Cristof, finish here. Aki, bring those upstairs. I want them all decoded."

Aki shut the door behind him, but he couldn't shut his ears to the scream that came as they walked out of the dungeon. It was a scream that could have been heard all the way into town, Aki thought. He wanted to add his own voice to it.

For the rest of the day, Aki bent over the missives that were meant for other eyes than his own. Once or twice, Mara appeared to see how far he'd gotten. Both times she'd left impatient and irritated. But Aki couldn't help it. The words refused to make sense to him. Everything refused to make sense. Felix's scream echoed in his mind, robbing him of the ability to concentrate on anything else. His impending execution only added to it.

There was nothing he could do about it. No way he could get out of his role in it. Mara meant to drag him down just as far as she could take him, and he had no choice but to go along.

But it was Felix. The one person at the academy who'd gone out of their way to welcome him.

Aki shook away the memory. Forced his eyes to read the coded message before him. It would be a quick, clean death at least. A mercy, almost, after what Cristof had done to him. Aki knew what it was like to suffer so much that death held a strange appeal.

But it was Felix, who'd tried so hard to forgive him. Who was willing to give him a second chance when almost no one else would.

Aki shut his eyes to keep them from burning.

And he was back in that arena, lying on the ground, pain tearing through his arm. The others holding back guilty laughter at the trick they'd played on him. Felix was at his side, worried, distressed. Horrified at the lack of honor among his fellow apprentices.

Aki slammed his fist into the table and opened his eyes. It was the wrong thing to think of now. The wrong memory to pull up.

It was only then that he became aware of Sebastian's presence. The man was sitting some distance away from him, just watching. Aki didn't know how long he'd been there, but he could guess Sebastian's purpose. Mara was having him watched.

Sebastian leaned forward as if to say something and Aki hoped that whatever it was it would be enough to drag him out of the misery that held him now.

But Sebastian didn't speak. He looked away. He looked at the ceiling, the floor, out the window, anywhere but at Aki. And then he got up and left and Aki was left alone with his wretched memories and the burden of knowing there was nothing he could do to stop anything.

He dreaded the coming of night. Yet night still came. As darkness settled over the castle and all but the men on guard duty retired, Aki withdrew to his room. There was no hope of sleeping tonight. Not when he knew what the morning held. Mara would drag it out, too. She'd turn it into as great a spectacle as she could. She would reveal who he was to everyone who watched and his fate by her side would be sealed.

He lay back on his bed in the darkness. All he wanted now was for this nightmare to be over. Mara's leash was getting tighter by the day. He had no choice but to obey her.

"You always have a choice, Aki. It's mindless obedience that makes a slave..." Master Wehr's words slipped in between his darkest thoughts.

Aki almost laughed at the memory of them, spoken in response to his anger over being bound in service to King Darien. Only the laugh that welled up in his throat was horribly close to hysteria. How could he ever have been angry at the idea of serving King Darien? The man had given him his life back.

No choice, he'd told himself all day. But there, in the darkness of his room, he knew he was lying to himself. Kings might not be able to put the needs of individuals first, but he was no king. And what did it matter if he accomplished anything else if he let his own friend die?

His boots were already laced up, his feet were already moving across the floor when he realized what he was doing. In his hand was a satchel that Colin had taught him to always carry with him on a mission.

The courtyard was empty, only the walls guarded. He crept across it, keeping well within the shadows. Mara didn't even bother to put a guard at the door of the dungeon. Her only prisoner was in no condition to escape on his own.

Aki was inside, shutting the door behind him, shutting himself into the inky blackness of the dungeon. His own breathing was loud and raspy in the silence. Leaning against the door to catch his breath, Aki's eyes gradually adjusted to the dark. One hand to the damp wall, cringing at the layer of slime he felt beneath his fingers, Aki groped his way down the side passage. When he turned the corner, a faint line of light showed beneath the door at the end of the hall. He made his way toward the light, toward Felix.

Chapter 49

I S IT MORNING ALREADY?"
Felix turned hideous, blinded eyes toward the sound of Aki's entrance. His voice broke over the words although he tried hard to keep it steady. He was no longer on his feet, chained to both posts. Instead, he sat, leaning against one. At first Aki thought he was unrestrained, but a closer look showed that his hands were shackled together and a short length of chain held him to just the one post.

Aki didn't know what to say. There weren't words that could make up for anything that Felix suffered. There was no explanation Aki could give him now that would make any sense or that Felix would believe. And he couldn't bring himself to look at what was left of Felix's face. Cristof had used a hot iron to blind him, and the resulting disfigurement was too painful to witness. Instead, he searched around for keys.

After only a cursory search, it was obvious Cristof hadn't risked leaving them behind. Aki went to the table and examined the tools on it. He selected a thin metal wire and returned to Felix.

Felix stifled a cry when Aki's hand touched his. He recoiled as far as his broken body would go, the chain clattering with every frantic movement.

"It's alright, Felix. It's just me," Aki said, although, after this afternoon, he wasn't sure there was much comfort in his reassurance.

"Is it time already?"

"Shhh...it's still the middle of the night."

"How could you do this, Aki?" There was so much despair, so much anguish in Felix's words that Aki turned away in shame, despite the fact that Felix couldn't actually see him.

"I'm going to get you out of here," he murmured.

Felix said nothing else. He was trying too hard to stay quiet as Aki's efforts shifted his now broken and mangled hands. Aki winced at the sight of them. At least they could be healed. His eyes were destroyed, sightless forever.

Aki's hands were anything but steady as he worked at the locks. He was hurting Felix no matter how hard he tried not to. Every movement he made jarred Felix's hands.

He tried not to jump every time a rat scurried off into some corner. As far as he knew, no one had seen him enter, but if they did, he would be hard pressed to come up with a reasonable excuse. His imagination filled in exactly what Mara would do if she caught him down here.

If only picking locks had been among his many lessons with Master Wehr and Colin, Aki bemoaned. No matter how he picked at them, they refused to open. Minutes ticked by and he only succeeded in frustrating himself and causing Felix far more pain.

"Someone's coming," Felix whispered through clenched teeth and Aki paused to listen as well.

There were footsteps coming. Whoever it was made no effort to conceal their approach. Aki was sure it was only one person. Cristof, maybe, coming to admire his handiwork before it was dead.

"Don't let them know I'm here," Aki said softly as he crawled back behind the heavy table and into the shadows. It was a poor hiding place. If they were coming down here to ease their suspicions, he'd be found out at once.

The footsteps stopped in front of the door Aki had carefully shut behind him. Aki watched as the latch was lifted from the outside. From his hiding spot he could only see the lower half of the man who entered. He didn't pause in the doorway but came straight toward Felix.

Aki sucked in a breath. His fingernails bit into the palms of his hands as he clenched them at his sides. If it was Cristof...

He could kill him.

He would kill him. Before he had the chance to hurt Felix again. Inching out of his hiding spot, one hand already drawing free the knife at his side, Aki watched as Cristof crouched down in front of Felix, something in his hand. He would...

"Here, drink," Sebastian's voice came softly across the room and Aki froze. "It will make it better for a while."

In the quiet of the room, Aki heard Felix swallow whatever liquid Sebastian offered him. Already half out of his hiding place, Aki didn't dare retreat as Sebastian stood up and stepped near the table. If Sebastian looked past it, he was lost. The quiet jangle of metal came from just above the table and then Sebastian was walking to the door, closing it behind him as if he'd never been there.

Aki waited. He waited until Sebastian's footsteps had long since faded and then he waited even longer. Felix's breathing evened and although Aki couldn't see his face, he could guess from the way Felix was slumped against the pillar that Sebastian hadn't given him just water to drink.

His legs protested when he finally stood upright after so long in his cramped hiding place. There, right in front of him on the table, was a ring of keys. Aki knew he hadn't missed seeing them before. Sebastian had put them there. Which meant, Sebastian knew he was there.

Aki's heart leaped to his throat.

He snatched up the keys and fumbled through trying one after the other in Felix's cuffs. Felix, though still awake, was too drowsy now to be of any help. At least he was quiet, Aki thought. Sebastian had given him tea to dull his pain. A merciful gesture that Aki hadn't thought the man capable of. His own experience with Sebastian had never revealed such a side.

At last, the chains fell away. Aki caught them before they clattered to the stone floor and alerted anyone lurking nearby. He stooped down to pull Felix's arm over his shoulder. The medicine was only so effective. As Aki pulled him up, Felix moaned and mumbled something incoherent.

Felix was taller than him and heavier and totally incapable of supporting himself or standing upright. Aki staggered a little under the burden of his weight.

Felix mumbled again and this time, Aki caught the last word, "...coming."

Without waiting to make sense of what Felix was trying to say, Aki started toward the door. It opened before he reached it. Cristof stood framed in it, his face still in the shadows.

"What have we here?"

Aki could hear the smirk in his words. Cristof had probably been watching for him to make just such a move. Waiting for an excuse to strike. Aki looked around but there weren't many options left to him. Holding Felix up prohibited him from reaching most of his weapons and by the time he put him down it would be too late.

"Not quite Mara's faithful little slave, are you?" Cristof made a show of looking around the room. "Looks like she's not around to protect you, either."

"Doesn't mean she won't be upset if you kill me," Aki said, backing up as best he could with Felix leaning on him. Cristof sounded like Cadoc. Standing there in the shadows, he looked like Cadoc. Aki tried to breathe past the frantic rhythm of his heart as every lurid memory he'd shared with that man assailed him.

"I don't think that's a good enough reason to let you live. You killed my father. Now it's time to...," Cristof's voice broke off in a startled gasp.

Aki's eyes widened as he watched Cristof stumble forward a step and fall to his knees, and then to his face, a knife in his back.

"You let him talk too much."

"Halle?"

"Well, are we going to do this or not?"

"Wait. How did you know I was down here?"

Halle came into the room and grabbed the lantern that hung near the door. "It really wasn't that hard to guess. Come on."

Aki shifted his hold on Felix to keep his balance. He stared at Halle and wondered once again how it came to be that they found themselves on the same side of anything.

"What about him? If Mara finds him...," the rest didn't need to be said.

Halle stared down at Cristof's body and Aki watched as the realization of what he'd just done sunk into Halle. His face went a pasty shade of green and he swallowed hard several times before turning his head away.

"I guess he'll just have to run away with the courier."

Before Aki could ask what he meant, Halle bent down and started dragging Cristof out the door with one hand, holding the lantern in his other. Aki followed.

"I'm assuming you wanted to put our newfound secret to use," Halle whispered over his shoulder, breathless already from his exertion.

Aki was too busy trying not to lose his balance to actually answer. He simply nodded his head.

The distance between them and the tunnel seemed to grow with every step. And Aki knew it would only get worse once they were inside it. Sebastian's gesture of kindness was probably the only way they would get through to the caverns without Felix waking the entire castle. As it was, Felix hadn't so much as whimpered, although Aki's care in moving him was, of necessity, less than careful.

The space became cramped very quickly, the air stifling, as they crawled through the last stretch of tunnel. Aki heard his own breath, harsh and panting, echoing in the tight space. Halle's wasn't any better. Aki tried to find a new position to haul Felix's unresponsive body in to relieve the aching cramp that took hold of his right arm and succeeded mostly in getting himself soaked with the small stream of water that drained down it. Ahead, he heard Halle kicking the grate open.

"This is as far as I'm taking him," Halle whispered out of breath.

Again, before Aki could ask what he meant, he heard Halle grunt with effort and watched Cristof's body roll over the edge of the chasm. Neither of them moved as a long moment of silence stretched out. A distant thud told them that Cristof's body had found its final resting place. Halle met his eyes and nodded. "Guess you don't have to worry about him hunting you down anymore."

"Now I just have to take care of the hundred other people who want me dead," Aki answered.

Halle laughed, a little shaky and breathless, and Aki found himself joining him.

"He was a lot heavier than I thought he'd be," Halle said at last, pausing for breath.

"Let's keep moving."

It was easier going once they were through the grate and onto the ledge. Halle came up on Felix's other side and between the two of them they made good progress. Aki wished there was a way to know how far the night was gone but he was left guessing, hoping that it wasn't yet dawn.

They reached the place where the two sides of the chasm joined and went into the open room. Here, Aki lowered Felix to the ground near one of the other openings and knelt beside him. With Halle holding the lantern over them, he got his first real look at what had been done to his friend. And in that moment, he wished it had been his knife that found Cristof's heart.

He slid his satchel off his shoulder and opened it. Inside were several small tins, an assortment of medicines Colin thought it was necessary to always carry with him, as well as bandages. Aki didn't think the bandages were nearly enough, but they were a start. He pulled his own water flask out and soaked a cloth with fresh, cool water. Beginning with Felix's face, he cleaned each wound as best he could.

Halle leaned over his shoulder, watching. After some time had passed, he startled Aki by speaking. "Are you planning on coming back?"

"Yes. I have to."

"Because Mother wants you to?"

Aki nodded, the closest he would come to lying outright. He opened one of the tins, the earthy scent of the salve inside blending well with the air around them, and applied it to the burns on Felix's eyes and face.

"She won't win."

Aki turned sharply at Halle's words. "What do you mean?"

"She never wins, Aki. And she's already coming apart. I mean, that attack on the town, putting her own men up against each other, that's insane. She's losing her control over them, and she doesn't even realize it. It's how it always goes." Halle moved around to the other side of Felix and sat down.

"She has enough of them. Sebastian will still do anything she says."

Halle let out a derisive snort. "For being right in the middle of everyone's secrets, there's a lot you don't know, isn't there? Sebastian doesn't listen to her because he's loyal to her. He listens to her so that he can stay close to his daughter."

Aki furrowed his brow in confusion but didn't look up. There had been too many secrets revealed to him about family. It wouldn't surprise him if somehow Sebastian was just another extension of that tangled web. At this point, he didn't see how it mattered. All Mara's talk about him being the lost heir and he was still nothing more than the story she'd sold the people. He'd done absolutely nothing that a leader would do.

But he was curious. When Halle didn't elaborate, he asked, "And who is this daughter he wants to stay close to?"

Halle laughed again. "You're half blind, aren't you? It's Karina, you idiot."

"What?"

"I guess there was some sort of family debt, or maybe he just made Father angry or something like that. I don't know. It happened years ago when Karina was just a baby. Father took Karina from Sebastian and his wife and eventually gave her to Mother."

Aki stopped wrapping the bandage over Felix's eyes and stared in open disbelief at Halle. He shook his head and went back to work.

"You are coming back, though," Halle repeated his earlier question and Aki nodded. "I'll cover for you until you do but don't stay too long. You can't be missing in the morning or there's nothing anyone can do to save you."

"Why are you helping me, Halle?"

Halle stood up and shrugged. "Why'd you ask Ritter to spare my life? Or put up with me all those days on the run? Or stand up for me when we were working together?"

Chapter 50

HALLE LEFT THE LANTERN BEHIND with Aki, insisting he didn't need it to feel his way along the rock wall. Aki sped up his work. Halle was right. He had to be back before dawn. Well before dawn. He stifled a yawn that threatened to split his face in two and rubbed a weary hand over his eyes. Beside him, Felix stirred a little.

Aki wished he would wake up before he had to leave. If he didn't, Aki wasn't sure what he would do. Trapped down here in a dark cavern without a clue as to how he got there. Aki could only imagine how frantic he'd be. Then Aki remembered that the darkness wouldn't make any difference to Felix. He would live, trapped in such darkness, for the rest of his life. There was no undoing Cristof's final act of cruelty. None.

Aki drew his knees up and rested his forehead on them, the full weight of Felix's fate coming to rest on him. "I'm sorry," he whispered. "I'm sorry I didn't stop him. I should have. I should have figured out a way to stop him."

Only lonely silence greeted his words.

Aki hated it.

There was only one way to keep himself from hearing it and that was to keep speaking. So, he did. Just like he'd done with Karina when they were running back to Bren, he talked to no one. Only this time, it wasn't interesting lessons in history or stories of people whose bravery always left him ashamed. Aki spoke the words he hadn't dared to even think since he arrived in Dorsten.

He spoke the truth.

And the truth was its own bit of comfort in the dark, lonely silence. It was its own bit of warmth against the cold cruelty of the circumstances he found himself surrounded with every day. The truth was a breath of free air, and he couldn't afford to bring it back with him to the castle. But for those few minutes he could savor it and he did.

The silence that followed wasn't quite so formidable and Aki made the mistake of shutting his eyes. It was a terrible mistake, and he knew it even as he succumbed to the temptation. Only for a moment, he told himself. He just needed a moment of respite.

He didn't wake fully the first time the blade prodded the soft skin beneath his chin. Nor the second. He didn't wake until a bright light shined directly into his eyes. And even then, the events of the past few days left him too scrambled and muddled to respond with much speed.

"Give me one good reason why I shouldn't just kill you now."

Aki's eyes were open then, squinting up at the man whose voice was so painfully familiar. Whose face was...

"Stephan?"

The blade at his throat withdrew slightly and the man standing over him shook his head.

"So, you know my brother. How's that? You're dressed like one of them. You sound like one of them. What do you know of my brother?"

Aki dropped his eyes. And immediately felt the prick of the knife against his neck once more.

"Stephan's... Stephan's dead. I," Aki scooted away from the knife and out of the blinding light. He looked around. Aside from Felix still lying beside him, there were now at least six other men in the room, including Stephan's brother, Norman, a man he'd only ever heard about and never met. "You just look like him. You look just like him."

"Dead? When? How? I've had no word. We've had no word of anything that's gone on in Dival."

"There's time for that later, Norm," another man spoke up behind Norman.

Norman nodded. "Let's get back to that first part then, shall we. What are you doing down here?"

Aki looked at the anger etched in the faces of all the men in the room. Most were old enough to have families. All had probably suffered under the reign of terror Mara had conjured up. Aki had spent a lifetime reading people, gauging the depth of their anger.

And Norman was right. He was dressed just like one of Mara's men. He had an accent just like Mara's men. He knew in that single glance that he only had one choice.

"Kill me if you want, but please, just take care of him," he gestured toward Felix. "He's Baron Orlander's son and a courier in the king's service. And he was my friend. He's on your side. Just keep him alive and give him to his father. Desmond's army isn't far. The baron will be with him."

The men exchanged looks and Aki knew his death wouldn't happen immediately. He'd bought enough time to talk and that was all he needed. He silently prayed that was all he needed.

"And just whose side do you think we're on?" Norman asked.

"Not Mara's. That's all that matters. She's the one that wants him dead."

"So, he's the one that's supposed to be executed in whatever's left of town. And who might you be?"

"The one who's supposed to execute him," Aki answered miserably.

A collective gasp rippled through the group. Norman studied him a little more closely, using the tip of his blade to tip Aki's head back to get a better look.

At first, Aki was confused by the reaction. Then he remembered. Mara was going to use the morning's execution as an opportunity to finally unveil him to the people. He was no longer going to be just a character in a story she made up, but flesh and blood, the living, breathing heir come to rescue them from the tyranny of the southern royals. She must have spread word about it. And somehow these men in front of him must have heard.

A germ of an idea sprouted up in his mind, the first seed of hope in an otherwise hopeless task.

"You're the lost heir everyone's been going on about?" Norman asked. "You're Sybil's son?"

Aki hesitated, partly because of the familiarity that Norman spoke his mother's name with and partly because his answer would mean everything. Knowing that whatever answer he gave now sealed his road. There wouldn't be any turning back. If he acknowledged his heirdom, his claim, then he would never be allowed to throw it off.

He drew himself up the best he could while sitting under their scrutiny, met Norman's eyes evenly, and said, "I am. My mother was Sybil Bayner. I am Lord Bayner's heir."

"Aye, I can see it," Norman nodded, a strange brightness filling his eyes. "And if that's the truth, then it's your side we're on."

Aki absorbed the words. His side. Well, at least they had a side. He wasn't sure what his side in all this was. There was the promise he had yet to fulfill, although it was too late now for Darien. There was Desmond, who he only wished to see dead. There was Mara, who's leash grew shorter and shorter each day. Where did he fall in all of that?

Mara couldn't win. But then, neither could Desmond. The prince had butchered Aki's own people in cold blood.

Aki thought of Alina, of Ophelia and little Boris, of Master Wehr. He thought of Halle, and even Karina. He thought of Lars and Faramund. He was on their side. Those were the people who needed to win.

And for the first time since his last conversation with Darien, Aki began to understand the words the king had spoken. Kings couldn't choose individuals over their kingdoms. They couldn't let their choices become personal - not for love, or for hate. But the moment they forgot that people were individuals, the moment nothing was personal anymore - that was the moment that bred tyrants. Because the burden of leadership was that you couldn't let yourself care, but if you kept yourself from caring, you became the monster. Two ends that could never meet and yet must always join together. A pendulum that could only be balanced for a moment or two without swinging to one side or the other.

Compassion is weakness. That's what Gundar used to say. Trust is for fools, Mara would say. But they both only had one half of the picture. Aki was tired of looking at that half.

Gathering himself up, he got to his feet. "If that's the case, we need to talk."

Seated on a rock, Aki watched as Norman sketched out a map of the castle, town, border woods and the great plains with a stick in the dirt. Norman said without looking up, "Desmond's army is a day, maybe two away."

"How many men are hiding in these caves?"

"Hard to say."

Which Aki understood to mean Norman didn't want to say. There was distrust still. He had to hope it wasn't enough to ruin them.

"No, it's better you don't tell me," he hurried on to say. "I can't have her finding out." He remembered the passing of time and stood up. "I have to get back before she misses me."

"Aki," Norman called after him, "we can hear everyone who comes down into these caverns. If it's ever more than you or that friend you had with you today, this one will be the first to die."

Aki looked past Norman to where Felix lay. He nodded. "Take care of him, please. And if he wakes, tell him... tell him I'll find a way to explain everything to him."

It was Norman's turn to nod and Aki turned and started the long trek back to the surface.

Alone, doubt crept in. He'd laid out a plan before the group of men. Gave them every detail he could think of. And they hadn't said much of anything, hadn't volunteered any information of their own. Most importantly, they had given him no confirmation that they intended to go along with his plan. If they didn't, Aki didn't even want to think about what would happen.

He hurried until he was half running down the ledge toward the still open grate. A few months ago, he would have expected Halle to betray him to Mara. He would have expected a greeting party of Mara's men waiting for him at the mouth of the tunnel.

But not today.

Today, Halle was on his side. Today, he had hope - that insane, fragile hope his mother spoke of. Hope that there was a chance to end the madness. Hope that his parents' sacrifice might at last become worth something.

As he left the dungeon behind him and slunk through the shadows back to his room, he searched the sky. There were a couple of hours left before dawn. He couldn't spend them sleeping, despite the exhaustion that dogged his steps.

Going straight to the bedside table, he pulled out a small drawer full of writing materials. It took him the full two hours to finish three letters and tuck them into an inner pocket of his clothes. By then, he heard the castle stirring. Guards on the walls were being changed. Somewhere below him, breakfast was being cooked. Mara would expect him to attend as usual. She would expect him ready for an execution. And that was exactly what Aki intended to be.

There was an uproar before he made it down the stairs.

"You've lost him?" Mara's voice was raised. Aki paused on the stairs. In his entire time with her, Mara had never raised her voice. Her anger was a bit more like ice than fire - cold and not easily thawed.

"I'm sorry, M'lady. I've searched the entire dungeon and there's no sign of him."

"Sebastian," Mara called, her voice echoing off the stone walls.

Aki heard footsteps hurrying toward the dining hall. He didn't envy Sebastian's position and he wondered once again about Sebastian's actions the night before. They didn't make any sense. Perhaps it was a coincidence that he'd offered Felix a drink then. Perhaps it was a mistake that he set the keys down on the table and did not pick them up again. But Aki didn't think so. Sebastian was too careful of a man.

"Were you not in command of the guard last night?"

"I was."

"And you saw no one enter or leave the dungeon?"

"I saw only one, Mara. Cristof entered the dungeon late in the night. I never saw him leave. And no one's seen him this morning."

"Cristof? Cristof would never do such a thing."

"You always say things like that, Mother, but Cristof was angry that you wouldn't let him kill Aki. Maybe he finally saw a chance to get even."

"If I'd wanted to hear what you had to say on the matter, Halle, I would have asked you."

Aki decided he'd waited long enough. He entered the dining room, his face carefully indifferent, as if he hadn't just heard the entire exchange and knew exactly what was going on and who was guilty.

"Where were you last night?" Mara turned on him before he was fully through the door.

Aki let a look of mild confusion pass over his face. "In bed, asleep. I didn't get much the night before, you know."

He noticed Sebastian stiffen at his words but looked past him to Mara. Mara's eyes narrowed. There were times when she could slip past his lies and see the truth. She was one of the very few people who could. But not this time. Too much was at stake this time. When she'd convinced herself that he spoke the truth, she waved him toward the table, already laden with food.

She rested her head in one hand for a moment and then collected herself. "I'm sure you've heard a bit of ruckus this morning. It appears there won't be an execution after all. Our courier friend has disappeared. As has Cristof."

"What?"

"Yes, it appears there is a traitor in our midst. Perhaps you'll get to execute him instead, just as soon as I discover who it is."

Aki slumped into his chair and stared down at his plate. "What of your other plans for the day?"

Mara tapped the table with her fingertips. "The townspeople have already been advised to gather. I suppose it wouldn't do to let them down entirely. With Desmond's army as close as it is, they need to meet you. That will go ahead as planned."

Nodding, Aki began to eat. Halle caught his eye only briefly across the table but there was a small, conspiratorial smile in his eyes.

"You'll have to speak to them, of course."

Aki's spoon dropped to his plate. "Speak to them? You mean, make a speech?"

"Yes, of course. You didn't honestly think I was going to do all the work, did you? I've sold them your story, today you'll sell them yourself."

"What do I say?"

"Oh, tell them a couple of stories that will make their hearts bleed. Show them that you're really just one of them, that you understand the suffering they've endured."

"I don't really enjoy telling those stories."

"Then make one up, Aki, or I'll do it for you," she said darkly.

There was a platform erected between town and the castle, a platform whose purpose was no mystery to Aki. He followed Mara up the steps to the silence of the waiting crowd. It was a small gathering of people. Most, he guessed, were taking refuge in the caves like Norman. And some, of course, had been lost during the staged raid.

He barely listened to Mara's words. They were honey dipped lies at best. Words about how she had prayed the day would come when there would be someone to throw off the oppression of the southern kingship and bring peace between Dorsten and Aruuk. And then she was guiding him forward, a hand on his elbow, speaking the words that he had spoken just the night before.

"...Desmond's army marches on us even now, ready to force us into submission. But we no longer have to listen to that line of rulers. Not when we have our own heir. This is Lord Bayner's heir. The son of his daughter, Sybil Bayner."

There was absolute silence in the aftermath of her announcement. Mara pinched his arm and Aki took another step forward. The faces of the people swam before his eyes. All he could think about was watching them run, screaming, from the flames Mara's men had lit. He shut his eyes to drown out the image. Forced himself through the same list of people he'd thought of the night before. The list of the living. He added them to that other list, the one of the dead, and together, he found a purpose.

"I don't want to fight a war," he started and heard Mara's sharp intake of breath behind him. "But more importantly, I don't want you to fight a war. Not one on my behalf. It is true that Prince Desmond's army approaches. But I still don't want to go to war. War will cost us thousands of lives. It will cost us our towns, our farms, our families. I could not ask anyone here to make such a sacrifice just for me and my claim to a throne," he paused for breath, conscious of the growing tension radiating off of Mara. "I'm not worth that. Neither is Prince Desmond. But there is something I want. I want justice for those Prince Desmond heinously murdered in cold blood. I want justice for the towns ravaged by raids. I want justice for those families who have already lost people in a war that hasn't even yet started. And I can give you that. I can't give you much else, but I will give you justice."

He couldn't even bring himself to look at the faces of the people he'd just made promises to. Behind him, Mara fumed silently. In front of him, the townspeople listened silently. With nothing more to say, he turned and walked off the platform. It was only then that he heard a smattering of weak applause, no doubt from people who were afraid of the consequences of indifference. Someday, they would understand what that promise would cost him. Or maybe not. People didn't often see much that wasn't directly in front of them.

They were in the throne room before Mara's pent-up rage broke free. She spun around and struck Aki twice with the back of her hand. He stumbled back and held up an arm to shield himself from any more.

"What, exactly, do you not understand about our arrangement?"

"I did what you wanted me to, didn't I?"

"What I wanted you to? I want to go to war, Aki. I want to watch these pathetic, sniveling peasants slaughter each other in the name of a better future. And do you know why, Aki? Do you know why such a sight would be the most satisfying thing in the whole world to me?"

Aki, still nursing his smarting cheek, shook his head.

"Because those same low-minded people loved their peace and their comforts and their insignificant, worthless lives so much they were willing to sell girls like me, like your mother, in exchange for it. I begged my father to find some other way. I begged Darien to help me escape. And they both turned their backs on me. They chose everyone else over me. My own son chose you over me. Have you any idea what it was like?" Mara's voice caught but she didn't stop. "Have you any idea what it is to share the bed of a monster, always fighting to stay in his favor? Have you any idea what it's like begging your son to do whatever it takes to stay alive and having him turn his back on you? That's why these people are going to destroy each other. That's what I want, Aki. That's all I've wanted for years."

For that one moment, Mara was nothing but her pain and her pain was her. It consumed her until there was nothing left but that pain. She could no more separate herself from it then cut out her own heart. She no longer knew how to live without it.

Aki saw the crack in her impenetrable mask, the chink in her armor. There were tears in her eyes. Tears of rage and heartache and fury and injustice and anguish. Tears he'd never seen her shed before. Oh, she'd had tears before, cold, false tears conjured for the benefit of another. But never, never indulged in for herself.

For that one moment, Aki knew her. He knew exactly what she lived with every single day.

Aki let his hand drop away from his face. He stepped toward her.

"Mara, you know I know what it's like to suffer. I told you before, I'm yours. I don't have anywhere else to go. But listen to me just this once." He paused, waiting for some acknowledgement on her part. She didn't nod or say anything, just watched him, waiting, rebuilding the wall she'd temporarily let crumble. He went on, "If we fight, if we go to war, Desmond will just remain behind, protected by his men. Yes, he'll watch his kingdom fall apart. Yes, he'll watch his armies destroyed. That's not good enough for me. I need to kill him. It's not enough for him to just die. I need to be the one to do it. And our people need me to be the one to do it. I won't rob you of your war but let me first kill the prince."

Her moment of weakness passed, Mara wiped away all trace of her tears as she considered his words. He stood quietly, submitting to the study that seemed to reach all the way into his soul. He watched as a smile, crueler and colder for the frailty she'd just displayed, lifted the corners of her mouth.

"You want to challenge him? Fight him one on one in the manner of the old kings?"

"Yes. I think his pride and his hatred for me will not allow him to refuse. And I know I'm better than him."

"And have no aversion to killing," she added wryly. "It ought to be public. The young prince should die in front of a crowd. It would not only solidify your claim by eliminating his rivalry, it would prove to the people that you have not only the skill but the courage to lead them. An excellent message to give them."

Aki held his breath as Mara hovered over the idea, turning it into her own. It had to become hers if she was going to do it. Mara never did anything that she didn't fully want to do.

"And do you really think he will not be able to refuse?"

"If, in our challenge, we state the desire to spare our peoples from further bloodshed and make some insult against his pride, he'll be compelled to agree."

"Then I shall write it at once. You will kill the young prince and then we shall go to war."

Chapter 51

THE CIRCLE OF MEN AROUND Prince Desmond leaned in, waiting for him to read aloud the contents of the letter sent to them through the hand of an official emissary. Desmond, for his part, had no intention of reading it out loud. It was an insult. An affront to his intelligence and courage.

"As the men leading your armies to battle, it would be beneficial for you to share any pertinent information that letter contains," Captain Tyrrel broke the anticipatory silence.

Desmond looked up, his face flushed with a mixture of anger and humiliation, and found that the captain merely gave voice to the thoughts of all the others.

"Oh, fine. Read it out yourself, Captain." He tossed it to the man and folded his arms over his chest while the captain cleared his throat and began.

My Dear Nephew,
It has come to my attention that the reputation surrounding myself and the heir, Aki Gundarson, is one of bloodlust and murder. I find that quite unfair when I consider the massacre that you only very recently ordered on the old border of Dival. Surely such an act is equal to any atrocity we are accused of committing.

To set that story straight, I have a proposal. It was long a tradition of the old kings to spare their armies from battle, and subsequently death, by solving their rivalries in single combat. Aki Gundarson wishes to avoid this senseless loss of life. He wishes to spare as many people from war as he can. I can only hope you wish the same for your people.

And so, he is offering this challenge - single combat between heirs. Such an act will not only spare many lives but will also provide a display of the courage that is much needed in running a kingdom. The winner will be the undisputed ruler of these united lands and no further conflict will be necessary.

Of course, if you feel your abilities or courage to be somewhat lacking, well, that is what we have armies for, isn't it?

We await your answer by nightfall.

Mara

"Please tell me you're not planning on accepting this," Captain Tyrrel said, looking up from the letter. "It would be madness to do so, Your Highness."

"And why's that?" Desmond had no intention of accepting. Not really. But he sensed a reason in Captain Tyrrel's words that he wouldn't like and that made him want to hear it all the more.

"He will kill you."

There it was. Desmond pinched his lips together. He looked around the group of men - Captain Tyrrel, Baron Orlander, and a handful of others who commanded his army. None of them but the captain met his gaze. Desmond could read their unspoken agreement. They agreed with the captain, not just that he shouldn't accept the challenge but that if he did, Aki would doubtless kill him. They had little faith in his abilities.

More than that, though, he read their disgust. And their blame. They'd been looking at him like that since he'd ordered the old fort burned down. Even Baron Orlander, the one who ensured his order was carried out, was ashamed of it.

"I did what needed to be done," Desmond said to the unspoken accusation. "Leaving so many of them alive behind our army was inviting trouble."

There was no response from those gathered around him. Most were too preoccupied looking at the ground.

Desmond balled his hands up into fists at his sides. He tried to quell the heat growing inside of him. They were ashamed of him. Ashamed of what he'd done. Ashamed that he lacked the skill to even consider Aki's challenge.

"Your Highness, might I suggest that, as Captain of your guard, Captain Tyrrel can legitimately fight for you. In which case, it might not be a bad idea to accept."

"While I hide like a coward, just like she implied I am? How does that seem like a good idea?"

"Your Highness, you cannot win. Not against him," Captain Tyrrel said flatly. "I've trained both of you and he's by far the superior swordsman. He will destroy you before you have a chance if that's what he wants."

"And that makes me a coward, unworthy of rule. That's what it would be perceived as, wouldn't it?"

By their silence, he knew their answer.

"So, we refuse. It's what you have an army for," Captain Tyrrel said.

There was something about being told what to do that irked him. There was something about being told what to do by Captain Tyrrel that was even worse. The man just had a way about him of making Desmond feel completely insignificant and useless, as if he was incapable of coming up with even a single good idea.

"I will think on it before I answer tonight."

"You cannot accept, Your Highness."

"And you cannot tell me what I can and cannot do. The last time I checked, that was not your place, Captain."

Captain Tyrrel's lips pressed into a thin, disapproving line.

"See that the man who brought this is well guarded until we are ready to reply, Captain. I think that is more in line with your job than trying to order me about."

Captain Tyrrel stalked away, and Desmond knew he had not heard the last of the captain's opinion. He retreated to the safety and privacy of his tent before anyone could add their voices to the captain's.

He wasn't left alone long. Tristan invited himself in after no more than an hour had passed. Since the incident at the old border fort, Tristan had become almost flighty in his presence, as if he half expected Desmond to set fire to him. Desmond hated it. Even now, Tristan's smile was nervous, questioning, unsure. Desmond motioned for him to sit down. After his altercation with the captain, he was glad of Tristan's company.

"He wants to fight you himself," Tristan said.

"It's spread around camp already, has it? And what do the men say about it?"

Tristan grimaced with discomfort. "I'd prefer not to repeat their words."

"Oh, just say it. It's not like I can't already guess. Aki's made this a matter of honor, as if he had any. And yes, I can refuse. I can refuse and have the entire world think I'm a coward who hides behind an army, who can't stand up for himself. I can refuse, and Aki looks like the benevolent leader who wants to prevent bloodshed while I'm the one who's murdered innocents and left my army to die."

"What would your father have done?"

Desmond shook his head and looked away. "We weren't the same people, my father and I. Never were. He would never have...," Desmond started to say that his father would never have order the murder of innocent people, but that wasn't a point he wanted to reiterate at the moment. "He'd have never let it come to war."

"There is a certain cleverness to cowardice."

"I'm not a coward, Tristan," Desmond yelled, kicking a clump of grass.

"Forgive me. I'm merely trying to point out that avoiding a fight isn't always the worst option. I haven't seen him fight but I've heard he'd be a formidable opponent for you. There's no need to run headlong into death when you have a thousand men here to do it for you."

"And that's the problem. Because no one else will see it like that. My men won't. They'll just see that I care more for myself than them."

Tristan leaned forward. He ran his tongue over his lips several times and fiddled with a blade of grass he plucked up from the ground. "You know, there's more ways to win a fight than just skill."

Desmond found himself moving closer, lowering his voice at the tone of Tristan's words. "What do you mean?"

"Accidents happen, Your Highness. Accidents that might turn a fight to your favor."

"What sort of accidents?" he was whispering now, his heart racing with a little thrill at the solution he saw Tristan laying out before him.

"Let's just say, were you to accept his challenge, and were you to be losing that fight, I could perhaps, at some prearranged signal, cause some unnoticed interference. You would still get the killing blow and you would be the hero of the hour."

"And everyone would have to recognize that I did, in fact, defeat him." Desmond smiled. Aki dead at his hand. No one would ever again be able to dispute his right to rule. And it would be justice for Father. "Could you really manage something like that?"

"It would be my pleasure to. Now, you just have to convince your not very convincible Captain Tyrrel that you want to go along with the challenge."

Desmond stood up. "I don't need his permission. All I must do is write a reply and send Mara's messenger back to her. There will be nothing anyone can do to stop me after that."

Chapter 52

IT SEEMS YOU WERE RIGHT. With a little motivation, Prince Desmond was unable to resist the chance to kill you himself." Mara looked up from the reply the prince had sent less than an hour ago. "Now, I trust you weren't exaggerating your own abilities in a match against him. It wouldn't do to have you killed by him in front of an entire crowd of people."

News of the prince's acceptance had melted away what was left of Mara's anger over Felix's disappearance. It was as if he'd never existed at all.

"We should plan it for three days from now. And, of course, we'll be sure to let everyone know about it."

"Three days?"

"Yes, that should be sufficient time for everyone to arrive. We wouldn't want those from Aruuk to miss out."

Aki exchanged a confused glance with Halle. He didn't risk speaking out again, not with as shifting as Mara's moods were lately.

"The two of you can stop trying to guess from one another," Mara said sharply, and Aki dropped his eyes to the table. "It's not that great a secret, although it does give us a considerable advantage. I made sure Illsen received word of what the prince did with those of our people who settled in his lands. As you can imagine, they were less than happy."

"They're coming with an army?" Halle asked.

"I wouldn't call it an army. More like reinforcements."

Aki continued to stare down at the table. It was all happening too fast. He was still reeling from the events of the past few days. There wasn't time enough to think. He was drowning in Mara's schemes. He needed time. And space. Too much was happening. Too many pieces still needed to be fit together if he was going to accomplish anything at all.

Mara noticed his silence. He felt her gaze settle over him and shut down the thoughts that were running wildly through his mind.

"Is something troubling you?"

"No. I was just wondering if, perhaps, Lars was with those that are coming?"

Mara raised a disbelieving brow. "He is a son of Gundar. Of course, he is among those coming."

"And they'll be here in three days?"

"They'll be here sooner than that. By tomorrow evening, I expect."

Nothing more was said on the subject that evening. Mara wrote another letter, establishing the details of the single combat and sent Sebastian with it. As much as he hated the risk of it, Aki caught the man before he left and added his own letter and instructions with it. He could only pray that whatever had moved Sebastian to conceal his efforts to help Felix would be enough for Sebastian to listen to him now.

Aki waited until midnight had come and gone before creeping back down to the cavern he'd left Felix in with Norman and the others. It was empty this time, but Aki hadn't really come down to talk. He could hear their voices coming through one of the smaller tunnels leading off that first cave and he was sure they heard him. He left the second of the three letters he'd written on the same rock he'd sat on the night before and then returned above ground.

After three almost sleepless nights, Aki did not wake until late the next morning. By then, Sebastian had not only returned, but was pounding on his door. Which was, in fact, the only reason Aki woke up when he did.

"Mara's looking for you," Sebastian said when Aki cracked the door open, still half asleep.

Aki nodded and, looking down, realized he'd been too tired to even bother undressing the night before. His clothes were rumpled and wrinkled with sleep, but he decided that keeping Mara waiting was a worse thing. He started down the hallway, only to be stopped by Sebastian's hand on his shoulder.

"I know what you did the other night," the man whispered so close to him that Aki could feel the hot touch of his breath on his ear. "I'll make it up to you if I ever get the chance."

He was gone before Aki could turn around and ask him what he was talking about. It was Aki who should be thanking him for not telling Mara that he and Halle were in the dungeon the night before. Unless Sebastian had some strange connection to Felix, the man's words simply didn't make sense. He pushed them away almost immediately. There were just too many other things clamoring for space in his thoughts.

"I'm sorry I overslept," he said as soon as he was in the throne room with Mara.

For once she wasn't seated on the throne that she insisted was actually his. Her back was to him as she stood in front of one of the broad windows that bathed the room with light. From it, the view that was captured had mountains to the one side and the flatlands and woods on the other.

"I've dreamed of this day for so long," Mara said softly, almost as if she'd forgotten that Aki was there. "I never imagined that you would be the one to give it to me." She turned now, the exhilarating thrill of victory already lighting her face. In her hands was Prince Desmond's agreement to their terms. "After you finish off the prince, after they all destroy each other in fruitless battle, I will have everything I ever wanted. No one will ever forget that I existed again."

"Just two more days."

"Yes, just two more days. Two more days and my vengeance will be complete, the line of Divalian kings broken irreparably." She broke out of her euphoric daze and looked at the letter in her hands. "You'll need someone to stand with you at the duel. I think Sebastian would be the best choice."

"What will he do?"

"You don't even know how this sort of thing is done, do you? I forget how little real training you had. It will be Sebastian's job to ensure that the prince carries no other weapons than the one we've all agreed on. And the prince will have a man who does the same with you. They will also both be present to ensure that there is no foul play during the fight, no interference from others."

Aki nodded his understanding. He waited until he was absolutely sure that Mara was through speaking. He inhaled deeply. "I would like to ride out and meet Lars. If you would allow that."

"Why?"

"I want to see him. It's been a long time. And I would," he hesitated then made up his mind to just go on. The worst she would do was hit him again. "I think, if he's going to be here, I'd like him to stand with me."

"Oh, would you?" Mara's voice was instantly cool.

"He's my brother," Aki said weakly.

"He's not really. You know that. But I suppose I can't see any harm in having him do it instead of Sebastian."

"And I can ride out to meet him?"

He saw her hesitate, biting her lip as she thought about it.

"Please, Mara."

"Don't beg. You know it doesn't work on me and I hate it." She sighed. "Only if Sebastian goes with you. I can hardly afford to have you running off moments before my revenge is complete."

Aki blew out the breath he was holding.

The air in the mountains was fresh and crisp, cooler than the sweltering heat that hung over the flatlands. Despite how much he hated every moment of his childhood in the mountains, Aki couldn't hate the mountains. Not in the summertime when they were teeming with life and beauty and rugged strength. A breeze carried the scent of wildflowers on it and swayed the branches of trees as it brushed past them.

Aki kept Sky at a brisk pace, the comfort of riding again after so many days of being cooped up inside the castle almost enough to carry away the burden of decision that he carried about with him everywhere now. They passed streams full of clear, sparkling water singing their way merrily down the mountainside. They wound up the pass road that Aki had traveled less than a year ago with Prince Desmond on their way to Illsen.

It was early afternoon when the jangle of horses' bridles and the clopping of horses' hooves on rock reached his ears and Aki nudged Sky into a canter. Around the bend they went and straight into the lead horsemen. Lars was among them.

Under Sebastian's watchful eye, Lars and Aki rode together some distance ahead of the rest of the group.

"I wouldn't have come if it hadn't been for Sasha," Lars said soberly after they had caught each other up on the last few months. "I can't believe he's dead. I can't believe the prince killed him. He saved their country."

"What are you going to do in Dorsten?"

"Stop Desmond. That's all that really matters. He can't be allowed to win. Not after what he did."

"Mara can't win, either, Lars," Aki said quietly.

Lars gave him a solemn nod. Sebastian moved a bit closer, and Aki turned the conversation to anything other than the impending conflict that was about to embroil them all. Every time he looked over his shoulder at Sebastian, the man looked like he wanted to speak, but he never did. Aki couldn't forget the words Sebastian spoke into his ear just that morning, words he still didn't understand. Sebastian had been too careful to keep his distance coming up the mountain pass for Aki to ask him about them, either.

When at last Sebastian fell back a way, Lars, looking straight ahead, said, "You're planning something, aren't you?"

"How do you know?"

"The look on your face. It's the same one you get when you're plotting some spiteful revenge," Lars said, laughing.

Aki gave him a halfhearted smile. "You're right, I guess. I'll need your help, though." He looked back up the pass to the hundred or so men who followed. "Do they listen to anything you say?"

"I'm a son of Gundar. If it's reasonable, they'll listen."

"It's reasonable. Make them listen."

Chapter 53

DESMOND WAS WIDE AWAKE when the sun rose. Sitting outside his tent, he'd watched its coming. It would be someone's last sunrise to witness. His. Or Aki's. The thought made him sad. He frowned to himself. He oughtn't to be sad over Aki's death. Aki was his rival, his enemy. Yet, the word last kept popping up every time he noticed something. The last sunrise, the last night, the last chance to listen to the song of the birds.

So many lasts.

Desmond had never given much thought to death. Now it was all he could think about. It wouldn't be his own today. Tristan would see to that. Who could have guessed that his life would be in the hands of a man he'd only known for a few months? It made his head spin to think of all that had transpired in those few months. If Tristan weren't at his side today, Desmond didn't think he could overcome his fear enough to even get to his feet. Because sitting here, thinking of all those lasts that were Aki's this morning, Desmond knew he was terrified of dying.

Even now, knowing that Tristan would not really let him die, he was terrified. It crept over his limbs and turned them to jelly. It crept over his heart and made it run wild.

Captain Tyrrel saw him sitting there outside his tent and turned his steps toward him. Desmond both wanted and didn't want his company at the moment, but Captain Tyrrel was never one to leave that choice in his hands. He envied the man his steadiness, his calm. He was irritated by it.

"Your Highness," Captain Tyrrel inclined his head in a slight bow.

"You're about to say I shouldn't have agreed to it."

"It's a little late for that. No, what I was about to say is that the terms don't actually clearly specify that it's to the death."

"Traditionally, it is."

"Yes, traditionally. But in reality, it wasn't put in writing. There's no shame in losing and asking for mercy."

"He murdered my father, a man who had spared his life. I doubt very much that he would extend mercy to me. And how would I ever show my face again anywhere if I had to beg for my own life?"

"It goes both ways, Your Highness. If, on the narrow chance you are winning, you don't have to kill him."

"You want him alive?"

Captain Tyrrel sat down on the ground beside him and stared across the small meadow between the castle and town that was to be the meeting place of the two rivals. For a long time, he didn't speak and for once Desmond didn't mind that his question had been ignored. He was enjoying the silence when Captain Tyrrel said quietly, "What I want is not the question. But I know this, Your Highness. It is a terrible thing to kill a man, to steal the life from inside him. It will haunt you for the rest of your life, no matter how deserving the death may have been. And I fear you would come to regret it."

The captain's words took him back to that room in Illsen, to the look on Aki's face. Whatever else he believed about Aki, he believed that was the first time he'd ever killed anyone. And he believed the captain's words. But none of that mattered. There was no room left for mercy. And Tristan would ensure Aki's death.

Chapter 54

FOR A DAY THAT HELD SUCH dread for everyone, it was about as perfect as it could be. The sun rose in a clear sky of bright, deep blue. It was warm but not blistering hot the way it had been the last week or so. A few stormy hours during the night had driven away the excessive heat.

Aki stared out of his window past the wall and out into the grassy field that stood between the castle and town. It would be there that they met. There, in the small meadow, where Aki would either fail or succeed in ending what had started long before his own life began.

He'd been awake for a while now, unable to sleep any longer. His hand found its way to the pocket that contained his mother's letter. For a moment, he just fingered it, drawing comfort from the fact that it existed at all. Then he pulled it out, smoothed the wrinkles in the paper, and read it. He didn't really need to look at it anymore, the words were forever imprinted in his memory, but there was something about seeing his mother's smooth, neat handwriting that helped quell the nervous fluttering in the pit of his stomach.

Hope.

It was what his mother had lived for. Insane, wild, fragile hope. That the sun would always rise, that the darkness would always fade, that day would always follow night. Hope that there was a difference to be made. That one person could make that difference.

Hope was what his mother had died for.

When he read through it a few times, he put it away again with a sigh. He wasn't ready for this day. There was nothing he could do to make himself any more ready. For once, he left all but his father's sword behind in his room.

Breakfast was impossible to swallow down past the lump that was lodged in his throat. His only comfort was that Lars was now with them. The other Aruukens had stayed within the mountain pass where Mara wanted them, hidden from view of the Divalian army. Her own men were a mixed group representing Dorsten, Aruuk and even a few from Karu. They weren't real soldiers. Most could boast of no skill other than ruthlessness and brute force. Thugs, for the most part, who acted only in their own best interest.

Mara was particularly snappish, he noticed. She was irritated at the slightest provocation. Her fingertips never stopped tapping the table until Aki found himself becoming very annoyed with it. He didn't need her nervousness on top of his own. And she wasn't the one who would most likely be dead by nightfall.

She looked over and noticed that he was only picking at his food. Her attempt at a reassuring smile was more sickening than optimistic. "You are really better than him, aren't you?"

"Yes."

"Well, there's nothing to worry about. Besides, if, on the slight chance things go wrong for you, I have a plan to ensure your victory."

"That's cheating, isn't it?" Lars said.

"Oh, the way that word gets thrown around," Mara let out a laugh that wasn't at all amused. It was high pitched and almost squeaky. "Call it whatever you like, Lars, I intend to win this day."

"Yes, but my purpose is specifically to make sure no one cheats."

"You spent too much time with Sasha. But no matter. I won't risk your precious conscience for this. Will it make you feel much better if I promise to have no part in interfering no matter how it all plays out?"

Nothing more was said on the subject but Lars and even Halle were scowling the rest of the meal and Aki wished they wouldn't. It wasn't how he wanted to think of them. It wasn't how he wanted to remember them. Mara excused both them and Karina as soon as the meal was over. She motioned Aki to stay where he was.

He was seated at her side, only the corner of the table between them. Reaching across she took his hand in hers. "Lars doesn't need to know about this. Should the fight go ill with you, you have but to signal my man on Desmond's side. He will know what to do."

"You have a man on his side?"

"Of course. How else do you think I've known everything that goes on? I have spies everywhere but this one in particular has endeared himself to Desmond. He will be near enough to change the course of the fight, should it come down to that. If you feel you are losing, loudly ask for a respite of five minutes. Whether the prince agrees or not, Tristan will know what to do."

"You think of everything, don't you?" Aki asked, absorbing her words without any sign of their significance to him. "I suppose there's no way to lose, then."

"I won't lose, Aki."

Aki turned away. There was so much hope and triumph and vindication on her face that it was painful to look at. He was so used to hating Mara that it was strange to pity her on this day when he would bring everything she'd worked for crashing down around her. It made him almost consider throwing his plans to the wind. He understood her now, at least a little. Understood her pain, understood the fear that spurred her every decision. Whether he wanted to admit it or not, he shared a lot of common ground with his grandmother.

"Anton would have been so proud of you today," Mara said, a slight tremor in her voice at the name of her firstborn son. "It's only fitting you should choose his weapon to fight with today."

Aki stopped the grimace that wanted to cross his face. What he was now, standing in front of Mara, was not the sort of person he wanted his father to be proud of.

"It's time," he said.

"It's time," Mara repeated, an anxious smile flitting across her face. She pulled the thin veil she'd chosen to wear down. It was sheer enough to catch glimpses of her face beneath, but heavy enough to keep anyone looking at her always guessing as to her expression or thoughts.

The meadow was already filling with people when they arrived. Halle and Karina and Sebastian all right behind Mara, with Lars and Aki hanging back, and a dozen of Mara's most trusted men, including Ritter, behind them. The bulk of her men were some distance behind them, waiting, Aki knew, for the moment the prince fell dead. Mara had no intention of honoring the agreed prize.

Prince Desmond and his own men were already waiting for them, an intentional fact on Mara's part. The bulk of the prince's army also stood ready at a distance. Aki wasn't sure if the prince meant to honor their agreement or not. If Aki succeeded, he wouldn't ever have the chance to find out.

Gathered around the actual space marked out for the fight were a handful of furtive townspeople. Aki heard quiet conversations taking place all around and guessed that most of them centered around Prince Desmond and himself. Although it made no difference on the outcome he intended, Aki did have a moment's curiosity about who they hoped would win this combat. Rumors here had not been kind to Desmond, but they hadn't been wonderful for him, either.

From the Divalian men he heard murmurs.

"Murderer."

"King killer."

That was what the Divalians thought of him. They wanted him dead. Anger and hatred seeped out of their gaze. Aki took a deep breath. He guessed that it was only the rigid discipline maintained by Captain Tyrrel that kept several of them from breaking ranks and killing him right then and there. King Darien was a beloved king. It only made sense that his men wanted a chance to take their revenge. And if he ended this fight they way he intended to, they were likely going to get to satisfy that desire.

He sensed Lars' presence directly behind his shoulder and knew Lars wanted to speak.

"I hope you know what you're doing," was all Lars whispered as Mara addressed those gathered.

Aki ignored her words on purpose, shut them out of his mind so that he wouldn't have to be distracted by them. Turning to Lars, he said, "I do."

And he did. For once, every decision that he was making this day was his own, entirely his own. He wasn't Mara's slave or puppet, and he wasn't Darien's either. With that knowledge came an utter peace that he'd never known before. He turned to Lars, a letter in his hand.

"If it turns out I don't, though, find a way to give this to Alina."

"Aki, don't," Lars started to warn but Aki just shook his head.

"Promise me, Lars. That's all I want."

Lars, biting back whatever else he wanted to say, nodded his acceptance and promise.

Mara was done speaking. A thunderous silence filled the air in the absence of her voice and Aki looked around one last time before stepping forward, Lars right behind him.

From the other side Desmond did the same, followed by Captain Tyrrel. Aki stifled his relief at the sight of the captain. It had been a guess and a hope to think he would be the one with the prince today.

Whatever Captain Tyrrel's thoughts were as he approached Aki, Aki could not guess. The man's face was set in marble. Aki stood still as he came up to him, his own face veiled. Captain Tyrrel reached first for the sword on his back. Sliding it free, he examined the blade for any poison that might have been smeared on.

Aki found it amusing in that moment, when they were both getting ready to kill each other, that it mattered how they accomplished it. Dead was dead; however it came about didn't change that. He was a little surprised, though, that Mara hadn't tried something like that.

"I read an interesting letter the other day," Captain Tyrrel murmured, his head down, his moving lips hidden from anyone's gaze. "It made some wild claims of service and asked for what some might call disloyalty and disobedience to the prince. I'm just not sure if I can trust the writer. It's a little hard to know what to believe when there's a rumor about you killing the king. Everyone here wishes to see you executed."

"I have no other proof on me now other than what I gave you. And none of that can refute the story that I killed the king."

Captain Tyrrel returned his sword and began his search for hidden weapons. Since he'd been the one to teach Aki where to put his knives, Aki didn't think it should take long, but the captain moved slowly, methodically.

"I can't go against the prince."

"Master Wehr told me once that it was unquestioning obedience that made one a slave. I've never thought of you as being a slave - not even to the prince."

"I'm not," Captain Tyrrel bristled slightly but Aki saw the doubt in his eyes, the uncertainty, and Aki knew he'd said enough. "Tell me this, will you kill the prince today?"

"No."

Captain Tyrrel finished his search and met Aki's eyes for the first time. "In theory I'm telling you the rules of this combat right now, understand?"

Aki nodded.

"Whether I want to go along with what you asked of me or not, I'm not the only one you must convince. Any order to stand down on my part will be quickly undone by the baron."

Aki nodded again, looking over at where Baron Orlander stood without turning his head. The baron's face was set hard with hatred, but Aki saw the grief behind that.

"Tell the baron, Felix is alive. I do not say this as a threat but as a fact. If my plan does not succeed today, he won't be able to find his son. Tell him I can answer any question he wishes to ask me if I'm alive by the end of this."

The captain was studying him hard. Too hard. Aki glanced around to see if anyone was noticing. Either the captain satisfied his own unspoken questions, or he came to the same realization Aki had. His face went indifferent.

"Why are you telling me this now?"

"King Darien said to tell no one that I did not trust completely."

"And you trust me why?"

"You don't like me. But you have never used that as a reason to treat me unfairly. One more thing," Aki said. "Tristan is Mara's man, and he will try to kill Desmond if I do not. But you must let him try or Mara will be too suspicious."

To anyone not paying attention, nothing about the captain changed. Aki noticed the stiffening of his back and the slight widening of his eyes as Aki's words became clear to them.

"It doesn't have to be to the death," Captain Tyrrel said as he got ready to walk away.

A moment's worth of sadness slipped inside the calm that surrounded Aki. He shook his head slightly. "I doubt very much that I'll be alive when the sun goes down tonight no matter how this ends."

Chapter 55

WHY DID LARS HAVE TO BE the one with Aki today?

Desmond shifted from one foot to the other as he waited for Lars to approach. He'd seen the brief exchange between the brothers and despite everything else he should have been considering at that moment, such as how he was going to survive long enough to give Tristan a chance to act, he wondered what was in the letter and who it was meant for. He wondered what secrets it contained.

Beyond them, Desmond got his first glimpse of his aunt. Well, what he could see of her anyway. A thin veil covered her face, tugged gently by the breeze but never enough to reveal her full face. She'd addressed everyone gathered just moments before. She'd made beautiful promises of peace and unity. She'd commended Aki on his desire to save the land from further bloodshed. It was enough to make Desmond sick.

And then there was Lars. Desmond couldn't keep the heat from rising to his face as Lars stopped in front of him. He remembered the last words they had exchanged on that cold mountainside a lifetime ago.

"I wasn't aware that you were involved," he said, trying to preempt any lecture that might be coming.

"Neither was I until we received word of our people being butchered. That sort of involved me."

Desmond swallowed down the lump that always threatened to choke him when mention was made of the massacre he'd ordered. He dropped his eyes.

"At least I didn't murder the king," he said.

Lars gave him a derisive glare. "Neither did Aki. You should have learned to read through Mara's lies and then perhaps you wouldn't be here. You sent her the man who did the deed, the one you spared from your fire to send word to us. He's the one who killed the king."

"I don't believe you."

"You never believe the right people. Just the ones who tell you what you want to hear."

With that, Lars finished his search and stepped back, leaving Desmond standing alone. Captain Tyrrel was also finished with Aki.

Sweat dampened his hands as he pulled his sword out. It made it difficult to grip the hilt firmly. Desmond found himself staring down at the blade that suddenly felt clumsy and cumbersome. Its weight was more than he remembered it being.

He let the tip of it touch the ground to keep it from shaking in his hand, but the tremor wasn't in the blade. It was in his arm, traveling through his entire body as the reality of what he was about to do set in. The ground blurred in front of him, and he brought the back of his free hand up across his forehead to wipe away the beads of cold sweat that gathered there.

At some point he would have to force his eyes off the ground. Force his eyes to meet his opponent's. Desmond squeezed them shut for a moment, hoping that his vision would clear. He wiped his forehead again, but it didn't matter. He was hot and then cold again. His heartbeat in his throat, forming a lump he couldn't swallow down.

Tristan might fail.

The thought took over everything else inside of him.

Tristan might fail and Desmond might die.

Today might be his last day. His last sunrise. His last moments.

In the moment it took to think it, his life - all of its failures and successes - paraded before his mind. He wasn't ready to die. He was afraid of it. Afraid of just the possibility of it.

He wanted to drop the sword in the dust and run. He turned to find Captain Tyrrel. Hoping to ask if it was too late for the captain to fight in his stead. His mouth was like sawdust. No sound came out despite his best efforts.

Tristan was standing there. A smile on his face that Desmond found cold and treacherous in that moment. It couldn't be, though. Tristan was the one who'd convinced him to fight. Tristan would not fail.

Across the open space, Aki waited. Desmond couldn't help but be a bit envious of his composure. From that distance, Aki almost appeared bored. Certainly, he wasn't paralyzed by the same fear that gripped Desmond. And Desmond almost pitied him for that. He was so sure of winning, so sure that he was better than Desmond, that he carried no worries into this combat. It would be the last time he underestimated Desmond. The last time for anything.

A murmur broke through the haze of fear that held him bound. The crowd was shifting as Mara stepped forward, a simple cloth held aloft in her hand.

"To settle once and for all the question of succession between two recognized heirs, you all are witnesses to this fight of tradition." Her voice, not raised but still carrying easily over the gathering, was tight with tension. She glanced in Aki's direction, speaking unspoken words through her silent gaze. "May the truest heir win."

With that, she dropped the cloth.

Desmond knew he had only seconds before he died. Knew he had to do something to stop that from happening. Aki's sword was already coming at him like a streak of silver through the air.

He tried to remember anything Captain Tyrrel had ever taught him but even his thoughts were held in this fear bound paralysis. His own sword came up, but it was sluggish, as if he were trying to drag it through mud. Way too slow. It would never stop Aki's in time.

His eyes shut without asking his permission. Tristan would never be able to act in time. All Desmond needed to buy him was a minute or two and he couldn't even manage a second or two.

Yelping, Desmond's eyes flew open again, staring down at his arm. He expected to see blood drenching his sleeve.

There was nothing. Nothing but a tingling pain that came from having been struck hard with something blunt. His eyes met Aki's, close enough now to read in them the hatred that had been born in the council room so many weeks before, the hatred that was strong enough to kill.

"Fight me," Aki said quietly enough that no one could hear him. "Isn't that what you've wanted all along?"

Chapter 56

THERE WERE NO CHEERS.
No shouts.
There was nothing, really. Nothing beyond the clang and screech of metal blades colliding. Desmond was at least trying now, trying because Aki wasn't giving him any other choice. He pulled each blow, letting only the flat of his sword ever touch the prince.

This was control.

This was order.

Aki reveled in it, in the quiet that filled him. After weeks of chaos, after weeks of running, of hiding, of pretending, he was done. The sword in his hand put him back in control. It made him want to test that control, to push himself faster and faster until the blade was nothing but a blur, whirling through the air as an extension of himself. It made his senses come alive. Every sound, every sight, every touch, he knew them all. His blood thrummed in harmony to it.

In front of him, Desmond retreated. Aki could see the sheen of sweat that coated the prince's face. It wasn't as much from his exertion as it was from his fear. Prince Desmond was afraid of him. And with good reason.

Aki wanted to kill him.

If he let his mind wander toward the news Finn had carried across the great plains, the match would be over. If he let himself think of that day in the council room when

Prince Desmond lied and sent Aki fleeing for his life, the match would be over.

Instead, he blocked all such thoughts from his mind. He needed this to last. Time was what his plan required and only he could give it that.

He sent Desmond's sword spinning out of his hand and watched as the prince scrambled to retrieve it. A flush rose in Desmond's cheeks when Aki disarmed him again.

It was too easy.

Prince Desmond had never even entertained the idea that he might one day be fighting for his life. Aki always had. The third time the prince's sword left his hand, someone in the crowd let out a short laugh. Desmond's face was red all the way to his ears as he picked his sword up yet again.

Embarrassment feeding his fury and temporarily drowning out his fear, Desmond attacked with a wildness that lacked any skill or cunning. It was fueled purely by his anger at the humiliation of being laughed at. Aki beat him back and by the time the prince's fury had spent itself, Desmond's breath was coming in short, heavy gasps.

"Why are you doing this?" he bit out between clenched teeth.

"Why did you lie?"

The prince made no answer.

Desmond blocked him, but only barely. He stumbled a little as he stepped out of Aki's reach. Aki followed. Closer and closer they inched toward the Divalian side of the circle, Desmond always retreating. It was where they needed to be, it was where Aki wanted them to go and so far, he'd gotten everything he wanted in this fight.

In Aki's peripheral, he could see Captain Tyrrel standing apart from everyone. Risking a brief scan, he spotted Baron Orlander, the same anger and grief still stamped on his face and Aki decided Captain Tyrrel hadn't had the chance to tell him about Felix.

Tristan was not far, a smile on his face that Aki thought wasn't entirely unlike the look wolves got when they were circling fresh prey.

It was Tristan he was waiting for. And Norman, he thought. If Norman was going to go along with his plan, Aki needed to give him enough time to succeed. He could only hope that the single conversation, coupled with the letter he'd left for Stephan's brother, was enough to convince him to act.

On the other side of the circle, Mara watched, seething, as Aki threw away chance after chance to finish the prince off. He was winning. Anyone could see that. He never lost the upper hand, but he never pressed it, either.

"What is he doing?" she whispered.

"What he said he would do," Halle answered with an indifferent shrug. "You know if he'd killed him in the first few seconds, they'd have all been screaming murder."

"He's just playing with him."

"I don't know why it bothers you so. He'll clearly win, and this is rather amusing."

Aki was too far away to hear the exchange but not too far away to hear Mara's voice call out, "Finish this, Aki."

Desmond, already scrambling for footing and to keep his sword up enough to even hope to block Aki, turned his gaze briefly in her direction. Before he could recover, Aki took his chance. His sword dropped, sweeping Desmond's legs out from under him. The prince landed with little grace on his back on the ground.

There was a shift in the air at the change in the fight, as if the entire gathering of people were leaning in, waiting with bated breath for the next move. The sword in Aki's hand was suspended above Desmond. Desmond's own sword was on the ground just beyond his reach. His fingers scrabbled across the ground to reach it, but it was too late.

Tristan was at Desmond's side before Aki could act.

His hand was on the prince's arm. To anyone beyond them, it appeared he was helping him up. To Aki, the tiny, silver blade that darted out and nicked the prince's arm was Mara's assurance that this fight ended her way. She wasn't waiting for him anymore. He'd known it was coming, but it was too fast for him to stop.

What he hadn't known or expected was Desmond's response.

Desmond's eyes widened, horror stricken as he realized what Tristan was doing and he uttered the words that Aki was sure were never meant to be spoken aloud, "You're supposed to be killing him."

Time stopped as Desmond's words filtered through the understanding of those close enough to hear them.

Tristan jumped back, leaving the prince on the ground, a satisfied smile on his face as he lifted his eyes to meet Mara's across the circle. It was the last thing he did before Aki's blade met his wrist. This time, Aki didn't turn the sword. This time, he let it slice clean through. He let the severed hand fall to the ground, the small, hidden knife now exposed for all to see.

"What are you doing, Aki?" Mara called out across the space.

She wanted to cross the space and strike him, Aki was sure, but even she was bound by the rules of tradition that governed their combat. And Mara couldn't break them right now. Not in front of so many people.

In front of him, Captain Tyrrel was already pulling a howling, bleeding Tristan back, out of the circle. Captain Tyrrel looked up long enough to meet Aki's eyes and Aki knew he'd heard Desmond's last words as well. And he was furious at them.

With one hand pressed over the thin slice Tristan had made on his arm, Desmond pushed himself up onto his knees. He wasn't even looking at Aki, he was staring at the cut in ever growing despair. The arm that was wounded hung completely limp and immobile by his side. He struggled to get one foot solidly on the ground in front of him.

"Get your sword," Aki said, his voice hard. There was poison on Tristan's knife. Poison Desmond fully planned on crippling Aki with. The realization of that obliterated every other thought for a moment. He'd known Mara would do something like that, but the prince?

With one frantic look at Aki, Desmond tried to reach for his sword, but his fingers refused to close around its hilt.

"What's happening to me?" he cried out as his leg gave out beneath him and he collapsed once more to his knees. "I can't feel them. I can't feel my hand."

"What you planned on having happen to me, apparently," Aki snapped. There was no effort to keep his voice down.

"I didn't. No, I didn't. I would never have killed you. It was all Tristan's idea. He said... he said," a sob choked the prince as he strained to move his arm, to get to his feet, to do anything at all. "He said..."

"He said what? That he'd poison me so you could kill me?"

"No," Desmond protested, "no. Just so that I could win. I wouldn't have killed you. I swear it, Aki. Why can't I move?"

It was true. Desmond's limbs refused to obey him. He was still on his knees, one hand still clutching the wound on his arm, the other still uselessly extended toward his sword.

"Pick up your sword," Aki repeated.

"I can't. I can't move." Desmond's eyes were wide now, his skin a pasty white as blood drained from his face. There was a tremor in his voice and tears of helplessness and fear in his eyes as he spoke. "Aki, don't kill me. Please. I swear I never meant to kill you. Spare me. You've already won."

All around them, people were pressing in closer, tightening the circle that enclosed the two. Captain Tyrrel was there again, standing next to Lars. Neither made any move toward Aki and Prince Desmond.

Aki saw none of them.

Only the prince. The prince who had lied. Who had carried his lies with him for weeks. The prince who'd planned on poisoning him to win. The prince who'd burned an entire group of men alive on an angry whim.

Anger rolled over him, as black as any abyss he'd ever looked into. And he let it. He invited it. It wrapped itself around his heart, coiled up inside of him like a serpent waiting to spring. It tightened his fingers around his sword as he flipped his hold on it and brought the weapon up, ready to plunge into the exposed neck of the prince. The strangled sob that escaped Prince Desmond's lips broke the tense silence that hung over the group.

From across the space, he could sense Mara's triumph. She stood on the brink of her own victory. One he could hand to her. And despite everything she'd ever done to him, he almost wanted to grant her this one final prize. He almost wanted to let her win just once in her life because he knew what it was like to lose over and over again. His sword still poised to strike the final blow, he turned to where she stood.

It wasn't her that he was looking at, though. It was beyond her. All the way back to the castle, he let his eyes wander. The castle had flown the black flag with the silver wolf's head on it for weeks. Now, however, it was the gold and scarlet banner of Dival that waved above its ramparts. Aki stifled the smile that crept over his face at the sight of it. Norman had decided to go along with his plan. He lifted the sword just a little bit more.

"Captain?" Desperation shrouded that single word as Desmond's wild eyes sought Captain Tyrrel's in a plea for intervention.

Captain Tyrrel shook his head. "It's what you agreed to, Your Highness."

"I'll do anything you want, Aki. Just please don't kill me. Please."

"Then tell everyone the truth," Aki answered. He had to end this quickly. Before Mara grew suspicious.

"What truth? That I lied about you in the council? Is that what this is all about? I lied, alright," Desmond forced his voice louder so that the others could hear. "I did send you back to my father. You didn't run away. Is that what you want?"

Still, Aki waited, his sword still suspended above Desmond's exposed neck. Mara called out to him, "Kill him, Aki."

"Please, don't." Desmond looked up at Aki.

Aki shook his head. There was more Desmond needed to tell. "You knew." It was all he needed to say. Desmond's face, already washed out with the death he was facing, went gray. Although he couldn't really move, there was an unmistakable slump of defeat

"You didn't have anything to do with his disappearance. I knew that."

"How?"

Desmond shut his eyes, ashen now. He couldn't see his own people behind him, but he knew they were there. Knew they were listening to every word. But it didn't matter now, not when his life lay entirely in Aki's hands.

"Because it was me," he whispered, his eyes still closed. He felt the effect of his words in the atmosphere around him. "I let the men in. It was Tristan's idea, though, not mine. And I never meant for any of this to happen."

Looking from Desmond to the Divalian men behind him, Aki saw the effect of the prince's words on them all. Captain Tyrrel's usually placid face was overshadowed with shock and confusion. Baron Orlander couldn't decide which one to look at - his eyes darted between Aki and Prince Desmond. Likely, he couldn't decide what to believe, either.

Behind him, Aki could almost hear Mara's silent glee. She'd known all along how Tristan had found a way to get inside the king's rooms that night. Forcing the confession from Prince Desmond just added another layer to a victory she was so sure Aki was handing her now.

One moment his sword was in the air, its tip bearing down on Desmond's neck. The next it was buried several inches deep in the earth by Desmond's knees. Desmond let out a final cry as the blade descended, straining to move but still held immobile by the poison from Tristan's cut.

Chapter 57

T HIS FIGHT'S OVER," AKI said. He looked around at the spectators of his triumph. "Is there anyone who would argue that I didn't win?"

Utter silence met him. No denial, no acceptance. Men on both sides still rested their hands on their weapons, waiting for the moment when this brief reprieve fell apart. They would kill him in a second, the Divalians would. More than one was stepping forward. He was guilty in their eyes now not only of killing the king but defeating their prince.

Aki looked to Captain Tyrrel, wishing he could, just once, read what the man was thinking. Wished he knew if the captain would stand the Divalian army down. Wished he knew if the captain would recognize him as the winner and, by default, the leader.

A miniscule nod from the captain was the only assurance he had that Captain Tyrrel would not allow the others to act just yet.

He looked at Lars, whose face was lined with unspoken worry. He knew what Lars was thinking and it didn't make matters any better. Lars was afraid for him. Aki appreciated the sentiment, but he was scared enough for himself that he didn't need anyone else helping him.

The Divalian men shifted warily, waiting on Captain Tyrrel or Prince Desmond or someone to tell them what to do.

Aki had bought time enough for Norman. Now he needed it for himself. All of his planning had led to this moment, but now that it was here, now that he was staring its success in the face, he felt like a child among adults. Completely inadequate and uncertain. Even Desmond seemed to know what to do better than he did. The prince had dropped his head since his confession and wouldn't meet anyone's gaze, but Aki hadn't missed the relief that swept over Desmond's face when his sword hit the earth. Now, he remained quiet, doing nothing that might make Aki change his mind.

"What are you doing, Aki? This isn't what we planned," Mara said, stepping forward. Her veil pulled against her features with the movement, showing the outline of her face. Aki could well imagine the expression she wore. To anyone else, the mask would still be unreadable. But Aki had seen it crack before and he knew it was only moments from splitting wide open. He hated himself for what he was about to do next. He hated that he actually pitied her at that moment. She wasn't worthy of it. Perhaps that's what made her so pitiable.

"Didn't I win, Mara?" He risked turning his back on the Divalians, trusting Captain Tyrrel to keep them in control, or at the very least to keep them from killing him. "Isn't that what I said I'd do?"

"Kill him," she bit the words out, still coming toward him. "Kill him now."

Aki swallowed back the urge to just give in and obey her. It was what he'd always done. As instinctive as drawing in breath, he fought it now. Fought it by not moving as she swept over to him. Her anger took more courage to face than Desmond's sword, he decided as his heart hammered in his chest. Still, he willed himself not to flinch when she got close. Her hand was up already, ready to strike.

"How dare you. I gave you protection. I gave you this. You think you can stop what I've begun just by sparing his life?"

Her raised arm moved to hit him, but, for the first time in his entire life, Aki stopped her. His heart skipped a beat as he did it. It felt so wrong. So completely out of place as he caught her wrist in his own hand. It was so unlike anything he'd ever done with her, so unexpected that Mara yelped in surprise. Beneath her thin veil, shock and fear flickered in her dark eyes. She tugged at her arm to free it, but he held it firm.

"Mara, stop. You can't win."

She was shaking her head, still staring at her wrist in his grasp, a sound that was somewhere between a laugh and a sob and a yell coming from her. "Let me go," she said, her voice a pitch higher than usual. "Take your hand off me at once. Sebastian! Halle!"

Aki looked beyond her, praying neither made any move to help her. Halle scuffed the ground with his foot and refused to look up. Sebastian looked from Aki to Karina and Aki saw the man waver in indecision.

If his eyes held any power at all to speak for him, he was practically screaming at Sebastian to do nothing. One move on Sebastian's part could be enough to snap the tension that held everyone in place. There would be nothing but bloodshed and death after that and all Aki had worked for in the last weeks would be wasted.

His sigh of relief when Sebastian made no move was audible.

"Halle, fight him. Do something," Mara's voice rose even higher. She pulled still against Aki, her efforts growing frantic. "Stop him."

"I don't think I'd like to die today, Mother," Halle said reasonably.

"Worthless son," Mara shrieked. A trembling took hold of her entire body. "Don't do this to me, Aki. It's all I have left. Let me go. Let me finish this."

"Mara, just stop. Look around you. You can't win," Aki repeated, saying each word slowly. She was coming apart right in front of him, her wall of ice and stone crumbling as he watched. There had been so many moments in his life when all he wanted was to see her brought low. But now? Now there was a pang of guilt that came from being the one behind her defeat. "You don't hold the castle anymore. You don't hold the town anymore. The Aruukens do not fight for you. What's left of your men are surrounded and badly outnumbered."

Mara twisted around to see. An awful keening came from her as she took in the sight of the castle. Her stronghold, now out of her reach. Without another word,

Aki released her arm. She stumbled forward a step toward her side, a beseeching hand outstretched for anyone to act, to help, to come to her side. They parted in front of her, looked away from her in shame and rejection.

And that was the final blow. Mara sank to her knees. Her hands clutched at her hair, tearing at it as she screamed her rage. Over and over again, she screamed. Incoherent, deafening. Full of all the pain she'd nurtured all those many years. Pain Aki knew, pain he understood.

"You've ruined me," she cried. "You've ruined me."

Aki wanted to turn away, wanted to close his eyes and shut his ears. Victory was supposed to feel better than this. Triumph was supposed to be intoxicating. But all he wanted was to crawl into some hole where he didn't have to witness Mara's undoing.

A shifting of bodies behind him gave him a good excuse to turn. Desmond still knelt helpless on the ground, his eyes bright with apprehension and shame as he watched the scene unfolding before him. The others were transfixed as well. Most still had a hand on their weapon, but none had drawn. The thin thread of control that had held them back was still at work. Aki knew he had to do something to keep things this way.

Only Baron Orlander was not held spellbound by it all. He shoved his way past the others, pushing those aside who weren't quick enough to get out of his path. He ignored Desmond on the ground. Aki braced himself at the dark look in the baron's eyes. But it wasn't Aki he reached for.

Mara's screams had died to moans. She rocked back and forth on the ground, her hands still tangled in her thick, black hair, murmuring the same words again and again, blaming Aki for her defeat. The veil was gone now, and her face was white as snow. Cold, bitter tears fell from eyes that saw nothing but years of hurt and betrayal.

There was nothing but furious grief on the baron's face as his thick hand closed around Mara's neck. He pulled her half up, his face close to hers as he said, "You're the one who ordered him killed? You're the one who had my son murdered?"

"Enough, Baron." Aki's sword was in his hand and held against the baron's neck before he knew what he was doing. "I didn't get to kill the one I wanted to today, and neither will you."

Baron Orlander let Mara drop and turned on Aki, quite unfazed by the presence of the sword. "You think that's all you need to do? Win a fight and then we all forget everything you did and pretend it never happened? Is that what you want? You killed the king. We ought to be taking your head, not watching you humiliate our prince."

"Felix is alive."

Blinking in stunned disbelief, the baron froze. The hand that held Aki by the front of his shirt went slack. "Don't do that. Don't give me hope just to save your own life."

"He's alive," Aki repeated. "And as to what I want, it is just to end all of this." He took a deep breath to steady himself as he looked around. He had to say something. The atmosphere was rife with suppressed malevolence waiting to be unleashed. The air hummed with the desire for violence. "I won the combat between Prince Desmond and myself. According to our agreement, that makes me the undisputed heir." He bit his tongue to keep from turning it into a question. No one would believe it if he didn't.

There was a ripple of dissatisfied mutterings among the Divalians, a general consensus that Aki should be executed right then, but a withering look from Captain Tyrrel silenced them. Aki wished he could thank the man right there and then. Captain Tyrrel might not be on his side, but he had enough honor to make sure Aki was heard out.

Instead, he blew out a long breath. "I know the rumors that have been attached to my name in these last weeks. I know that not one of you believes I am fit for anything aside from an execution. Baron," he faced the man directly, "if I turn myself over to your side and submit to whatever justice you deem right, will your army return home without a fight?"

It had to come from Baron Orlander. He embodied all of Dival's desire for war and he was Captain Tyrrel's counterpart, the only one aside from Prince Desmond who would override the captain's commands.

Baron Orlander stared hard at him. "Does Felix truly live?"

"He does. Badly injured but he's alive."

"And what army answers to you?"

"The Aruukens, for now, and the men of Dorsten. They recognize me as an heir even if you do not."

"If you surrender yourself to us, they will attack. You'll accomplish nothing but your own death. That is what will happen to you, you know that, right? We will kill you."

"They will not attack, no matter what you do to me. Unless," Aki kept his voice steady and his gaze even, knowing that if anything was going to go wrong, it would be now, "you fail to meet my terms."

"Your terms?" Captain Tyrrel spoke up from where he stood listening in.

Aki looked around. Everyone was listening, hanging on every word he said. Not just the Divalians. Lars and Halle and Sebastian and Karina. The townspeople who'd gathered. The handful of Mara's men who'd accompanied them. Even Mara, although she was once more on her knees, her face shielded from sight by her hands, had grown quiet to hear what he had to say. Their eyes made him want to wither into the ground.

So much depended on this moment. Aki silently whispered the names on his list. The names of those who had to win. The names who were the only reason he could make himself go through with what he was about to do. People he might very well never see again, or who he was seeing now for the last time. It was for them that he went on.

"My terms," Aki repeated firmly. "First of all, you won't kill Mara."

"Aki..." Captain Tyrrel started.

Aki shook his head. "No. She doesn't die. She's paid a high enough price for the peace of this kingdom; she doesn't pay again."

There was bewilderment at that, but Aki didn't think it was a good time to explain. He had an audience, and he wasn't sure for how long. It wouldn't do to waste it on history lessons.

"Anything else?" Baron Orlander was still wary.

"Desmond doesn't get the crown. He lost. He's done at least as much damage as I've been accused of. Instead, he stands trial not only for what he allowed to happen to King

Darien but also for the order he gave to murder innocent people. Choose someone else to be your king, someone who's actually worthy of the title instead of just someone born to it."

"You're asking that we undo generations of tradition and succession. That's not an easy thing," Captain Tyrrel said.

"It can be. Is there really anyone here who thinks Desmond's fit to rule?" It was perhaps a little unfair to pose such a question right after Desmond's humiliation and confession and while he was still helpless to even get to his feet. Aki didn't care, though, and he could see the Divalian men considering his question. Not one spoke up on the prince's behalf. Not even the prince.

Desmond's face went from pale to brilliant red at their silence. But even in his anger, Aki saw his shame, saw his guilt and then, his acceptance.

"And lastly, the people of Dorsten need their own voice in your council, unless they wish to break their union now that King Darien is dead. If that is the case, they must be free to choose their own leader. Agree to all of that, and I'll surrender myself to you, I'll... I'll submit to any punishment that's deemed worthy."

"And Felix is still alive?"

"Yes, Baron Orlander. He will be with the men who now hold the castle."

Captain Tyrrel stepped forward. "You've left yourself completely out of your own terms, Aki. You know you face death if you come with us?"

This was the part of the plan Aki had known he would have to face. The part he'd dreaded more than any other. There was a fluttering of nervousness inside him that had been getting stronger as he spoke. It made him want to be sick now.

Hope, he whispered to himself. The same hope that made his father and mother deem their own lives less important than his. He'd called it foolishness. And it was a little foolish, and a little wild, and a little intoxicating. But it was all he had to offer these people, to offer anyone. It was the difference he could make.

"If by killing me, your justice is served and there is no more need to go to war, then do it. I will not... I cannot ask anyone else to fight and die for me. I've enough people on that list as it is, I don't need to add an entire army. All I can ask for myself is this, let me live long enough to stand trial in Bren. I will answer any questions regarding my actions there. Will my surrender be sufficient to make you go home in peace?"

The baron and captain exchanged an inscrutable look. Aki looked beyond them to Desmond, who was watching him with an intensity that made Aki want to disappear. There was confusion in the prince's face. Confusion that slowly shifted into understanding as he realized just what Aki was doing, what he was offering. Desmond lowered his gaze at last.

"Aki, who holds the castle now?"

"Norman Turston, former captain of Lord Bayner's, and his people."

"I've heard of him," Captain Tyrrel said. "He recognizes your authority as heir?"

"He does."

Captain Tyrrel nodded and looked once more at Baron Orlander. Then he turned his attention to Prince Desmond. There was a great reluctance on the prince's part to look back up. There was still indecision on the captain's part.

"Your Highness, what you said during the fight, was that true?"

Desmond's reluctance extended to his voice. His whisper was barely audible as he answered, "Yes."

"All of it?"

"I never meant for all of this to happen. I never meant for him to die."

"You have a lot to answer for, prince. An awful lot. As do you, Aki."

"Which I'll do, if you agree to my terms and decide not to execute me immediately."

"And if we don't?" Baron Orlander asked.

"Then you will likely kill me right here and now, and then there will be a battle, possibly an entire war, and a lot of men on both sides are going to die and perhaps you'll decide to marry off one of the princesses in hopes of ending it, but you'll really only be starting more problems. And we'll keep repeating the same thing over and over again and hope that one time it will work out better. That's what will happen, Baron. That's what's already happened, isn't it?"

He knew the story well for Master Wehr had taught it to him early on. The tale of twin princes, heirs to their father's kingdom, rivals for his crown. Their rivalry had divided the kingdom into two - Dival and Dorsten had never truly been one since that day.

"I'm offering you peace and justice the best way I know how, Baron. Believe me, this isn't something I want. I know every one of you here wishes to kill me. And even if you choose to wait, I'd rather not go back to Bren and face another trial. I doubt I'll find much mercy there no matter what I say. I don't exactly have a lot of people on my side. But starting a war is a worse solution."

Aki meant the words more than he'd meant most anything else he'd ever said. So it hurt a little when Captain Tyrrel started laughing. Not a half smile or a short bark of laughter that was instantly smothered, but actually laughing. Aki just stared at him.

"I'm sorry, Aki, but you do realize that you have more people on your side right now than anyone else here, don't you?" Captain Tyrrel was shaking his head as he laughed. He grew sober again after a few moments. "I don't think any of us can argue that a solution that doesn't involve war is the best. You did win the fight, and would have won regardless of Tristan's involvement, and that puts you in a position to demand terms, I suppose. And it puts us in the position of obeying those terms."

Chapter 58

NOTHING WAS EVER AS SIMPLE as imagined. Aki watched as Mara's men were disarmed. He caught sight of Ritter among them but either the man didn't see him or was choosing to ignore him. Aki thought it was likely the latter considering the fact that he'd stood before them only a short time before and explained the change in their circumstances.

Leaderless, surrounded completely by the Aruukens who rode with Lars, facing the Divalian army and with their castle stronghold returned to Dorstenian hands, Aki had offered them the choice between fighting and surrender. Mercenaries whose greatest cause was money, they weren't particularly interested in testing the odds against them.

"Someone else can oversee this," Baron Orlander said just behind him. "You said we cannot enter the castle without you."

Despite the baron's brusque tone and still wary manner around Aki, there was an impatience in his request that sprung solely from hope. Felix lay inside the castle if Norman had followed Aki's instructions.

"Go on, Aki," Lars said. He hadn't left Aki's side since Captain Tyrrel officially acknowledged not only his victory but his demands. "I'll finish this. They're probably getting anxious in the castle, anyway, and I'm sure the prince would appreciate an actual room to recover in."

Aki didn't miss the smile on Lars' face at the mention of Prince Desmond. Nor did he return it. He couldn't. After everything that had happened, he felt a bit wooden, going through the motions of what was apparently expected of him, knowing all the while that, although everyone around him would be able to enjoy the peace he'd just bought them, Aki's fight was far from over. He still had to face yet another trial in Bren if they decided to keep him alive long enough for that. A trial that he had slim hopes of coming out of without a death sentence.

Soldiers parted before him as he led the way through the stiffly mingling armies back toward the castle. It was true that he'd asked Norman to let no one into the castle unless he accompanied them. It had been a purely selfish request. Aki wanted to live a little longer. There'd been no way to know whether they would decide upon a summary execution for him or not. By ensuring that they needed him for at least a little while, he'd bought himself a few extra hours of life.

The bridge was drawn up, the gate shut fast when they approached. It was just him and Baron Orlander. Captain Tyrrel would follow shortly with a small group of soldiers escorting Mara and Sebastian as Aki had asked him to, and, of course, Prince Desmond. Karina, keeping a safe distance between herself and any soldier, was behind the captain's group.

Norman was looking down on them from the wall and acknowledged Aki's presence with a nod. He shouted an order down and then disappeared.

"I will kill you if you're lying about Felix, agreement or no agreement," Baron Orlander said as they waited.

"Baron, whether you choose to believe me or not, Felix is one of the few people I think I could truly call a friend. I would not lie to you about him."

"I hope not." It wasn't malice in his voice this time, only hope tangled up in anxiety.

"He is injured," Aki said carefully. There was no kind way to tell the baron the truth. "He was only kept alive for questioning."

"They tortured him?"

Aki nodded, watching as the bridge settled onto its stone base and the gates, groaning on their hinges, opened.

"Tell me."

"He never told them anything."

"What have they done to him?"

Before Aki had a chance to answer, Norman was crossing the bridge to meet them. He was only a few years younger than Stephan but his resemblance to his brother was such that Aki felt like he was staring at Stephan each time he saw Norman. It was both a comfort and a heartache.

"You succeeded, I see, my lord."

Aki gave him a quizzical stare at the title. It didn't belong to who he was, to who he'd ever been. He was tempted to say something to that effect but decided it might be better for Baron Orlander to hear for himself that Aki was, in fact, an heir. "Thanks to you and your people. Did you lose any?"

"You were right in thinking Mara would leave very few behind. You were also correct in assuming she knew nothing of the secret entrance you and your friends discovered. We took them completely by surprise. A few of ours are wounded, but none are dead."

"And you brought Felix?"

Norman nodded. "He's upstairs in one of the bedrooms. We've had a doctor see to him and my wife's with him now. I'll lead you there now if you'd like."

It had been just a few hours earlier when he'd walked down these very stairs with nothing but a promise to fulfill and a plan, a plan that hinged on so many people he wasn't sure he could count on. He supposed he ought to add some of them at least to his list. It was hard to add anyone, though, when there was still the great, big empty space left by Sasha. No one would ever be able to take the place of the very first person to show him real kindness.

"He's right in here," Norman said, stopping in front of one of many identical doors.

Baron Orlander started to open it, but Aki stopped him.

"Baron, there were things done to him that he won't recover from. You should know that before you see him," Aki said, keeping his voice low so that no sound of his words would carry into the room.

"What things?"

"When he refused to cooperate, he was blinded with a hot iron. He'll never see again."

There was something terrifying about watching a man like Baron Orlander break down and weep. Aki turned away, not because he was ashamed of the man, but because it was what he'd wanted to do and couldn't. He'd let Cristof do it, he'd walked away and left his friend to the mercy of a man who knew none. Coming back for him later wasn't enough. He should have found a better way.

Baron Orlander remained in the hallway outside of the room for several minutes. When it became clear that he wasn't going to enter until he'd composed himself once more, Aki pushed the door open and let himself in. He hadn't seen Felix since that night, and he wasn't sure if Felix even remembered that thanks to Sebastian's timely and merciful interference.

Felix was lying on the bed, a bandage wrapped around his head, covering where his eyes should be. But he wasn't asleep. Aki could see that right away. He turned his head with painstaking care at the sound of Aki's feet crossing the floor. There was a woman sitting beside the bed that Aki guessed was Norman's wife. She watched him without a word and a fond smile graced her face after a moment, as if she were smiling at someone she remembered and was glad to see again.

"Who is it?"

"It's me, Felix. Aki."

"They said you would come back."

Aki was relieved to hear no anger in Felix's voice. "I've come back, and I've brought your father to see you. He'll be in soon."

Felix turned his face away toward the light of the window. "I don't know if I want him to see me like this."

"Felix, I'm sorry. I should have..."

"Norman read your letter to me. And I heard everything you said in that cave, though," Felix paused, frowning beneath the bandage, "I do not think you meant for anyone to hear you then."

Aki frowned in turn. Felix was right. When Aki had broken the silence with his own voice, he'd said words he'd never meant for another to hear. He'd just needed to hear them out loud himself, he needed to remind himself of his real task, of the truth beneath all the lies he was living.

"I'm sorry I didn't stop Cristof. I should never have let this happen to you."

"Please, just stop. I feel sorry enough for myself as it is. I don't need anyone else doing it for me."

Aki hesitated. The question that burned inside him was one he wasn't sure he wanted the answer to. But his time was limited. He wasn't sure how long he'd be allowed to wander freely about since he'd officially turned himself over to the custody of the Divalian army.

"Do you believe me?" It sounded like such a simple question, but there was so much Aki needed Felix to believe.

"I wanted to believe you when you first translated that letter. I'd been staring at it for days. I knew what it said. And you read it all wrong. That was on purpose, wasn't it?"

Aki nodded, then remembered that Felix couldn't see the gesture. "It was."

"Is it all over then?"

"It is. And," Aki turned to see the door open again, "I think your father is here to see you now."

The baron's face was still suspiciously red, as were his eyes, but otherwise he looked unchanged. He paused in the doorway, taking in the sight of his youngest son on the bed, accepting what his eyes were telling him was true.

"Father?"

"I'm here, son." The baron was across the room in an instant, pulling Felix up into his arms. "We thought the worst for so long."

"I'm not sure how much better this is," Felix whispered. "I'm blind, Father. I'll never...," he choked on the words.

"But you're alive."

Aki slipped out of the room quietly. The woman, sensing her presence unneeded, was not far behind him.

Waiting outside the door was not only Norman but also Captain Tyrrel. Whatever conversation they were in the midst of stopped abruptly when they noticed Aki's return. By the hard set of Norman's jaw, Aki could guess that he was displeased about whatever they were talking about. It was a look he'd seen so many times on Stephan. It was about the only look Stephan had worn around him since

Sasha brought him home from Karu. Aki didn't like seeing it now. He didn't like being reminded of Stephan's disapproval.

"You never said how much he looked like Sybil." It was the woman who spoke first, breaking the brittle silence of the moment.

"Well, it's not like we've had a lot of time in the past two days to discuss it, Lydia."

Lydia reached a caressing hand to Aki's face, her eyes misty and distant. It wasn't him she was really reaching for, Aki realized, but that knowledge didn't keep him from flinching away. That was usually enough to remind Alina that he disliked being touched, but Lydia didn't seem to notice.

"You're Sybil's son, alright. She'd have been proud to see you here today."

"You knew my mother?"

"Knew her? I practically raised her, boy. She was as much my daughter as any of my own. 'Twas a sad day, indeed, that Lord Bayner chose to send her north. I never thought I'd get to meet her child, though. I told Norman he ought to have brought you back with him the other day, but he said you wouldn't have considered it. But now we have you here to ourselves. Norman and I served the Bayner family for many years. I'm sure we'd both be happy to do so again."

Aki drew back out of her reach uncomfortably. He hadn't prepared himself for such a reaction from anyone. There was an awkward cough from Captain Tyrrel and Norman stared hard at Aki. Lydia seemed to notice for the first time that something was amiss between the two men. She looked expectantly from one to the other, even including Aki in her questioning gaze.

"It seems we won't have him, after all, since he's bartered his life away to keep the peace."

"You told him the terms?" Aki asked the captain.

"We were discussing them just when you came out."

"Why'd you tell them you'd surrender yourself to them, Aki? You're our heir, we would have fought for you."

"That's just it, Norman. I couldn't ask you to do that. I couldn't ask you or anyone else to die for me. You don't even know me. You know whatever version of me Mara sold to you."

Norman shared more than just a similar face with Stephan, Aki realized. He shared his tenacity and ability to drive his point home rather excessively. Aki wanted to shrink away as Norman repeated story after story that Mara had told about him and asked after each one if it was true. They all were. Mara hadn't needed to make up any stories to exaggerate the difficulty of his life. He'd had plenty for her to choose from.

"And it is true that you agreed to surrender yourself to the Divalians if they would go home in peace?" Norman said at last.

"It's true," Aki answered, his voice small, his eyes fixed on the floor. Mara had shared even the worst moments of his time in Aruuk. Even dead, Cadoc was still haunting him. Out of the corner of his eyes, he saw Lydia's hands clasped together over her mouth in horror and tears in her eyes.

"Then I suppose I do know a bit what sort of person you are. And believe me when I say, we would willingly have gone to war to support your claim."

"I've made my terms, Norman. I can't undo them. And even if I could, I wouldn't. I don't want a war. I never did. I just wanted to keep my promise to King Darien and stop Mara. You'll be free now to choose who leads you, whether that's someone from Dival or one of your own. Just, please, choose someone good. Someone who won't be looking to start a fight every chance they get."

Norman gave vent to a sigh of frustration that Aki didn't quite understand. "I suppose I should go and make sure your brother, Lars, doesn't need any help."

Lydia followed him, leaving Aki alone with Captain Tyrrel. He scuffed at the stone floor with the toe of his boot, unwilling now to meet the captain's eyes, unwilling to face what he was sure was coming.

"You don't get it, do you?"

"Get what?" Aki looked up, annoyed at the captain's tone.

Captain Tyrrel didn't answer. He just shook his head in bemusement and gave Aki an odd look. That only worsened Aki's irritation. He was likely on his way to die unless he could convince the council of the truth and he thought the least Captain Tyrrel could do was explain himself. His annoyance wasn't enough of a motivation to compel the captain to speak, though.

"What are you going to do with me now?" Aki asked, unwilling to wait any longer.

"What should I do with you?"

Apparently, Captain Tyrrel meant to test whatever was left of his patience. "Why are you asking me? That's not my decision to make."

"Isn't it? Haven't you been making all the decisions here today?" Now Captain Tyrrel had the gall to look amused.

"Not out of choice," Aki protested. "If I'd left it up to everybody else, we'd still be fighting, and people would be dying. I just did the only thing I could think of to stop it."

Captain Tyrrel shrugged but didn't speak again.

"So, you're just going to let me do whatever I decide? You're going to trust me to keep my word even though it means I'll likely die? You're not going to lock me up or put me under guard?"

"Do I need to?"

"Well, it would be in my own best interest to run away."

"Will you?"

"You don't have any reason to trust me. No one does," Aki said quietly.

"Maybe not. But, if you were going to run, you'd have done it weeks ago. Besides, I think you earned a bit of trust today by not killing the prince. You can't tell me you didn't want to."

"It wouldn't have solved anything. Besides, I made a promise not to. Where is he, anyway?"

"In a room, recovering. The poison's not fatal nor, according to our doctor, is it permanent. I'm sure he'll heal from that a lot faster than he'll recover from his wounded pride today."

"What about..."

"They are locked up. We may have agreed to spare her life, Aki, but that woman has a lot to answer for."

Aki leaned his head back against the wall, shutting his eyes. Shutting out those moments when she'd shattered in front of everyone. She would blame him for her defeat.

"You may want to talk to Norman. He is of the mind that any trials that are to be held, should be held here, in Dorsten." Aki opened his eyes to look at the captain. "He's not wrong."

"That's not my decision to make," Aki said, repeating his earlier words, hoping Captain Tyrrel would take them with more seriousness this time.

"If it was?"

"If it was," Aki gave it a moment's thought. His planning hadn't gone far enough into the aftermath of his success to help him now. "If it was, I'd agree with him. Dival only had a part in this. Dorsten and Aruuk ought to have a say in the outcome as well. They lost the most people."

"Then it seems we all agree on at least that one matter."

"What difference does it make?"

Slapping his hand to his forehead, Captain Tyrrel let out a sigh of frustration not entirely unlike the one Norman had given vent to a few minutes' prior. "You won, Aki. That makes the difference. You won, and if you want the trial to be held here, if you want everything to be done here, that's your decision to make. Prince Desmond may not have intended to abide by our agreement, but I will not break it. We agreed that the winner would be the undisputed heir."

"Wait," Aki held up a hand to stop the captain from speaking anymore, "wait. That's not what I intended. That's not at all what I intended. I can't be the one who decides. It can't be me. It shouldn't be me. I only challenged him to stop Mara from starting her war. I didn't really mean it."

"And here I thought Prince Desmond was the only one who hadn't thought this all through. What, exactly, did you expect?"

If Aki hadn't known better, he would have thought Captain Tyrrel was struggling to keep his face sober. It was so unlike the captain that Aki almost forgot what the man said.

"Honestly, I thought I'd already be dead, or at the very least, on my way back to Dival in chains."

"I'm sorry we've disappointed you're rather bleak expectations." Captain Tyrrel was definitely amused.

There was no mistaking the way the corners of his mouth twitched upwards. "Perhaps when calculating your plans, you ought to have left room for the possibility that not everyone wanted to see you dead. Although, I can't say that the sentiment among my men isn't that you should die. Regardless, it is still your decision to make. Certainly no one else is in a position to make it."

"Neither am I. I'm wanted for treason again."

"You want to stand trial, don't you?" Captain Tyrrel gave him a searching look.

"I want to prove my innocence. That's the only way to do it."

"They might not believe your proof."

"It's all I have," Aki said, knowing it might not be enough. That had been the danger of his plan. All the proof in the world might not be enough to change the minds of those already ill disposed towards him.

"Where is this proof that you claim to have?"

Aki grimaced. "It's a letter. It was written by King Darien the evening before he disappeared. It explains everything - why I'm here, why he sent me, what he wanted me to do. I left it with Alina."

"I knew she was lying," Captain Tyrrel muttered. "She said she hadn't seen you."

With an apologetic shrug, Aki went on, "King Darien's secretary, Jarvis, witnessed him write it and give it to me that evening."

Everything hinged on that letter, and Jarvis' testimony. It was his way home, King Darien had told him that night. King Darien had promised to leave him a way home in exchange for Aki's promise. Aki hadn't known at the time what was going on. And King Darien had, as he'd already discovered, decided not to tell him the truth about his relationship to the royal family. Aki still wasn't sure if he was angry about that or not. His only consolation was that the king, although he knew who Mara was, knew nothing of the history between her and Aki. Aki still wished the king would have mentioned who was behind everything. It might well have altered his own choice.

"You didn't kill him, did you?"

Aki shook his head. "He spared my life. Why would I want to take his?"

"Because of your bond of service to him."

The laugh that rose up inside his throat felt strange after so much solemnity, but Aki couldn't help it. Captain Tyrrel raised his eyebrows at the sound of it. Rolling the sleeve of his shirt up, Aki held his arm up for the captain to see. "I've spent more of my life as a slave than free, and I will forever bear the marks of those that owned me. One of them I helped escape Bren when his life was endangered, and I just bargained for the other one's life today. No, Captain, my bond of service to the king would not have been sufficient reason for me to want him dead."

He wasn't sure whether or not Captain Tyrrel believed him. It didn't really matter, anyway. It was whatever assembly of men that came together to try him believed that would make all the difference. But he wanted the captain to believe him, wanted someone to know him well enough to know that he would never have done such a thing.

Tired all at once, Aki started to walk away. If he wasn't to be locked away by the captain, he was about to lock himself away in his room. He wanted to be alone. He wanted to rest.

"Since you're neither dead nor in chains, you might want to take some time to think about what happens next," Captain Tyrrel called after.

So much for rest.

Chapter 59

A DEEP THROBBING PAIN BEGAN at the back of his head and wormed its way all the way to the front, making Desmond reluctant to open his eyes when he heard footsteps in the room.

There was no one he wanted to see. There was no one he wished to speak to. Not one person had stood up for him, but he couldn't even really blame them. He'd confessed to everything just like Aki had wanted him to. Just the thought of Aki left a bitter taste in his mouth. Desmond had never been so humiliated in his life. He'd never been so afraid for his life. The memory of that fear, of his helplessness in the face of it, burned like a hot coal inside his chest. He would never forget it.

"Awake, Your Highness?"

Desmond groaned at the sound of Captain Tyrrel's voice. If any strength had returned to his limbs, he would have covered his face but the best he could do was turn away from the captain's gaze. Too late, he remembered that the motion gave away his state of wakefulness. For over an hour, he'd pretended to be asleep still just so that he wouldn't have to acknowledge anything that had happened during this dreadful day.

"We need to talk, Your Highness."

"What is there to talk about?" Desmond snapped, turning back to face him. "About how Aki stripped my throne and crown away from me? About how he made a complete fool of me in front of everyone? It's bad enough I had to endure it. I'd rather not discuss that."

"I think you know what I came here about."

Desmond swallowed hard and stared at the blanket drawn up over him. He knew, alright. He knew, and he wished the poison had taken away his ability to speak. His position would be far less uncomfortable if his mouth had been sealed shut. He silently cursed Aki all over again for forcing the words from him.

"You know, he could have killed you today. He was well within his rights to do so."

"So I should be eternally grateful for his mercy? How benevolent of him to humiliate me but keep me alive. Once again, he's made himself the hero and I'm everyone's villain."

"You ordered the murder of his people, Your Highness. And lied about him. And made plans with your friend, Tristan, to disable him in your fight. And, apparently, you knew something of your father's disappearance that you chose not to share with the rest of us, leaving us to believe that it was the courier who was behind it. I believe those facts have more to do with everyone's perception."

Finding great interest in the blanket, Desmond refused now to raise his eyes. There was nothing he could do to refute the captain's words. He'd condemned himself during those agonizing moments when he was more helpless than a baby.

"Tell me the truth about what happened with your father."

"I'd rather not."

"Your Highness, don't make this harder than it has to be. You've already admitted your part in it. Just tell me exactly how it happened and why."

For a long time, there was silence. Desmond had no intention of speaking and the captain, apparently, was equally determined to stay until Desmond changed his mind.

All Desmond could think of was the trial Aki made Captain Tyrrel and Baron Orlander promise he would face. The threat of that trial loomed large in the forefront of his mind. Desmond had never even considered the possibility. It made him wonder whether it was mercy or something more sinister that made Aki choose to spare his life.

"I didn't know what they were planning," he said at last, breaking the loud silence between them. "Tristan wasn't the only one that came back with us."

"I know. I was there, remember."

"He suggested I invite them. I had no idea they were working for that woman. How was I supposed to know? They wanted to look around and I showed them... well, I showed them more than I should have. I didn't mean anything by it, though."

"You showed them how to get to your father's rooms?"

"Yes."

"When?"

"That day."

"And you didn't bother to tell anyone about this when your father was missing?"

"How was I supposed to tell you that it was probably my fault? How was I supposed to admit that to our people?"

"So, instead, it seemed like a better idea to send us after the courier, wasting our time and endangering your father's life."

Desmond turned away so that the captain wouldn't see the tears of shame that burned in his eyes. Tears he hadn't let himself shed yet for his father. "I didn't know anyone wanted to kill him. I didn't know about Mara or anything. He never told me any of it, even though he knew. I was just afraid of anyone finding out that I'd been so... foolish." The word hurt to say.

"And what would you have done if we'd apprehended the courier before he made it north?"

"I don't know. I don't know what I would have done, Captain. I didn't think. I was just scared, alright. I was afraid of what the people might have done if they thought I was responsible. They loved my father. They wanted someone to blame. And that couldn't be me. You understand that, don't you? I didn't actually think through what I would do if you'd brought Aki back."

"Perhaps not, but what was that you said at the end about how you lied to the council about him? Was that true?"

He didn't need to answer for the captain to see that it was true. His own guilt was written plainly on his face. Captain Tyrrel sighed, resting his hands on his knees and leaning back in the chair he'd taken, his expression grim.

"I don't want to stand trial," Desmond whispered. Just the thought of it made him sick. Trials were something criminals endured. Not princes. It wasn't the thought of being in front of so many people, it was the knowledge that all those he would be in front of thought horribly of him.

"The terms are already set, Your Highness. You lost and he won. If you'd wanted a different outcome, perhaps you should have listened to the advice of everyone but that spy, Tristan's, and not agreed to the fight. You placed the entire kingdom in the balance of that fight against all of our better judgment. You've only yourself to blame now that it's out of your hands."

"You wanted him to win," Desmond said accusingly. "You never really believed he was guilty."

"If you remember, Your Highness, I was quite adamant in advising against the single combat. And that had nothing to do with his innocence or guilt, just the certain knowledge that he is a far superior swordsman than you have ever allowed yourself to become. That said, I never believed he acted alone, nor did I believe everything that woman said. I told you before that it didn't all add up." Captain Tyrrel got to his feet. "There are those who favor a joint trial conducted by representatives from Dival, Dorsten and Aruuk. If I were you, Your Highness, I would give some thought toward making amends if you can."

It was doubtful whether he could give his thoughts to anything else with that news. It was one thing to be tried by his own council. He had men like Gregory on his side there. He couldn't imagine facing people like Lars. It was a waking nightmare.

Chapter 60

IT WAS ONLY A LITTLE PAST midday when Captain Tyrrel approached the familiar door. Knocking, he stepped back and pulled the letter he'd carried with him out of his pocket. He could hear footsteps crossing the room to reach the door moments before it was swung open. It wasn't Alina who met him. Nor was there any warmth in the look the young woman gave him. Dressed in the somber black of someone mourning, she held a small baby in her arms. Captain Tyrrel cursed inwardly. He'd forgotten about Sasha's wife. Sasha's widow, he reminded himself.

"Are you coming for us this time?" Ophelia Gundarson wasted no time in pleasantries.

"No." Captain Tyrrel looked down at the letter in his hands. He wasn't one to fidget, but under Ophelia's grief-stricken eyes, it was impossible not to. He twisted the letter around in his hand. "I need to speak with Alina."

"I don't believe there's anything left for you to say that I'm interested in hearing," Alina's voice carried across the room as she approached. Standing beside Ophelia, she glanced down at the letter. "What is it? Have you come to tell me he's dead?"

"He's not dead. He sent me to deliver this to you."

"And since when does Aki tell you what to do?" Alina's face darkened with suspicion, but she took the proffered letter.

"Since he won."

Alina rubbed her hand over her forehead and stared down in confusion at the letter. "How?"

"I think that's better answered if you read that first."

Alina didn't wait any longer. In front of both him and Ophelia, she broke open the plain wax seal and read. It was a lengthy missive, totaling several pages full of writing. Captain Tyrrel could only assume that Aki had written out an account of everything that had transpired in the past weeks. From time to time, her expression shifted - sometimes a small smile, sometimes a frown. More than once she brought her free hand up to her forehead and smoothed out the wrinkles that creased her skin there.

At long last, she folded the papers back together.

"I'm going," she said to Captain Tyrrel before he had a chance to speak.

"Going where?" Ophelia asked.

"I'm going with you back to Dorsten."

"You can't," Ophelia beat Captain Tyrrel to the words. "Whatever that letter says, it's probably not true."

"I can assure you it is," Captain Tyrrel said.

Ophelia turned cold eyes to him. "Just like it was true that you only had a few questions for...," she stopped, shaking her head as tears pooled in her eyes. "You didn't even give us the chance to say goodbye. You just took him. You just lied to me and took him. And now he's gone. He's gone." She was crying now, one hand over her mouth. But her words still came, rising up out of a great well of sorrow. "He's dead and my son will never know his father because of you and that murdering prince. I hate you. I hate you. I know I shouldn't, but I do. I can't help it. I wish... I wish..."

Captain Tyrrel looked down, away from her weeping. He knew what she wished. And it was deserved. "I am sorry for what happened and for my part in it. I had no idea that the prince intended to...," the words wouldn't come. Not without the memory of hearing the screams of those trapped inside the inferno. Not without the sickening odor of burning flesh filling his mind. All of it happening while he stood by and watched, stood by, and did nothing. "I'm sorry."

Ophelia just turned away, unable to stem her grief. Captain Tyrrel was tempted to add to his words, to tell her that he hadn't taken Sasha straight to the other Aruukens. That the prince had wanted him brought to Bren and questioned in case he knew anything of Aki's whereabouts or who Aki was working with. He wanted to suggest that perhaps Sasha had not yet been taken to the old fort when the prince had ordered it burnt to the ground along with its occupants. But he couldn't give her hope that wasn't really there.

Aki was right. Prince Desmond had done too much harm to be given the crown. He'd wrecked entire lives in a fit of anger. His brief legacy was one of death, destroyed families and broken homes. But the men who stood by and watched, including himself, were just as guilty. It made passing judgment on anyone from the other side considerably harder. Who was to say that Mara's crimes were worse than the prince's?

"I'm going," Alina repeated. "If he's alive, I want to see him. And I'll not surrender anything he gave me to your safekeeping. I'll take it myself."

"It is several days journey across the Void."

"Captain, it could be on the other side of the world. I'm going."

He'd heard the same steel in her voice before, when she refused to acknowledge that Aki had visited her before running to Dorsten. He knew there was no arguing with it. And with a resigned sigh, he nodded. "Hamo's coming too. As are three other members of the council and the late king's secretary. I'm sure we can make arrangements for you to accompany them."

When Captain Tyrrel left the farm, he turned his horse toward Bren. It wasn't part of Aki's instructions to go there, but he had to know. He had to be certain before he made preparations to return to Dorsten with the people Aki had sent him to collect.

Bren was a town on edge. Captain Tyrrel and the handful of men he'd selected to accompany him were the first of the army that had marched away weeks before to return. Even in the darkened streets late at night as they rode through, he caught sight of faces pressed against windows, peering through the darkness, a thousand questions waiting to be answered. Word of their arrival spread like fire and by morning it was no secret. What did remain a secret was the outcome of their army's endeavors. Aki had begged him not to say a word to anyone aside from those on his list.

Inside the castle, Captain Tyrrel sought out the jailer. An elderly, balding man who was afflicted with a perpetual wheeze in each breath, the jailer was easy to find. Captain Tyrrel interrupted him on his morning rounds. The jailer paused long enough to inquire what the captain wanted.

"Several weeks ago, I delivered Sasha Gundarson to you."

The jailer nodded.

"I just need to know if he's still here or if he's been sent with the others."

"He'd be dead now if he was. At least, that's the story going around. Prince Desmond wanted to send a message. Is that true?"

"It is."

The jailer shook his head in disgust and started to walk on. Captain Tyrrel leaned against the wall. He shouldn't have even hoped. He'd only come all this way to satisfy his own conscience, anyway. Even if Sasha had somehow still been alive, a hundred others weren't. He'd heard them die.

"Aren't you coming?"

Captain Tyrrel looked up to find the jailer standing several paces away, waiting for him.

"Where?"

"To see him. That's why you're here, isn't it?"

Chapter 61

AKI SHUT HIS EYES, LETTING THE sun warm his face. Today was the day. Captain Tyrrel had arrived late the night before and promised that the others were only a few hours behind him. For two and a half weeks, Aki had been both dreaded and longing for this day to arrive.

Now it was here.

Resting his hands on the stone ledge of the window, he looked out past the wall to the small meadow where he'd ended Mara's dreams and brought Desmond to his knees. Where he'd offered up his life in exchange for peace. Today was the day he discovered whether that price would be required of him. He ought to have been afraid. Instead, he was just impatient to have it over with. The waiting was wearisome.

At the far end of the meadow lay the town, half burnt but free of the presence of Mara's raiders. The group from Dival would pass through that town. They were the reason he couldn't tear his eyes off it.

Alina was with them, Captain Tyrrel had said. She'd insisted on coming and bringing the letter he'd left with her rather than entrusting it to anyone else's care. He hadn't even dared to harbor the hope of seeing her again. Whatever decision was made today, he was glad to have the chance to explain things to her himself. She would believe him. She always had. Even when he'd shown up in the middle of the night, telling her he was a fugitive but that he was innocent. She was the closest thing to a mother he'd ever had.

Thinking of her arrival inevitably led his thoughts toward the other woman responsible for raising him. Mara. It had been Captain Tyrrel's suggestion that he not make any attempt to see her or speak to her until after his trial. A suggestion Aki was very willing to heed.

"Aki?" Halle's voice came from the other side of the door.

In the days that followed Aki's victory in that meadow beyond the castle, Halle had kept himself scarce and Aki hadn't sought him out. He'd seen Lars and Halle together from time to time, but there was a distance now between the three of them that had not existed before. Captain Tyrrel didn't need to suggest that, it just sort of happened.

Halle had the door open before Aki could answer.

"What is it?"

Halle shut the door behind him and found an empty chair to make himself comfortable in. He fiddled with his hands for a long moment before speaking. "You made a lot of bargains with them."

Aki waited, watching him expectantly.

"You didn't happen to, you know, maybe include me in any of those bargains?"

Letting out a deep breath, Aki ran his fingers through his hair and frowned. With everything else to think about, he'd entirely forgotten Halle's sentence and the fact that Halle was a wanted fugitive himself.

"Sorry," was the best he could manage. "I didn't think about that."

Halle slumped down a little further into his chair, stretching his legs out before him. "I helped you save the courier."

"I know. Maybe we can just tell them that, and, of course, they'll know you didn't have anything to do with the king's disappearance. Maybe that will be enough to overlook the fact that you ran away."

Although Halle nodded in agreement, Aki could see quite plainly that he didn't like the sound of Aki's words.

"Even if they do, I'll just be taken back to Bren and locked up every night and left to beg on the streets during the day. I don't want to spend the rest of my life there."

Halle looked past him out the window. "I want to go home."

That was a sentiment Aki understood better and better with each passing day. He wanted to go home to the only place in the world where he was comfortable. He wanted his small room and the barn full of horses and the smell of Alina's food cooking that always filled the house. His greatest desire now was to be allowed to disappear into obscurity and return to that place. His days as a courier were irrevocably over. Keeping the farm for Alina was the most appealing plan of all.

Looking back at Halle, seeing the dejection on his face, Aki said quietly, "I won't stop you if you leave, you know. Keeping you here wasn't part of any deal I made."

Halle took a moment to think about what Aki was saying, then nodded, a rare smile on his face. He hauled himself up to his feet and started for the door, turning once he reached it to say, "You know, maybe it's not such a bad thing we didn't kill each other when we had a chance."

"Maybe not," Aki answered.

"Although, you still shouldn't have let them hurt me so much. If it's up to you, you ought to drown Ritter a few times and see how he likes it."

That was it, he realized as the door closed behind Halle. That was goodbye. As much of one as they were able to say to each other. He had no doubt that Halle would be gone long before anyone remembered he'd been there. To his surprise, the thought made him sad. Which, in turn, made him strangely satisfied. Because today, Gundar lost. The hatred he'd stoked between them since the time they were boys, knowing full well their relationship to each other, had, at long last, petered out. And even though he was dead, Aki felt free of the man who was his grandfather for the first time in his life.

Chapter 62

THE HUM OF CONVERSATION THAT echoed off the walls of the throne room died away as Aki's presence was noticed. At the front of the room, the dais with its three seats was unoccupied. Instead, everyone was gathered around the three tables pushed together in the center of the room. Five men sat at each table. Five senior clansmen from Aruuk, five senior councilmen from Dival, and five men from Dorsten. Norman was among the Dorstenian men and had helped in selecting the other four.

Somewhat separated from the others at the far end of the tables, sat Jarvis, secretary to the late king. Aki had only seen the man up close once, the evening of the king's disappearance. Aki hoped he was more honest than Gregory. Gregory's absence this day was part of Aki's choice. Although he was one of the longest serving councilmen, Aki refused to have him take part in this trial. The man may not have lied directly, but he'd let Prince Desmond's lie go unchecked.

Aki made his way through the quieting crowd and toward the single chair that faced the mixed tribunal. He'd allowed himself only two decisions regarding this day. Who from Aruuk and Dival would sit in judgment of both Desmond and him and who would face that judgment first. Everything else, he'd left up to the men now responsible for dispensing some form of justice.

As a hush fell over the room, Aki searched the sea of faces for familiar ones. Alina and Lydia were seated together off to the side of the tables. Seeing their worry, he attempted a reassuring smile in their direction. Neither of them looked even a little reassured.

He turned his attention back to the men in front of him. And frowned. Baron Orlander was not yet in his place. In the three weeks it had taken to organize this, Aki had seen little of the baron. The man rarely left Felix's side and Felix had yet to leave his room. Aki hadn't spoken to him since the day of the fight.

There was an impatience in the room as others also noticed the empty chair.

"Captain, perhaps you could go and remind the baron that his presence is required here?" Jarvis said from his seat at the very far end of the table.

"There's no need for that," Baron Orlander's voice came from the back of the room. "I'm here."

Aki turned with everyone else.

A path was cleared for the baron. He was not alone. His upper face still concealed by bandages, Felix leaned on his father's arm, allowing him to guide them forward. Despite what he faced, Aki smiled to see him up at last. The baron led his son to a seat near Alina and Lydia and then joined the others at the table.

Knowing the truth didn't make this moment any more palatable than the memory of his first trial. Still, Aki managed to keep himself from fidgeting in the moment of anticipatory silence that followed Baron Orlander's arrival. At least it had been his own decision that saw him here.

It was more than just his life and Desmond's that hung in the balance today. Everyone in the room knew it and it made the air alive with uncertainty. Today, Dorsten and Dival would choose. Today, they would either maintain their union and find a leader together or take separate paths. Desmond wouldn't be among those to choose from. Not if they kept to his terms.

Jarvis cleared his throat, an action that was quite unnecessary for collecting everyone's attention, but very necessary to collect his composure. Jarvis wasn't used to being the one to speak in front of people. The only reason he was doing it now was because everyone had agreed that someone needed to direct the events of the day and he was unfortunate enough to be selected for the task. He was on his feet, a paper in his hands.

"Aki Turston," Jarvis coughed over the name. He'd insisted the day before that Turston was not his legitimate name, that he should instead go by his family name of Bayner or at the very least, Gundarson, but Aki refused. "In the terms laid out here, you have agreed to not only answer any and all questions regarding your actions in the last year but to submit yourself to any judgment issued by this tribunal. I believe the foremost question in everyone's minds is, why did you run the night of King Darien's disappearance?"

Aki looked down at his hands. He looked back up at the men in front of him. Most of them, he did not even know the names of - Hamo, Baron Orlander, Norman and Faramund. The others were strangers to him.

"In a meeting earlier that day," Aki chose each word carefully, "Prince Desmond accused me of stealing an incomplete letter written to his father, King Darien, describing our success in the north." He'd rehearsed this so many times. Even while he was running, not knowing who or what was waiting for him in Dorsten, he'd gone over these words, words King Darien had told him to speak if he was ever given the chance. "He accused me of taking that letter back to Bren and delivering it to his father without permission. As this amounted to a breach in my bond of service to the king, it would likely have resulted in my execution. Those of you who were there," he looked between the five men from Dival, "know that the king had me removed from the council room at that time."

He waited for some sign of acknowledgement from the men of Dival and was satisfied when two or three of them nodded. They were the ones he was speaking to mostly, the ones he had to convince.

"After that meeting, I had a private audience with King Darien himself. He was well aware that his son lied to the council about me, but he refused to publicly refute the prince."

"A fact that no doubt infuriated you, giving you good reason to raise your hand against the king," one of the Divalian men Aki didn't know said. "You are simply convincing us that you had a good reason to act against him."

"In that conversation," Aki went on, ignoring the man, "King Darien gave me two choices. He knew that if I remained in Bren, my life would be forfeit. He offered me money and safe passage out of Dival to anywhere I wanted to go."

There was disbelief on most of their faces, but Aki had expected that. He forced himself to ignore it.

"The second choice wasn't all that different from the first except for this - I would run away still as far as everyone else was concerned but not where I wanted. He was well aware of the trouble that was building here in the north. Trouble that seemed tied both to the Dorstenians and the Aruukens. But he was blind and deaf to any details thanks to the ruthless murder of every courier and traveler who tried to cross from the province of Dorsten to Dival. He thought that if I were a fugitive of the crown, an enemy to the royal house of Dival, there was a chance I could make it north. And being able to speak and understand Aruuken like a native, I would have been above suspicion. The second choice was to serve as his spy in Dorsten. But that could only be accomplished by cutting all ties in Dival first."

"And you expect us to believe that you, a proven traitor, chose continued service to the king? That you chose to risk your life here rather than run and hide?"

"No. I don't expect you to believe me at all. Neither did he. Which is why that conversation did not take place in a room with just the two of us. He had a witness to it. A man who was not only there for the entire conversation but who also watched King Darien write a letter of explanation and give it to me."

"Who?" came the terse question.

"His secretary."

All eyes turned now to Jarvis. Aki hadn't spoken once to Jarvis since his arrival with the rest of the Divalian group. He'd been almost afraid to. Afraid that the man might not be as trustworthy as the king thought him to be, afraid that he might let some harbored ill will toward Aki overshadow the truth. But there was such an openness in his face, an honesty that could not be mistaken as he nodded.

"He speaks truly. I was there. King Darien," Jarvis' voice shook a little over the name and Aki realized that, having worked so closely with the king for so many years, the man was likely very close to him, "did offer the choices Aki has described. He did not feel he could expose his son's dishonesty without causing more harm than he could afford. It was a difficult choice for the king. And, I might add, a difficult choice for Aki."

Aki looked back down at his hands at the secretary's words. It had been an impossible choice. He remembered sitting there, in that small office, everything inside of him sinking at the king's offer. He'd hesitated. More than just hesitated. He'd begged King Darien to just tell him what to do, to make the choice for him because he knew what he wanted, and he knew he shouldn't want it so badly. King Darien had refused.

"I know what I'm asking of you," he'd said. "I can't order you to do this."

Aki had made his choice that night, and with it, a promise. The promise King Darien wanted.

It was Baron Orlander who spoke up next, saying, "Where is this letter of explanation?"

"Most likely, conveniently lost where it can never be found again," another councilman said.

"Unfortunately, even if his copy were irrevocably lost," Jarvis said, "the king didn't rely on just one." From the pocket of his shirt, he pulled out a sealed letter and handed it down the table. "King Darien understood the risk of what he was asking and wished for the truth to be made known even if Aki Turston did not survive to tell it."

"I still have mine, as well," Aki said, taking out the one Alina had brought with her. "It's not something I was likely to misplace, you know."

Baron Orlander collected the two letters and broke them both open, spending a moment comparing them before reading aloud from one of them.

"To whom it may concern," he read, his voice loud enough to be heard all the way through the room. Aki sucked in a deep breath and waited. He didn't actually know what the letter said. He only knew that King Darien had promised it would be a way home for him. "In light of recent events and news we have received from the northern province, I find it necessary to employ Aki Turston, now known to me as the grandson of my sister Mara, as my eyes and ears in the north. He has willingly agreed to act on my behalf and in my service.

"It is my greatest desire to be able to say these words myself after we have achieved success against those who move against us. However, that possibility is not great. If this is being read, then it is because I have failed in my own attempt to bring about peace. No one should carry the blame for my death. The choices I am making now are my own and are for the good of the people.

"In order to act as my spy, it is necessary for Aki to appear, once again, as a traitor. He understands this. However, I wish it to be known to all, whether he succeeds or fails, that Aki Turston has only acted in accordance with my request. Should he succeed, I would strongly advise the council to reconsider the sentence imposed on him in his prior trial."

Baron Orlander set the letter down on the table in the hush that followed.

There were many moments of his life when Aki wished he could vanish, not only from everyone's sight, but from their thoughts as well. Few moments, though, could compete with the strength of that desire now. He was the center of everyone's fixed attention. And the letter had evoked as much disbelief as it had trust.

"That's a nice piece, however you're the one who killed him in the end. I believe that negates any protection that letter was attempting to offer you."

"I didn't kill King Darien."

"Where's the proof of that? Another letter?"

Aki let his head drop. There wasn't any proof. Mara had made sure of it. Halle could have vouched for him, or Karina. But Halle was gone, and no one was going to listen to anything he said anyway, and who knew what Karina would actually say if she were asked.

"The proof is in the fact that he was not even at the place of execution when it took place." Looking up, Aki saw Norman speaking. "He was with two others down in the caverns that run beneath the castle and into the mountain.

I and several others heard and saw them down there. Unless he has the incredible ability of being able to be in two places at once, I'm not sure how it's possible for him to have been the one to execute the king."

"Mara said he didn't really kill the king. That's why she was going to make him execute me. To prove he was on her side," Felix said quietly from his seat. "I suppose she didn't mind admitting the truth in front of me since I was supposed to die the next morning."

"He was supposed to kill you?" Hamo spoke up for the first time, addressing Felix instead of Aki.

"He was. Instead, he saved me."

Felix's words brought about the first real consideration of his innocence since the trial began. At the table, a quiet discussion was taking place. Aki waited for more questions, but none came. That made waiting almost unbearable.

He thought there was more he needed to say, more that he needed to explain. They weren't even aware of the promise he'd made the king that night, the promise that made him offer himself up in exchange for continued peace. They didn't know about the many hours awake late at night trying, and often failing, to think ahead of Mara. Then he decided that none of those things really mattered to them anyway. If they didn't believe the word of King Darien, if they didn't believe Jarvis and Norman and Felix, then they would never believe him.

Across the room, he could see Alina. Lines of worry furrowed her brow and, although they lay still in her lap, Aki could see how clenched and white her hands were.

In front of him, the discussion grew in intensity, but not sound. He was still deaf to the arguments being made for or against him. There were some things he didn't need to hear to understand. Baron Orlander spoke very little at all, spending more time with his eyes fixed on his youngest son than participating in the debate. When he did speak, though, the other four invariably listened. Aki thought it must have something to do with the fact that he, out of all five, was the most directly impacted by Mara's work.

And it was Baron Orlander who at last rose to his feet and held out his hands to silence the swell of whispered conversation in the room. "There are still many things left for us to discuss, including the terms you set both with Prince Desmond before your single combat together and with Captain Tyrrel and myself after your victory. Those conversations are for another day. However, I think we have satisfied ourselves of at least one fact today."

He paused and Aki wanted to shout at him to just say it, to just say whether Aki was going to die or not, whether he was condemned for treason or acquitted of all guilt. He'd waited for three weeks to find that out and these last few seconds were longer than any of that time.

"Unless we are to discredit the word of men who have always been known to us as honest, we must conclude that you did indeed act in service to our late sovereign and that at no time, even the time of his death, did you raise your hand against him. Even without the word of trustworthy men, it would be difficult to dispute the fact that, without your intervention, none of us would be sitting here today. We would, instead, be engaged in a war that served no purpose other than our own destruction. Therefore, it is our decision that the accusations made against you in Bren are not valid. And you are not guilty of treason."

Chapter 63

"IT IS TIME, YOUR HIGHNESS."

"And if I choose not to go with you, Captain?"

"Don't make this harder than it needs to be. If you choose not to go, you will be forced to go. I hope you have more dignity than that."

Desmond wasn't sure if he did or not. His legs were lead weights, though, when he tried to move them. They refused to obey him.

"What, exactly, am I facing?"

"A less public affair than Aki has just faced. Yours will have no audience, only the men selected to judge you."

"Of course he did that. It makes him look better than me. Just like everything else he's done so far."

Captain Tyrrel didn't say anything. He didn't need to say anything. Desmond could read his answer in the way he stood, not speaking. Trying once more to get to his feet, he was almost surprised to find that they did indeed work.

"I don't want to do this."

"A fact you've made very clear on several different occasions, Your Highness. However, as you agreed to the terms of the fight, you are now bound to the decisions that follow."

The hallway Desmond followed Captain Tyrrel was empty, much to his relief. In the past three weeks, he had not ventured outside the privacy of the room he'd woken up in after his humiliating fight. Shuttered up in that room with nothing but his thoughts for company, Desmond

380

wavered between bursts of fiery anger and sullen self-loathing. He couldn't deny that he'd made decisions that were quite terrible in the eyes of everyone around him. Nor could he accept that there were any other choices he could have made.

They were outside the door before Desmond could work up the nerve to ask, "Is Aki going to be in there as well?"

"He is not."

For one moment, wild hope flared up inside his chest. If Aki was not there to tell the truth...

"I will be in the room, Your Highness," Captain Tyrrel added as if he'd read the thought in Desmond's mind.

The hope guttered out at once. He distracted himself from what lay on the other side of that door one more time. "What did they determine about Aki?"

"That he was truly only ever working on your father's behalf."

"Of course, they believe he's innocent," Desmond muttered under his breath.

"Should they believe any differently?" When Desmond lowered his head, Captain Tyrrel sighed. "You did send him with the letter to your father. Your father did send him as a spy to the north. He did effectively end what could have been a disastrous conflict. And he didn't kill you when he had not only the opportunity but reason to."

"And what about him killing my father?" Desmond almost choked on the words. It was too much to wrap his mind around – the thought that he would never see his father again, never get to speak to him again. Especially after their last words together.

"He did not kill the king," was Captain Tyrrel's only response.

Desmond thought back to what Lars had told him right before the fight. Perhaps it was true. And that just made everything worse. Because, if it were true, Desmond had a hand in his own father's death. If only he'd never thought of burning that fort down.

It was quiet in the room when Desmond and Captain Tyrrel entered. Gregory wasn't among those sitting at the tables. Desmond swallowed back the disappointment he felt at the man's absence. Gregory would have at least given him another person to help share the blame.

S. T. Hobbs

To his consternation, Lars was among those in the room. His sole purpose was to translate between the Aruukens and everyone else, but Desmond wasn't sure whether, given the choice, he would not have preferred Aki to act in that capacity. He hadn't been given any choices these past three weeks.

"We've decided that the best way to do this is," Baron Orlander said when he was seated, "is for you to simply tell us your version of what happened."

Desmond pressed his hands together to still them. Speaking slowly and pausing often to give Lars the chance to translate and forever conscious of Captain Tyrrel's presence, Desmond did as they asked. It had been one thing to confess out of a desperation to save his own life. It was quite another entirely to recount his decisions without any immediate threat to his person and in front of a roomful of men who took each and every word that came out of his mouth and weighed it. And it was another thing to listen to what he was saying and realize fully for the first time what a terrible thing he did.

By the time he was finished, he could not meet the gaze of any other person in the room. All he could think of was that day, that dark day, when he'd ordered so many lives extinguished. When he'd stood and watched the building burn, a furious satisfaction growing inside him as he finally struck back at their enemy. Struck back by turning the innocent into nothing more than fodder for his anger and fear. No amount of shame or remorse could take that day back.

His voice was barely a whisper as he finished, his eyes riveted to the floor in front of him. A burning heat rose in chest and all the way up into his face as the men before him broke into discussion.

Sitting farthest from him, the Aruukens who sat in judgement of him were the hardest to meet the eyes of. He knew, without Lars' translation, exactly what they wanted done with him. He could only hope that the others would disagree.

Chapter 64

THE HIGHEST TOWER OF THE castle was still dwarfed by the size of the mountain rising up behind it. Still, it was the furthest Aki could get from anyone inside the castle. A hot wind blew across it, bringing with it grim clouds that promised rain and blotted out the stars from the night sky.

Alina had retired more than an hour ago and Aki had wandered up to the tower afterwards. Somewhere in the heart of the castle, the futures of three countries were being discussed. Aki gave the talks little thought. His part in buying their peace was over. It was up to them to decide their next steps. He only knew what his would be.

Home.

He'd go home. And even if he was offered a chance to resume his training as a courier, he was going to turn it down in favor of staying home. There was nothing more he craved than obscurity. To no longer carry the weight of anything greater than the farm.

The entire plan had been growing on him since he'd left his trial many, many hours before. For hours, he'd talked it over with Alina, convinced her it was really what he wanted. Convinced her that he was ready to leave as early as this afternoon. It was her idea to wait, to at least see what direction their new world would take before running home. Aki had only reluctantly agreed.

Distant thunder rolled across the sky. The first few drops of rain splattered on the stone around him, but Aki made no move to seek shelter inside the castle. Inside people would find him, would want to speak to him, to question him. He was thoroughly sick of it.

A creaking of a door turning on its hinges made Aki turn around and watch as Lars stepped out onto the tower.

"So, this is where you're hiding," he said, looking around.

"Are they done?"

Lars shook his head and joined Aki at the low wall that encircled the top of the tower. It was too dark out to see anything beyond the courtyard that was lit up with torches, but Aki wasn't really there to look at anything specific.

"They're not, but we are. At least until they've decided who they're going to appoint as a new ruler."

Although they were both leaning on the wall, facing the darkness beyond it, Aki could sense Lars' eyes on him.

"What?"

"You haven't sat in with them at all, have you?"

"No."

Lars shrugged and turned, leaning his back against the stone wall, and facing the door again. "Halle's gone."

"I know. We spoke."

For a few moments the only sound was that of a few more raindrops falling and thunder that was growing closer by the minute. Lars scanned the sky and shivered as the rain increased.

"We're going to get soaked if we stay out here."

"No one's forcing you to stand out here."

"What is wrong with you?" Lars turned to look at him sharply.

"Nothing."

"Right. Because standing out in the rain in the middle of the night as far as you can get from people is something you do all the time. You won today, Aki. Why are you acting like you lost?"

"Tired, I guess." The problem was that tired didn't even begin to express the paradox of weight and freedom that hung over him. Because, now that it was all over, now that there were no other obligations left to fulfill, the final cost of the last few months became a reality. There was so much he'd lost forever.

"Well, I'm going in."

It was sometime after Lars disappeared back through the door that it swung open again. Aki didn't bother to look at who stood there.

"I'm coming in," he called over his shoulder, expecting it to be Lars again.

"Good, because you're needed."

Aki turned then and found Captain Tyrrel standing in the open doorway. His face fell in confusion at the captain's words.

"I thought I was done?"

Captain Tyrrel opened his mouth to speak then snapped it shut again. Opened it one more time then shook his head and turned to head back down the staircase. Dragging his feet, Aki followed him. Several times on their way down the very long staircase, Aki was tempted to ask the captain the reason for his strange behavior. Each time he convinced himself that he wasn't actually that curious.

When they entered the meeting room, it was too late for Aki to ask although there was no convincing himself that he didn't want to know now. Captain Tyrrel did not linger in the room, shutting the door quietly behind him as he left Aki standing alone in the middle of it, facing the mingled group of men from Dival and Dorsten.

"Come in and sit down, Aki," Hamo said.

Aki walked to the nearest empty chair in a daze and sank into it, avoiding the gaze of the others. Apparently, he wasn't the only one ill at ease, though, because several long seconds dragged by in a heavy silence. A chill crept up his spine as he sat there, a premonition that things weren't over yet, despite the course his trial had taken earlier that day.

"Captain Tyrrel said you needed me," Aki said when he could bear it no longer. He addressed Hamo because that was easier than talking to the entire group. "Do you have more questions?"

Hamo shook his head. "No, not questions. Well, not questions of the same nature, at least."

"We've a difficult task in front of us. A difficult decision to make. One you put on us when you made it part of your terms that Prince Desmond forfeited his right to the crown," Baron Orlander said.

Aki bit his lip. Part of him wanted to take it back, to tell these men that they could stick whoever they wanted on the throne, even the prince, just so long as he was left alone. But he couldn't. He couldn't because of the same list of people he'd held close through this entire ordeal. They didn't win with Desmond on the throne.

"That's left us in a bit of a predicament. We need a ruler. A successor to our late king. Preferably someone who shares royal blood. That will make the smoothest transition, we believe," the baron went on. "Unfortunately, it is not just Dival that must be considered, but Dorsten as well and even Aruuk."

"I think we've all come to the agreement that our two countries are stronger united. And under the right leadership, we're better for such a union," Norman said. "You laid out in your terms that Dorsten is to have an equal voice in the Divalian council, which is definitely a welcome change by those of us living on this side. Under such terms, and with the right leader installed, we intend to maintain our union."

Aki looked around, trying to decipher from the faces of the men about him what was coming next.

"And, of course, there is our treaty with Aruuk to consider. They've made it very clear what they want in order for us to keep that treaty intact," the Dorstenian man beside Norman said.

"I don't understand. What do you need me for? None of this is something I can decide."

Hamo leaned forward, folding his hands in front of him on the table. "Aki, we must seat a king on the throne that all three will accept. Anything short of that will likely undo all the work you've just accomplished here. We are not so far removed from being ready to slaughter each other that we can be reckless and careless about choosing who wears the crown."

This time, Aki squirmed a little in his seat as he looked around at the others, his mind already filling in the words they weren't saying.

"As you know, King Darien left no other direct heirs aside from Prince Desmond. By royal blood alone, the next closest male kin would, in fact, be Mara's son, Halle Gundarson."

Aki stifled the laugh of disbelief that threatened to burst out. Halle? King of Dival? It would have been a slightly terrifying thought if it weren't so ridiculous. Besides, Halle was gone. Probably somewhere in Aruuk by now and with no intention of being found.

"Yes, we feel the same," Baron Orlander said, noting the change in Aki's expression. "Besides his... well, his lack of qualifications, he would only be a Divalian heir. We think we have a better alternative."

"Who?" Aki felt sick as he said the word, sick with fear that he already knew what they were going to say. He was already shaking his head, already trying to deny it.

"You. You are a direct descendant not only of the Divalian royal family but of Lord Bayner and Chief Gundar of Aruuk," Hamo said. "The Aruukens have already stated that they will reestablish the treaty if you are seated on the throne. The Dorstenians will keep the union if you are seated on the throne."

"No. No," Aki said, pushing his chair away from the table, pushing himself out of it and backing toward the door. "It can't be me. I'd be the worst. I... no, it just can't."

"Aki..."

"No. Pick someone else. Pick someone who's actually good. Pick anybody. Just not me."

"It's too late for that. You're the only one born that can claim to unite the three ruling families."

"I was never supposed to be born," Aki cried. "It was a mistake. And choosing me is a mistake. I'm not... I can't..."

He was gone. Out of the room. Out of their sight. Fleeing down the hallway and up the long staircase that led him as far away as he could get. It didn't matter that it was raining or that behind him someone was calling his name. Calling for him to come back. What mattered was that he wanted to go home. He wanted to leave all of this behind him. He wanted...

Aki wasn't even sure what it was he wanted now.

To be free of making choices that involved other people, that was what he wanted. To be free of the burden of that, of the weighty responsibility that came with holding the lives of others in his hands.

"Aki, come inside," Captain Tyrrel's voice was almost bored as he stood just inside the doorway, safe from the rain. "Standing out there isn't going to change anything."

The stairwell was only dimly lit making it difficult for Aki to see much more than the shadows on Captain Tyrrel's face as the captain sat down on one of the steps and motioned for Aki to join him. In his hands, the captain spun a folded piece of paper around that Aki recognized. It was the letter Aki had sent to him through Sebastian begging the captain to keep the army in check, to stand them down, and to trust Aki.

"I take it they told you."

"It can't be me, Captain. Anybody but me."

"Well, not anybody. I'd rather not have Mara. And there's a few other people that I can think of that would be worse than you."

Aki rewarded the captain's attempt with a half-smile.

"Why can't it be you?" the captain went on. "It makes sense that it is you."

"Because of who my parents and grandparents were? That's a ridiculous reason. How does that make any sense to anyone? I wasn't even supposed to be born. I wasn't meant to exist. And I'd be an absolutely horrible king. I can't tell people what to do, I can't make decisions for them. I'm the one who couldn't even find enough courage to tell the truth when it mattered, remember?" He slid his hand against his pocket as he spoke, feeling for his mother's letter. Realizing that his clothes were damp from the rain, he pulled it out for safekeeping.

"There's more to it than just who your parents and grandparents were, although that fact does matter to people. Aki, three countries were ready to go to war over the havoc Mara caused. They didn't want to find out the truth. They didn't want to try to negotiate. Not one single person looked for a way to end it. Except you. And I know you're about to say you only did it because you promised King Darien you would." Aki pressed his lips together, holding back those very words. "But he gave you a choice that night, and you chose this. Now, I know that we've known peace for a long time under King Darien and that limits my experience, but I can honestly say I've never seen or heard of anyone accomplishing what you did that day.

Three armies met, fully prepared and wanting to fight and you turned that around."

"I just want to go home. I just want to leave all of this behind. I don't want to be the one in charge."

"That I can understand." Captain Tyrrel turned to eye him in the uncertain light. "You've had an eventful life."

"Something like that," Aki muttered.

Captain Tyrrel let out a rare laugh. "You do realize that's why half the people around here want you. Mara played her game a little too well, you might say. These people, the people of Dorsten, they're still fighting their way back to a normal life. She ravaged their land quite thoroughly. They want someone who knows what it's like to suffer. Do you know why?"

"Because it's what Mara told them they should want."

Shaking his head, Captain Tyrrel said, "No. She didn't need to convince them of that. Hope. They want hope and when they look at you, they see it. You survived when you shouldn't have. You've succeeded where you shouldn't have. And you belong to them."

The letter in Aki's hand was heavy all of a sudden. The words that he'd memorized weeks before sprung up in his mind unbidden.

"I can't tell you what to do, but I think you should at least talk to the men you chose to make this decision. You trusted them enough for your trial. Maybe trust that they might actually know what they're doing now."

With a heavy sigh, Captain Tyrrel stood and waited. Aki hadn't planned on going anywhere just yet but when it became clear that the captain wasn't going to move until Aki came with him, he grudgingly got to his feet.

"Not tonight, by the way. They've decided that any further discussion can wait until tomorrow."

That was a relief in and of itself. It postponed any decision on Aki's part for a few more hours at least. And when morning came, he could only hope that they would come to their senses and realize what a terrible king he would actually be.

Captain Tyrrel was apparently determined to make sure it was his room he went to and not another hiding place because he led Aki all the way to the door. Aki opened it but before he stepped in, Captain Tyrrel laid a hand on his shoulder to stop him. Aki tensed at the touch and froze so that he wouldn't pull away.

"There are a couple of things I want you to think about before the morning. First of all," he held up the letter he'd been holding onto the entire time they were talking, "I'm pretty sure the person who wrote this and the person standing in front of me right now are the same. You keep saying you can't make decisions for anyone else, but you've already been doing that. And secondly, you should know that Aruuk will only reinstate the treaty broken by Prince Desmond's actions if we appoint you to the throne. They made that quite clear today. According to them, you were the only involved party that looked out for their interests and the only one they trust to not betray the terms of the treaty. They will also relinquish their claim on Prince Desmond's life only if you are named the successor."

"And I'm supposed to sleep after all this?"

Captain Tyrrel was audacious enough to smile. "If you make up your mind, you'd sleep easier."

Aki shut the door in his face.

Chapter 65

"YOU'LL HAVE A REGENT, OF course, until you're of age." Jarvis shifted through the same small pile of papers over and over again as he talked, never once looking up. "That'll be until you're twenty, which is..."

"A bit less than three years, still. What's a regent?" Aki asked, feeling like a fool for even having to ask. Age had never made any difference in the rule of Aruuken Chiefs. If they could take and hold the power, it was theirs by right.

"Someone who will serve as," Jarvis paused in his shuffling, frowning down at the papers as if offended by the order they now found themselves in, "a guide, I suppose you could say. Something a little more than an advisor and a little less than a sovereign. While you'd still carry the authority of a king, a regent, in extreme circumstances and only with the approval of the council, can overrule decisions you might make. Their most important function is to lend the experience of age and time to a young sovereign."

"And who is the regent?"

"Oh, there isn't one in particular. Darien, I mean, King Darien," Jarvis' voice quivered a little over the name the way it always did now, "he never had one. He did not ascend to the throne until he was almost thirty, so he had no need of one. I think, traditionally that is, the regent is picked by the sovereign and approved by the council. They cannot be a family member, if I recall the laws regarding them correctly. Nor can they be someone who also presides on the council. I'm sorry. It's been many, many years since we've had a regent. Certainly not in my lifetime. I'll have to clarify the laws regarding them once we return to Dival."

Jarvis continued to shuffle the papers, flipping through them like he expected the words to rearrange themselves into a more pleasing missive and frowning often when they didn't. Aki wanted to reach out and snatch them away from the man.

It was unfair to be so irritated with him, Aki knew. The man grieved for his old king and friend. Having to sit here and pretend like Aki was anything other than a very poor substitute was likely requiring all of his many years of experience and training in the king's court to accomplish. Jarvis of all people had to know that they were trading an excellent monarch for one whose only purpose now was to maintain the peace that was still so delicate.

"I'm sorry about the king's death," Aki murmured.

Jarvis looked up and gave him a fleeting sad smile. "I knew. He told me that he intended to go to his sister and try to settle things. I knew, at least I suspected, that things might not end well. Mara was never one to forgive easily."

"I'm still sorry it happened. He was a good king."

"Yes. Yes, he was a very good king. And a good friend. If he'd been less than either of those things, well, he would never have left."

Aki glanced down at the long table at where the others were sitting. It wasn't all ten men, just three or four. Aki had spent all morning with the ten. He'd spent all morning listening to their attempts to convince him. He'd spent all morning pretending it wasn't working. But in the end...

In the end, it was Captain Tyrrel's final words from the night before that decided him. It was the words his mother had written, both in the final entry of her journal and in her letter to him. It was the promise he'd made King Darien a lifetime ago - the promise to do whatever he could to keep the peace. He'd thought his part was over. He wanted his part to be over.

Jarvis, at last fed up with his own nervous fiddling, gave the papers a final straightening and pushed the whole stack of them out of his own reach. "Everyone here is of the mind that we should wrap things up as quickly as possible and make our way back to Dival. Bren, to be precise. The people of Dival, and even the outer reaches of Dorsten, will, no doubt, have heard rumors regarding the king's death and the appointment of a successor. We need to assure them that the matter is well in control and that there's no need for panic or chaos. The last thing we need is that."

"I doubt I'll get much of a welcome in Bren," Aki said under his breath, wondering for at least the millionth time in the past half hour if he was not making perhaps the gravest mistake of his life.

"Well, that's not necessarily true. See, Mara's not the only one who can tell a fine story. By the time you reach Bren, you will, we hope, be seen only as a hero to our people."

Aki scoffed at the thought and turned his attention to the large window that overlooked the meadow.

"Laugh all you like. We need the people unified, or as close as we can get them to unity. This divisiveness Mara nurtured has only the power to destroy, which is what she intended. She revealed discrepancies, inequalities, problems that all existed well before she came along. She merely used them, not created them. Those things don't just disappear. They must be fixed. We'll eat ourselves up inside out if we can't find a way to put a stop to it. You managed to point us in the right direction, but we're far from through this. Besides, it's no lie we'll have told. Only the truth told in the very best light."

"So what? We're leaving here now?"

"Not quite so fast. There are a few matters yet to be seen to here. You have faced your trial as has Prince Desmond. But in our custody, we have Mara, and also the men who fought for her. Something must be done with them."

"Like what?"

"That, Your Majesty, is for you to decide."

Aki grimaced at the words, at the title. It wasn't his. Not really. Even Jarvis knew it. He gave the words a funny twist when he said them as if they tasted sour in his mouth.

"You will, of course, have these men," Jarvis motioned toward the other end of the table, "to help with that decision. And you must also give some immediate thought as to who shall serve as your regent. That will need to be decided expediently for the assurance of everyone."

"Anything else?" Aki asked wryly.

Jarvis threw a quizzical glance in his direction then gave a quick shake of his head. "At the moment, no. But it might... No, never mind. It's not my place."

"What? What were you going to say?"

"Only that it might be easier, at least a little so, if you were to truly accept what you are now. There will not be, probably for the rest of your life, any days that pass that don't require many decisions from you."

Not exactly the words Aki wanted to hear and definitely not what he wanted to think about. There was that regret again, swift to rise to the surface of every other thought and emotion, telling him he should have run away in the night rather than stay and allow himself to be convinced. He looked up to find Jarvis watching him discreetly, waiting to see his reaction to the secretary's words of advice.

"Do I have to decide any of that this afternoon?"

Jarvis gave another quick shake of his head. "Tomorrow. I believe that was the consensus of your council members. They would like to begin the journey back to Bren by the end of this week."

When Jarvis got up, picked up his collection of papers and removed himself from the room, Aki folded his arms on the tabletop and laid his head down on them. It was less to rest than it was to prevent anyone else from coming up and speaking to him just then. His efforts were completely foiled when a chair scraped across the floor beside him, and someone lowered themselves into the seat.

"Falling asleep at the table definitely seems like a great start to your reign."

"Shut up, Lars."

"Very kingly words. I can see why you were the wisest choice."

Aki lifted his head enough to glare at Lars. "Just drop it, will you?"

Lars spread his hands out in mock innocence. "As you command." His serious expression melted into a grin a moment later. "Seriously, you look like they sentenced you to die, not gave you the crown. You might want to fix that before you leave here."

"And you're telling me this from your superior age and experience?"

"Age, no. Experience, most definitely. You're forgetting I went back with Sasha when he took over Aruuk as Chief. It wasn't what he wanted either. But he'd have been murdered the first day if he'd acted like that. These people might not resort to murder, but you'll never succeed facing it like this."

Scowling down at his arms still resting on the table, Aki knew Lars wasn't wrong. He straightened in his chair and let his hands drop to his lap. Lars tipped his chair back and put his feet up on the table.

"Next thing you know, they'll be trying to marry you off to some princess or nobleman's daughter."

"No," Aki said flatly.

Lars only laughed, loud enough that it drew the attention of the others in the room and Aki jabbed an elbow into his side to make him stop.

"What are you going to do now?" he said, to change the subject.

"Stay close enough to keep annoying you."

"What do you mean?"

"Well, Aruuk wants someone to travel back and forth between Aruuk and Dival, just to keep an eye on everything and, since I speak both languages, I was the logical choice."

"So, you'll be around? A lot?"

Lars shrugged. "I don't know how much, but this isn't the last time you'll see me. I'll be around whenever they decide you need a queen."

Chapter 66

AKI EXHALED DEEPLY AS THE key turned in its lock.   Although Captain Tyrrel and two other soldiers stood in the hallway behind him, Aki entered the dim room alone. Light from the hall spread across the stone floor, revealing the cell's sole occupant.

Still clothed in the now filthy, ragged dress that she'd worn three weeks before on the day she'd expected her greatest victory, Mara didn't even turn to look at him.

"You don't have to do this," Captain Tyrrel said quietly enough that his voice wouldn't carry the short distance.

But he did. He knew he did. If he couldn't face her again, he would never be able to face anything at all. Besides, somewhere deep inside him, next to all the hate he'd harbored all those years under her care was a small pebble of pity that didn't make any sense but refused to leave.

He took another step forward, motioned for the others to close the door behind him.

Still, she sat unmoving on the cold floor. Her black hair hung limp and tangled around her face. Beneath it, her face was cold, pale, and devoid of even hatred. Aki had never noticed the passing of years on her features, but here in the dungeon, she looked old. Old and worn completely through. Her eyes, listless dark pools that stood out in stark contrast to her pallor, stared at nothing at all. The only flicker of movement she betrayed was the steady rise and fall of her chest with each silent breath she took.

"Mara," Aki said, stooping in front of her. She gave no sign that she heard him. "Mara, look at me."

A moment passed and then another.

Mara looked at him.

And Aki almost wished she hadn't. Still, he didn't turn away as he was used to doing under Mara's gaze. Of course, she'd never looked at him quite like that before. It took him a moment to realize what had changed in her expression. It was fear. She was afraid of him. Afraid of the power he now held over her.

In that moment, Aki knew, with a surety that he'd never known before, what he was going to do with Mara. And no voice on the council would change his mind.

Rising to his feet once more, Aki held out his hand. "Come, Mara. This is no place for you."

She flinched, actually flinched, when his hand came close to her. Confusion overlapped her fear as she stared at it and then up at Aki. He nodded, waiting. Waiting until, at last, Mara slid her own hand into his.

On her feet again, some semblance of her dignity returned. She pulled her hand away from him, smoothed out the tattered remains of her dress and straightened her shoulders.

"And what place is for me?" There was ice back in her voice, but it was so brittle, so close to shattering into a thousand broken pieces. "What will the new king do with me?"

"He will take you home."

"That word means nothing," she whispered, anguish raw in her eyes now.

"Not yet. But I hope it will."

He led her out. Out of the dark dungeon and back into the light of the sun. Turning to Captain Tyrrel, he said, "Take her. Put her in one of the bedrooms upstairs and post a guard. See that she's well taken care of. No one is to enter or leave that room unless it's me."

Although Captain Tyrrel raised his eyebrows at the request, he gave a slight bow with his head and took Mara by the elbow to guide her off.

"What are you going to do?" he turned to ask Aki.

"There's one more I need to speak to before we begin."

He wasn't dreading this meeting quite so much as he'd dreaded the one with Mara, but he wasn't looking forward to it either. Once more, he waited patiently while another door was unlocked, another cell opened.

The prisoner in this cell was bound to the wall by a heavy chain around his neck, keeping him well out of reach of the open doorway. He looked up when Aki entered and stiffened at once.

"You must have worked your way through that list of people you hate more than me," Sebastian said as Aki approached and sat on the small stool that was left in the room. Sebastian made what was meant to be an imperceptible attempt to move further back against the wall. He pointed to the iron band around his neck. "Was this just the beginning? Payment for what I did to you?"

Aki ignored his questions. "What you said to me that day, just outside my room, what were you talking about? You said you knew what I'd done the other night and that you would find a way to make it up to me."

Some of the trepidation left Sebastian's posture at Aki's question. He slumped a little and lowered his head. "You were given my daughter for a night, and you didn't lay a hand on her. That's what I meant."

His daughter. Karina. Aki remembered the brief revelation by Halle in the caverns the night they rescued Felix. There'd been so much else demanding his attention since then that he'd forgotten all about it until now.

"Does Karina know?" he asked quietly.

"Know what? What Mara sent her to you for? What you were supposed to do with her? She knows."

"No. That you're her father."

Pain flashed across Sebastian's face. Regret. Shame.

That was answer enough for Aki.

"You're going to tell her."

"No."

"She deserves to know."

"No. You don't understand. She's known me her whole life. She just hasn't known who I was. She knows what I've done."

"I don't care. You're going to tell her. She deserves the truth, and she deserves to hear it from you."

"I can't."

"You can either do it alone with her, or you can do it in front of the men who will judge you."

Sebastian's head sank lower. "Is this how you plan to begin your revenge?"

"It's not revenge, Sebastian. And it has very little to do with me. I'm simply trying to fix some of the many things that Mara has broken." Aki paused, waiting for a response but none came. He went on, "I've lived my entire life wishing I knew my father for even one day. Wishing I could have met him just once. And you're not going to be such a coward that you'll put Karina through that for the rest of her life. She's free now. You're free now. Start over. Begin again."

"This is what you call freedom?" Sebastian gestured once more to his chain.

"Yes." Aki pulled the key he'd brought in with him out of his pocket and unlocked the chain. "This is exactly what I would call freedom. You will accompany us on our return to Bren. There, you will find work, any work that is honest. If you choose, I will give you a job. If you prefer, you may find your own. You'll find a place to make your home. And you will make a life for your daughter and, hopefully, for yourself."

Sebastian didn't move. He just stared down at the empty chain now lying across his lap. He stared at it as if he'd never seen such a thing before.

"Why?"

"For the kindness you showed Felix. For the secret you concealed on my behalf."

"I don't deserve this," Sebastian murmured.

"No. But I don't think most gifts are deserved. The only reason I'm still alive today is because someone thought I was worth a second chance. I'm just passing that on. Don't waste it. Tell Karina the truth."

Shutting his eyes, leaning back against the wall, Sebastian nodded. "Take me to her and I will."

It was midmorning before Aki joined the others in the throne room. He ignored the dais and sat instead at one of the tables still set up for their use.

"I trust you've given some thought as to what you might decide today," Hamo said as he sat down next to him.

Aki nodded. He'd barely slept last night because of that very reason. He stared straight ahead even though he could sense Hamo's eyes on him.

"Today's not about revenge, Aki."

"I know." He turned to look at the older man. "But it is about justice, right?"

"Yes."

Today was about a lot more than justice. Aki could tell from the way everyone was pretending not to watch him. Today was about him. It was about seeing what kind of king he would be, what path he would set himself on. Even Alina, who had slipped into the room mostly unnoticed, was watching him intently.

With a nod to Captain Tyrrel, Aki began the proceedings. The captain opened the door to allow the first man to be led in and Aki looked up a moment later to see Ritter standing in the open space before him. The same patient, self-assured smile on his face that he'd worn the night he'd questioned Aki and half drowned Halle. Aki was glad to start with him.

Jarvis, seated on Aki's other side, read out the charges against Ritter. Ritter was one of her leaders, one of the men who bore the heaviest responsibility for the raids and the murders and the terror that had enveloped the land.

"There's no use, really, in you trying to deny any of this," Baron Orlander said when Jarvis was through.

To Aki's annoyance, Ritter's smile widened a little. "I wouldn't think of trying to deny the truth."

"Good. That makes it easy. We can get straight to the matter of your sentence," Norman said.

Ritter didn't look at either Norman or Baron Orlander. His gaze continued to rest on Aki, as did his ingratiating smile. Aki remembered how tempted he'd been that night to tear that smile off the man's face. The temptation was even stronger now.

"For these so-called crimes I've been accused of committing, I accept whatever punishment your new king wishes to bestow on me and beg that he would find it within himself to show mercy." Ritter made a mocking bow toward Aki.

Norman started to speak again, but this time, Aki cut him off. "You don't want me to do whatever I wish to you," he said quietly. "My brother, Halle, was of the mind that I ought to drown you a few times to see how you enjoy it. Accompanied, of course, with the same delicate efforts to awaken you from time to time that you imposed on him."

Ritter's eyes darkened but his smile remained intact. Aki felt Hamo's hand on his arm but shrugged it away. If they wanted to see what kind of a king he would be today, he meant to show them exactly that. And he'd already had his fill of mercy.

"I'm not opposed to the idea," Aki said, keeping his voice casual, noncommitted and had the satisfaction of watching a seed of doubt creep into Ritter's eyes. "You're from Aruuk, Ritter. You know how they do things there. Punishments always fit crimes. For instance, I spilled hot broth on the Chief's arm. He had me beaten with hot iron rods." Aki would have been mortified to share such a story just a few weeks ago, but since Mara had made them all public knowledge anyway, he decided he might as well use them to his advantage. "As you can imagine, I never spilled another thing, hot or cold, on him."

There was a stunned and rather uncomfortable silence in the room when Aki paused for breath. Ritter's smile had faltered a little with the telling of the story and he tried now to restore it to its previous belligerence.

"Although they can become too brutal, I don't entirely disagree with the principle behind such punishments."

"Your Majesty," Ritter said the title with a mixture of disgust and dwindling confidence, "unlike everyone else, I am not so easily frightened or intimidated by you or your stories. After all," Ritter took a few small steps forward, "you're the one who succumbed to my questioning in the face of your brother's discomfort after having claimed you cared nothing for him. Mara didn't make you kill the king because she knew you wouldn't. You broke the one you were meant to kill out before you could be made to do it. You didn't kill the prince when you had the chance. See, I don't think you have it in you. You won't kill me, and you won't have me killed. You're sitting there only because of the people around you. So why don't you let them finish this."

Several of the others started talking at once, but Aki held up a hand to silence them, praying inside that they would heed him. When they did, he leaned back in his seat and stared hard at Ritter.

"I'm not going to have you killed. See, Ritter, your death, while it might be satisfying, would be entirely wasted and useless. It would mean absolutely nothing. Nothing to me, nothing to the people you helped murder, nothing to the families left behind, nothing to the towns and villages you burned and looted. And I can't have that. So, your punishment isn't going to be death. It's going to fit your crime."

Ritter's smile disappeared entirely, wiped clean off of his face in a flash. He looked around the room, but Aki continued to stare at him. Ritter tried to muster some of the bravado he'd carried in with him, straightening his shoulders and letting out a disconcerted laugh.

"And what is that? Lock me in a burning building like the prince did? You condemned him for that."

"Those were innocent people. Enormous difference. But no, that's not what I've decided. I've decided that you must never again be given the opportunity to hurt so many people again." Now Aki leaned forward, savoring the moment even if he'd told himself he wouldn't. "I'm going to give you a choice. You can either join your men in rebuilding the same towns and villages that you destroyed, replanting the crops you ruined, for however long it takes and when that is complete you will remain in prison for whatever the rest of your life happens to be. Or, to ensure your harmless existence in this world, you will lose both hands."

Now Ritter's face was white, any cockiness washed irrevocably away. "You wouldn't..."

"Why not? You're a mercenary. A sell-sword. Kind of hard for you to wield a sword without your hands. A fitting punishment for your crime. Besides, you have a choice."

"No pity today, Aki?"

"The only times I've met you before, you didn't seem like a man who was much interested in pity. Although, if you chose the second option, you'll have to become well acquainted with pity, won't you? Because you'll be spending the rest of your life relying solely on the kindness and compassion of everyone around you. A difficult task for a man who's made killing his living. So, what do you choose, Ritter?"

Ritter ran a nervous tongue over his lips as his eyes darted to the other men around the table. Rubbing his hands together, he tried one final time to muster a smile, but it was a pained, twisted grimace that came out instead. "Don't they have to agree with all of this?"

"Ask them if they do," Aki said. It was a risk to dare him, to dare the others in the room. But it was a risk Aki was going to have to take at some point anyway if he was to lead anyone. "Ask if any of them disapprove of your sentence."

In the absence of any sound, Ritter looked from one face to another, searching for a sign, any sign, that gave him hope to continue his argument.

"Does anyone disagree?" Aki asked when it was clear Ritter wouldn't say the words. No one spoke up. "So, what do you choose?"

Now, at last, Ritter had no choice but to fully accept his defeat. His entire demeanor shifted as that realization crept over him. "I have no choice but the first option. I will help to rebuild what we've destroyed."

Satisfied, Aki nodded to the captain to lead Ritter away.

"After what we were told you did this morning with Mara and Sebastian, I was afraid we were going to have to convince you that you couldn't just show mercy to everyone," Baron Orlander said as they waited for another to be brought in. "I guess I was wrong."

It wasn't quite what Aki wanted to hear. He wanted just one of them to assure him that he'd made the right judgment, that it was just and not vengeful. And he didn't want to stoop to asking any of them. That would ruin what he was trying to accomplish today. But he did steal a glance, first at Hamo, and then Alina, and neither of them looked at all unhappy. In fact, Alina caught his eye as he looked in her direction and offered a small, very satisfied smile. Aki decided that was the best reassurance he could get.

They did not finish until late in the evening and by then Aki was more than ready to retreat to the privacy of his room. A headache had been growing steadily between his temples as the day had worn on, the sort that wouldn't go away without a good night's sleep. Privacy would have to wait though, he realized as he saw Karina standing in the hall outside his door, waiting for him.

"They won't let me see her, Aki," Karina said as he approached. "I just want to see her. Why won't they? Tell them I must, please."

"You can't, Karina. I told them not to let anyone in to see her."

"But it's me. What do you think I'll do?"

"Karina," he said slowly and carefully, "you would be the last person I would allow in to see her."

"Why? Don't do this to me, Aki. Please." Karina wrung her hands together as she fought back tears that threatened to choke her up. "She's like my mother. You can't take her from me. Please, Aki, please don't do this to me."

"Because, even if you don't want to, you do what she tells you. You're dangerous around her even if you don't mean to be. You have family, Karina, but it's not her. It won't ever be her again."

"Who? Sebastian? I don't even know if he tells me the truth."

"He does. What he told you today is true."

Karina just stood there, looking as lost as a small child. "Then what am I supposed to do?"

"Come with us back to Bren. Give Sebastian a chance to be a real father to you."

"But I've never lived apart from her. I don't know what to do."

"Then you can learn, just like everyone eventually has to. It might be hard for a while, but you'll see in the end it's better this way. Both for you and for her."

Chapter 67

HOME.

The word had never meant so much to Aki as it did now. It danced inside his head. Sang to him across the wind. He was almost home. The very air smelled different, sweeter, richer than it did a day ago. There was the faint hint of salt from the sea still clinging to the breeze.

Around the next bend of the road, Aki knew, Stephan's farm would at last become visible. And even though it was no longer the place where he would live, it was the only place in the entire land worthy of being called home to him. Stopping here had been a source of disagreement between him and a few of the men, including Captain Tyrrel. They wanted to ride straight for Bren and make his reign official.

It was Hamo who convinced the others to allow him this one day.

Only a little more than half of the army had returned with them, the rest staying behind to ensure Aki's judgments were carried out. He had offered the same choice as he'd offered Ritter to all of their captives and found them all inclined to make the same decision Ritter had. Now, most of them had continued on to Bren with the rest of the councilmen, leaving Aki alone with Captain Tyrrel, Alina and a small contingent of soldiers the captain insisted on for a guard.

The house came into view and Aki didn't wait for anyone else. He didn't need to even prod Sky. His excitement had long before trickled down to the horse and as the old familiar place neared, she broke into a gallop, leaving all the others behind.

Leading Sky into the barn, loosening her saddle, taking off her bridle, brushing her down until her coat shone, it all seemed like the most normal thing in the world. He knew the others were caught up to him because he could hear them outside the comfort of the barn walls, but no one intruded on him.

When Sky was in her stall, content to chew on the hay Aki put in with her, he slipped out the back door of the barn and made his way across the pasture. There was a mound of earth there, grown over now and with a sapling sprouting from the very center of it. It was toward that mound that Aki turned his steps.

He came to a halt beside it and sat, his back to the woods, facing the barn and the sloping pasture and the house beyond them. For a long time, he just sat there, feeling the warmth of the sun on his face, savoring the quiet sounds of the farm.

"I wish you could have been here, Stephan," he whispered after a while. "I think you might have actually been happy with me."

There was no voice to answer him but just being here was a comfort. And now that he was here, Aki thought they might just have to drag him away if they wanted him to leave.

It was with grudging feet that he made his way out of the house the next morning. He wouldn't come back here. Not like this, anyway. Each hour they moved further away from the only place he really wanted to be, the harder it became to convince himself that he made the right choice.

Late on the evening of that day, Aki knocked on the front door of Atticus Wehr's house. He waited only a moment before it was opened. Master Wehr didn't give him a chance to speak. His arms pulled Aki close in an embrace.

"I thought I'd never get to see you again." Master Wehr's voice was muffled against Aki, and he stepped back, his hands resting still on Aki's shoulders. "Yet here you are. And not just returned, but the one everyone's talking about."

Master Wehr stepped back, and beckoned Aki in. He turned away to wipe his eyes.

"Are you alright, Master Wehr?"

"Yes, yes. A bit of dust in my eyes, I think. Come in, come in. It's not every day one gets to host the king in one's own house, now, is it?"

"I could never be your king."

"King to all, Aki. King to all. That's what you must be. That's what we need. Oh, but there are a lot of stories going around about you. I'm flattered you remembered me in the middle of it all."

"I wouldn't be where I am if it weren't for you. And I don't think I can go any further without you."

Master Wehr squinted at him in puzzlement. "What do you mean by that?"

"I mean," Aki said, trying to keep his voice from sounding desperate, "I mean, I need a regent. And I've been told that I can pick anyone, so long as they are no family of mine and they do not already serve on the council. That severely limits my choices. But even if I had a thousand others I knew to pick from, I think I'd still be here, asking you."

"To be your regent?"

"Yes. I know you were going to retire when you finished training me. And I'm sorry that I sort of failed as your student and ruined your perfect record. But I hope you'll forgive that and agree. They said I should pick someone that I knew to be honest and just and loyal to the country. And you were the first person I thought of."

Aki waited. He twisted his hands up into knots while he waited and moved from one foot the other. At first, he thought Master Wehr looked like he planned on refusing. And although he couldn't very well blame him for that decision, he desperately hoped it wouldn't be his final one. He had no other ideas when it came to choosing a regent.

Still without answering, Master Wehr held up a finger. "Wait here a moment. I've something of yours that ought to be returned."

While Aki puzzled over what he could possibly be talking about, Master Wehr left the front room and reappeared a few moments later. He took Aki's hand and pressed something into the palm of it.

"You gave up much to save us from a futile and costly war. More than I think you could possibly guess would be required of you in the beginning. It would be very selfish of me, indeed, to not aid you in the sacrifice that will be the rest of your life. If you truly choose me, and the council approves, I will gladly serve as your regent."

Aki's eyes were strangely misty as he stared down at the ring now resting in his hand. His mother's ring.

"Thank you. For keeping this and for agreeing to come with me. And for everything else."

In the early morning hours, he stood on a small balcony that overlooked the sea. With Sybil's letter in his hands, he made a new promise. One that wasn't meant for anyone else to hear. A promise to always look for the light that chased away the darkness. A promise to remember the dead, but to live for the living. A promise to never forget the power of a dawn.

Epilogue

THE BALDING MAN WHO APPROACHED Aki late on the evening of his first full day in the castle was familiar. And not in the sort of way Aki wished he was. It had only been about a year and a half since he had been in that man's charge.

The jailer bowed his head as he approached. Aki still hadn't decided what the proper response for such reverence was since he was so used to being the one who bowed. It was only made more uncomfortable with the knowledge that he'd been a prisoner in this man's care. One look at the jailer's face told Aki that the older man remembered him just as clearly.

"Your Majesty," the jailer said. "Have you any orders for me?"

Aki's forehead wrinkled in a confused frown. He started to shake his head but stopped himself to think. "Is there any reason I should?"

The jailer pressed his lips together and drew in a long, wheezing breath. "It may not be my place to inquire, but...," he hesitated, and Aki motioned for him to go on, "Were you made aware of the fact that your brother, Sasha Gundarson, is being held here?"

Aki's hand found the wall beside him as the man's words sank into his understanding. Alive. Sasha was alive. Aki's breathing grew heavy with the heady hysteria that threatened to make him laugh outright. Sasha was still alive. And he was here.

"How?" the word escaped his lips before he knew what he was saying. "Why?"

The jailer's mild face showed a bit of slight puzzlement at Aki's reaction. "He was brought here for the prince to question regarding you. He was never taken with the others."

"He's here? Where? What's been done with him? The prince didn't hurt him, did he?" Because if he had... Aki left the rest of that thought alone. He stopped speaking for a moment to collect his thoughts and then drew himself up. "Take me to him."

"As you wish."

He knew the staircase that wound its way up to the tower cells. He'd walked them before as a prisoner, condemned for treason. He wanted to run past the jailer now, take the steps two or three at a time. It was all he could do to hold himself at a more dignified pace. He was the king, he reminded himself, and kings didn't run up staircases.

"He's in here," the jailer said as he unlocked the door.

Aki froze on the threshold of the cell. Inside, Sasha was getting to his feet, confusion written on his face.

"Aki?"

The sound of laughter was a shock to Aki's ears. Even more shocking was the fact that it was coming from him. It was shaky and wild. And he couldn't stop it.

"You're alive," he said at last, an utterly unnecessary observation but one he couldn't help making. "I thought you were dead. Lars thought you were dead."

Sasha shook his head in disbelief, his eyes not leaving Aki's face. "What did you do?"

Still laughing a little, Aki answered, "That's a really, really long story."

Other titles by S. T. Hobbs

The Divalian Chronicles –

Prequel ~ The Thief and the Slave

Book 1 ~ The Traitor's Alliance

Book 2 ~ The Last Chief

Book 3 ~ The Courier's Apprentice

Book 4 ~ The King's Successor

The Oracle's Odyssey –

Book 1 ~ The Forgotten Curse

Book 2 ~ The Fallen Gates

Book 3 ~ (Coming soon) The Fates' Finale

www.ingramcontent.com/pod-product-compliance
Lightning Source LLC
Chambersburg PA
CBHW030246270626
47156CB00020B/117